FILTHY SEX

THE FIVE POINTS' MOB COLLECTION: FOUR

SERENA AKEROYD

COPYRIGHT

COPYRIGHT © 2021 by Serena Akeroyd
   All rights reserved.
   No part of this book may be reproduced in any form or by any electronic or mechanical means, including information storage and retrieval systems, without written permission from the author, except for the use of brief quotations in a book review.

AUTHOR'S NOTE

My darlings,

Welcome back to Hell's Kitchen.

Please be advised: this book is the **most violent** of them all, so have a care when wandering into this tale...

And for your reference, you will come across this word: *céilidh*. Just pronounce it kay-lee. :)

I'm sure you'll remember, but here's a recap:

Aoife - Ee-Fah

Eoghan - Owen.

Aela - Eh-Lah.

I truly hope you love Brennan. He's one of my personal favorites now. And please, as you dive into this book, have an open mind about people's kinks. :) I know some of you won't like the verbiage used, but it's what Brennan's leading lady likes, which is all that matters.

If you're curious about the universe crossover, then find that here: linktr.ee/SerenaAkeroydReadingOrder <3

Much love,

Serena

xoxo

PLAYLIST

If you'd like to hear a curated soundtrack, with songs that are featured in the book, as well as songs that inspired it, then here's the link:

https://open.spotify.com/playlist/1206t1LEjQDvpwQUFCCnSW

THE CROSSOVER READING ORDER WITH THE FIVE POINTS

FILTHY
NYX
LINK
FILTHY RICH
SIN
STEEL
FILTHY DARK
CRUZ
MAVERICK
FILTHY SEX
HAWK
FILTHY HOT
STORM
THE DON (Coming Soon)
THE LADY (Coming Soon)
FILTHY SECRET (Coming Soon)

PART 1

"Maybe you are searching among the branches for what only appears in the roots." – **Rumi**

ONE
1995
BRENNAN

UNCLE FRANK'S hand tightened on my shoulder, prompting me to peer up at him.

"Your da won't ask, but are you okay?"

Was I okay?

I wasn't sure if he was joking or not, so I just stared at him in confusion.

Nothing about this situation was okay.

Ma was...

I swallowed.

She was in the hospital.

My already crazy father was close to losing the few marbles he still possessed.

The city was drenched in blood, and I was about to commit mass murder.

And my uncle was asking if I was okay?

I tilted my head back around, staring at a sight no fifteen-year-old should ever have to witness, but this was my punishment.

I should have gone into the dress shop with her. I should have gone *inside*. I shouldn't have rushed off to catch the bus for school. I should have made sure Ma was safe. That was my job—to take her to her shop every morning.

My throat closed at what she'd endured because I'd fucked up.

I didn't feel my own bruises, didn't feel anything really. Just knew that nothing was okay about this situation. Nothing at all. And that was safer. Being numb right now was a hell of a lot safer than the alternative.

Surrounded by busted up cars, mountains of them, Da jumped out of the CAT tractor. Clouds of dust burst around him in eddying flurries that settled on his shoes when he moved to stand in front of a car crusher that diminished his larger-than-life frame. His arms were folded over his chest as he watched me, a bitter hatred etched into his features that I knew he'd always feel for me because of what I'd done to Ma, and that was when Frank nudged me forward.

"Go on, it'll take a few minutes. You've killed before, Bren. This is just like that."

This was nothing like before.

Nothing.

What was it with Uncle Frank today? Was he out for an award for Understatement of the Year?

Holding my arm tight to my side, the cast heavy thanks to my broken arm—one of Da's first punishments for this mess and no less than I deserved—I swallowed, but stepped forward, knowing I had no real choice.

Suspended above the car crusher, was a thin concrete block about eight feet long. It reminded me a little of the clothes line on the rare occasions when Ma hung out some laundry in the yard, except, instead of clothes, there were seven men dangling down, their feet trapped in the block. Most of them were conscious, Da wouldn't get his fun otherwise, but some of them were fortunate and hadn't woken up yet.

They never would either.

"Get in the cab," Da hissed, pulling me by the ear when I didn't move fast enough, my head tipping back as I stared up at the men who'd defiled my mother.

I bit the inside of my cheek as I scurried away, darting into the cab before he could clip me again. A clunking sound echoed around it as my cast collided with the side of the door, and I almost howled as the pain slalomed inside me, winding me with its force.

Simultaneously, my nose began bleeding once more, and whether that was from the pressure of knowing the horrific fate I was about to let these men endure, or from the fact Da had broken it yesterday, I had no real way of knowing but I grabbed the paper towel I was carrying for this purpose and jammed a chunk inside each nostril.

As I plunked down in the CAT's bucket seat, Da climbed up the ladder beside me, his feet hooked into the rungs as he hovered in place. Unsure of his next move, I held my broken arm closer to my side, the pain still ricocheting through me was enough to make me feel like I could pass out, so I didn't need him adding to that by grabbing a hold of it or anything.

All around us, there were motes of dust and debris, shards of metal and boxy squares of wreckage that glinted under the hard glow of the spotlights. Uncle Frank was watching from a distance, while my da's crew, Mark O'Reilly, Tony Hannaway, and Paul Claren, were somewhere in the vicinity, keeping the scene secured.

"All you need to do is release the pincers," he told me.

Their deaths wouldn't make up for what they'd done to Ma.

They wouldn't pay for their sins by dying no matter what Father Doyle said. Da believed that bullshit, but I didn't.

Knowing it was pointless to argue, I licked my lips and raised my other hand to do as he bid.

Before I could tap the button, he told me, "You could have prevented this, Brennan. Remember today. Your ma would be safe at home if you'd just done as I fucking asked you. Women, be they your wife or your mother, are queens. They're to be protected and sheltered at all costs."

As much as those words resonated with me, I wanted to ask why he'd laid Ma's responsibility on my shoulders if she was so fucking important to him, but I knew why.

Sure, I still went to school, but that was only to keep up appearances. Plus, he wanted his sons to rub shoulders with Manhattan's elite, so off we went to learn BS we'd never need, before our real jobs started once that shit was over and the uniform was off.

To him, I was a made man.

To him, it was my duty to protect her.

He wasn't wrong.

I should have waited in the shop with her until Stephen arrived to take my place. It was my fault we were running late. She'd told me twice to get up, but I'd ignored her, and she'd paid for that when I darted off to catch the bus.

I was a bad son.

A terrible one.

I licked my lips as I let my gaze drift over the Aryans. They'd almost killed Ma, had done things to her that I'd heard Da sobbing over last night as he got drunk in his office.

They deserved to die.

My hand hovered over the button, but I kept my gaze trained on them as I lowered it.

When the pincers flared wide, the men screamed, but not for long as the mechanical jaw chewed them up and spat them out.

Blood spurted everywhere like a geyser. Da and Uncle Frank laughed, but me?

I just puked.

TWO
2009
THE FINAL JOURNAL ENTRY BY MARISKA VASOV

I NEVER IMAGINED *there'd come a day where I wanted you to read these journals, my darlings, but I hope you read about the mistakes I made and I pray that they don't lead you down the same path I took.*

When you were a little girl, Camille, and Inessa was barely two, I was at a political fundraiser with your father, and that was where I met him.

He was only in his early twenties, and shouldn't have held any power in that space, but Brennan O'Donnelly dominated the room. He commanded everyone in its vicinity. Truly, I've never felt anything like it before—he drew me to him like a moth to a flame, and I've never been more okay with being burned.

Brennan is a man like no other. Even if I was only an affair, a change of pace—an older woman, a married one at that, making our time together charged and heated with the fear of us being caught—he was different. So unlike any other man I've met in this world of ours. He was honorable. Kind, in his own way. A modern day protector. Whenever I was in his arms, I wished that I was his. That we could be together, that my fate wasn't tied to Antoni's, but... that simply wasn't to be.

I don't like sharing my secrets with you, not when they cast me in a painful light, but the truth is, I need you to know about Brennan. About the kind of man he is.

Decent.

Generous.

Honorable.

Don't mistake him for not being dangerous, because he is. He's just not like your father.

Accept this now, my darlings, that we are broodmares to men like Antoni. Our worth falls to the fruit we can bear, and I'm sure you know this by now that it's the sons who matter. I wish that weren't so. I wish that you hadn't been raised in a world like this, but you have. We don't just have glass ceilings, but glass cages.

It distresses me more that I have to tell you I knew from early on in my marriage I would die in childbirth. Carrying Camille and then Inessa wasn't easy, and my doctors advised against having another child. Of course, with no son, that was never going to happen.

Brennan was a spotlight in the darkness. A chance of something more in the middle of a life that I knew was coming to an end. Getting pregnant again felt impossible, and with each passing day, I knew I was becoming surplus to requirements. Call him my last act of rebellion, but I'm hoping he will be your savior.

Just before we parted ways for the final time, I was desperate to protect you. So certain that your father would have me killed for an inability to get pregnant again, I knew I'd be leaving you at his mercy, so I pleaded with Brennan. My daughters, I said to him, are unsafe in their father's household. If anything happens to me, I need you to protect them. I need you to promise me you'll watch out for them.

Things ended badly between us, there's no doubt about that. He'd been pulling away from me for a while, and then he came to me, bruised and beaten, his wrist broken, his nose and a few ribs too. I had a feeling his family knew who he was seeing. I was devastated about losing him and said some things I shouldn't... But despite all that, despite the hard words we spewed at each other, he still made me that promise, and I know he will uphold it. All this time later, I trust him more than your father, and I haven't seen him in six years...

Somehow, I survived our break up, I survived the long wait between Inessa and Victoria. No one was more surprised than me to be graced with another beautiful daughter, but your father still didn't have his son...

Antoni discovered I'd had an affair recently. I don't know how, nor do I want to. Information is passed around like popcorn at the cinema in this world. It doesn't matter that it was a long time ago, he's not the kind of man to forgive or forget. I can see the hatred in his eyes and know that he's been waiting for any excuse to pull the trigger, but I lied, and told him I thought I was pregnant again. To my misfortune, he came with me to my doctor's appointment yesterday and discovered that lie.

I know my time remaining is short, and I can only pray that my end is swift. There will be nothing I can do to protect you, my darlings, but Brennan will.

Camille, I know you, naughty little minx, are aware of where my journals are, so I hope you find these soon after I perish.

You must tell Brennan that he promised me. His honor will never let him rest if he breaks that promise—that is the kind of man he is. The kind of man I'm entrusting your safety to.

Know, my darlings, that I love you all. That you were the joy that made my days. That, without you, my life would have held no meaning.

I would like to hope that I can watch over you, but if God isn't so kind, then that might not be something I can do. I pray nightly that I'm wrong, that I'm good enough to enter the kingdom of heaven just so I can see you become the beautiful women you are destined to be.

I love you. There are no words to express how much.

Ever yours,

Mama

PART 2

AIDAN JR
THE SUMMIT

When the four families who reigned over New York banded together, it meant shit had gone down.

Not just *regular* shit, either.

That was our stock in trade.

Extortion, thieving, drugs, prostitution, they were our shares. Our commodities. Our products, as it were.

Every man in this room was wanted by some law agency or another, and with the crimes we'd committed, we'd all be locked up for the rest of our natural lives if we were ever arrested—that was a given.

What was also a given?

Not one of the four leaders from the four families—the Irish, the Italians, the Chinese, or the Russians—would ever see the inside of a prison cell.

They'd never be punished for their sins.

And considering I was the heir to the Five Points' throne, I wasn't about to complain about that. I didn't want to spend the rest of my life in a Supermax, jacking off to the sounds of people walking down the corridor outside my cell because that was as much human contact as I was allowed in a twenty-four hour period. Painting the walls with my shit just to have *some* method of communication.

Even if the lower ranks did get sent to jail, we worked deals for them. No one ever served what they were supposed to—take the old Don's heir. That cunt Gianni Fieri had died in prison, but not because of his sentence—he probably wouldn't have served even an eighth of it if some clever bastard hadn't broken his neck.

Until recently, the last few years, at any rate, I'd been quite happy with the status quo.

Then I'd been shot.

Then I'd nearly lost my mobility.

Then I'd become hooked on pain meds.

As I sat here, around a table with the four most powerful men in the state, their heirs and trusted advisors grouped around them, as we discussed a war that we were fighting on too many fronts, all I could think about was the Oxy.

It was there, a siren call in my head. A song that made me want to close my eyes to chase away the nausea that plagued me.

The shakes would come soon, the nausea shortly after. Sometimes, they mixed themselves up, and I'd find myself puking as I shook like I was having a seizure. Then I'd take a pill, and everything, all my worries, would disappear.

But this morning, I had to focus.

Especially when Rex, the Prez of the Satan's Sinners' MC, stormed into the warehouse where we were gathered, raised his guns and took his shots. It was like something from *Kill Bill,* only Rex wasn't wearing a yellow catsuit.

His slaying of the Italian fuckers wasn't a part of the official program, but the Irish were the only ones who knew to anticipate Rex's arrival. We'd planned it.

The Italians had to suffer.

They had to be made to pay.

Their Don was dead thanks to my youngest brother.

Now his successors were dead, his *consigliere* too.

As I smiled at the bloodshed before me, satisfaction filling me at the sweet taste of vengeance which definitely was better when hot, I concealed my hands, which were starting to tremble, and for a while, I lost myself to the biting need to pop another Oxy.

The bodies were dragged away by two guys from the Chinese camp, and Rex took a seat after my father explained why he'd helped our ally infiltrate the Summit, sacred territory according to our unwritten laws, and why he'd allowed him to shoot the men from the Italian contingent. I managed to make a few comments, but I was well aware that I was wading deeper into the mire of the Oxy's call.

Because the Italians were mutually loathed by the Chinese, the Irish, and the Russians, there wasn't much concern about their brutal murder or the man who'd done the murdering. Business quickly took center stage, and it was then the New World Sparrows found themselves under the spotlight. And though the need was painful, I knew I had to focus, knew I was too weak to endure the siren song of the opioids that were taking over my life.

My attention here was imperative.

The New World Sparrows, or NWS as we'd started calling them, were our biggest threat.

So, I caved in.

I slipped a pill out of the bottle, carefully tumbling the round tablet onto my palm with as little noise as possible as my beads of poison rattled against each other, then I drew it into the nook of my fingers. Pretending I was covering my mouth, I slipped it between my lips and swallowed it dry.

The nausea soon went away.

The shakes stopped.

My brain cleared up shortly after, and I managed to tune in properly.

"What kind of group is this? One that exists in the shadows and uses criminals they've blackmailed to do their dirty work?" Vasov, the Russian leader, sneered. "This sounds like a children's story. You're making it up."

Rex pressed his elbows to the table and retorted, "You can think what you want, Vasov, but they're real. They've existed for far too fucking long, managing to escape our attention. Now we know about them, we can work on eradicating them."

Vasov mocked, "I'm the king of cocaine on this godforsaken island, I don't need to do shit. I'd just bet that you want us to waste *our* resources on hunting down this fairy story so you can grab—"

"You're a moron, Vasov," Zhao, the Dragon Head of the Triads, snarled, not letting the Bratva Pakhan finish. "You just proved how out of touch you are. Cocaine *isn't* king in Manhattan anymore. Hell, it isn't king in New York." His lips twisted. "Heroin is the new emperor." His eyes narrowed, his smugness overpowering thanks to the strong poppy routes he'd spent decades cultivating. "And long may it reign."

Vasov slammed his hand against the table, his outrage clear, and when he surged to his feet, I was the only one who could possibly understand the agony he endured when he realized, too late, that he'd *forgotten*.

My patella had been shattered, my other leg hit too, muscles torn and shredded, bones in my femur forever damaged like it had been under a butcher's knife.

His kneecaps, on the other hand, had been decimated by a sniper's bullets.

The sharp cry of pain had me wincing, while the rest of the men, my father included, looked upon him with feigned disinterest.

Did he but know it, Vasov had just shown weakness amid this pool of sharks.

They'd scented blood, and now they were going to be out to get him. *Prick.*

Rex, however, had different priorities than territory that had nothing to do with him. He was based in New Jersey, the lucky bastard, and had no jurisdiction in our city. The only reason he was here was because when Declan had explained the particulars to Da, in Da's eyes, the man's cause was a worthy one.

A good son, Aidan Sr. had declared, should and would kill to avenge his mother's honor.

And that was why Rex had the blood of three men on his hands.

Because my da had allowed it.

Wasn't he kind-hearted?

"You're not getting the bigger picture here. I've got my people looking into this group, but I'm telling you, they're more dangerous than you want to think."

I cast my father a look, felt Finn, my best friend, tense up at my back, because *we* knew he was right.

We were the ones who'd recently been affected by these NWS cunts, we'd been touched by them, and had almost lost my nephew and sister-in-law as a result.

We knew they were a shadowy organization that worked amid the Alphabet agencies—at least, that was what we'd come to believe. For all we knew, they were everywhere. In the jails, in the courts, in the churches. Wherever corruption ran rife in this city, hell, this country, they were probably there. Nibbling away at the foundations of democracy while pretending they were its face.

Fucking bureaucrats—couldn't trust any of the cunts.

My mouth twisted into a sneer at the thought before I asked, "How do we eradicate them?"

"We have to find them first," Rex pointed out. "We need to band together to do that." He peered over his shoulder at the fresh dead who were bleeding out onto the warehouse floor. "All I do know? The *Famiglia* was their front. You can't trust any of the Italians."

"Like we didn't know that anyway," Zhao said wryly.

Rex shook his head. "You wanna watch your ties as well, Zhao."

"What's that supposed to mean?" The Triad leader's eyes narrowed at the Prez, and his advisors started cracking their knuckles.

Because, yes, that would terrify the leader of the Satan's Sinners' MC. Jesus Christ.

"It means that Triads in China have trafficking links to some of the *Famiglia's* subsidiaries..."

Zhao's frown darkened. "I know nothing of this."

"A hacker friend of mine made the discovery. Don't believe me, then gimme your email and I'll send proof over."

"Can we get back on track?" Da snapped, his disinterest in this topic clear. "The Sparrows are our biggest threat right now."

"Yes, and you've just taken off their head," Vasov rasped, sounding winded and looking like death from his recent attempt at standing, "which means they're going to take note."

"We've drawn them out of the shadows," Da concurred, gleefully rubbing his hands together like he'd just decided we were all going on a vacation to the mountains. "Let the fun and games begin..."

THEY MIGHT HATE ME NOW, BUT MY SISTERS NEED ME.

THREE
CAMMIE

"WHERE ARE YOU GOING?"

I turned to my baby sister, Victoria, who was scowling at me from the doorway.

My bedroom was a thousand shades of puke—I meant, pink—as if Bratva princesses could only like this color—and once upon a time, I'd fit in here.

Exactly like Victoria did.

She'd just turned fifteen but looked like some kind of bizarre politician's wife in a gray pencil skirt with a neatly tucked in pink shirt and pearls around her throat.

Pearls.

She was either a First Lady-in-the-making or an upper class secretary.

Who bought her clothes now that Mama was gone, I had no idea. I couldn't see that slut, Svetlana, our new stepmother, going into the kinds of stores that stocked outfits such as this one. She dressed like a stripper who'd landed on her stacked heels in a pile of money.

A part of me wondered how she'd managed to snag my father who was notoriously marriage-shy after Mama's death, but then, I really didn't want to know how she'd hooked the biggest whale of them all.

Shuddering at the thought, I dropped my gaze from the vanity mirror and twisted around to look at Victoria and not her reflection.

Her concern was clear.

It was also warranted.

Just not today...

I wafted a hand down my outfit. "Can't you tell?"

She frowned. "You're coming back, aren't you?"

As if *he'd* let me run... I didn't say that though. Just smiled at her. "Of course. I'm only going for a ride. If I don't get out of this house, I'll scream."

Her nose crinkled in a way that told me she agreed. One hundred percent. But was too scared to admit it out loud.

That was the kind of household this was.

We were scared.

All the time.

From the outside looking in, the Vasovs were industrial tycoons.

But from the inside?

We were Bratva.

Scum.

Dangerous and endangered.

Living our lives on the knife's edge, never knowing if today was our day to die.

Once upon a time, I'd thought it was only the men who had to subsist like that. One foot in the grave and the other foot in a jail cell, but it wasn't just them.

Victoria and I would never go to prison, at least, not for the Brotherhood's crimes, but death could come to us at any moment.

Just like Mama.

Raped and slain in her own house.

Fuck, I hated this property.

I'd never understood how, when my father proclaimed to love her so much, he could stay here. Had never understood how he allowed his daughters to remain in the residence where such tragedy had happened...

It was one of the many reasons I loathed him.

Why, one day, if he wasn't careful, I'd be the one to eliminate him as easily as it was hitting backspace on a keyboard.

Palms growing sweaty with a cocktail of nerves and wishful thinking that it'd be so easy to get rid of him when it was anything but, I reached up and tugged on the star pendant I'd purloined from my father's safe when I'd stolen one of my mother's necklaces for my sister, Inessa.

"What's that?" Victoria asked, stepping into my dressing room and not stopping until she could lean over and peer at the pendant. "I remember it. Just not..." Her brow puckered. "I don't know where I remember it from."

Of course she would.

She'd been a toddler when Mama died. Would have remembered the tiny star as Mama put her to sleep or played with her.

But I didn't tell her that, nor the thought processes that had led me to a conclusion that was beyond unpalatable.

"It's something I bought myself the other day. Isn't it pretty?"

Victoria's frown only deepened. "Did Mama wear something like that?"

"I don't remember," I lied, and I reached for her hand and tugged on it. "Come riding with me?" I asked, by way of a distraction.

Victoria was not the world's most natural equestrian. If anything, she was terrified of horses, and they sensed that fear like they were starving predators, not man's best friend.

And yes, horses were so much more man's best friend than dogs.

Horses were life.

As expected, she staggered back, slipping on this morning's edition of the New York Times, her fingers forming the sign of the cross like I needed exorcising. I grinned at her as she scampered away without another word.

I sucked in a relieved breath for her questions to have scampered away too, then leaned over to grab the paper. I'd already done this morning's crossword which was why it was on the floor, but I could imagine me slipping on it next.

The last thing I needed was a concussion because I'd banged my head on the bed frame—that would be just my luck. I'd end up married off to my worst enemy while I was unconscious or something. Father was, after all, an opportunist.

Shuddering at the thought, I turned to face myself in the mirror.

My appearance wasn't satisfactory, but then, it never was.

Even after I'd had surgery, and my tits were bigger than before, I wasn't happy with them. I still felt flat-chested, and I knew that I probably always would feel that way. Just like I'd never feel pretty. Just like I knew I could get addicted to surgery, to make-up, to everything that was false in an effort to shore up a self-esteem that had been dumped in the Hudson years ago.

The only thing that had saved me from getting addicted to going under the knife was my empty bank account. I'd hoarded every cent to get the money together, and when I'd found myself in dire straits later on, I'd regretted how much money I'd wasted on my appearance.

With or without them, everyone else might look at me and see an ice princess, delicate features, a pretty face, long, silken blonde hair, and a body that would make a pin-up envious, but I saw...

I swallowed.

A hag.

A walking vagina.

A womb that my father had repeatedly tried to sell.

My mouth tightened at the thought, my palms stinging as I dug the tips of my nails into the ragged flesh there, and I looked away from the mirror.

I'd had compliments about my appearance, and I knew they were true. When I'd found sanctuary in West Orange, at the Satan's Sinners' MC compound, the only territory I knew my father would never dare infiltrate, the only place that, in his eyes, would truly sully me, I'd been popular. So popular that it had scared me.

I'd been a virgin when I went there.

Nyx, the club's Enforcer, had actually popped my cherry without even realizing it. He'd also popped my heart, because I'd loved him for nearly as long as I'd been at the compound. When he'd told me that no other brother was allowed to have me, I'd thought he was claiming me.

I was wrong.

He hadn't made me his Old Lady, just his slut.

Turning me into a walking vagina once more, except this time, I was less of a commodity without my hymen.

After he'd claimed Giulia as his Old Lady, and I was no longer under his protection, everything had changed. His brothers got the go ahead to have me when he was done with me, which had about broken me, and I'd ended up giving Sin a blowjob to get him away from me.

When I hadn't been able to put out, I'd known my time at the club was over. Then with Dog, I'd outright rejected his advances. When he'd punched me in the stomach as punishment, he'd just fast forwarded things.

I was back home.

Back where I never thought I'd be again, and I was only welcomed because Father had almost died. I wished he had. Wished we'd buried him, then, maybe, we'd be free.

The desire to reach into my vanity to unveil my box of freedom was a strong one. To lift that lid, to stare at the gleaming metal, to sink it into flesh and to let my pain and anger run free with my blood, but I was going to the stables today.

That had to be catharsis enough.

Storming out of the dressing room, I grabbed my purse, which rattled with its contents, and slung it over my shoulder so that the strap settled between my breasts.

Peering out of the door to my bedroom, I saw that the coast was clear from relatives—there was a guard sitting on a stool at the other end of the landing, but he didn't count—and I headed out.

The grand staircase was worthy of a mansion back in Moscow, one that had seen the Romanovs themselves wandering down those grand sets of steps, but it led to a home that belonged in a thrift store. An expensive one.

Cheap tack was everywhere, which had me wondering what on Earth my father was thinking. Mama had tastefully decorated this place to suit a man of his standing. Svetlana, in barely no time at all as his wife, had ruined that and turned it into a tart's paradise. Mama's style might have been out of date, but by comparison to this mess, it was a dream.

Mouth pursing at the thought, I crossed the floor that was carpeted in zebra-print, and made it outside without crossing paths with the wicked witch.

We were the same age, but while my life hadn't been easy, it had definitely been harder on her. Every time she looked at me, I felt her resentment, but I didn't understand why.

We were the same.

To the Bratva, we were just cunts to be plowed and filled with seed.

Mama had failed to provide a son, so I knew Svetlana would be used by Father. That was probably why he'd married her. He still had time to beget a son...

Pakhans didn't tend to be hereditary, but my father had done the Bratva proud. He'd established the Brotherhood on the East Coast in ways Moscow appreciated, and had stayed at the helm for an unheard of amount of time. Moscow's pleasure and the city's fear of him meant if he bred a boy child, and managed to live long enough for that son to get to adulthood, my brother might, just might, take over Father's throne.

God help him.

As I darted across the way to the garage, I took note of my surroundings. The courtyard was still stained with the blood my father had spilled when he'd been shot here—my one regret? The sniper hadn't aimed higher. Like, at his chest. Or even his skull. That would have solved all my problems.

Sighing with regret, I made it to the garage and headed to a Range Rover without seeing anyone but guards.

I'd gotten used to living without them, had adapted to a life where they didn't follow me everywhere, but it was a small price to pay.

I was back in the center of the war zone.

Not that I'd have been safe back at the Sinners' compound.

They'd just been bombed.

My father had been shot at his home.

Was anywhere on the East Coast safe?

I thought about the rough tenor of Nyx's voice the last time I'd spoken to him on the phone. When he'd answered, my heart had soared, only to hear his lack of interest, to recognize that it was a token call.

He didn't give a shit about me.

Nobody did.

That was why I had to protect myself. Do what no one else would—have my back.

With the engine idling as I waited for my cell to connect with the dashboard, I watched as, unbidden, a guard settled beside me in the seat, and I left.

We didn't speak.

I didn't even know his name.

We ignored one another as I drove toward the Belt Parkway, my end destination, Forest Park.

A few minutes into my thirty-minute ride, my playlist paused with an incoming call. Seeing Inessa's name, I answered and immediately spoke in French.

"*Bonjour, ma soeur.*"

She hesitated for a fraction of a second, before replying in that language too. "Who's there?"

"God only knows. I haven't bothered learning their names. They'll all be dead before this crap is over with the Italians."

French, as always, was our secret language. The only means of having any privacy in our godforsaken lives.

"Cammie," Inessa chided with a small laugh. "Since when are you so gloomy?"

"Since Father tried to force another engagement ring on my finger." I shuddered at the thought of Abramovicz's hands on me. It was bad enough whenever he kissed my cheek in greeting before we sat down to break bread, but for him to have outright access to me whenever he so chose?

No.

Nope.

Niet.

Just wasn't going to happen.

That was why I had a plan, and it was going to work.

There was no alternative. It worked or I slit my wrists.

Simple.

"Not that again," Inessa replied, but her tone contained every shred of revulsion that I felt.

I wouldn't be surprised if she'd had to face that horrendous prospect before Father had shoved her onto the Irish to make an alliance with them.

"Yes. Unfortunately. Abramovicz graced us with his presence at dinner last night, which was where Father made the announcement.

"Seems that Svetlana doesn't like me lounging around the place, and Abramovicz is still willing to take me off Father's hands even though he won't bloody the sheets with my virginity. And yes, that *is* a direct quote from him. He told us that as he picked salmon out of his teeth."

Inessa growled under her breath. "I hate that bitch, and I hate that bastard too. Why won't he just die already? He's ancient."

"Maybe I'll be lucky and he'll have a heart attack soon. As for Svetlana, I fantasized about drowning her in a bowl of borscht, but what can you do? I don't want to end up with a bullet from Father's gun between my eyebrows."

"Yes, I'd prefer your brains not to be splashed over the dining room. She might have made the place look like a casino in Vegas, but I don't think that would do much for the decor."

My lips twitched but because I could feel myself getting mad, I knew I had to change the subject before I hightailed it off to the state line—guard be damned. He was both my protection and my jailor, after all.

"As wonderful as it is to hear from you, and to practice French again, why are you calling?"

Inessa and I weren't exactly close. Victoria had forgiven me for abandoning her, but Inessa hadn't. I'd barely spoken to her since I'd returned home. I couldn't blame her, just wished she didn't blame me.

I'd taken my chance to get out, and I'd been a fool to think anything would change when I returned. But when your haven became your hell, sometimes it was easier to go back to the devil you knew...

Fool me once, shame on you.

Fool me twice, shame on me.

She cleared her throat, rupturing my thoughts as she admitted, "I'm in Texas."

"You are? Why?" I sputtered, her revelation filling me with both envy and surprise.

None of us had traveled anywhere other than New York or Moscow.

That was literally it.

We weren't allowed anywhere else, which was why West Orange, just across the state line in New Jersey, had felt both liberating but as daring as I could brave it.

"For a wedding. An MC wedding. It's strange. They're getting married in a kind of garden."

"Not a church?"

"Well, no. It's more of a blessing. She's marrying three men."

My brows rose. "Three?"

"Yes. It's... It doesn't matter." She sighed, then her voice turned hushed, "Cammie, I've done something stupid."

"Like what?"

"I let Eoghan shave me last night."

My brows lowered. "Let him shave you? Your legs?"

She hissed under her breath. "No! Between them."

A smile danced along my lips. "Oh."

"Yes, oh," she grumbled.

"What went wrong?" My grin widened. "Assuming something went wrong...?"

"It's itchy," was her short reply. "And if you're laughing, I'll kill you."

"I'm not laughing," I countered, barely managing to hold back a chuckle. "Don't you have any aloe vera?"

"I'm dressed for a wedding, Cammie. What about that sounds like I'm packing aloe vera?"

"Can't you go to a drugstore?"

She hissed once more before begrudgingly admitting, "He used his shaving foam... I think I might have had an allergic reaction or something."

My eyes flared wide. "Are you being serious?"

"Yes!" she snapped. "Cammie, I wouldn't have called you if I wasn't being damn serious."

That stung, but I got it. I'd left her when she needed me the most, but I'd had to think of myself. I'd have been as little use to her as Abramovicz's child bride as I was incognito at the Satan's Sinners' MC compound.

At least after a stint there, I was alive. As Abramovicz's wife, I'd probably have hurled myself down the stairs by now.

"Have you told Eoghan?"

Because he'd asked me to steal her one of Mama's favorite necklaces for a birthday present, I had some insight into their relationship. I knew Eoghan wasn't a bad husband—well, bad in our world was a little different than the regular one—but only someone who gave a fuck about their woman would bother to do something like that.

Which was exactly why I'd done it too. The danger to myself be damned. I loved my sister. It fit that Eoghan did as well, and that we'd worked together to make her happy.

"No," she growled under her breath. "Why would I tell him?"

"Because he's your husband?" I retorted. "Aren't man and wife supposed to share things like this?"

"I just wish I'd let him wax me," she wailed. "That would have been less painful than this."

"Inessa, if it's that bad you need to tell him, for God's sake." My hands tightened around the steering wheel, forcing a shiver out of me as pain whispered along my nerve endings like the sweetest of caresses.

"I can't!"

Whatever I'd expected today, without a shadow of a doubt, I hadn't thought I'd be talking about my sister getting her vajayjay shaved by her husband. Did she have to be so stubborn about this?

"He might need to take you to the ER," I pointed out.

"I refuse to go to the ER over a—"

"A, what?" I countered, even though I got it. Well, not entirely, but I *was* a woman. No one wanted to go to the ER over something like this.

"You know what," she snarled, and in her voice, I heard humiliated tears that made me annoyed at myself for being amused earlier.

Uncertain about what to do, especially when we were this far apart and knowing she was really desperate to be calling me, I said, "I'll tell him. Let me break the news. That'll spare you."

"You're kidding, right? Then he'll know I told you I let him shave me last night. H-He—" A sob escaped her, one that was quickly choked back.

"*Malyshka*," I soothed. "What is it?"

Her gulp was so loud, it was audible. "H-He doesn't want anyone to see my vagina. That's why he shaved me."

I blinked, then rolled my eyes. Then winced as a wave of misery hit me.

The green kind.

I'd have loved for Nyx to feel that way about me.

To not want anyone to see my pussy.

To feel that possessive of me that not even an esthetician could prod me between the legs.

That was how things had gotten so complicated, and gone so wrong. I'd thought he wanted more from me, more than any other woman when he'd told me no other brother was allowed to fuck me. I just hadn't realized he did that with all the clubwhores he'd slept with.

He used them exclusively until he was bored with them.

Just like he'd grown bored with me.

Squeezing the wheel again, the physical pain easier to deal with than the emotional, my throat clogged with tears as I rasped, "Is it really that bad?"

Silence.

She didn't reply, not for the longest time, and only the fact the SUV's dash remained lit up with her name on it let me know she hadn't cut the call.

"Yes," was her miserable whisper as she accepted her situation.

"Sweetheart, you and I both know things are dire if you called me. You have to go to the doctor's... You know you have to. Embarrassing or not."

"I don't want to," came another miserable whisper.

I couldn't even begin to imagine how an allergic reaction would unfold down there, neither did I want to know, but Inessa was my baby sister. She needed my help, and I couldn't give it to her. My support, on the other hand, was something I could freely offer.

"I know you don't, *malyshka*, but hey, it might bring you closer! You should be able to share anything with the man you care about and who cares about you, shouldn't you?" And it was evident to anyone with eyes that Eoghan had strong feelings for my sister.

Oddly enough, I wasn't jealous about that. Just the possessiveness.

I didn't want to be loved. Love was toxic.

I wanted to be owned. Owners looked after their property.

I just wanted to choose who I belonged to.

"Yes," she said thickly. "I know you're right... But it's so mortifying."

"I know it is," I soothed. "But I promise, it's no worse than how itchy you are."

Every woman knew how godawful that kind of thing was. Never mind without an allergic reaction ramping things up tenfold.

She sucked in a breath. "The service is over so maybe we can cut out soon."

"Screw politeness, Inessa," I grumbled. "What if you go into anaphylactic shock?"

"That would have happened last night," she replied absently. "But it is bad... Okay. I'll tell Eoghan." A groan escaped her. "Thank you, Cammie. I guess I knew I needed to talk to him all along but I'm not sure if I would have."

"What are big sisters for?" I queried lightly, even if my heart ached for the years we'd lost, the time and the closeness that we'd never been destined to have. Where she only called me when things were bad, not when things were good...

I half-expected her to reply with all the bitterness she felt at my abandonment, but instead, she whispered, "You're right. They're for calling with post-depilatory disasters."

My lips twitched. "Let me know when you're at the ER?"

"Okay. I-It might take a while. You know how long it is before you get seen."

I snorted. "*Malyshka*, if you think Eoghan isn't about to move heaven and earth for you, you're crazy."

A soft laugh tittered down the line, one that told me she knew I was right.

As we parted ways, the ache in my heart was strong.

I was glad for her. Truly, I was. I just...

A sigh rushed from my lips.

If wishes were horses, beggars would ride.

I was no beggar, but I'd spend the next few hours riding. That wasn't much consolation, but it was better than the alternative—spending another moment under the same roof as Svetlana the Slut.

FOUR
BRENNAN

"WHERE'S YOUR MIND AT, BREN?"

I tried not to yawn, especially not at the moment when Ma was scowling down at me, because she had the uncanny knack of reading every cue I gave off with an accuracy that was practically mystical.

If I yawned, she'd think I was stressed. Not tired.

If I shivered, she'd think I was feverish. Not cold.

And the bitch of it was, as crazy as it seemed, as nonsensical, she never got it wrong. I didn't know if that was because we were close or whatever, but she always knew.

My yawn might be founded in a lack of sleep, but mostly it was forged from stress.

The last month or so had not only been a nightmare on the work front but on a personal front. Especially when the past and present were colliding and not in a very helpful way.

My regrets were coming home to roost.

In more ways than one.

I'd made it a practice not to regret much in my life. As a general in the Irish Mob, there was plenty to turn me maudlin, but Mariska was a memory that was pretty much laying eggs in my fucking head.

Of late, the family had been turning to me with all their problems, because Aidan Jr. was out of it. I'd always been the go-to fixer, slapping

Band-Aids on situations left, right, and center, but that was nothing to now.

Not when we were knee deep in a war with fucking ghosts.

"I'm just tired."

Ma sniffed at me. Lena might be nearing seventy but she was as shrewd as ever. "Pull the other one. I won't tell your Da. You know that."

I winced. "It's nothing to do with work. Anyway, we're not supposed to talk about shit like that."

She rolled her eyes. "I know more than your father would like."

"More than any of us would like. The last thing we want is you in danger."

Her shrug had me frowning at her. "I lived far longer than I ever expected I would."

The irritating thing was, I knew this had nothing to do with the reason she and I were closer than most mothers and sons.

That was what happened after what we'd gone through together. Instead of blaming me for being a shit son, she'd taken me under her wing, and showed me I wasn't. She'd had faith in me and the promise I'd made her, unlike Da who trusted me with business but who'd never trusted me with her again.

Still, she wasn't talking about that.

Just the fact she was Aidan O'Donnelly's obsession. His weakest link. The reason he'd trigger a war the likes of which New York had never seen before.

One that made the current pissing match between the Italians and the Russians look like two kids involved in a fistfight on a playground.

"Sorry, Ma," I said gruffly.

"You don't have to be." She tilted her head to the side, then leaned over to cup my cheek. "Takes more than bloodshed and bullshit to make those shadows appear under your eyes. Are they to do with Junior?"

I frowned at her. "No. Why would it be about him?"

Contrary to what Da thought, the world didn't revolve around his heir.

I loved Aidan Jr. but I resented the preferential treatment he got when I was the one doing all the fucking work. Da had never really forgiven me for what the Aryans did to Ma though, and it was a constant uphill struggle with him sometimes.

"Your father might be in denial about how many pills that boy's popping, but I'm not." She pursed her lips in disapproval. "We should never have called him Aidan. It was just asking for him to be as stubborn as his da."

"Not sure addicted and stubborn are synonyms, Ma."

"Maybe not. He's got a strength of will that beats even you, Brennan, but he's letting those pills win. The only reason I haven't raised the subject with Senior is because I know he'll push."

"I'm surprised you don't think that isn't what Aidan needs."

She shook her head. "You have to let them bottom out. I—" It was the faintest of hesitations, but because I knew her so well, I sensed it. "—read it in a book."

Narrowing my eyes at her, I asked, "You read it in a book? You sure about that?"

She huffed. "I'm not in the habit of lying to you, Brennan."

"I don't think you are," I countered, still squinting at her, but I wafted my hand in a circle in front of her face. "What was that about?"

Her scowl made an appearance, but I was long past the age where that scowl was enough to have my knees knocking with fear. I faced bigger boogeymen every day of the fucking week now. I wished she was the scariest thing I'd seen in my life.

"What was what about?"

"You hesitated." My voice was flat. "You didn't read that in a book."

Her mouth tautened into an irritated pucker. "No, I didn't," she conceded.

"And don't say you saw it on Oprah," I countered immediately. "No BS, Ma."

"I spoke to my psychologist about him."

Her words had my eyes flaring wide. "Are you shitting me? I thought you'd stopped visiting him years ago." She'd seen Da getting stabbed by a rival and, as he phrased it, had taken a funny turn.

One diagnosis of PTSD later, some prescription meds that Da got on the black market, and no more visits with a practitioner who could spill the family's secrets.

Or so we'd thought.

Jesus.

"Does Da know about this?"

I saw the anger whisper over her face. Over the years, I'd learned to be wary of that look. Redheads and their tempers—nothing beat it. I almost pitied our money man, Finn, his Aoife because her hair was redder than a rose. I just couldn't imagine her slapping their son Jacob, not like Ma had slapped us and clipped us about the ears.

I wasn't saying we didn't need it, because that would be a lie. We'd been a bunch of five—six after Finn moved in with us—rowdy boys, who knew that we owned Manhattan. That level of power quickly went to a kid's head, but our folks had been swift to nip any mutiny in the bud.

Nepotism might be a key factor in our world, rebellion when it came to the Irish fighting for their freedom, but within the ranks, obedience was expected.

We'd learned that at a very young age.

"I'm not, as you so eloquently put it, shitting you, Brennan. When have you ever known me to do that?"

She'd kissed the Blarney Stone, and I felt no compunction in telling her that, only, my cellphone buzzed. Which was what saved both our asses.

Hers, because I could tell she didn't want to talk about having another therapist.

A fucking therapist.

The Alphabets wouldn't think twice about turning a shrink.

Mine, because it'd been a while since she dragged me from a chair by my ear, and I didn't feel like a repeat.

When my phone buzzed again, I frowned as I checked my messages.

The first one had my mouth tightening.

Forrest: *Coullson is on the move.*

Me: *Heading to his usual spot?*

Forrest: *Looks like it.*

Me: *Keep me in the loop.*

Forrest: *Today the day?*

I shot Ma a look, saw the defiance in her eyes and had to wonder what the fuck she'd said that might be used against us... Now was not the time for family secrets to be spilling out from the core unit of the King and Queen of the Five fucking Points.

Me: *Time we broke ranks and started the ball rolling.*

Forrest: *Gotcha. I'll be in touch.*

Before I could read the second message, Ma's hand reached for mine.

"It was twenty-five years ago."

Guilt hit me. Like a fucking sucker punch. I closed my eyes and squeezed her fingers. "I'm sorry, Ma. I forgot." How the fuck had I when it was my living nightmare? Twenty-five years ago she'd been taken hostage.

Because of my fuck-up.

She shook her head. "You don't need to be sorry. I know the family is piling too much on you." Our gazes clashed and held as she whispered, "Brennan?"

That her defiance had disappeared, slipping away like sand in my hand, being replaced with a cocktail of guilt and shame, had me frowning with concern. "Yeah, Ma? What is it?"

"Do you ever—" She released a shaky breath. "Do you ever regret what you've done?"

I blinked, because I knew she wasn't talking about the Aryans. About my letting her down.

What I'd done?

I'd killed for the family. Slaughtered for us, truth be told. My hands weren't just covered in blood, my fucking soul was too. But that was nothing to what I'd be willing to do.

When you were born into the Irish Mob, there was but one route in your life—to follow in your father's footsteps. To become a soldier for the firm.

I wasn't like Declan who'd questioned his place in the Points, nor was I like Eoghan who'd tried to live his life in the regular army—not just an illegal one. I knew my place. Had accepted it a long time ago. But regrets?

"Yeah, I have regrets," I told her softly, frowning when her manicured nails, the clean white tips, dug into my palm.

"When I was a girl, I used to believe that going to church was enough. You did something wrong, you went to confession. That was how it worked. It's what your father believes." Her brow puckered. "It's what I believed but—"

"What have you done wrong, Ma?" Deciding to lighten things a little, my grin made an appearance and it turned rueful. "Apart from give birth to five knuckleheads?"

She'd normally have narrowed her eyes at me, but this time, those bright green orbs were wide with distress, and business aside, concern had me asking, "Is the therapist helping?"

My cellphone buzzed again, and I knew why. This time it'd be another of my buddies on my crew—Bagpipes. That he'd messaged at all was enough for me to know she was on the move. Which meant he'd be awaiting further instruction.

Mouth tightening, I ignored my phone, and gently coaxed, "You don't need to talk to strangers, Ma. I'm here."

"I-I can't get clean, Brennan. I can't seem to shake it off. Your father made it sound so easy, but sometimes, there's no going back, is there?"

My brow puckered as I wondered where this was coming from.

She'd seemed all right on Sunday, the last time I'd seen her. A smile on her face, her hair neat and tidy even after cooking for all of us, her trim figure shown off in a blouse and skirt with low kitten heels that made her look ten years younger than her real age. She'd joked and chivvied us like usual, hugging Jacob, trying to get to know Seamus, teasing Inessa and Aoife... normal.

"Sometimes, no, there's no going back," I agreed, twisting my hand in hers so I could grip her fingers.

I had no idea what would make her feel dirty outside of what she'd endured during her abduction, but I didn't think she was going to tell me. Da, on the other hand, she might. Father Doyle didn't seem to have done the trick.

"Does Da know what's on your mind?"

My cell buzzed once more, and her fingers clamped down on mine before she surged to her feet and darted over to the other side of the kitchen.

A kitchen she, with her pearls and chignon and designer dress, didn't fit in at all. But I knew the homeliness of it comforted her. It reminded me of the one in our second cousin's cottage back in the Motherland. We'd stayed there only briefly, but Ireland was in my blood as a result.

And not just because of the money we sent back to fund its freedom, either.

"It's okay, Brennan. You're busy. You need to deal with business."

"No, don't be—" I scowled when my phone started ringing, not just buzzing this time, and I picked it up, snapping, "Bagpipes, can't you take the fucking hint?"

"She's going to the stables, Bren. You told me to tell you if she went back there."

My brows furrowed because I couldn't fault the fucker for obeying orders.

Did Camille seriously have to go riding right this goddamn second?

"Shit," I rumbled under my breath. "She got a death wish or something?"

"Or something," he agreed. "Want me to bring Tinker over? Make sure things are copacetic?"

Pinching the bridge of my nose, I leaned into my elbow that I stacked on the table. My brain raced as I thought about the best move to make.

Somehow, she maneuvered around Italian territory without getting into too much shit, so if I sent a bunch of Pointers over there to protect her, it might cause raised eyebrows and draw attention to her—the last thing I wanted.

The *Famiglia* might be fucked now we'd chopped off their Don's head and had shoved their potential leaders off this mortal coil too, but that didn't mean two more fucking heads weren't about to pop up.

Goddamn Hydra.

Pushing a Bratva princess into Italian territory was a disaster waiting to happen. I had no idea why her father let her breach that uncharted border, but until she was mine, I had no rights over her.

A fact that was starting to piss me off.

My jaw worked as I asked, "What car you riding in?"

"The Beemer."

"The one with the stolen plates?"

"Yeah."

I dipped my chin. "Okay, follow her, but keep a low profile."

"Can't exactly do that when she's on a fucking horse, Bren. What do you want me to do? Go riding with a bunch of five-year-olds?"

Despite the severity of the situation, my lips twitched at the thought of Bagpipes, so named for the size of his gut and an unfortunate incident on his wedding day with a musician, trying to blend in among a bunch of kids.

"She usually deals with tack, doesn't she?"

"I don't fucking know what that is."

I grunted. "The saddles and shit. Not talking about the state of your apartment, Bagpipes."

"Kerry-Louise has got great taste. Fuck you, Brennan."

Grinning again, I cut Ma a look and saw she was standing at the sink, her hands gripping the sides as she stared out of the window and onto the expansive yard. I didn't think the pool was what had her so engrossed, though.

If anything, she was lost to me.

To the house.

To New fucking York.

What was going on with her?

The question plagued me even as Bagpipes growled, "Brennan? What the fuck do you want me to do?"

"Not get shot," I said promptly. "She's been managing to keep her ass in one piece without our interference. Just sit on her car. Make sure she doesn't go anywhere without you there tailing her. Got me?"

"Yeah, I do." He cleared his throat. "You coming over?"

In the Five Points, family was more than just blood. It came in the shape of a five-pointed star too. Bagpipes and Forrest were a part of my crew, but they were friends as well. Because I'd set them on innocuous jobs they gave me shit about, I'd enlightened them about the status quo.

They thought I was fucking nuts, but who were they to argue?

I answered to three people in this world.

God.

My father.

And Father Doyle.

Two of them, I ignored, but Da? He wasn't the kind to let anyone ignore him. Not unless you wanted a knife between the legs.

My only saving grace was that Camille was family now, and Da wanted my balls right where they were so I could spawn the next gen of O'Donnellys. A poor fucking bunch of kids who'd take over the helm when we croaked—thirty years earlier than we probably should thanks to the shitty life we led.

Heaving a sigh, I muttered, "I'll be over if I can make it."

He grunted. "See you later, then."

He didn't tack on, "Dumbass," but I heard it all the same.

If I hadn't known something was wrong with Ma, I'd have known it when she didn't ask me about the phone call... her focus was still on the back yard.

Frowning, I got to my feet and moved away from the scrubbed oak kitchen table, toward the island which I rounded, before I headed to the wide porcelain sink she was gripping like it was a life raft to cling to.

I moved to her side, slung an arm about her shoulder, and pressed my chin to her head. "You can talk to me, Ma."

She cleared her throat. "I had some good news, by the way. Mary Catherine gave birth to a boy. Isn't that wonderful? Her mother's a real piece of work, but she was always such a nice girl—"

"Ma," I grumbled. "I like Mary Catherine too, but for God's sake, I ain't interested in her right now. Talk to me. What's going on?"

"Some things a son shouldn't know about his mother," was all she said.

"You could kill someone and I wouldn't give a fuck, Ma," I argued, my tone waspish with irritation. I felt her shoulders bunch thanks to my hold on her.

"You need to get going, son."

I did. She wasn't wrong.

But...

"You seemed fine the other day."

She tilted her head to the side. "Some days are better than others, aren't they? You know that as well as I do, son."

At her words, I just blew out a breath, tilted my head so that my cheek was resting on the crown of hers this time, and I stared out the window too.

Because she wasn't wrong.

Some days really were better than others, and there was nothing I, or anyone else, could do about it.

FIVE
BRENNAN

THE RIDE back to the city was a pain in the ass. A necessary evil since we'd moved the folks upstate for their safety, but a pain nonetheless.

Because Aidan Jr. was a fuckwit and wasn't pulling his weight, I was the one managing his load as well as my own, and that load wasn't exactly fucking light. Not in the middle of a war. Not with all this shit going down with the New World Sparrows.

Goddamn Sparrows.

Who named a secret organization after a fucking bird?

A tiny little fucker too.

Not a dirty great eagle or some kind of vulture, but a sparrow?

Shaking my head, I settled into my seat for the annoying, traffic-jammed ride ahead. One hand on the steering wheel, the other leaning on the door of my Mercedes-Maybach GLS600, which was just fresh in and still with that new car smell. Driving down the highway toward home, I tapped a button on my steering wheel which had the music soaring so loud it made my ears ring.

Audioslave.

No better soundtrack to cure me of my fucking mood.

What with the birds, those greasy Italians, and a fiancée who didn't know I was stalking her ass, who didn't even know she was my fiancée, and Ma who was going all 'one flew over the cuckoo's nest'—birds were fucking haunting me at the moment—I needed something to stop my ears from bleeding.

Tension lines bracketed my mouth as I scanned the rear-view mirror, checking on who was following me. I usually had a Fed tail, but I didn't mind because we had the Director in our pocket, and I preferred them there. It was easier when they were out in the open, made it simpler to control the fuckers.

Of course, they didn't mean to be so visible, but the useless pieces of shit needed to go back to Quantico because I could tail someone better in my fucking sleep.

Before I'd climbed into my new SUV, Forrest had confirmed Coullson's location, which made that my end destination.

Just because I wanted to head to the stables in Forest Park didn't mean I could.

I had outstanding debts that were racking up, debts that had been as much on my shoulders as whatever sins were weighing down Ma.

Funny how the shit you got up to as a kid could come back and haunt your ass when you least expected it.

The Russians and the Irish had always been enemies.

I'd never thought that would change.

Then, shit had.

The Colombians had tried to gun down the family at Finn's wedding, and we'd teamed up with the Russians to stamp them out. Ever since, we'd been on a recruitment drive, and with our numbers finally healthy—economic downturns were always great for getting people onto the wrong side of the tracks—we no longer needed our allies as much, but that didn't mean we weren't stuck with them now.

Eoghan was married to one of them.

Not just fucking married, either. *He loved her.* It was clear whenever he looked at Inessa. The possessive stamp on his face, the way his hand rested on her, how he was always turned into her, an arm slung about her shoulders, around her waist...

My baby brother had an issue with sharing and hand-me-downs.

Inessa was his. No one else's. And whenever he was with the family, he made that clear.

I'd just never thought that Mariska's daughter would be my sister-in-law.

And I never thought, that last day in our usual room in the Ritz-Carlton, when we'd split up, my body nearly broken from the beating Da had given me when he'd found out who I was screwing, the promise she'd made me give her would come to pass.

As enemies, there wasn't shit I could do to help.

And that wasn't me being a chicken shit either.

The Russians were cunts. Dirty fuckers with no honor. No code. And, without a code of conduct, there might as well have been rabid jackals roaming the streets.

But as allies? I was honor bound to take action.

Honor bound to do as Mariska had made me promise—take care of her girls.

Speaking of 'no code,' my phone beeped with an incoming message, one I read when there was a lull in the traffic.

Lyanov: *Svetlana Vasov's pregnant. Antoni's crowing about it. Says it's a boy.*

Shit.

That was going to fuck with my timeline.

Me: *Appreciate the intel. Keep me in the loop.*

I'd been sowing seeds for a long while in the Russian camp, and with this one revelation, the fortune I'd spent might have just paid for itself.

Arriving back in the city faster than anticipated, I was glad to have shaved off some minutes—time was precious at the moment. As was the element of surprise—and Lyanov's news had put the wind up my ass and my foot firmly on the accelerator pedal.

As I pulled up alongside Elemental, a valet appeared, hovering in place as I opened the door when the coast was clear, and dangled the keys for him to snatch. Using a valet meant I'd have to sweep my car for bugs later, but it was better than having to park in the sardine cans they called parking lots in this space-poor neighborhood.

I didn't need to warn the kid that I'd have his head if he scratched the paint job. The second his eyes collided with mine, his gulp told me he knew who I was.

Most people in the city were aware of the O'Donnellys. Especially this close to our home turf—Hell's Kitchen.

The kid swallowed once more as he reached for the keys, and I let them drop into his palm before I rounded the fender and stared up at the club.

It was on the border between our territory and the *Famiglia's*, but ever since the Satan's Sinners' MC had joined our side in the war against the Italians, their hacker had joined forces with my brother, Conor, and had started stirring shit with their gambling businesses. Shutting down casinos, draining the bank accounts of their illegal gambling dens, sending cops to their whale poker games on massive busts...

Their losses were approaching the eight figures—that was how much damage this Lodestar bitch and my younger bro had done. As a result, the Italians had started shedding real estate, and we were snapping it up.

Their financial losses were our gain.

Still, that the club had changed hands hadn't hit the news. Our legit front, Acuig, hadn't been buying up these pieces of property, shell corporations had. That was down to Conor and Finn strategizing long term.

I had no idea as to their end game, but I didn't need to. Just like they didn't need to know why I was here today.

It sure as fuck wasn't a spot check by the new management...

Elemental was lit up in light bulbs, raw, old-world glamor that fit the esthetics of the place. The doors were swathed in red velvet curtains, and as I walked in, the heady scent of incense overwhelmed my senses— musk and sandalwood. Overpowering smells. Smells that made me want to sneeze.

I fucking hated perfume.

A glance about the front hall revealed a porter's chair by the door which was manned by a bouncer who barely fit on it. He kept his gaze trained on the door, which told me he wasn't interested in registering my identity—smart man.

Any trouble that went down today would bypass everyone's attention.

Even if a server witnessed it, they'd never go to the cops.

Not unless they had a death wish.

As I headed down the corridor, the coat check attendant kept her face turned away too as I strolled down the rich burgundy carpet and toward the inner sanctum of *Elemental*.

A quick check of my phone had me seeing Forrest had sent another message.

Forrest: *He brought Frederica. They're in the back.*

Me: *Perfect. Just in the lobby. On my way.*

Tucking my phone back into my pocket, I smirked to myself, satisfied by the success of today's plan. Something I'd been working on since Declan and I had learned about the Sparrows from Caroline Dunbar—a dirty Fed.

We'd had several lackeys working to bring down Coullson, and in all honesty, that the fucker had picked Frederica would give us even more leverage than we'd be getting with a regular hooker.

Barely refraining from rubbing my hands together, I focused on the club once I pushed open the doors.

Even at this time of the day, it was busy.

The rich bastards who frequented *Elemental* weren't worrying about their nine-to-five jobs, that was for fucking sure. These were trust fund brats with nothing better to do with their days than waste their ancestors' hard earned cash.

Cunts.

I hated this type of place and the type of person who used it. Waste of space morons with their minds high on blow and their cocks riddled with Chlamydia.

Pulling a face, I stared over our new domain. A domain that contained at least one person who *should* be worrying about his nine-to-five.

Elemental, on the surface, was a regular club. There was a large expanse of space where people were dancing. It was dark, pitch black, with strobe lights that lit the place up, and a DJ played earache-inducing tracks that had everyone twerking like they were in a strip show. I saw a few people sniffing from small bottles—poppers—and saw others snorting white marching powder—coke.

The folks here were still dancing from the night before.

That was the kind of place *Elemental* was, a modern day *Studio 54*.

The party never stopped until you passed out.

But this didn't interest me.

This was all for show.

Around the back of the room, there was a low lying wall that cut off the dance floor from a corridor. It meant I could walk around the atrium without being accosted with high dancers, and because I wasn't in the best of moods, that stopped any bloodshed.

For the moment.

I knew that the 'Fire Exit' sign led to an inner courtyard. The health inspector saw what they were supposed to see—a short path that led to another door which took people out to the street.

Me? I saw the wall opposite and registered that the arched door which looked like it had been bricked up forty years ago, was a front.

I moved over to it, tapped on it once, and Forrest pulled it open for me.

Tipping my chin at him, I stared over the real reason people came to *Elemental*, and the real reason why people spent tens of thousands of dollars on becoming a member.

It was a fancy sex club.

As I scanned the scenery, nothing impressed me that much.

But maybe I was just fucking jaded.

The place was segmented into three, and truthfully, I couldn't deny it was a neat set up, especially as, from my vantage point, I could see what was going down in each part and could make my decision about which one I wanted to approach.

Each had a stage at the head of their section, but the one to my left had a string quartet on there while some burlesque dancer messed around with a bunch of fans. The audience used chaise longues to watch the show, lounging around like they were fucking Ancient Romans as they sucked on ornate bubbler pipes that had a haze hovering below the ceiling like a dense smog.

The middle stage had a large movie screen on it, except, there was nothing playing—the action was going down in front. A large bed housed four women, each of whom were going down on each other in a kind of human centipede formation that held no interest to me.

I didn't even tip my head to the side or squint harder.

I never had liked doing shit in public.

What I preferred required privacy.

The seats in that segment reminded me of a vintage cinema, red velvet, upright, and the viewers weren't eating popcorn, that was for fucking sure. I had no idea what they were munching on, and neither did I want to goddamn know.

The third section was a little different. Instead of bright reds, scarlets and rouge, it was burgundy and maroon. More like blood than anything else. The dried stuff, not the fresh kind.

On this particular stage, there were three guys tied to St. Andrew's crosses. A woman, dressed up to the nines in leather, was paddling them with a spiked cat o'nine tails. The spikes weren't dulled, either. She drew blood with every strike.

Here, the audience were seated on, what could only be called, mattresses. They were circular, and reminded me of those sun loungers that were like a shell—the ones that came with a roof? Well, these had roofs too, but they also had curtains. A soft squeal confirmed what was going down within the privacy of the one nearest to me.

"Let me guess," I directed at Forrest. "He's watching the chicas on the middle stage?"

Forrest's lips twitched. "Nah, he ain't that kind of politician."

"Ya mean he ain't a hypocrite?" I shoved him in the side when he smirked at me.

"He's all that and more, I promise. He's one of them." Pointing to the stage with the Domme and her subs, he said, "Sanctimonious prick is over there."

"You sure Frederica's in with him?"

He scowled at me. "You think this is my first fuckin' sting, Bren? Shit. What the fuck do you take me for? An amateur?"

I had to grin at his umbrage. "Forrest, you're too good at your job."

"Remember that when you're handing down bonuses," he grumbled. "You think I'd have let you waste your time by coming here if we couldn't twist it to our advantage?"

"Shit always goes wrong," I reasoned, even though I knew he was right.

"Not on my watch."

Forrest had never let me down, so it wasn't like I could argue with him. Instead, I straightened my shoulders, swept a hand over my cuffs, and asked, "Which cabana?"

"The largest."

"Of course," I said with a grunt.

I wasn't the type of man who judged other people—only those who were fucking hypocrites, and this place was hypocrite central.

Coullson had been coming here long enough for Forrest and Tinker, another guy on my crew, to get to know this place real well over the past two weeks.

We'd known for a while that anyone from politicians and celebrities to business tycoons, all had memberships here—and it wasn't for the tunes being played out front—which was why I'd encouraged Conor and Finn to shell out top dollar to buy it.

Blackmail was dirty work, but someone had to do it.

"You sure you want to start the ball rolling today?"

"Yesterday's Summit was illuminating." My brothers and I had been called to the parents' place for a briefing on what went down. I'd stuck around for a coffee with Ma—I was glad I had now. "We need to get shit rolling." I cast him a look. "Be better if we had our ducks in a row and we can do that once we have key players on our side."

He shrugged. "You're the boss."

That I fucking was.

Heading toward the darker section, I made my way to the largest cabana. There was no missing it, nor was there a way to miss the fact that it had a central view of the stage. It was the same color as the walls, a deep, dark red, but it had gold trim that was illuminated in the low lights.

As I moved around to the front of the cabana, bunching the fabric so I could make a small gap in the curtains, I shook my head at what I found.

Coullson, the Mayor of New York City, the renowned anti-gay Christian, was sucking Frederica's dick.

I rubbed my chin as I cast a look at Frederica. She was good—didn't tense up or anything. Her smirk lit up her eyes, but she moaned and groaned like the great actress she was while Forrest took out his phone and started taking snaps like he was on the set of a GQ shoot.

The soft sound didn't register with the Mayor who was really getting into sucking Frederica's dick, but the flash? That did.

He tensed, then turned, cock still in his mouth.

Forrest took another picture.

"That's the money shot right there," I rumbled, shooting a grin at

Forrest who turned the phone around so Coullson could see himself with his lips stuffed full of Frederica's wiener.

"I think you're right. You can still make out who's doing the sucking. I think I'm a fucking artist."

Laughing, I nodded. "You're right, Forrest. I think you could make a real exhibition out of that shot. Could take center stage." At that, Coullson spat out Freddie's cock. "Think he's finally figured out that we ain't servers, bro."

"Never let it be said the Mayor ain't smart."

"Keep your fucking voice down!" Coullson snarled, peering around like people might hear, not registering I was the shark amid the guppies.

My lips curved. "I think you're misunderstanding the situation, Mr. Mayor. You don't control shit anymore." I took a seat at the edge of the cabana. "I control you."

WHERE WOULD THE HORSES BE
WITHOUT ME?

SIX

CAMMIE

I'D DISCOVERED THE 'RIDE BACK' project when I was sixteen, and had to do an essay in school about a charity that meant a lot to me.

I'd been a brat. A spoiled rich kid who knew that she could have whatever her heart desired, just not her father's respect, so I'd spent his money like it was going out of style.

That Papa could handle. Giving me love was too much hard work. Buying me Chanel purses like they were holding a 'closing down' sale was well within his limitations.

I hadn't given a shit about anything, hadn't even given a crap about my grades, but then, I'd stumbled upon a charity that was only a half-hour drive from our house. When I was a kid, Mama had taken us horseback riding, but just like parental love, that had died with her.

Finding that charity had been pure happenstance. I was threatened with after-school detention for a month if I failed to hand in any other projects after weeks of completing no homework, so I'd done a rudimentary Google search, my intention to write a twenty-word essay—most of those words being the charity's address.

Then, I'd visited the site.

That was when something had clicked with me.

The 'Ride Back' project was a way of getting disabled kids, vets, seniors, and at-risk teenagers onto a horse's back. For strength and agility training, but also to help them be a part of a group. It was a form of therapy that was proactive, and horses were angels sent from above. Always understanding, always willing to listen, and far more affectionate than most people knew.

I could have done my research online for my essay, instead, I'd visited in person.

For the remaining months of that year, and all throughout Senior year, I'd gone to the stables to volunteer at least three times a week.

The horses, not even my sisters, had been what I missed the most when I was in West Orange.

So near to them, yet so far.

In the early days, when I hadn't been under the Sinners' protection, the urge to visit them had been strong, but I hadn't dared risk coming to my father's attention. Instead, I'd tried to stop missing my four-legged friends—spoiler alert, I never had—and I'd worked my butt off at the local cafe to make ends meet, pulling shifts at a nearby bar in the evenings until late. Back then, the Sinners' MC hadn't owned their own bar, so when they weren't at the clubhouse, that was their local.

That was where I'd met Nyx.

That was where my life had changed, and not exactly for the better.

The only joy in this interminable situation I found myself in was the horses.

As I ran a hand over Terry's head, the Palomino's long lashes fluttered slightly as I whispered, "I brought my baby a treat."

The dry, yet somehow wet, raspy, but somehow soft, mouth brushed across my palm as I held out a couple of sugar cubes. The sensation tickled, making the sore flesh there stir to life as the rigid cubes rubbed against the Band-Aids that were already starting to wrinkle and rise up from my skin.

My back pocket was loaded with treats—Band-Aids too—but not just for Terry, for all my favorites—all twenty of the horses stabled here, each one a retired racehorse the program had rescued.

On the ride over, I'd stopped off to grab some carrots, apples, and sugar cubes because I was a sucker for these beauties.

Terry neighed softly, his head butting my chest, nuzzling into me like he remembered me from before.

I wanted to think that he did, but I'd been gone a long time, and these guys had so many people on their backs.

Was it stupid to want to be special to a horse?

Was it stupid to want to be special to someone?

Teeth tugging on my bottom lip, I ran my nose along Terry's, then murmured, "Let's get you ready... after I hand out my goodies."

I hadn't meant to time it this way, because I had no problem with mucking out stalls, but I'd arrived just after the stablehands had finished up so my time here today would be a lot less stinky than usual.

I wasn't a regular volunteer.

Father, with the obvious aim of buttering me up so I'd marry his prick of a Sovietnik without too much of a fuss, *ha*, had reinstated my allowance, all of which I'd plowed into the charity who needed it more than I did.

The perks of being such a big donor was that I could roll into the stables whenever I wanted, unlike the other volunteers who came in on a rotation.

I took my time, moving down the aisle, treating them all and stroking them, chatting a little with each before I made my way back to Terry who, though I shouldn't have favorites, was my numero uno.

For a few minutes after my return to his stall, I just stood there, swaying with him as he nuzzled into me.

He was the most affectionate, but Princess Plum was as well—she was more demanding though, always wanting more apples.

Reaching up to fondle his ears, I murmured, "Okay, enough relaxing."

He neighed like he was in agreement, making me smile as I pressed a kiss to his nose.

Before I went through the motions of setting him up for a ride, I checked my phone, wanting to make sure I hadn't missed Inessa's call.

I wouldn't be surprised if she forgot to phone me when she was in the ER, because I wasn't a priority, but I was pleased to see she'd messaged.

Inessa: *At the ER.*

Seeing she'd sent that ten minutes ago, I quickly tapped out: **Me:** *Everything okay?*

Inessa: *Eoghan's raising hell. They keep wanting me to talk to a nurse first. He's insisting on a doctor. A FEMALE doctor, too. *sighs**

My lips twisted.

Me: *As predicted.*

Inessa: *Yeah. You were right. Not just about that... He was mad I didn't tell him sooner.*

Me: *Of course he was. He loves you. He wants what's best for you.*

Inessa: *:/ I guess I'm not used to being a priority.*

Eyes stinging, I replied: **Me:** *None of us are, malyshka. I'm glad you've found someone who treats you right. <3*

Inessa: *Thank you, Cammie xx GTG. Doctor's here at last. Eoghan's already started giving her the side eye and she's only just poked her head around the curtain.*

Me: *LOL. xoxo*

Inessa: *TTYL xoxo*

I tried not to take too much comfort in those 'xoxo's but I did. If I could rebuild my relationship with Inessa, then at least one part of my life would be on track.

With a happy sigh, and now knowing that she was being treated and in her husband's care, I prepped Terry for our ride.

The second we were outside, my butt perched on his hind, my shoulders straightening and my hips turning both loose and relaxed while my core remained engaged as I started to sway with him, I took my first real breath. A deep inhalation and a deep exhalation.

The oxygen flooded my system as I looked around the beautiful Fall day.

The trees had already started to turn, the leaves were a bright red—the ones that remained on the canopies anyway. The grass was green, the sky was blue, and I...

God, why did I just want to cry?

Being alone, being amid nature, not having anyone watching me, the ability to be free, even if it was for a handful of moments... it felt both torturous and delightful.

The land belonged to the stables, one of the few remaining in the area with so much free space to roam. Terry knew all the trails like the old pro he was, so I let him guide me, knowing I'd be safe with him, but not having to focus drew my mind to my circumstances.

"I should never have come back to the city."

I whispered the words to myself as I let my head fall back, the white clouds so blinding that my eyes stung behind my shades—at least, that was what I told myself.

Yeah, I'd blame the sky.

Right.

I'd given Victoria my telephone number only recently, because I'd been missing my sisters something fierce. It was horrible to admit that being Nyx's goddamn sex toy had been enough to keep me going, to stop me from feeling lonely.

"Too pathetic to live," I muttered under my breath, forcing myself not to tug on the reins—my agitation at my own stupidity wasn't something poor Terry should have to handle.

My stupidity was repaid by Victoria's call a few weeks after I'd given her the number, when she'd told me Father had been knee-capped. She'd expected me to come home, and like a fool, I had. That was what family did, wasn't it?

We came home in times of trouble.

We didn't expect that a parent would sell us off while they were still in casts from surgery.

Mouth tightening at the thought, I finally focused on my surroundings and noticed we'd gone so deep into the trail that Terry had started to wander back toward the stables.

My back was starting to ache, which told me I needed to visit more. Thanks to years away from the saddle, I wasn't able to ride as long as I'd like, and sometimes, it wasn't easy sneaking out of the house. I was a grown ass woman, capable of going wherever the hell I wanted, but the truth was, if someone spotted me in the hall, I was obliged to talk with them.

And that, sometimes, was more than I could muster.

In high school, thanks to my heritage, I'd earned that most boring of titles—Ice Princess. Maybe I *was* that. Frigid, too. Or maybe I was just anxious. So eager to escape the necessities of human convention that I preferred to stay in my room. To live inside my four walls where I didn't have to break bread with killers, where I didn't have to wander past a room where my mother had died in a pool of her own blood and Italian cum.

The pain that thought triggered was like when Father slapped me across the face, and my gasp was so sharp that Terry paused, hovering slightly, waiting for further instruction. When I didn't give him any, he carried on his path, and I just let him.

I didn't stir him out of the gentle walk and into a canter.

I just allowed him to lead me back to the stables, where the ripe scent of horses and the pungent stench of hay welcomed me like a warm embrace.

My thoughts were too dark for this crisp, bright day, but they were weighing on me like clouds that were heavy with rain. Plaguing me and giving me no escape in the one source of joy in my life—my horses.

As I tended to Terry, giving him some more carrots in gratitude for his having taken good care of me, brushing him down and giving him extra hay, I switched focus.

Too often, I found myself stuck in the past.

But this was my present.

And I had to make sure that my future was brighter.

That meant exchanging one killer for another—not that great a bargain, but at least this one was nearer my age than the grave and, according to Mama, was a decent human being despite his career choices.

It was time I made my move. Father and Abramovicz weren't going anywhere... Not like I'd hoped.

I just prayed I wasn't too late.

Now Svetlana wanted rid of me, only God knew how quickly Father would act.

With a soft kiss to his nose, I departed, leaving Terry behind for another day. I'd been so absorbed in my thoughts that I didn't realize just how quiet the stables had grown, though, so when I twisted around, and I saw him, I staggered back in surprise.

Whatever I'd expected, it wasn't that I'd see Brennan O'Donnelly leaning against the door to my stables.

Had I magicked him into being with my thoughts?

If only wishful thinking really worked that damn way.

It took me a second to regain my composure, before I tipped my chin up as I watched his gaze dart over me, around me, taking in the situation, my location, and while it wasn't the best timing, not with my hair probably a mess from the helmet I'd worn, and my jodhpurs scuffed from the few tasks I'd completed around Terry's stall, I'd take it.

Snagging an invitation to Inessa's place was one thing, trying to ensure her brother-in-law was there as well, another. And while I had no idea why he was here, that wasn't going to stop me from taking advantage of this good fortune.

As I straightened my shoulders, I was fully aware that my future was on the line with this conversation.

But I'd walked naked amid a bar full of men.

I'd sucked Nyx off in front of his brothers.

I'd lived with bikers with more blood on their hands than motor oil, and I'd survived not only a poverty-stricken life, but one with the biggest cats of them all—clubwhores.

After that, this was a piece of cake.

One Irishman wasn't enough to scare me. Nor would he turn my head. Where this situation was concerned, I was like Terry. One destination in mind. Except, my trail wouldn't end at the stables...

"I have a favor I'd like to call in."

SEVEN
BRENNAN

HER COOLNESS, her calm, her resolve, all of it keyed me into the impossible—she knew about us.

About Mariska and me.

Of the many directions I could have anticipated this conversation taking, *this* wasn't one of them.

"How?"

It was the only question I was really interested in.

The favor? Less so. Favors were dull, a common commodity in my world.

No, what I found fascinating was *her*.

She reached up and tugged on a chain around her neck. As she let the silvery metal slide between her fingers, I saw the tiny star. Platinum. Tipped with emeralds.

My lips tightened at the sight of the stupid gift I'd given to someone I'd thought I'd loved at the time. I'd been too young to recognize it for what it was—a crush a guy had on a beautiful older woman. One who wasn't a whore. One who knew how to suck a cock, and who was mature enough to take her own pleasure.

She'd been my Mrs. Robinson.

I'd been infatuated.

I knew that now.

The gift was a sign of my recklessness, however, and I didn't appreciate seeing the proof of that in the flesh.

"She told you?"

"No." Camille shook her head. "She wouldn't have dreamed of sharing something like that with me."

"Then, I repeat, how?" If it sounded like it came out between gritted teeth, then so be it. I wasn't about to dig myself a deeper grave. I wanted to know exactly what she'd learned, and how, before I committed to anything.

It was just uncanny that she was talking of favors when the burden of Mariska's promise had been weighing heavily on me.

Coincidence.

Nothing more.

"I found this necklace first. And it triggered a few memories."

Her smile made an appearance, and it was uncanny how much she took after Mariska, while also being a thousand times more beautiful. It was like the difference between a candle and a thousand-watt flashlight.

One illuminated, the other laid everything bare.

And the most impressive thing of all was that she wore little to no make-up. Her skin gleamed with honest sweat, she didn't use any of that shit women wore nowadays—the stuff that crafted illusions about their bone structure.

There was no magic here.

She had a chin as sharp as an ice pick. A deep point that added to the fragility of her cheeks, making the arches seem impossibly high. They were slightly gaunt, like she hadn't been eating well. She had long blonde lashes that weren't tinted with mascara, and the greenest fucking eyes I'd ever come across. And I was Irish. Green eyes were our stock in trade.

Her brow was slanted, the temples delicate with golden hair wisping around in a chaotic mess that came from the helmet she'd been wearing, and it arched into a widow's peak that seemed to add to how many angles she had.

Her nose was streamlined, a delicate blade that bisected the two perfect halves, before it gave way to the delicious rosebud mouth that merely confirmed she was a china doll in the flesh.

Everything about her was delicate.

Feminine.

From the long, slender arch of her throat, to the collarbones that I could fit my thumb in. She had a tiny waist, slim hips, but her tits? In the modest camisole she wore, I knew they were fake. They had to be. No way could such a slim woman have that kind of rack.

More than that, beneath the straps of the magenta cami, there was no sign of a bra, but her tits, as well as the rest of her, were terminally perky.

She was, quite frankly, a walking porn star with the face of a princess.

Jesus.

How was this the first time I cast eyes on her?

"What kind of memories?" I rasped, trying to keep my focus on the matter at hand and not the semi triggered by the mental image of those tits of hers bobbing around my cock.

"I remembered her wearing it and touching it with a smile." Her eyes were stormy, more gray than green, as her gaze turned distant with thoughts of her turbulent past. "Knew that who'd gifted her it made her happy. She wasn't happy with Father. He can't make himself that, never mind anyone else.

"Then there's the fact that he'd never have given her anything like this. It's platinum, and the emeralds are real, but it's too discreet for him. He always wants to show off his power, his position. That's why half her jewels need to stay in a vault... This one stood out among her things because it didn't belong.

"Nobody would give her something this pricey outside of the family, and I was too young to gift her anything like that, so I knew it had to be a lover.

"The value as well as the memory of her smiling when she touched it led me on a hunt in the attics. I wish I'd read her diaries after she died, but it was too painful to even contemplate looking at them back then. That was why I hid them up there." A soft, sorrowful laugh escaped her. "She wrote in French, just like she taught us, and that was where I learned about her *meelyi*."

My jaw tensed as I recalled that endearment, something I hadn't heard in a long time. Something I hadn't wanted to hear either.

Mariska was, in my mind, locked away under the label 'big, fat mistake.'

Worse than that time I'd tried ecstasy and had almost died.

If she'd been clinging on to that necklace, it only confirmed how right I'd been to break things off when I had. If she could spend years pining for something that had amounted to an affair, I didn't need Camille to ram home how miserable her mother's marriage had been.

"She named me?" I whispered, rage making my voice quiet.

Her eyes were sad. "She did. In the last few passages. I recognized your name, not just because of Eoghan, but because you're in the papers a lot."

Guessed that explained how she'd recognized me when we'd never met before. A sharp hiss still gusted from my lips at Mariska's idiocy. "That was a stupid thing to do." No wonder she'd gotten her ass killed.

Tension filtered into her frame. "Everything about your affair was stupid. Dangerous. Still, it made her happy even if it killed her."

Mouth tight, I rasped, "You don't know that."

"Oh, I know it helped," she argued softly. "Those last few passages revealed she was aware Father knew she'd cheated on him at one point." Her brow puckered. "She should never have had Victoria. It put her life at risk. I didn't know until I read her journals, but she couldn't have any more children, which meant her usefulness to Father had dried up. He'd still wanted an heir, and she couldn't give it to him.

"That was why she urged you into that promise... because she knew he'd kill her when he found out—which he did. Years later, but she was right. And here's me, standing in front of you, hoping that you're the man of honor she painted you as."

If she'd have used any other fucking word but that one, *honor*, I'd have walked away. Promise or not, leverage was something I wielded, not something that was used against me.

Had Mariska been suicidal? Naming me in her goddamn diary? Did Vasov know one of the O'Donnellys had been boning his missus? What the fuck was our alliance about if he did?

This changed everything.

A few, fucking stupid diary entries tilted this already precarious situation on its head.

I scrubbed a hand over my face, before reaching down to massage the back of my neck.

Honor.

It was the one thing I tried to live by.

Big fat mistakes weren't the only things that littered my past. I'd taken a lot of missteps along the way, and the older I got, the more I survived, the deeper the desire had been to adhere to a set of standards that were of my own making.

One of those?

To face the past, to live up to it, and with any problems my youthful idiocy triggered, I had to deal with them head on. While, back then, I'd made that promise about Inessa and Camille as Victoria hadn't even fucking existed, honor demanded I protect her too.

Goddammit.

Gripping the back of my neck, I rasped, "What's the favor?"

For the first time, she wasn't confident. If anything, she was hesitant as she asked, "Why are you here?"

I frowned, pinning her in place with my stare. "Why the fuck does it matter?"

"It matters because when an Irishman approaches Italian territory to speak with a daughter of the Bratva, it doesn't bode well." Her chin tipped up again, another spark appearing in those stormy eyes, making the irises look like lightning sparked inside them. Fuck, she was pretty. "Before I tell you what I need, I want to make sure you weren't sent here to kill me."

I snorted. "That's a bit below my pay grade."

Her hands tightened into fists at her side. "I'm relieved to hear I'm so unimportant."

I shrugged. "If I were you, and considering the current situation, I'd be glad about that too." Before she could ask me again why I was here, why today was the goddamn day I'd decided to bring this shit to a head— and look what I got for trying to be as fucking honorable as her Ma had described—I rasped, "What's the favor, Camille?"

Nerves had her licking her lips. Those plump lips that parted just so, that made me think about pressing my thumb to the soft cushion of the bottom one, that made me think about watching her swallow me whole.

These weren't things I should be thinking of. Not with the daughter of an ex. Not with a daughter of the Bratva. And sure as fuck not with someone who thought I owed them.

God, I hated owing anything to anyone.

That was *not* how the O'Donnellys worked.

Owing her mother was bad enough, but marriage had seemed like the simplest way to protect Mariska's eldest from the wolves I knew were nipping at her heels.

I had no idea what she'd want from me, and could only imagine it would start a shitstorm—

"I want you to marry me."

For a second, I couldn't believe my ears.

Her favor and my reason for being here... it was improbable they were so aligned. Yet, the improbable had happened.

Here was me thinking she might ask me to kill her father for her, or Abramovicz, that cunt Sovietnik who was sniffing around her pussy like he was a tomcat in heat, but she just wanted me to marry her.

I saw the tension in her muscles, like she was just waiting to leap into the fray, to fight me on this. More than that, I saw the one thing she was trying to hide—*desperation*.

And like that, the balance tilted, slanting in my favor again.

I came here with this intention in mind, thinking I could kill two birds with one stone. Fulfill that fucking promise, and pick the woman I wanted to wed rather than have Da select one for me.

But now, I could have all that and more.

She wasn't going to argue about my claiming her.

In fact, her desperation was going to make this even sweeter.

Far better for her to be beholden to me than vice versa.

Like any Irishman, I could scent a pot of gold at the end of a rainbow, but I had a feeling my pot was filled with platinum instead.

I wasn't about to complain about that.

Did I look like a fool?

ONE FOOT IN FRONT OF THE OTHER...
TOMORROW WILL BE BETTER.

EIGHT
CAMMIE

THE WAY he stared at me was unnerving.

I was used to men being attracted to me. Used to seeing their eyes light up with desires I had no interest in allowing to flourish.

While I saw that in Brennan's, I also saw a mixture of annoyance, disdain, temper, and a flash of something I couldn't name.

I'd say it was triumph, but what about this situation was enough to make a man of his stature feel triumphant?

Nothing.

Not as far as I could see, anyway.

For days, I'd been wondering how I could meet this man, how I could start this conversation with him, and it seemed so unlikely that he was here.

Now I just had to get him to agree...

The urge to play with my bottom lip hit me, but I knew men like Brennan O'Donnelly were predators on the hunt for prey.

Any sign of weakness, even the slightest hint that the image I was projecting wasn't as confident as I was working hard to make him believe, and I knew he'd be on me like a ton of bricks.

"Why would you be asking a silly question like that?" he rumbled, sounding so damn Irish at that moment that it made me second guess everything I'd overheard Inessa telling Victoria about our new allies.

Oh, she was smart. Not sharing anything about business or the like, but she spoke of them with fondness, with witty jokes that told me humor was a part of their fold.

Totally unlike ours.

"Because you helped get my mother killed, and left three little girls without any loving guidance in this miserable world we live in," I told him woodenly. "I think you owe her enough to spare her daughter's life."

That had him rearing back, his shoulders colliding with the side of the door in surprise.

I knew it took a lot to shock a man like him—maybe I should get some kind of award?

Everything about him spoke of a cocksuredness that would, ordinarily, make me turn away from such a guy. But when the arrogance matched the man? That was like my form of heroin.

In someone who backed up their strength, their power, with every move they made, I wasn't sure there could be anything more attractive.

Nyx wore his power around him like a cloak. It hid a lot of vulnerabilities, some I knew because I'd been around him long enough to experience them in the flesh—on the rare occasions he'd let me sleep with him, he cried out a lot in his sleep, and I knew he had terrible nightmares. On top of that, I'd been there when he'd been inked. Each new tattoo a mark of a pedophile he'd slain in his dead sister's name.

He backed up his dominance with his lifestyle.

And Brennan was the same.

Except he wore a three-piece suit instead of a leather cut.

It felt disloyal to admit that I preferred the suit, especially how Brennan wore it.

He had close-cropped hair that was slightly tousled, in a way that had nothing to do with his hand running through it. But the cut was so good, so expensive, that it just added to his rugged appeal. He had gray-blue eyes that were shadowed by light brown brows, but that didn't mean I didn't feel like he could see into my very soul.

They were narrowed upon me, small striations having popped up along the sides as he frowned at me, evidently not appreciating my answer. His nose was long, and it led to a wide mouth, a flat upper lip with a prominent Cupid's bow, and a pouty bottom lip that made me think things I shouldn't be thinking right now.

Like, how perfect it would be to bite.

His chin and jaw weren't as stubborn as Nyx's, but there was power there too. A force of will that was different to the man I'd loved for years, but that told me he wouldn't take any shit.

I liked that.

I needed that.

More than I wanted anyone to know.

Unwittingly, an ember stirred to life inside me.

I didn't even register its existence, didn't acknowledge what I didn't sense, but it began to burn.

His long, strong form was so different from Nyx's. He wasn't bulky, but rangy, and it fit his tailored clothes to perfection. Though tall, over six feet at a minimum, the thin pinstripe added to his height, and made me feel like he was looming over me. Throw in a pair of Oxfords that gleamed so much it made me wonder if he had a spell on them that repelled the everyday dust from a stable, he was everything I wasn't at that moment.

Polished.

Pristine.

Perfect.

I finally bit my lip, my defenses quivering, and knew it wasn't my imagination when I saw his eyes darken.

"I didn't get your mother killed. She got herself killed."

Irritation had me spitting, "It takes two to tango."

"And we were both insane when we disregarded the risks for some momentary pleasure."

It was strange to think of my mother as a sexual being. In my mind, I still remembered her through the eyes of a teenager, where anything like that was disgusting in relation to your parents.

Mostly, I was perplexed by the distinct age gap.

For her, I understood it.

But Brennan O'Donnelly?

If he looked like this now, then I couldn't imagine him not being able to get any woman he set his sights on...

"Are you an adrenaline junkie?" I asked warily, because I'd already been in limbo with one of those and I didn't need it again. Not that I had a choice, of course.

Christ, my life sucked.

His scowl made an appearance. "What does that have to do with anything?"

"I'm just curious."

"Well, don't be." His mouth pursed. "I didn't get Mariska killed."

That he was repeating himself told me I'd struck a nerve.

Good.

"For the longest time, I believed the raid was just an unhappy twist of fate." Revulsion twisted its way inside me, unfurling like a snake uncoiling itself. "Her diary made me see things from a different perspective."

"I'd like to see this diary," he groused, shoving his hands into his pockets.

"You may." I smiled. "After we're married."

"We're not getting married."

"We are," I told him, my voice steely. "You *promised* her. It might as well have been a deathbed promise."

"Just six years before she died, hmm?" He arched a brow at me. "Why the fuck would you even want to marry me?"

"To spare myself from a marriage to my father's Sovietnik. You must have crossed paths with him at some point over the years. Can you blame me for resorting to blackmail?"

"So, I'm sloppy seconds?"

I shuddered with disgust. "You think I'd let that old pervert put his paws on me? I'd die first, and I will... I won't marry him."

His forehead puckered—he hadn't expected that answer. "You don't mean that."

"I do. I'll kill myself before I let my father control me to that extent. And his hold on me is nothing to what a husband's would be."

Just the thought of Abramovicz's sweaty form heaving on top of me made my skin crawl. But what was worse? Being his wife. Having to obey him. Having to appease him. It was either that or face the prospect of daily beatings, which ultimately resulted in my death anyway.

"You ran away before. Why not run away again?"

His question, and lack of concession, had me demanding, "And how do you know I've run away before? What the hell are you even doing here? You're not exactly dressed for a ride."

His top lip twitched. "I came to see you."

That had me frowning. "Why? We've never met before... have we?"

He shook his head. "We haven't."

"So why would you come to meet me?"

He ignored my question. "Why won't you run away again?"

My frown deepened. "Because Father won't allow that. Not again. His intention is to see this through." I tipped up my chin as I faced facts—my end was near unless I managed to convince Brennan to save me. "He'll kill me if he catches me running, and I'd prefer to control how swiftly I die, thank you very much."

"Wouldn't we all?" he rasped, before he surprised me by storming toward me.

It was second nature to back off, to acquiesce, and I stumbled against the stall door, jumping when Terry neighed and nuzzled his nose into my back. Brennan didn't even cast him a look, didn't stop until I was pinned against the wall and one forearm was pressed either side of my head so he was looming over me.

Maybe I was a product of my environment—I'd seen the caked on foundation Mama wore from time to time. Or maybe I was as pathetic as I feared... but the way he looked at me, his gaze raking over my features, seeming to expose every single flaw, every single nuance, God help me, it was, I recognized with some sorrow, the most intimate gesture of my life.

Nyx had had me in positions that would make the people who wrote the Kama Sutra feel faint, but he'd never looked at me. Sure, his eyes had been on me, but he hadn't seen the real Cammie.

He'd just seen a pussy.

A walking sex doll.

Brennan, well, he didn't see that. He saw something else. Something I couldn't put a name on.

He was so close that his silk suit brushed against me, his heat permeating the fabric so it burned me with its own brand too. He smelled like fire and sin and a whole host of other things I was pretty sure cosmetic companies didn't pack into their aftershave, but my visceral response to him was unnerving.

The man had fucked my mother.

He'd been one of the catalysts behind her brutal death.

And yet, he'd brought her joy. A kind of happiness that three daughters couldn't inspire in a woman—I'd read that in her diaries.

With that in mind, I rasped, "What the hell do you think you're doing?"

"I'm wondering if you know what kind of man I am, and if you're prepared for the repercussions of threatening me."

Anger flashed in my eyes. "I know exactly what kind of man you are." I could feel my lips curling into a sneer. "I'm just hoping you're worthy of the faith Mama had in you."

He tensed at that, and because I was so close to him, it transmitted itself to me, which, in turn, triggered a wave of emotions in me.

Relief.

Power.

So this was what it felt like to have it over someone, because with that slight gesture, he betrayed the truth.

Mama had been right to trust him.

Then, he destroyed that thought by moving slightly, and sliding one hand down to cup my cheek. He tipped my head to the side, his fingertips drawing the nerve endings to life. A shiver rushed through me as his breath brushed my mouth, before he let them trail up and over the curve of my jaw.

"Do you know you're playing with fire?" he practically crooned in my ear.

"I'd prefer to be burned by you than by *him*."

With our cheeks kissing, I released a shaky sigh when his stubble dragged against me, and though it wasn't comfortable, it had me clenching the muscles in my stomach in surprise. His lips whispered along the skin he'd just teased, before his hand slid down to my collarbone.

The tips of his fingers trailed there a second, making my heart skip a beat as the tiny hairs at the back of my neck stiffened with the delicious sensations that he forced on me with the simplest of moves. Then, he cupped me there, and his hand was so large that it covered the entirety of my throat.

His thumb pressed against my pulse, and I was well aware that it was fluttering away like the panicked beats of the wings of a trapped bird. He pressed down and murmured, "I need to work on my street cred if you're more scared of an old, fat fuck than me." Then he dipped his head and forced our mouths to collide.

And he stole my breath.

Robbed me of it like he was a thief in the night.

I hadn't expected this—*why would I?*

But a sharp gasp escaped me as he plunged his tongue between my lips with an ease that spoke of how comfortable he was in these situations, and reminded me of how *un*comfortable I was.

I'd never been at ease with my body, had always felt like something being fucked rather than someone, but even as my mind spaced, and my brain whirred, he retained my focus by pressing down on my neck. Almost as if he knew when my thoughts were drifting, I'd feel the heavy pressure at the same time as his tongue stroked along mine.

It was wet and warm, and unlike Nyx's kiss. I realized then that Nyx had always been disinterested in me, and had only wanted to fuck. Brennan, for whatever crazy reason, was into this.

More leverage over him, I thought, before he thieved me of that thought process by tilting my head to the side and pulling back, parting his teeth around my lip and biting down. That felt good and bad at the same time, and I registered the strange stirrings of warmth had begun to coalesce in my stomach as he let his free hand move down my arm, the calluses triggering a wave of gooseflesh into being as he grabbed my wrist and pressed it overhead. His fingers tightened on my throat in warning, and I knew he was telling me to hold it in place.

I obeyed.

I had no idea why.

But I did.

And when he did it again, with the other arm, in tangent with a biting kiss that made me melt into him, the gooseflesh didn't just roll down my bicep, but it surged along my shoulders, at my nape, along my spine, making me feel things I'd never felt before.

A soft moan escaped me as he pushed his dick into my abdomen, pressing me up against the stable wall so that I was literally between two hard places. The pain he triggered when he bit down again had me gasping, and he took advantage. He no longer simply thrust his tongue against mine, I felt like he was eating at my lips, supping from them like I was a cool, long glass of water and he was dying of thirst.

Robbing me of breath with that kiss as he tightened his grip on my throat, my mind was no longer capable of rational thought, it was awhirl, like a hurricane was blasting through it, but that was nothing to my body.

I'd never felt anything like this before.

Sparks of pleasure ignited behind my eyes as, with every kiss, the pain from his bite was renewed. God, it felt so good! I groaned, my back arching as I thrust my tits against his chest, needing more, needing something.

I'd never felt so empty in all my life.

He speared a thigh between my legs like he knew what I was experiencing, and for a second, it almost nudged me out of my headspace, before he tightened his grip around my throat once more, and my hips bucked as I dragged my core against him.

Was this dry-humping?

Jesus.

Was it supposed to feel this good?

His lips ravaged mine, plundering and taking, but was it really that when I wanted to give him everything anyway? Thoughts of leverage had disappeared, and all I could focus on was the delirious drug that was slaloming through my veins that he ratcheted up and up like he was increasing the dosage with each and every thrust of his tongue against mine.

For the first time, I struggled to free my hands from his grasp, even though I'd never been so happy to be pinned in place. It was of their own volition, nothing to do with me, as I chased more from him. The sensation of his hair against my fingers, the feel of his muscles as I clung to his shoulders to keep him close... to make sure he *never* stopped doing *this*.

Grunting, I fought back, my tongue tangling with his in the most intimate dance of all, unable to believe I was doing that, unable to believe the heat that was simmering with a life of its own inside my belly.

When he pulled back, he nipped at my lip again which had my head falling against the wall, the whisper of hurt making everything taste so much sweeter. I thought he was going to leave me, but he didn't. His mouth dragged down over my cheek, scraping me a little with his stubble once more, which made my nerve endings hyper aware, as he relinquished his hold on my throat and found it instead with his lips.

A soft nip preceded him cupping one of my breasts, and as he squeezed the pliant flesh, he nuzzled the spot where neck met shoulder before he bit down. Hard enough to make me cry out. His knee surged higher, pushing up against my pussy, and I could feel it.

All of a sudden.

I knew what that light at the end of the tunnel was.

An orgasm.

It might as well have been a damn unicorn.

Gasping, my head rocked against the rough wall as he bit me again, before his hand slipped between my thighs and he held me there.

I wanted to grind into him, grind *against* him, but I didn't. Couldn't. I could feel him pulling away for real, and my dazed eyes took that in as I saw the feverish heat on his face, which told me he was as into this as I was.

Maybe more if the thick brand of his cock against my lower belly was indicative of anything.

"W-Why?" I whispered, not sure what I was asking, whether it was about the kiss, why he'd stopped, or the way he still held me firmly by the throat and the pussy.

"Because I'm Catholic," he rasped, pinning me in place with more than just his body. I felt skewered in two as he grated out, "That means no divorce. That means forever, and forever is a long fucking time if we're incompatible." His hand pressed harder against my pussy, and shamelessly, I wanted to ride it, wanted to see these delicious feelings come to fruition. A hard bark of laughter filtered from him as he drawled, "Though I don't think incompatibility is going to be an issue... But whether you like the idea or not, Camille, there will be children. I'll save you from that fat fuck, and I'll stop you from having to sacrifice yourself, but—"

I blurted out, "I want children. And I don't want to get divorced." *I wanted more of this too.*

"You say that now."

Reality began to drift in, and the liquid heat that had overtaken my core started to grow cold. Somehow, that intense fire of before made the chill feel like ice was seeping through my veins, especially as I whispered, "Until Abramovicz dies, he's a threat looming over me."

"He's old. He'll die soon. Our marriage will outlive him."

I licked my sore lips. "I have a say in who'll own me. I'm okay with that."

His eyes flashed wide. "Own you? You're not a fucking slave." He moved his hand away. A moment ago, I'd have wanted to weep. Now, I was glad.

"I'm a possession," I told him simply. *A broodmare.* "I've had more freedom than Inessa had but you're still demanding children, aren't you? Whether I want them or not, that's still part of the agreement."

His brow puckered once more, and I could tell my verbiage put him on edge because his jaw rocked to the side like he was mad.

I'd even go so far as to say that it distressed him.

Wondering if he'd argue, I had to admit to being disappointed when, with a final squeeze to my throat, he pulled away from me, his arms jerking back with him as he let mine drop down.

At first, I thought he was going to slap me for my impudence, and it was second nature to shield my face, but before I could embarrass myself, I realized he was looking at the slimline watch on his wrist. Not like the bulky Rolex my father wore, but a thin leather one that was heavily wrinkled with age.

Vintage.

Vacheron Constantin.

In my world, the old was appreciated far more than the new, so my interest was piqued enough for me to make a mental note to Google the brand.

"Do you have somewhere to be?" I snapped though, surprising myself. I'd been reared to accept I wasn't important enough to deserve a man's full attention, but that kiss... I'd felt like I was the center of his universe.

I wanted that feeling again.

And again.

But that way danger lied.

"Always," he said simply, before his lips twisted. "But there's no time like the present."

Uneasy because of that non-smile, I swallowed. "For what?"

"To get our license." He smirked when I gasped, relief hitting me like a blow to the solar plexus. His answer, while unexpected, was wonderful. More wonderful than those sensations he'd stirred to life in me. "You're about to become an O'Donnelly, Camille. I hope you're ready for what that means."

NINE
BRENNAN

THERE WERE many laws we could break, a lot of bureaucratic hoops we could jump over, but sometimes, there were some rules you just had to follow.

Wealthy or not, when it came down to a marriage certificate, one had to show up at the city clerk's office, fill in an application, shove ID at a bored civil servant, and pay a fee.

Nothing in this life, after all, was free.

The thought was rammed home to me as Camille eyed the office with interest as I spoke with Forrest on the phone.

She was used to being dismissed which, in truth, made her perfect for the role of wife. I'd barely spoken to her since I'd given her a thousand dollars to persuade—i.e pay off—her guard into disappearing for a few hours, and she hadn't complained.

Not once.

Not that she had any right to.

She believed she was coercing me into marriage.

She didn't know that I'd come to the decision myself a month or so ago.

She didn't know that the decision had been brewing in my mind ever since Eoghan had told me his sister-in-law was back in the picture, and rumors had been stirring about Abramovicz making arrangements at their local church...

I had my fingers in every pie, especially with the Vasovs where Mariska's promise weighed on me like I was carrying the burden of the world on my shoulders.

Now that I'd clapped eyes on her, things had changed. My decision had morphed from a duty born of honor into that of desire ever since I'd seen that she was Mariska in the flesh, but... more.

Everything about her was sent to tempt me, and like the bad Catholic boy I was, I didn't avoid temptation.

I dove into it.

Headfirst.

Da might want to spend an eternity in heaven, but I was more than okay with hell.

Hot pokers up my ass might be uncomfortable after a while, but shit, a kink was a kink.

Still, it was ingrained in me to let her think I was doing her a favor. Everything came at a cost, remember? Well, in this instance, I wanted her gratitude.

Being grateful always made a person far more accommodating, and I wasn't sure how I wanted her to accommodate me just yet, but I'd figure it out soon enough.

By Christ if that kiss didn't make me even more eager to get the ball rolling...

A quick Google search had told me what we needed to do, but because I didn't carry a fucking printer around my neck, I had to wait to fill in the application at the clerk's office. I was annoyed at my lack of efficiency in not having the application printed out so that we were good to go, while also relieved because it didn't show my hand.

Having a marriage license application wasn't something most people carried around on the regular now, was it?

"Are you fucking listening to me?"

Not really.

I didn't bother getting mad at Forrest, even though my father would have beaten the shit out of anyone on his crew who spoke to him like that. But my crew wasn't like his. Wasn't like any of my brothers', either.

Mine were almost as close to me as my siblings were, which was really saying fucking something.

He'd been droning on and on at me for a while now, but my thoughts were firmly on the memory of her tit against my palm. Her lip between my teeth... She'd been so pliant. So submissive. Until she'd started fighting back.

Fuck, I didn't need to be getting a boner in this dump.

"I'm listening," I retorted, even though I thought it wiser to busy myself by looking around the paneled walls that were covered in cork bulletin boards, which were pinned with neon flyers advertising some shit or other, rather than study her ass. That mouth. Those fucking tits.

No.

Behave, Brennan.

Focus.

The clerk's office was the most plebeian place I'd ever been, and I frequented the goddamn docks for a living. Everything in here was mediocre, middling, and mildewed. Including the staff who were buttoned up—not just their blouses, but their mouths. Pursed like assholes, each of the three women were middle-aged and matronly.

A woman in her forties could be more banging than a bitch in her twenties, but these ones really needed to wear some fucking lipstick and take a goddamn chill pill.

I knew what petty tyrants looked like—I'd been raised by one—and these three were it to a T. They were also enough to quench any and all of my arousal.

"You really sound like you're listening," Forrest groused, making me roll my eyes.

The faint scent of chamomile, sunblock, and horses disappeared, jolting my attention toward the woman who was no longer at my side, but who was staring at one of the hot pink pieces of paper. Her brow was puckered as she read the stark black text, and though I had the chance to read it as well, I was more interested in her than in the flyer. Something I regretted when she unpinned it, folded it, then shoved it in her pocket.

The move drew my gaze to her ass, which had me peering over the rest of her once more.

She was, without a doubt, hot.

I mean, I'd banged pole-dancers whose asses weren't like Camille's, but it was more than that. There was something about the set to her shoulders, the tilt of her chin. Call me crazy, but I could see royalty in her.

Maybe Vasov's clan were fucking serfs—I didn't know, did I?—but Camille wasn't born to tend to the earth.

She was born to sit on a throne. And I wasn't talking the porcelain kind.

Did women like her even take shits? Did they puke or need to piss?

Biologically, they had to.

But Christ.

Such perfection...

It would be unnerving if the thought of destroying that wasn't so enticing.

Her skin was like fresh cream. Her eyes like gemstones. Her hair like spun gold. She was a doll. Pure and simple. A rich man's daughter who was reared to become a rich man's wife.

But I saw more than the surface.

I thought about those bright red lips being plump and sore from tongue-fucking her mouth for hours.

I thought about those cheeks being marred with mascara streaks from the tears she shed as she gagged on my cock.

I thought about those gemstone orbs turning glassy as she screamed out in orgasm.

Perfection was boring.

Dolls were boring.

Camille was not boring.

Tedious people didn't approach renowned Irish mobsters and attempt to force their hand into marriage. She was Bratva. She knew the rules of the game, but she'd broken them anyway.

If my mind wasn't already set on this path, there was fuck all she could have said to convince me otherwise.

Honor was important to me because of my past, but few people in my line of work felt the same way. Most grew hardened over time, and while I had, knowing I was the reason Ma had been abducted...

Christ, there was no denying it—it made me a pussy around women.

I'd admit it to myself, but no fucker else.

My past made me want to cosset and protect them. If that cosseting and protection also came with a side of blowjobs and cream pies, then that was no one's business but mine.

Plus the lady I was banging.

In this instance, for the foreseeable, it'd be Camille.

The second she'd spread her legs for me, at any rate.

And yeah, she'd spread them. It was a question of when, not if. I wasn't about to become celibate. Saving her from Abramovicz didn't come for free. But I didn't think she'd bitch about having to pay the price —not after what went down between us in the stables.

Most women would be squeamish about being with the guy who'd slept with her mother too, but that was the cruel reality of our world.

Survival meant more than polite niceties and societal dictates.

Protection meant even more than that, as well. I respected her for shoving that aside.

I liked an intelligent woman.

"You're seriously not listening to me right now, are you? For fuck's sake. This timing is so beyond bad—"

"Do you want a running commentary or something? Jesus. I'm listening, Forrest, I told ya." I tipped my cellphone against my shoulder as I grabbed Camille's arm, moving her back to my side in the line, and pointing at the desk when a space opened up.

She didn't dislodge my grip on her arm even though she stared down at it a touch vacantly. When her gaze drifted to mine, there was a gleam in her eye, one that I neither distrusted or trusted, just that I was aware was strange.

Inessa was a peculiar girl—I knew that from the random things Eoghan had pointed out about her. But who the fuck was I to judge?

I killed people for a living.

Dealt drugs.

Hit people up for protection money.

What about that was normal?

But Inessa had certain ways about her, was all I meant. It made sense that Camille would too.

"You can let go," she said softly, and though I knew I could because we were next in line for the clerk, and she had half a brain cell so could register that herself, I didn't want to.

A plan that was months in the making boiled down to the visit to this office.

Twelve weeks that were loaded down with stress and tension, concerns about a fucking cabal that had limitless power, and yet, she'd always been at the forefront of my mind.

Guilt—it wasn't often I felt it.

Wasn't often I acted on it.

In this instance, I did for one reason. A reason that, a year ago, would have been crazy to me.

I was ready.

Keeping her safe, protecting her from her father and his Sovietnik, didn't have to involve marriage, but I wanted a family. I wanted a wife. I wanted—fuck—what my youngest brothers had.

How was it that the babies of the goddamn family were the ones who'd settled down first?

I'd never been averse to the idea of getting married, but the bitches Da had shoved at me grated on my last nerve, and with the hours I toiled, with the dedication required for my position as the family's fixer, I knew Da, even though he'd never forgiven me for Ma, granted me a surprising amount of leeway.

Heirs were all he'd been talking about for the last couple of years, though, and Seamus, Declan's kid, had taken some of the slack off us all, but that was momentary.

Da would be sniffing around Aidan first and me next, but I didn't want what Eoghan had.

An arranged marriage to some Italian bitch whose virginity was being sold at St. Patrick's altar in the name of peace with the *Famiglia,* wasn't a sacrifice I was willing to make for the Points.

I wanted to pick my woman.

And I didn't want her to be pure.

Purity might be Eoghan's kink, but it sure as fuck wasn't mine.

I didn't want an angel in my bed.

I wanted filthy sex.

I wanted it every fucking day and every fucking night, and I needed a woman who could keep up. I knew about her past, and that Camille had been passed around by an MC might not be something my da would appreciate, but it meant she'd understand the needs of a man like me.

Something that kiss confirmed, enough to make my dick twitch again at the mere memory of it.

When the time came and she was pregnant and I visited a mistress, I knew she'd get it too. She was born into the life. She'd do her duty, just like I'd do mine. But as self-sacrificing as I was, dedicating myself to fucking a woman until she had a bun in the oven wasn't going to happen unless she'd take it any which way I wanted to give it to her... I had a feeling she was on board for that too.

The thought had me pursing my lips as Forrest yelled in my ear, "This is fucking pointless. I need you in Linwood, okay?"

My brow puckered as I said, "Why?"

"If you'd been listening, you'd know."

I grunted, because he wasn't wrong. "I'll be there before night falls."

"You'd better be. We got shit to do."

I cut the call before he could bitch at me some more, then turned to Camille and said, "After this is arranged, I want a full blood work—"

Her lips twisted and she tugged at the boxy leather satchel she had swinging off her shoulder. The clasp unlatched and she dug through the meager contents until she found a piece of paper.

"Here."

I stared down at it, saw she had a clean bill of health and asked, "How long have you been preparing for this?"

Unease had her features creasing. "I-I... the moment I got back to the city, I initiated the test."

"Why?" I scowled at her. "Did you fuck a guy with an STD?"

Her cheeks blossomed with heat and I realized I'd spoken a little too loudly. The office had been relatively quiet, no noise except from the women working the counter who muttered the same boring shit over and over again, but at my words, silence fell over the small room.

I shot everyone a glare, un-fucking-caring if I pissed anyone off or was being rude.

I was an O'Donnelly.

We ruled this city.

I just didn't appreciate the notion of being ruled by a fucking Bratva kid.

Like she read my mind, she simply stated, "No, but I wanted to make sure I was healthy. The second Father made murmurs about the arranged marriage, I sought solace in Mama's diaries... When I read about you, I knew I wouldn't have much time. Then, last night, the situation deteriorated." She tipped her chin up. "My stepmother says I take up too much space and I should have a household of my own."

Distaste had my lip curling. "Slutty Svetlana... Spread her legs for more sailors than an airport carrier can hold."

She pulled a face. "What on earth he married her for, I'll never know. Mistress, yes, but wife?" She shuddered, her distaste for the woman evident. Her mention of mistresses pleased me though. As I thought, she knew how this world worked. "But even though she put my freedom on a countdown timer, it was only a matter of time. I've been trying to figure out how to get in touch with you without raising any red flags."

"The luck of the Irish blessed you today then, didn't it?" I said dryly.

"Yes."

The simplicity of her answer confirmed I'd been right to behave as I had—she was grateful and wouldn't take this situation for granted.

She'd put pressure on me, had showed all her cards, but I still had the upper hand. That was exactly how I liked it.

"You were more than lucky," I rumbled. "Vasov shouldn't let you anywhere near Forest Park. Not with trigger-happy Italians roaming their territory. You weren't wrong when you said I could have been sent there to kill you. Just because that wasn't my intention doesn't mean it isn't some other faction's."

Like she read my mind, she simply stated, "I'm a child of the Brotherhood. You think I don't know when I'm being tailed?" She shrugged, moved something in her purse, then tipped it toward me to reveal a revolver. "I wasn't sure by who, but I came prepared."

"Apparently you've got better eyes than your guards," I told her, but I knew I'd have to watch her after we were wed. She might have come prepared but that satchel had been nowhere near her in the stables.

Guns were deadly, but they weren't when they were hanging on some coat rack ten feet away.

Sadness lit her eyes. "Can you blame me? After what went down in my own home?" She bit her lip. "I found her. She was..." Her eyes closed. "A broken doll. Covered in their—"

I reached up to squeeze her shoulder, unable to hear her next words.

It was too like what Ma had gone through for me to deal with, too similar except she'd survived, thank Christ.

I'd suspected for a long time, long before Camille had crossed my radar, that Vasov had made a deal with the Italians.

I hadn't loved Mariska, but the dishonor in what Vasov had done, not only in pulling a shady deal with the *Famiglia*, but for letting his own house, with his own daughters under that roof, purposely come under attack, was something that would haunt me.

In the wake of Ma's kidnapping, my father, while he was definitely a bastard, had started a war with the Aryans the city still remembered.

After Mariska's death, Vasov hadn't started shit with the Italians. And that was the most damning fact of all.

He was, and forever would be, bastard scum. Mariska had been right to leave her girls' safety with me.

"Next!"

The woman barked at me, her displeasure clear even as her gaze softened and she shot Camille a piteous smile.

I rolled my eyes at the display, because the clerks had been rude to every fucker in here, but I mentioned STDs out loud and all of a sudden I was the pariah?

"I need a marriage license."

Without moving, without even shifting her scowl from me, she slapped a piece of paper on the counter. "You need to fill this out." She raised a hand and pointed toward the door where the line had begun to strain out of the office's confines. "Then you have to get back in line again."

"We will. Thank you."

Politeness costs nothing, those were the words my maternal grandmother had tried to instill in me, but that wasn't exactly an easy lesson to learn when you had Aidan O'Donnelly for a father.

It pained me to let a petty tyrant boss me around, but I knew how this shit worked. Knew how people worked. She was too self-righteous to bribe, and would take too much satisfaction in telling me where to go. But, what she could do, was bury the application.

As far as I knew, once we left here, we had twenty-four hours until we could take the plunge, but petty bureaucrats made my insane father look self-sacrificing.

Camille surprised me by snatching the form before I could and then stalking over to the doors. I followed her and found her in the queue once more, the application resting on the side of her bag as she began to fill out her section.

Of course, she wanted this marriage even more than I did.

Her reasons were obvious, mine were vague. Even to myself.

But as I stared at the arch of her throat, the gentle fall of a few locks of hair from her messy bun, from the golden sheen to her skin that made her look like she was dusted in the precious metal, all I could see was what she'd look like under me.

Few women triggered my imagination.

The only time I got to be creative was when I was torturing people or figuring out a way to hide a body. I'd long since stopped dreaming, having goals. In my line of work, the main aim was to be able to get home at the end of the day. And I was okay with that. I was luckier than most, richer than most, and that came at a cost.

But when a woman inspired more than a yawn out of me, or irritation, it was worth pursuing.

Just like her mother had been at the time...

MAMA WOULD WANT MORE FOR ME. I
MUST MAKE HER PROUD.

TEN
CAMMIE

THE DRIVE back to the stables wasn't exactly excruciating but neither was it comfortable. Relief warred with my nerves, because as happy as I was to be escaping my father, Brennan was a stranger.

More than that, he was an enemy. Even if the Irish weren't technically our foes anymore, they'd spent most of my life as such and would remain that way until I was tucked safely in their bosom.

They'd accepted Inessa, so I didn't see why they wouldn't accept me. Especially when I'd do anything, and I meant anything, to make Brennan happy.

A happy husband was a means of survival.

If he was content with me, I'd live.

If he wasn't, then my usefulness would end.

Just like Mama...

He wanted kids—I'd give him kids. As many of them as he wanted, and when he grew displeased with my body, one that bore the signs of his offspring, I'd be grateful when he took to a mistress. I'd be safe.

I'd have a family.

I'd no longer be a Vasov.

I'd no longer be Bratva.

As I wondered if Inessa knew how lucky she was, I stared out of the window, trying to be as quiet as I could be. As meek as possible. I'd been trained for the role of timid, placid, *accepting* wife all my life, so this was no hardship, and I didn't want to do anything that would change Brennan's mind.

Twenty-four hours.

God, it was like a ticking time bomb in my head.

I hated that there was a waiting period. If we could have gone to the judge right then and there, I would have. I resented that I couldn't.

Goddamn rules and regulations.

My hands tightened into fists as I watched the city swirl by.

The time for hopes and prayers was gone. I'd seen how Eoghan cared for Inessa, and had to pray that his brother fell from the same tree.

If I was tying myself to someone as brutal as Abramovicz, then I'd end my life in a heartbeat. I wasn't about to be a man's punching bag.

No way, no how.

But that kiss... I didn't think brutality was in him. At least, not against women. He could have taken me in the stables, but he hadn't. Could have shown me what my new life was going to look like. Could have taken what wasn't offered, but he hadn't.

Instead, he'd made me experience things that might as well have been extra-terrestrial before—*arousal*.

"Are you okay?"

The question stirred me from my thoughts, and I turned to find Brennan watching me.

He did that a lot.

I could feel his gaze drifting over me in the clerk's office and on the journey to and from it. I didn't mind. I was used to being looked at like I was an inanimate object.

No thoughts in my head.

No dreams or wishes.

Just a vessel.

That's all I was.

My mouth tightened at the thought, the strange passion he'd stirred in me fading in a heartbeat as I thought about how I'd proven myself a long time ago.

I could have escaped the Bratva Brotherhood and made something of myself. I could have gone to a community college, could have tried to get a job. Instead, I'd become a waitress and then I'd become a whore for a biker.

I really *was* a vessel, a—

"Camille? Are you all right?"

I blinked at him, saw his eyes were trained on my hands and I gasped when I saw the blood peeking out from between the creases of my fingers and palms.

Embarrassment had me dithering, the tremor working down my wrist as I wondered how I could wipe away the blood with no paper towels in my purse.

My cheeks grew hot, my heart started to pound, and the nausea swirling around my belly made me wonder if I was going to puke all over my lap. Then, he reached for my arm and turned it over. He tapped my clenched fingers in a silent order when they remained furled, but I ignored it, and kept them tightly curled, knowing he'd see what lay beneath.

With his free hand, he reached over and tipped my chin up. His calluses against my tender skin had me shivering inwardly, before he rasped, "Tomorrow, you're going to be my wife. It might start out as an arrangement, but I will know everything about you, Camille.

"I'm not the kind of man who appreciates secrets. I prefer to know what I'm up against before I dive into anything. So don't try to bullshit me and paint yourself as being as meek as a Russian doll. You might con your father with that trick, but you won't fool me."

My brow puckered as I corrected, "*Matryoshka* dolls."

His eyes narrowed. "You know I wasn't asking for the correct terminology."

"What if I'm as boring as those nesting dolls? What if all I know is how to be meek? Mild?"

"A mild woman wouldn't approach an Irish mobster and force his hand into marriage." The simple statement had me cringing.

"For survival—"

He clucked his tongue. "Exactly. When we're under pressure, we're at our most interesting. When you were younger, you chose flight. Now you're older, you chose to fight." Brennan reached up and pressed his thumb to my bottom lip. It pulled away from my teeth as he dragged it down, and he stared at the slight opening before rumbling, "Now, you've won this battle because tomorrow, by this time, you'll be my wife. Just don't push your luck. Open your hand."

Pinching the tiniest piece of flesh on the side of my cheek between my teeth, I bit down and did as he asked. His gaze didn't move from mine for what felt like endless seconds, when a strange heat arced between us.

It was raw, which wasn't exactly something I was used to.

It was real, when everything in my world was a lie.

I wanted to ask him what he wanted from me, but that was a pointless question. I was forcing him into this, dragging duty up when a man like him should feel nothing of the kind. That he did should give me hope, but I'd long since learned that hope was more dangerous a drug than heroin—and I was many things, a fool, a meek doll, but I wasn't that stupid.

His glance finally drifted down to my hand, and he arched a brow at what he saw.

Without even looking, I knew what he was seeing.

Scars. Cuts. Fresh and old. Scabs. That was where the blood came from.

"You self-harm?"

I hadn't while I was away, but the second I'd returned to my old life, I'd returned to old habits too. "I wouldn't call it that."

His lips twisted into a snarl. "What would you call it?"

I blinked at him. "None of your business."

"That's where you're wrong, Camille. It is my business. These hands are going to be wrapped around my dick. They're going to hold my babies."

I could feel my forehead furrowing with a deeper crease at his response.

He raised my hand higher, twisting it left and right as the small puddles of blood dripped along the creases, gently raining down onto the leather seat between us.

"You've been doing this a long time."

"With a father like mine, wouldn't you?" I rasped, tugging at his grip.

"You think your father's a menace, what do you think mine is?" he rumbled, his gaze ensnaring me.

The question had me wincing, because, in this, we were equals.

Both our fathers were monsters.

"We all have an escape," I defended myself.

"Cutting isn't an escape." He squinted at me. "I see you slicing your palms, see the aftermath of it, I'll tie you to the fucking bed and—"

Irritation flashed through me. "And, what?" I leaned forward, pushing into his space, and with my other hand, I prodded him. "What will you do?"

"Spank you then make you come so fucking hard you won't remember why you were cutting yourself in the first place."

His statement had me rearing back, so hard and so fast that my spine collided with the door, but whether or not it was fate, my abrupt gesture was timed with the car's deceleration.

He moved forward, deeper into my space, and rasped, "You Russians might not take care of what's yours, but we Irish? Do." His gaze drifted behind me, to the stables' parking lot, and it gave me a lick of space to accept that his words hadn't inspired fear in me, just *need*. "Your driver isn't back yet. Go into the yard, and we'll wait out here until he comes back."

"I'll be okay—"

Anger flashed in his eyes. "Which part did you not understand? You're mine, Camille. By your own choice." He reached up and pinched my chin between his forefinger and thumb. "Let's hope, for both our sakes, you don't regret flying into my web."

"Your web can't be any worse than Abramovicz's," I whispered.

He shrugged. "I've had no complaints."

I gritted my teeth at the egotistical remark, but didn't say anything other than, "I'll be here tomorrow."

"Good. Be here at twelve. Make sure it's the same guard. And don't bring your cellphone with you."

"Why not?" I queried with a frown, especially as we'd already exchanged numbers.

"Because your old man's probably got a tracker in it. He did with Inessa. Caused a real shitstorm."

I winced. "I can see him doing that. We'll always be his property—in his mind, at least."

Eyes darkening, he tilted his chin down. "We'll see about that."

To that, I didn't utter a word, just slipped out of the car and headed toward the stables.

Though I really wanted to go back to Terry, to find comfort in my friend, I didn't bother because I knew the guard would be returning shortly, and I wanted to see if Brennan would stay.

The sound of a door opening and closing had me turning around during my short walk, and I saw Brennan quickly ducking out of the backseat so he could dip into the front with his man. Only, our eyes clashed and held over the empty space, long enough for it to be dangerous, long enough for me to feel things I hadn't anticipated feeling.

I wasn't scared.

Whenever Nyx had commanded me to his side, there'd always been a rush of fear that slithered down my spine.

We all knew Nyx was borderline insane. You never said no to him. Well, outside of sexual encounters—ironically enough. Nyx would slit his wrists before he forced a woman to have sex with him.

But though I knew Brennan was just as dangerous, and from his rep —just as deadly—I wasn't frightened.

Did a three-piece suit make that much of a difference?

Did Nyx, with his leathers and cut, his heavy boots and inked flesh, present more of a threat than a man wearing three-thousand-dollars' worth of tailoring?

Maybe to a layman on the street.

But I knew how venomous a person could be beneath the silk.

Prettying up the devil didn't take away from what that person was.

My father, dressed in Brioni and a hundred-thousand-dollar Rolex on his wrist, was more than capable of slicing someone from throat to belly. He just got someone else to do it so he didn't get bloodstains everywhere.

And rumors about Brennan, and his position in the Five Points, had always been rife.

No one knew what he did, not specifically, because he tended to be everywhere. But everyone knew that the Irish didn't work that way.

Each of the five sons had their own division, as they were their father's arms. Not just his heirs, but his generals. Each man had a crew who worked for them, and each one had distinct roles.

I didn't know what because the little I knew came mostly from the Sinners. In my household, business wasn't discussed with women. Not even in front of us. We were sent out of the room when Father had to talk with his Sovietnik and Obschak, his security and money men, over dinner.

The sound of a car's engine revving jolted me from the extended glance, and I shot a look onto the road, and saw the SUV was incoming. Brennan, also spying this, drifted into his seat, and within seconds, now my guard was back, he went, leaving me to return to the fold.

Not one part of me wanted to get into that SUV and head for the house.

The house because it was never my home. Not since Mama's death, and maybe not even before then. I'd worked hard to shield Inessa and Victoria from the truth of our parents' marriage, but there was only so much a teenager could do, and there'd been nobody to shield me from the sight of Mama's busted lips and the hours spent in front of a mirror as she tried to look her normal self.

Now I was older, now I understood such dynamics, I had to wonder what else had gone down between them...

A shiver whispered down my spine at the thought.

That was why I didn't begrudge Mama her affair with Brennan.

Why I wanted him for myself.

She would never have put herself in danger for a man who wasn't worthy, and I had to hope that he meant what he said—he'd keep me safe.

He'd protect me.

Because once I was married to him, I was his.

And even though I didn't know him, knew him only by reputation, and what there was of that was enough to terrify any death row inmate, I still preferred to be with him than remain under my father's roof.

With lead feet and dread in my heart, I made my way to the SUV, but when I reached for the car door, I caught a glimpse of my hands. The blood was drying, making the creases filled with it even more prevalent, and I sighed before turning on my heel and retreating to the front reception where there was a restroom, and thankfully, no one manning the desk who'd ask me awkward questions about my 'injuries.'

After washing up, I made a quick return, and found the driver's seat empty and the guard back as a passenger.

Grateful because I hated being driven as it gave me car sickness, I dipped my chin at him and murmured my thanks, "*Spasibo*."

"*Na Zdorovie*."

The drive home took barely any time at all, and within those moments, my head was caught in a whirl. Tomorrow, I wasn't free. I was exchanging one jail cell for another, but at least this jailor was handsome.

At least his eyes didn't spit evil.

At least he smiled, and was capable of gentle chivalry.

My mind whirred back to those moments at the clerk's office. He'd been a jerk, but when he'd put a hand on me, he hadn't left bruises behind. He hadn't dragged me toward him or toward the desk. He'd even got back into line.

A mobster—queuing.

I'd been hard-pressed not to laugh.

I doubted my father would have done that, was pretty sure his father wouldn't have done either. So why had he?

Once we made it back to the house, I dismissed the guard with a tight smile and retreated to my room quickly because I needed to get ready for dinner at seven. We dressed formally in this household, so I'd need to shower, do my hair and put on a full face of make-up before I'd be considered presentable.

As I stuck my phone onto charge, I eyed the device, wondering if Father was monitoring me, and if so, would he ask me why I went to the clerk's office today?

Could I trust the guard to be appeased by the bribe he'd been given?

I wasn't sure. Had no way of knowing for certain. I just had to pray that tonight's meal would go without a hitch. Had to pray that he wouldn't spring Abramovicz on us as a guest again—he'd done it twice this past week already.

Shuddering at the memories from last night of that lech's gaze on me, undressing me as he gorged on the *pelmeni*, traditional dumplings, I readied myself for battle.

My make-up was on point—looking better than a professional's by the time I was done. There were no signs of the fatigue under my eyes nor of the stress lines at my temples. I wore a slim-fitting Chanel dress and Prada heels, and made sure every single scab on my palms were covered with Band-Aids.

No one had ever cared enough to ask why my hands were always covered in Band-Aids, and I used that to my advantage.

Slice marks on my arms and legs would be noticed. My trunk too—with the skimpy outfits we sometimes wore to parties, of which there were many, from weddings to baptisms to celebratory occasions around a business deal—so cutting my hands had always been my thing.

And the best part?

It hurt.

All day.

Every day.

Whenever it got to be too much, I just had to squeeze my fingers. So hard that it would pop a scab, break already torn flesh and make them hurt all over again.

It was perfect. So beautifully ugly that it was my personal salvation.

A salvation I hadn't needed while I was away from this toxic household.

I thought about what he'd said in the car:

"Cutting isn't an escape. I see you slicing your palms, see the aftermath of it, I'll tie you to the fucking bed, spank you, and make you come so fucking hard you won't remember why you were cutting yourself in the first place."

Did he mean that?

God, I hoped he did.

I squeezed my fingers, feeling the ragged tissue protest the move.

Coping mechanisms... mine were so bad in the eyes of the world. Brennan dropped F-bombs like a priest prayed, but he didn't get side-eyed like he was a freak.

Me, I took a blade to my palm and I was the weirdo?

Still, orgasms.

I wondered what they were like. I knew that I'd been so close to experiencing one today. Would he make me feel that again? Or was it a one-time thing? I hoped not.

Once dressed, I eyed the time, and seeing that I had a few minutes to spare, I stared at myself in the mirror.

I'd pass.

My collarbone was a little too prominent which told me I needed to focus on eating over the next few days, and my wrists looked so delicate they could snap, but aside from that, I could have graced a catwalk. The heels were high, elegant and sleek, cupping my feet like slippers. The dress was tight, a rich navy that emphasized the gold in my blonde hair.

Biting my lip as I twisted around on my heel, I moved out onto the landing.

The staircase had a grand railing, like a massive semi-circle, and I leaned over it to peer down to the first floor.

All was quiet.

The place was like a morgue.

My heartbeat sped up, the response out of my control yet all the stronger for it, as my breath caught in my throat.

Morgues—how fitting that I lived in one when this place saw more death than life.

How was it Svetlana could bring herself to live here?

I'd whored myself out too, but the Sinners were honest with their sins. My father shielded his behind lies and boardroom deals that were founded in bullshit.

Give me the Sinners over the Bratva any day of the week.

Shuddering, and wishing that it was tomorrow already, I began the careful descent down the stairs. My heels were high, and it would be so easy to tumble down them. So easy to fall like Mama had.

I'd seen her crumpled form at the bottom of these steps far too often.

Nobody was that clumsy.

Mouth tightening, heart still pounding, and my skin clammy, the desire to dig my nails into my palms was a strong one. Nobody cared about a bunch of Band-Aids, but spilling drops of blood onto the hideous zebra-print rug in the hall? Staining the marble tiles? That was a surefire way to draw attention to myself.

Wondering how it was possible that I could be so much happier in a grungy clubhouse, surrounded by sex-mad bikers, most of them stinking of the road and motor oil, the scent of weed in the air and smoke on their clothes, than this manicured paradise, I entered the living room.

It was a grand affair with high, paneled walls that soared to a ceiling with intricate moldings and an authentic candelabra that had falls of crystal raindrops shimmering glittery light all over the parquet floor. It had never been my favorite place, even before Svetlana had gotten her grubby hands on it, but now it was like something from a strip joint.

What the hell Father was thinking was beyond me.

Had he lost more than his patellas during the shooting?

Everything was faux ornate now. High-backed chairs and sofas in the French-style, but made out of a weird kind of plastic, and in lurid colors. They clashed too—the chairs with the molding around the edges were like baby pink thrones, and the sofas were a chartreuse so bright it was enough to wind anyone with good taste.

A matching coffee table sat between them, and this one made turquoise look like it was muted.

When I thought about the antiques that had once graced this room, I knew that Father wasn't the only murderer in his marriage—Svetlana murdered good taste with every breath she took.

As I walked in, I saw her lounging against one of the two armchairs. Father always looked out of place when he was there, his ruddy cheeks, piggy eyes, and the belly that overspilled his pants no matter how much he spent on tailoring, made him, somehow, all the more uglier when he was surrounded by Barbie pink.

That wasn't a sight I saw often, however, as it was too hard for him to leave his wheelchair. Only at meals where he had business associates in attendance did he make that kind of effort.

Svetlana's focus was on her phone, her face down-turned as I took her in. Dressed in black, she looked more like a streetwalker than a Pakhan's wife. A part of me wondered if that was how Father had met her. It wouldn't be a stretch of the imagination, considering his line of work, but Pakhans didn't often marry dime-a-dozen whores.

Everything about their marriage stank, but it wasn't mine to dissect.

Her dress was so short that I could see her panties thanks to how she had her legs crossed, and the hem sat at hip-height, the PVC showing every single asset off to perfection. She was a beautiful woman, but life had made her hard—I knew how that felt.

I didn't begrudge her finding a sugar daddy. I just begrudged that she was mean to Victoria, looked at me like I was the slut who didn't belong here, and was always rude.

As my heels tapped against the marble floor, the clicking sound giving way once I was standing on a priceless carpet that appeared to be one of the only things Father had deemed worthy of protecting from his new wife's interior design disaster, she didn't bother looking up from her cellphone, just murmured in Russian, "Someone's gonna get reamed tonight."

My nostrils flared, concern hitting me like my father's fist to my gut. "Abramovicz is coming for dinner?"

She peered up at me, a malicious sneer on her lips. "By the end of the night, you'll wish that was all that had happened."

My pulse had calmed down some as I'd made my way into the sitting room, but now, it was back to racing like I'd been running. My stomach churned, and I could feel cold beads of sweat gathering at the back of my neck, my temples, and under my arms.

Svetlana wasn't warning me—she was telling me she was going to enjoy whatever crap Father was going to hurl at me. She was building up the anticipation. Encouraging me to dread what was going to happen, just so that she could see me hyped up, panicked.

Scared.

Svetlana wasn't to know that the only thing that would scare me was being locked in the house so that I couldn't escape tomorrow.

Being imprisoned here had happened before, so I saw no reason why the threat was off the table.

Did he speak about business in front of her?

Even as I was perplexed about how she knew of Father's plans, I didn't have time to puzzle over their odd dynamic, not when my time felt like it was running out.

I'd been about to take a seat, but at her words, I remained standing, and drifted over to the fireplace. Either side of it, there were console tables, two massive displays of flowers looming over them in vile colors that clashed with the bright pink and reds. I didn't even know royal blue tulips were a thing, but seeing them here, I wished they weren't.

I'd been punished a thousand times by my father.

I knew what he was like in a rage, and while he was just as evil in a wheelchair as he was out of it, these past few weeks, he'd been crueler than ever before. As if the weakness inherent in being injured was making it necessary for him to terrify the men under him.

In the power pit he existed in, it made sense.

But I was his daughter. Not one of his soldiers.

And that was why I picked up the small crystal pyramid that decorated the mantelpiece.

I'd never armed myself before. Never even thought about fighting back. But tomorrow... I had to cling to it. Had to protect myself. I needed to make sure that I could run.

The perimeter wasn't water-tight. I knew of at least two different ways that I could get off the estate if I needed to, so if Father came at me with his cane, if he beat me with it, I could defend myself before running off and finding one of those exits.

In my head, I planned my route. I wasn't wearing the best shoes, and it was cold out, the autumn nights already starting to turn chilly. It was getting dark, twilight past us, and I'd left my phone upstairs—dammit—so I wouldn't have a flashlight with me.

Neither would I have any money.

If things turned bad, and I could only reason that Svetlana's smug smirk was indicative of how bad it really was going to be, I was screwed.

The minute I retaliated against whatever Father was going to do, Svetlana would call for the guards, and I wouldn't have time to head upstairs for my phone and purse, wouldn't have time to do anything other than run for it. Even the car keys to the SUV I used were in my purse. Along with my revolver...

Dammit.

I was screwed.

Temptation hit me to retreat upstairs, just so I could get my things, but I didn't have time.

The second the pyramid was in my hands, I heard the faint squeal of the wheels in his chair. The sound had me tightening my grip on the impromptu weapon—a memento from when Father had taken his new bride to Egypt, yet another break from his old habits, taking her somewhere that wasn't Moscow—and the pointed tip dug into my palm. The pain grounded me. Centered me in a way that few would ever be able to understand.

The catharsis came at a moment where I needed to be ready, mentally prepared for whatever could be hurled my way.

I'd never thought the cuts would give me an advantage at a moment like this, but I knew I'd never seen anything as clearly as I did now.

Father wheeled into the room, a nasty scowl on his face, Maxim, his guard, at his back.

I'd known Maxim for years. He was one of Father's projects. Some Bratva boys showed a special talent for certain aspects of the life, and leadership cultivated that. In this instance, Maxim had come to the Pakhan's attention.

I wasn't sure I wanted to know exactly why Maxim was a part of Father's special guard.

He'd always been pleasant to me, and God knew, pleasant was hard to find under this roof.

"Where is she?" Father snarled.

I hadn't been hiding, but I realized that I was tucked away, sheltered by the natural nook formed by the fireplace, which jutted out into the room. Because the candelabra was old, it didn't exactly illuminate the space very well, but that didn't make me invisible.

Svetlana peered up, her attention veering from her phone as it ping-ponged between Maxim and her husband. She twisted around to point at me, a scowl on her face, one that made me wonder if Father's eyes were failing him or something because she saw me quite clearly, before grumbling, "She's right there!"

I took the opportunity to slip out of my high heels as Father's gaze darted over to me, and his hands tightened around the wheels, his knuckles bleeding white as he surged halfway across the room. Maxim's face was blank, but when I cast him a look, there was something in his eyes... something that put me even more on edge. Which, truly, shouldn't have been possible.

The tip of the pyramid dug ever deeper into my palm, until I could feel the blood soaking through the fabric of the bandages that covered my wounds. Nerves had me whispering, "Good evening, Father." I felt like a coward for shrinking in on myself, for my shoulders hunching, as the desire to disappear into the damn wallpaper overcame me.

I'd spent a lifetime trying to hide, but it never worked out. Unless I was with someone like him. Someone dark and dangerous. Someone more powerful than the Bratva Pakhan. Only then would I ever be safe from the monster who had sired me.

His nostrils flared as he maneuvered around the furniture like it was a NASCAR racetrack, and when he finally reached me, it hit me then.

He was in a wheelchair.

He was injured.

He couldn't walk.

After that display, I had a feeling he was badly in need of glasses, just too prideful to wear them, and I was still terrified of him.

I could run away, just dart out of the room, but Maxim was here. And Victoria wasn't. She'd made no mention of going for a sleepover earlier, which was something she would have shared with me if this wasn't impromptu.

That indicated what was going to happen.

Father was going to beat me. Or maybe Maxim was if Father couldn't manage it.

I could run, but Maxim would catch me. Would bring me back.

And like always, as was my new normal now, Svetlana would cheer on from the sidelines like the demented harpy she was.

Hatred surged inside me like lava bubbling in the pit of a volcano.

The desire to make him scared, to make him hurt, to terrorize him, to make them all scared was so overwhelming that it made my cheeks flush with color when, seconds earlier, I knew I'd paled.

The Irish were worse than the Bratva.

They were smarter, more devious. They ruled with iron fists but diversified. They had power in unusual places, where we scurried about in the shadows, they were New York's darlings. Not necessarily the older O'Donnelly, but the sons for sure.

Aidan Jr. and Brennan were considered eligible bachelors in need of snatching up by Park Avenue Princesses, and the A-listers who had attended Inessa and Eoghan's wedding hadn't been there for the Vasovs —but for the O'Donnellys.

That was power.

That was protection.

And it was within my grasp. Within my reach. I wasn't about to let anything get in my way.

As he slid toward me, his wheelchair making him faster even as it was harder for him to maneuver through the many pieces of adult Barbie furniture, most of which he collided with, I sucked in a sharp breath, curling my feet into the rug as I murmured, "Is something wrong?"

"Why were you talking to that O'Donnelly cunt today?"

So, the bribe hadn't been enough to keep my guard quiet.

I should have known.

Inside, I squirmed, but outwardly, I presented as calm a facade as I was able and rasped, "You mean Brennan? He uses the same stables as me."

Svetlana snorted. "A likely story." She surged to her feet, smoothing down her dress that was more like a napkin, and murmured, "I'm bored. And hungry. Your heir wants dinner."

Gaze whipping around to face her, I caught her just in time for her to pat her stomach. The smugness in her smile made sense now.

I'd already been useless to my father if I wasn't going to marry his Sovietnik and tighten his links with his Two Spies—his generals—but now Svetlana was breeding, and if she gave him a son, then my already precarious situation was a thousand times worse.

And that was nothing to Victoria's position in this family.

She wasn't in physical danger—she was too good a girl for that—but I could easily see her being married off before she was ready.

Inessa had been fortunate to hit eighteen before she was forced to tie herself to Eoghan for life. But Svetlana would want Victoria out of the house as soon as she physically could, and once I was out of the picture, there were only two years before she could legally, with his permission, get married to Abramovicz—unless he died first.

I had to pray that was the case, had to pray that Victoria would be safe from his clutches because seventeen was far too young to wed anyone, never mind an old man. Yet even as I thought about that thorn in my side, I realized that Abramovicz was only a part of the problem.

My father was the real thorn.

One that dug so deep into my skin that it made the razor blades that cut through my flesh like a fork through buttery lobster appear dulled.

He'd always be a danger to my sisters.

Even after she'd married, I knew he'd caused Inessa problems. Had known that without Brennan confirming it today.

The second I was under his roof again and he was back from the hospital, his first item of business had been to work on tying me to his Sovietnik.

My being in danger was one thing, but once Svetlana had his brat, Victoria's safety would be in jeopardy too.

I needed her out from under this roof.

I needed her away from the poison that was our father.

My mind was so slow that it felt like it was sludging through mud, but time wasn't as kind. If anything, it flew, so damn fast that, within seconds, he wasn't ten feet away from me but three. The wheelchair hurtling toward me, making me feel like a pin at a bowling alley that he was trying to ram down.

I stepped out of the way, huddling into the nook, but his hand reached for mine, his fingers digging into my wrist as he jerked me down.

"Why the fuck were you conferring with the Irish? Did they ask you to spy on me?"

Saliva spattered from his mouth, splashing me with his acid. I struggled, trying to get him to let go of me, knowing his grip would leave bruises in the morning, but the more I struggled to free myself from his iron grip, the tighter his hold became.

And then he reached for my other hand.

The one holding the pyramid.

His eyes glinted with malice as he snarled, "And what do you think you're going to do with that?"

He'd hurt me worse over the years than a too-hard grip to my wrist.

He'd slapped me, hit me with a belt. He'd choked me a few times, especially those initial occurrences where I'd refused to marry the man he'd picked for me and just before I'd run away to the territory of the biggest baddies I could think of, far away from his reach, deep in a land that offered more protection in its public park than most Russians had in the comfort of their own homes with the doors fully locked.

I knew what it was like to be terrorized.

Saw the same shadows in my younger sister's eyes, and knew Inessa was just as polluted with our father's toxicity, and I knew it was my fault.

I'd never protected them.

I'd left them.

I'd let my younger sister protect the baby of the family. I'd run away, I'd abandoned them. I knew what I'd left behind, too. That was why I never pushed Inessa. Why I understood her lack of interest in me, and why her call today had come as such a surprise.

I'd let them down.

I'd relinquished them to this monster's care.

And when I thought about how Mama had done the same, something inside me snapped.

Just as he was snarling, "Hand me your belt, Maxim," something clicked inside my mind.

He was going to hit me with it.

Like I was a naughty little girl.

He was going to beat me—again.

Just like he'd beat my sisters—again and again.

The only one of us who was safe was Inessa.

But I had to change that.

I had to.

I felt that click in my mind as though it were a visceral entity. As though I'd switched on a light. My movements weren't wooden, if anything, I drifted through the next steps like it was a dance.

I jerked my arm high, out of his grasp as I darted backward. Not far, just enough to evade his grip, to pull my wrist free as he struggled with me to gain a hold of the crystal pyramid, but this time, I was stronger.

I had to be.

Mine was a fury born of desperation.

Because, once this was done, I had a safe haven to retreat to.

Brennan O'Donnelly would protect me from the Bratva, from the repercussions of what I was about to do. But more than that, he'd protect Victoria too.

So it made my next step easy.

I brought the ornament down.

Hard.

Let glass collide with bone.

Allowed blood to spurt.

Let his rage-filled roar wash over me.

Allowed Svetlana's stunned shriek to pierce my ears.

And I did it again.

And again.

And again.

Until my palms weren't the only part of me that were bloody. Until the enemy inside my gates was gone.

Until the threat to me and my sisters was silenced.

Forever.

ELEVEN
BRENNAN

AS WE DROVE AWAY from the stables, Bagpipes muttered, "You can't trust Russians."

I snorted. "Dipshit, you think I didn't know that?"

"I'm your buddy. Your crew. I got your back—she don't. She's got your dick in a twist—"

My scowl darkened. "You can't seriously think this is my dick doing the talking." I mean, it was definitely chatting up a fucking storm now I'd seen her in person, but Christ, I wasn't that fucking dumb.

"I don't fucking know, man. I just know you're gonna wed some Bratva bitch without your da's permission. That means you've lost the fucking plot or something."

I shrugged. "Da owes me some slack. Been taking up the reigns for Aidan for a while now, plus I've been keeping the boys in line."

"Senior owes no one shit. You know how he works."

Pursing my lips, I muttered, "I do."

"And you're still okay with going ahead with this anyway." He shook his head. "You suicidal or something, man?"

"Nah, just got some old debts to pay off."

"Since when do the O'Donnellys owe anyone? Usually the other way around, ain't it?"

My crew and I were tighter than my brothers with theirs, but even though I'd come up with them, even though we'd come up together, that didn't mean they knew all my secrets.

One of the main reasons behind my break up with Mariska was that Da had discovered I was screwing a Bratva woman, and had beaten the shit out of me for it. That would be the first time he'd broken my wrist but it hadn't been the last, one of his usual punishments for not toeing the line when I was younger.

The family had kept our affair on the downlow. No one without an O'Donnelly last name knew I'd fucked around with a Pakhan's wife. At the time, Forrest, Tink, and Bagpipes had jeered at me for boning an older woman, but I'd lied to them, told them it was the mom of a kid we'd gone to high school with. Now, my lies were coming home to roost where my friends were concerned.

Nose crinkling at the thought, I stretched my legs as I rumbled, "What the fuck's Forrest's problem anyway? He's been nagging at me today like we've been married for thirty goddamn years."

"Says you ain't thinking properly, ain't taking all the risks into consideration, and I can see where he's coming from too. Your head's been stuck in the clouds for a few days now."

I scowled at him, but it missed the target because his focus was on the gnarly traffic that snagged us in its clutches as we headed toward Linden Blvd.

This was technically not our territory, but we'd had a place here for decades. It was rumored that Da had been burying people around this neighborhood for the past forty years, but Aidan Sr. wasn't exactly the type of guy you could have a Q&A session with. If I'd asked, he'd have told me that the eighties were a completely different time.

Which didn't answer my question. Nor did it delete my worries about the corpses that might pop up at any fucking moment.

The Hole was a part of the city that wasn't really on anyone's radar. It wasn't hooked up to mains water, and because it was below sea level, it often flooded. On top of that, it wasn't just the graveyard for our enemies, but also dumped cars. Those vehicles came in useful for us. On top of jacking a bunch and shipping them out to NJ for the Satan's Sinners' MC to strip down for parts so they could stuff 'em full of product, we supplemented those with the abandoned junk cars we found in the neighborhood.

It was a community fucking service, not that we got any thanks for it.

The area was a shithole. More water than tarmac, fewer homes, and bad cell service. There were small housing estates that neighbored it, but that was what made it a great place for us to lay low.

No one was interested in The Hole.

Why would they be?

I'd made it my base when I'd come of age, taking over this small slice of hell because it was away from my da. We had a better relationship now than we had when I was a snot-nosed kid, but I thought most of us did to be honest. I didn't think he'd ever view us as equals. We'd always be his blue-eyed boys —even if we didn't all have blue fucking eyes—but as we grew older, as we reigned over our own parts of the firm, well, his respect had to be earned and we'd done that with every drop of blood we'd shed for the Five Points. All of us had bled for the family. Some of us more than others.

Not just like with Aidan, who'd nearly been crippled in a drive-by shooting, but with Finn who'd almost lost his wife in that same attack.

The sacrifices we made to be a Pointer were many. As I grew to know Seamus, Declan's teenaged son, I had to admit he was one of the reasons I wanted to settle down. Why I was ready to wife someone who knew the score, and who wanted the same things as me—a family.

"You've been weird ever since Shay turned up," Bagpipes muttered, disarming me with how his mind was running on the same track as mine. "He's a cool kid, man, but fuck, it's turning your head."

I scowled at him. "The hell is that supposed to mean? You accusing me of being a pervert or something?"

Bagpipes' eyes rounded at that, and he gaped at me, long enough for a car to honk their horn at us and for him to swerve off the other side of the road and back onto our lane. "No way am I accusing you of being a pedo, man. Fuck. I just meant, it's making you have some kind of biological clock malfunction or something."

"Since when do you even know what a biological clock is?" I grumbled. "And it ain't got nothing to do with my age."

"No? Well, at least you admit something funky is going on."

I gritted my teeth, not liking being questioned, but Forrest, Tinker, and Bagpipes were my friends. Brothers of choice, if not of blood. They had my back, and with the situations I got them into, they deserved to know the full truth. Even if that truth wasn't all that flavorful.

Reaching up, I rubbed my chin, feeling the beginnings of a beard start to creep in. With Camille's lips looking like a peach that was still on the tree, I'd never be able to kiss her with stubble. Not without wanting to taint that creamy skin.

The prospect of my cock between her lips, against that molten hot cunt of hers, between her tits, had me reaching down to adjust myself as discreetly as possible.

I'd gotten more than I'd bargained for with that kiss back at the stables. That was for goddamn sure.

Knowing I needed to shift focus before I started waxing fucking poetical about her taste, I muttered, "You've met Shay. What do you think of him? Aside from him being a cool kid."

Bagpipes hesitated, and that hesitation was exactly what I'd banked on. "I mean," he started, before he cleared his throat. "He's, you know, cool."

My lips twisted. "He ain't Points' material though, is he?"

Bagpipes winced. "Didn't want to say nuthin'."

"Why? I didn't slice your hand off for insinuating I was a kid fucker. Why would I stab you in the leg for saying exactly how it is where my nephew is concerned?"

Because we pulled up at a red light, Bagpipes shot me a glare. "You make me feel so comforted."

"Well, that's my job in life, ain't it? Not to give you nightmares?" I told him drolly. "But I think we all know getting him involved with the shady side of shit is a fuckfest just waiting to go down. I also don't think Declan really wants that for him, and I think he'll either go to loggerheads with Da, or the issue won't be an issue if Da dies. He's an old bastard. Can't live forever."

Bagpipes scowled as we set off again, the lights changing which heralded a bucket load of horns as we didn't move fast enough—aka, at the speed of fucking sound.

New Yorkers—Jesus.

Not for the first time, my thoughts drifted back to Ireland.

I'd been there once. One fucking time. But it was like my brain constantly rewired itself and plunked me back there.

To a world where everything was green. Where the rain came down in torrents and made everything sparkle. Where it was a pleasure to tuck yourself away in front of a fire when the weather outside was abysmal. Where life, on the whole, felt so much simpler.

Jesus, maybe Bagpipes was right. Maybe I *was* starting to get weird.

Maybe I did have a biological clock ticking away.

Forty fucking years on this planet and I didn't have that much to show for it.

Sure, I rode a Maybach, my place was in Carnegie Hill, and I had enough material possessions to make a Sheikh jealous... but while that might have been enough at one point in my life, it just wasn't anymore.

I was tired. Of the bullshit, of the life. And things weren't going to get any better. Not when we had a bunch of Illuminati fuckers sniffing around our assholes, just wondering if they could shove a ten-inch dildo up our asses without us noticing.

Aidan was a liability, Declan's heart had never been in it, Eoghan and Conor were ripe for action, but they weren't soldiers like Aidan and Declan were. That meant this entire shit show fell to me. Finn had lost his edge when he'd married Aoife, preferring to ride a desk and get rich by evading taxes, and while that was all grand, it meant that I was the one who had to deal with the mean fucking streets.

I pinched the bridge of my nose, pinching off the pressure at the same time. I wasn't about to let it get to me, not when there was too much at stake. Ma had had a hard life without things ending like this, and I refused for the family to live in fear of a shadowy organization that pulled strings better than a server pulled pints of lager in a bar.

"Where's your head at, man?" Bagpipes asked softly. "Why are you going through with this shit?"

"Because I can. Because seeing Shay, knowing that he has a future that has nothing to do with the Five Points apart from familial ties gives me hope that if I have a kid, they don't have to follow in my fucking footsteps."

I wasn't surprised when he fell silent. Wasn't surprised when I saw he'd blanched a little. What I'd just said was tantamount to mutiny in my family.

We both knew it.

Just like we knew he wouldn't say jack. Not even to Forrest or Tink.

Clearing my throat, I muttered, "Don't worry about it, Baggy. Everything will turn out all right."

"It always does," he agreed.

Neither of us mentioned how many poor fuckers would die before the shit turned out right in the end, though.

In fact, neither of us said all that much as we made it down trash-filled streets, roads lined with dumped cars that we'd be sending over to West Orange to facilitate our trafficking product up to the Canadian border.

As always, at least three streets were bogged down with water because not only were we about thirty feet under sea level, this area wasn't hooked up to drains.

Nobody gave a fuck about The Hole, and that was why I'd made it my home away from home.

Dirty water splashed in cascading waves wherever we drove, and when Baggy pulled up outside our warehouse, I sighed and, thinking back to what I'd heard Forrest grumbling about on the phone, muttered, "She's in there, I assume?"

"Demanded to speak with you."

"Probably prefers talking to me rather than Declan."

"Yeah," Baggy agreed. "Let's face it, Dec don't give a shit about the business, but once she screwed his son over, she became a walking target."

I hummed under my breath. "She still is one. Nobody touches a fucking O'Donnelly and lives without regretting it."

His nose crinkled. "Bitch lost a couple of fingers and a thumb, Brennan. Probably has to pick her nose with a back-scratcher—I think she regrets it."

"She will before we're done with her."

"Wonder how she explained her injuries to her superiors."

Uncaring, I shrugged. "Probably told them she accidentally sliced them off when she was cooking."

Bagpipes snorted. "Don't fucking cook much, do ya?"

"Nah, too worried about cutting off a finger."

As he grinned back at me, I slammed the door shut after I got out, hearing the driver's door bang closed a few seconds later.

The yard was as muddy as every other part of this dump, and the outer walls of the place looked like they were about to seize under all the asbestos, but once I walked up the three stairs to the low porch, and headed inside, it showed a different side to things.

The front half was for business.

Where people came to talk to me, to curry favors, to petition our help. We were a little like a feudal system for our clients who paid us protection money. Da was proud of our service. Unlike the other fuckers who took businesspeople's money and didn't give a shit if they were hit up or if they were raided by the cops, Da provided a different kind of protection.

We cost twice more than the Russians and the Italians, were a little cheaper than those Triad cocksuckers, but we were worth it.

Unfortunately for me, I was the one who mostly dealt with angry bakers who'd lost their permits, and flustered jewelry store owners who'd been dealing with a spate of robberies.

Fun.

"What's going on?" I asked when I saw the fourth man in my crew, Tinker, hovering by the stairs, waiting on me to show up.

It felt like all three of my guys had been dithering around as I hauled my ass across the city, but they didn't say anything.

We were best buds, shot the shit like we were brothers, but they knew when I was boss.

"Caroline Dunbar wants to see you, but so does Anthony Isaac."

"Jesus Christ," I ground out. "You can't be serious?"

Tink shrugged. "What do you want me to tell you? The bastard's whining about a shipment of some kind of fucking snake that's gone missing. He wants your help with Customs."

"Pass him on to Da. He's the one with friends there."

Tinker's eyes widened a little before he smirked. "He'll love you for that. Shouldn't you get him on your good side if you're about to—"

I raised a hand to stop him from finishing that sentence, then glowered at him. "Shut the fuck up, Tink. Christ, we've got enemies in our midst."

"They're upstairs," he argued, but he did as I wanted—shut his trap.

Loose lips and all that.

My den of inequity had once been a haulage warehouse before Da had gotten his paws on it, but Uncle Paddy, his brother, had reno-ed it to the hilt before he got shot by an Albanian back when I was thirteen. Now, it looked like an eighties' bordello, but I wasn't interested enough in the building to change anything.

Bright red walls with intricate brocade detailing in black, brassy gold light fittings, and a rich crimson carpet that had worn down over time—a hooker would more than feel at home in this shitpile.

I walked up the stairs to my office, the only room I'd adjusted thanks to the invention of the Internet, and as I opened the door, murmured, "Send Dunbar in first. Tell Isaac to go to Da."

"I thought you were joking," Tink muttered.

"No. I'm not dealing with Customs Enforcement or who the fuck ever over a bunch of goddamn snakes. Da's got more time on his hands than I do."

"Yeah, but you're not the one who'll have to handle Senior when he blows up over Isaac calling him."

My lips curved into a gleeful smile. "That's what happens when you forget to get Mary-Joseph an anniversary present."

His eyes narrowed upon me. "You're fucking with me. She got you involved?"

"I'm a friend of the family, ain't I?" My grin widened. "Serves you right."

A storm cloud crossed over his face before he grumbled, "Motherfucker," under his breath and hurried over to the unofficial waiting room.

With Baggy at my back, I slipped into the office and walked directly to my desk. As I took a seat, I saw Baggy was laughing too.

"Brennan, the savior of Pointer's womenfolk."

I mockingly wafted my hand, waving like a royal would. "Just send my info to the Vatican. I'm sure they'll be ready to canonize me."

"I'll bet." Baggy snickered, then his tone dropped. "You noticed Tink's been quiet?"

Shrugging, I admitted, "Wasn't altogether surprised to get that call from Mary-Joseph, no."

"Think they're having marriage troubles?" Baggy rubbed his chin. "She's a cunt, but he ain't much better. Love the man like a brother, but wouldn't want to be married to him."

I snorted. "Me either. But, whatever it is, ain't like they can divorce. Just got to put up and shut up."

"That's what I don't get, man. You're fucking free to do what you want. Your dad ain't tugging on you to get married, so why are you tying the knot when you don't have to? We're all stuck with our women until death do us part, and let's face it, they're going to be the ones who survive us so they're the ones who get to dance on our graves even if they make us fucking miserable."

I knew he was right.

I did.

But...

"It's time."

That was as much as I'd give him, and it was just enough because a knock sounded at the door a few seconds later.

Baggy opened it, and in the hall, the corrupt bitch who'd almost cost my nephew his life stood there, both scowling at me and hovering like she was too afraid to do anything about it.

She was a Fed, which technically gave her power, but the O'Donnellys existed in a parallel universe of technicalities.

One pissant Federal agent meant jack shit to us, what with Da having the Director on speed dial. And yeah, that was the kind of phone the old man had. God forbid we trusted him with a smartphone.

Rocking back in my desk chair, I nudged the mouse to wake up my computer as I called out, "This had better be good, Dunbar. I thought Declan made it very clear that you weren't to get in touch without good reason."

Her jaw tensed. "Trust me, I wouldn't be here otherwise."

Curious now, I arched a brow. "Do tell."

JUST BECAUSE NYX DOESN'T LOVE
ME, DOESN'T MEAN I'M UNLOVABLE.

TWELVE
CAMMIE

IT HAPPENED IN A FLASH.

One second Father had his hand on mine, his fingers digging into my wrist like he could shatter the bones with his hold alone, and the next, his head was a bloodied mass and Svetlana was screaming like she was a banshee on Red Bull.

It was her screams that brought me back to life. That robbed me of the daze that had seen me slam a glass ornament into my father's skull so many times that—

I peered down at myself, saw the blood and matter, tiny pieces of brain and God knew what else, coating my Chanel dress. My mouth widened in a scream, I could feel the noise building up in my lungs, just waiting for me to erupt, only, I never did.

A soft popping sound caught my attention, and I knew what it was. Even though I was only a daughter of the Bratva, not a soldier, I knew that sound.

We all did.

When I stared over at Maxim, I almost expected the gun to be aimed at me. But it wasn't. Smoke curled about the gun's muzzle, and as I watched, his hand lowered, before the gun returned to the inside pocket of his expensive suit. Within seconds, a cellphone was in his hand, and dazedly, I let my glance drift from him to Svetlana.

To a sight I prepared myself to behold.

Her face was, quite frankly, gone.

Vomit bubbled up my gullet and the need to puke was a strong one. To let it out. To let everything out. But I didn't.

Couldn't.

I'd just killed my father.

And Maxim, his loyal soldier, had killed my stepmother.

Not me.

I'd been raised in a violent world, one where I knew that my death would be the prayer on someone's lips, where my end could be abrupt and painful and out of the blue.

But Mama had been left like a broken doll, and these two weren't.

They'd been butchered in violence.

A violence spawned by me.

I raised my hand to my mouth to stem the flood of tears that longed to break through, but as I did, the scent of iron on my lips had me juddering in reaction, my hands dropping to my sides, fingers trembling as I evaded their slickness. A slickness that had nothing to do with the cuts on my palms, but my father's.

I'd killed him.

I'd fucking killed him.

My knees caved in, any starch in them disappearing as my brain tried to come to terms with what my hands, my body, *my heart* had done.

As I stared at the grim pitting on his skull, as I stared at the mush of flesh that was the remainder of a man I'd loved at one point in my life, I knew this was it.

The day I'd die too.

"He's dead."

Maxim's voice was clear, loud, even, in the room.

I flinched with both words, especially as they were spoken in English and not Russian.

As I watched droplets of blood course over my father's face, like some kind of carved fruit decoration to celebrate Halloween, I heard him rumble, "I'll get her out of here. You'll have to be fast. I'm going to have to spin this." Then: "No, she's dead too." He grunted. "I'll expect more than just a favor when it comes down to it. Alliances were forged, but they can be forgotten over time, O'Donnelly."

That was all it took.

Just the mention of the last name that would be mine tomorrow for me to feel like I was splintering into a million pieces.

The relief was insane. The O'Donnellys, the Irish, were no safe haven. They were, if anything, a den of vipers that could bite me and poison me the first chance they got, but they'd protected Inessa. They'd welcomed her into their fold.

I had to pray that they'd do the same for me.

Even if they couldn't forgive me for not being the virginal bride they might have wanted for their son, their bitter dislike of me was better than the toxic shelter of this house.

"She'll have access to a car. You can make your own arrangements where you want to pick her up."

Maxim moved toward me, and I tensed up, unsure if he was going to stick to his words—a backstabber could never be trusted, even if that backstabbing was in my favor—and I watched as he arched a brow, a sneer on his lips as our eyes clashed and held before he strode past me and moved toward the wall.

At first, I wondered what he was doing, then, I watched as he tucked the cellphone into his throat, clutching at it with his shoulder as he drew a pen from his pocket and began digging through the drywall to snag the bullet.

He was lucky that Svetlana's taste was worse than my mother's. This room had been painted a pale wintry peach, one that was barely ripened, in her time. Now? It was a sea of busy floral patterns. The one that held the bullet was a mass of black with vibrant pink roses that, oddly enough, matched the godawful Barbie furniture, but hid the bullet hole.

"Victoria is at a friend's house. It was pre-arranged. I can bring her tomorrow." He shrugged. "Well, whatever. I can give you the directions. I'll expect you to uphold your promise where that's concerned as well."

What promise?

Where what was concerned?

After he pried out the bullet, I watched him toss it on his palm a second. Tiny dust particles bobbed and swayed here and there with it, hovering in mid-flight before cascading down, thanks to gravity.

It felt like time had been freeze-framed as the bullet danced in the air, and then it restarted with a screech as he finally put the phone down and murmured, "We have to get you out of here."

My mouth felt thick as I rasped, "You're working for the Irish?"

Maxim's brow puckered. "What made you think that?"

Did he think I was stupid? "You just got off the phone with one of the Pointers."

"I did. But that was different. That was for you." He pursed his lips.

I had no idea what was happening here, no idea whatsoever but the one thing I did know? He was lying.

But what the hell could I say when he was obviously helping me?

I had no loyalties to the Bratva. The Brotherhood had kept me fed and clothed for the largest chunk of my life but that didn't mean that I owed it anything.

If the wedding still went ahead tomorrow, I'd switch allegiances in a flash.

Which, I supposed, didn't make me sound very loyal, but loyalty wasn't something you could buy or intimidate out of another person. It had to be earned.

But the sheer fact that he was going to protect me, simply because of a promise he'd made my mother, Brennan O'Donnelly had already shown more integrity than my father ever had.

Which meant whatever he wanted from me, whatever he needed, I'd do it.

My heart ceased to race now I knew that, as untrustworthy as he clearly was, Maxim was going to help me escape.

Sharing a fate like Svetlana's wouldn't have come as a surprise to me, but Maxim evidently had other plans.

My bottom lip trembled a second before I firmed it, then toughened up.

I wasn't alone anymore.

I was going to be an O'Donnelly, and between my leaving Brennan and now, he'd obviously concocted some kind of deal with Maxim. A deal that had been enough to turn him, one of my father's most trusted *boyeviks*.

Unsure if I wanted to know the details when, from experience, I was well aware that it was better to stay out of things like this, I whispered, "Did you have to kill Svetlana?"

"Of course I did," he said with a sneer. "You killed the Pakhan. Do you think she'd stay quiet? She'd have run you to the ground as soon as spit on you."

I thought of the baby brother or sister she'd been carrying, a child who'd put Victoria's life in danger, who'd triggered the flipping of that switch in my brain and as horrendous as it was, as evil as it probably made me, I couldn't find it in me to be regretful.

That child, had it been a boy, would have perpetuated the nightmarish Vasov legacy.

As it stood, the only Vasovs still living were the unwanted girl children. But we knew what it was to love thanks to Mama. We could change things. Could alter that legacy, imbue it with love.

I wanted that.

More than I could say.

My gaze flittered over Svetlana. She was sprawled backward on the uncomfortable armchair she was so proud of, her legs splayed, her arms wide, her face just... *gone*.

My father wasn't much better.

His head was a pulpy mass that reminded me of ground beef. His brain was—

I snapped a hand up to my mouth again, but the metallic tinge to the air had me gagging once more.

"I need to get cleaned up," I rasped, staggering upright, uncertain if I could stand to be in here much longer.

"You have five minutes," he ordered. "I need you to look presentable." He grabbed my arm and hauled me closer to him. When his hand came to my chin to force me to look into his eyes, I jerked back, but his hold on me tightened. His eyes were dark and stormy as he intoned, "I'm doing you a solid, Camille. I'll expect your help when the time comes."

Fear had me flinching in his hold.

Maxim wasn't a man I knew well, but I'd seen him come up through the ranks, and like most teen soldiers, his life and devotion to the Brotherhood inspired pity in me. Duty to the Bratva wasn't love from a family, but they acted like it was.

The Bratva wouldn't hug you at night or congratulate you on a win.

They'd just coat your soul in blood and get you locked away in a cell for a lifetime...

God, was that going to be my fate?

Was he about to blackmail me?

"What kind of help?" I whispered. "How can I help you?"

"When the time comes," he repeated, "you'll know."

Maybe I was feeling brave, either that or stupid, but I rasped, "I owe you—"

"Bet your ass you do," he interrupted.

"—but I will never spy against the O'Donnellys."

His lips twisted. "The Bratva bitch is capable of loyalty, after all."

"Like you can judge," I snarled.

"My loyalty is to the Bratva. Not to an individual."

I swallowed. "Well, I'm the opposite. I'm loyal to the people who count, and no one besides my sisters ever has under this roof." I knew that I had to go, that time wasn't on my side, but... "Why, Maxim? I thought you loved him."

He hitched a shoulder, his gaze darting over to my father. "He was becoming a liability."

I frowned—was that his justification for this treachery? For helping me when, by all rights, I should be on my knees, his gun burrowing into my nape as I awaited my punishment?

"In what way?"

His eyes settled on mine. "When we were at the hospital, they did some scans, some bloodwork. We learned he had some cysts in his brain."

Mouth gaping, I snapped, "Are you being serious?"

"Well, there's no reason to lie about it now, is there?" he retorted waspishly. "Not when some of those cysts are probably decorating that fancy dress of yours."

I blanched, feeling as if my entire body was turning pale at his callous words.

"He was dying?"

Maxim shook his head. "No. They were benign. But they were pressing onto certain areas of the brain and it was causing issues."

My brow furrowed as I thought about how his gaze had drifted around the room as he looked for me earlier. And now I thought about it, he'd been clumsier recently. Dropping things and getting furious about it, like it was someone else's fault...

I'd thought it was from the pain, or his meds, or maybe his just not being used to using a wheelchair, but this changed my perspective on the matter.

"With his sight?"

"That, and the way he was letting that bitch lead him around by the dick," was all he said before he shrugged. "He earned my loyalty, but the Bratva is more than just one Pakhan. The Bratva is who we must protect."

God, he sounded exactly how Moscow wanted their men—indoctrinated.

"Not we, *you*. I'm telling you, Maxim. If you ever call on me to spy, I won't."

A gleam of something—I had no idea what, and I had no desire to know either—appeared in his eyes. "Shame your father was so intent on tying you to that old fat fuck."

I pulled back out of his hold, aware of what he was saying and seriously not wanting his mind to go down that route. Women in the Bratva were vessels.

Against their wills.

The last thing I needed to happen tonight was to get myself raped because Maxim thought I should be grateful to him.

"I-I'd best clean up."

His eyes darkened, not out of arousal thankfully, but in warning. "Be fast. Dress like you're heading for a party."

"Who are you going to blame this on?"

"That's for me to worry about." His lips curved down into a grimace. "Go on. Don't come back here, Camille. Ever."

I grabbed his hand. "You'll make sure Victoria gets back to me?"

"You didn't care before when you ran away."

"I always cared," I snapped. "Sometimes self-preservation is the only way you can come back at all."

He arched a brow, his disbelief evident, but I didn't bother to defend myself.

If he thought I'd have done Victoria much good as a child bride to a Bratva money man than he could go on thinking that.

"I'll look after Victoria," I told him gruffly.

"And that's where you'll need to remember the favor I've done you tonight."

It didn't take much to figure out the path his mind had taken him down. "You're too old for her."

He smirked. "Brennan O'Donnelly is sixteen years older than you. I'm only fourteen years older than Victoria. I'll wait until she's of age, but do not turn her against me."

For myself, I was scared. The ramifications of tonight were immense, but, at that moment, I didn't care what this bastard had against me. What he thought he could hold over me. Didn't care that the gun he'd used to murder my stepmother was back in his pocket, and didn't give a damn that he could easily press that to my temple and whisper, "Night, night, Camille," faster than I could run out of here...

At that moment, I was an older sister. At that moment, I was the only protector my baby sister had.

Pulling free of his hold, I snarled, "I won't turn her against you, but neither will I lie to her. I won't help you either. If you think you can turn up three years from now when she's eighteen and haul her down the aisle, you're mistaken. You want her, you'll court her. You want her, you'll make her want you." I shoved a finger in his chest, prodding him as I rasped, "She won't be like Inessa or me. I won't allow it."

"You're not the one holding the cards, Camille," he warned, his voice a low rumble. The hiss of a threat whispered along my nerve endings, but I didn't care.

I'd never had anyone back me up. Never had anyone protect me.

Until tonight.

Until Brennan O'Donnelly.

I wasn't sure how, didn't care if I was being honest, but his backing gave me more leverage than I might have otherwise had.

"Neither of us are," I told him coldly. "Seems like both of us are dancing to the Irishman's tune."

And with that, I twisted around, picked up the heels I'd discarded earlier, and rushed over to the door.

Seeing that the coast was clear, I made my escape to the staircase, wondering how, in the past twenty minutes, everything, my life, my whole world, had morphed into something that belonged in a true crime novel.

THIRTEEN
BRENNAN

"THAT WAS UNEXPECTED."

I rocked back in my seat, shooting Bagpipes a glance before I murmured, "Damn right it was."

"What do you think happened?"

"With which problem?" I asked wryly. "Dunbar's or Lyanov's?"

Bagpipes rolled his eyes. "You said it yourself. She's a rat—should be used to being tailed."

I smirked at him. "What did she expect us to do? Babysit her?"

Bagpipes sniffed. "Stupid bitch. Losing digits all over."

"Huh?"

"Digits... ya know. Like numbers? IQ points?"

"Ain't got time for your weird sense of humor, bud."

He flipped me the bird, but said, "Wonder why she killed him."

"No idea." I scraped a hand over my jaw. "Just grateful I set that particular wheel in motion a few weeks ago. I must be a psychic."

"More like psycho." Bagpipes chuckled before leaning over, his elbows coming to his knees, as he rumbled, "That's two families with unstable leadership."

"Things are going to get rocky in NYC," I agreed. "Probably a good thing that the Summit went down before this happened."

Bagpipes winced. "Jesus, yeah. With both the Italians and the Russians floundering, you know what that means?"

I rolled my eyes. "This ain't my first time, Baggy. Territory grab."

"We have the men now," he pointed out, and he wasn't wrong.

Uncle Sam didn't know it, but in our particular district of New York, we were one of the biggest employers out there.

Funny how shit like that worked out, when the Irish fucking Mob gave out better goddamn benefits than legit corporations you knew you were living in a messed up country that needed change.

Not that we were going to get it with Alan fucking Davidson as POTUS. All those promises he'd given the American people... all of it bullshit. Typical politician. That's why I had no faith in the system. I didn't like my world, but give me that over butting heads in the Senate. At least I could leave bruises. Those fuckers just left The Capitol feeling like their asses had been reamed.

Drumming my fingers on the table, I pondered my next move. This had altered the situation dramatically, but it didn't change what was happening tomorrow. Made it easier, in fact. Plus, with Vasov out of the picture, we could earn some more territory out of it, *and* retain an alliance with the Bratva if Maxim Lyanov managed to make it to the top of the tree.

There was a reason I'd thrown a lure his way—he had potential. That was why Vasov had kept him close. With no boy children, he'd had to mentor someone. Of course, that meant Lyanov had crosshairs on his back now Vasov was dead...

As always, the minutiae were enough to trigger a headache. And I didn't have time for that.

"I need to get going."

"You're going to meet with her?"

"How else would she know where my apartment is?"

"You could text her," he said dryly.

"And they say chivalry is dead. She just murdered her father," I drawled as I reflected on how his murder changed the status quo.

Altered the balance.

Would she still want to marry me?

She might think, with him gone, that the threat was gone, but if anything, Abramovicz could still swoop in and snatch her away...

My hands curled into fists at the thought.

She was a burden. A guilt trip. A promise owed, a favor outstanding. None of which sat well with me. But this afternoon, when I'd seen her fucking palms, something had tripped inside me.

Those hands of hers were ravaged.

They weren't the lily-soft digits of a woman who'd never done a day's work in her life. They weren't soft and silky. They were callused and rough with scars. Self-inflicted ones.

The thought of her doing that to herself filled me with a rage that was unnecessary considering how little she meant to me—she was, for all intents and purposes, a stranger.

She wouldn't be for long, but that was exactly what she was right now.

She shouldn't inspire anything other than apathy in me, but that was the last thing I was feeling.

Getting to my feet, I said, "Don't say a word outside of the crew."

Baggy frowned. "Why not? This is good news."

"Because I'm not saying shit to anyone about anything until she's my wife."

Concern had him sighing. "Because you think your da will make a stand and not let you marry her?"

"I don't think, I know," I said grimly, before I twisted my wrist until the bone cracked.

The joint was weakened from how many times Da had snapped it over the years—until I'd fought back. The satisfaction of breaking his nose was tied with the fact he'd recognized I wasn't going to take his beatings anymore. One year, my wrist had been broken so often, I'd worn a cast like it was a fucking fashion accessory.

My father was capable of many things, and stopping me from marrying the woman of my choice was small fry for him.

Bagpipes' frown darkened. "If you knew what a pain in the ass wives are, you wouldn't be so militant. I'm only trying to protect future Brennan here."

"From Da or her?"

"Both of them. He'll just beat the shit out of you, or," he amended, "have one of his men hold you down so you can't move."

We shared a glance, both of us knowing my father was capable of that—that was how he'd gotten Eoghan down the aisle.

"I doubt it. He's left me alone since the broken nose incident."

"True."

"What do you think Camille will do?" I prompted with a laugh. "Beat me with a rolling pin?" I mocked, both of us grinning because that was a famous story in our family.

Ma had beaten the shit out of Da with a rolling pin in the early days of their marriage, and had earned his love and a lifetime's devotion in the process.

"You think all wives are like your ma. Trust me, they ain't. They won't slap you around the face before they suck you off."

My nose crinkled. "You talking about my ma and cock-sucking in the same breath?"

He arched a brow. "She made five sons. I know Aidan Sr. likes to think he's holier than thou, but I'm not sure his bride is capable of an immaculate conception."

"Maybe the first time, just not the fifth," I joked, but I folded my arms against my chest as I queried, "What makes you think I'm going to hold Ma up as the perfect wife?"

That had him rolling his eyes. "Because we all do. Trust me, we should never have left home. At least our mothers made our beds for us without nagging our asses off about taking out the trash."

Lips twitching, I murmured, "I pay you enough to install a garbage disposal unit. Anyway, don't you have a shoot?"

"Sure, but when a man gets home, he don't wanna be dealing with a bag of messy fucking diapers." He stretched his arms out in front of him and cracked his knuckles. "Trust me, you should stay away from that bitch. Whatever magic she's got between her legs, it ain't worth it. Stay single."

Dryly, and knowing he meant well, I merely said, "I've made my choice, and I'm going to stick to it."

"You're asking for a whole pile of shit to fall on your head."

I smirked at him. "Isn't that what we do best? Dig our way out of landslides of crap?"

My cocky retort had him rolling his eyes. "One day he'll stop cutting you so much slack."

"What day is that? When Aidan pulls his head out of his ass and cuts out the drugs? Like that's going to happen any day soon. I'll stop rocking around like I'm the heir to the Points when Aidan steps up and takes it back.

"You know I don't want this much responsibility, but I've taken it all on the chin, accepted that I'm one of the few who can manage the workload. If Da doesn't want his house of cards to come tumbling down, then he'd better accept that on some shit, I ain't about to let him have his way."

Sighing, Baggy just grumbled, "You're a braver man than me."

After I rounded the desk and made my way to the door, I clapped a hand to his shoulder and told him, "Brave? Nah. Just as whacko as he is."

My bud snorted out a laugh as we left the office together. He headed down to the parking lot to sweep my car for bugs, while I hovered in the hall when I caught sight of Tinker hefting a baggy in his hand. The way he was holding it had me veering toward him, the problem of my future bride shelved momentarily.

"Tink? What's up?"

"That feel light to you?" He tossed me the baggy.

"I'm not a set of scales. You're the human fucking computer." I threw it back to him and asked, "You think the *Demonios* are short-selling us?"

He shrugged. "Either that or their delivery man is taking a pinch here or there."

I eyed the many and varied crates in the stock room, some of which contained drugs, others contained guns. There were all kinds of shit inside them, some I didn't even want to know about. We had our own little import business going down. The more exotic shit interested me the most—and I wasn't talking about Colombian marching powder either.

This place was Tinker's domain, and while I'd been teasing about the human computer shit, he somehow managed to keep track of everything in our stock without computerizing any of our records, and had the knack of being able to heft something in his hand and figure out the weight.

To the nearest ounce.

It was insane.

If the fucker ever decided to do the crazy thing and 'retire' from the Five Points, I was pretty sure he had a career on *America's Got Talent*.

"I can talk to Juan Alonso—mention we've got product on the loose?"

Tink shook his head. "This is the second time it's happened, but the measurements are marginal. Before we accuse the psychotic fuckers who are willing to dip their faces in ink, let's maybe accuse their equipment?"

"Sensible," I agreed with a hidden grin, because he wasn't teasing. "What about here? These accurate?" I asked, eying the bags full of cash that the Dominicans gave us to launder through our fronts. We'd be shipping this out across Hell's Kitchen in the AM, so I knew it would have been processed by now.

"Their counting machines work plenty fine."

"Good to know." I moved over to the crates that were wadded down with bank notes—my favorite kind of exotic product. Only I found a little extra something too; a catalogue.

"What have we got here?"

"A thank you from the Yakuza. One of the runners just brought it over. Was going to bring it upstairs once I'd finished here."

I arched a brow. "They heard about my little collection?"

"They'd be dumbasses if they didn't know you collect rare denominations."

"Think they're tailing me?"

"Maybe. There was a reason you were caught with your pants down in that sushi restaurant," he pointed out, making me roll my eyes. "But I've had three separate guards on you ever since, and they've found no one so I'm not worried. But I did get Conor to scan your computers, make sure there were no trackers on there."

Knowing he would have the situation in hand, I hummed, a tad disinterestedly, as I opened the catalogue and eyed the coins within them.

They were vintage.

South African.

Even better, they were twenty-four carat gold.

And not just your average Krugerrand.

I wasn't like Declan—didn't collect things for their beauty, or for an artistic interpretation that would bring harmony to my environment... or whatever bullshit excuse he gave for spending a wasted fortune at Sotheby's.

Me? I liked my investments to be portable.

I liked them small.

I liked them to be in a safe at home so that if shit came to shit, and this far, it never had gotten so bad where I needed to run, but if I had to, then I could open my strong box, grab my catalogues of coins and have about five million I could trade in.

Personally, I thought that was a lot fucking smarter than investing six hundred thousand in an antique wardrobe some ancient Chinese dude had stored his clothes in. Couldn't exactly heft that around on your back, could you? But what the fuck did I know?

"Anything nice in there? I didn't look seeing as it was a gift to you."

I shook my head at his words, still, after all these years, unable to believe just how trustworthy my crew was. I treated them right, even gave them an equal status to speak up and discuss shit with me—which wasn't common in our world—and I paid them well, but that didn't make loyalty any less of a commodity.

They never let me down though, ever. And considering the mess we were in, our world at war, appreciation hit me harder than it usually did.

"You should pick one," I said gruffly.

Tink, who was bent over a crate, the rough wood snagging on his suit coat, his head inside it as he reached in to grab the baggies at the bottom, froze then snapped up. "You sick or something?"

I scowled. "No. I'm fine."

"You sure? I'd check if you have a fever, Scrooge, because we all know you hoard that shit like it comes from a unicorn."

"Unicorn manure," I mused. "The most precious shit in the world."

Tinker snorted, but he tipped his head to the side. "You serious about the coins?"

I shrugged. "Consider it a 'thank you' gift for all the overtime."

His brows rose higher but he replied, "Well, it's appreciated."

I just hummed. "Make sure Bagpipes and Forrest pick one too."

"Will do." He dipped his chin in a nod, but I could sense his surprise.

I definitely wasn't a miser, but he wasn't wrong. I safeguarded my future with high insurance premiums, the likes of which didn't depend on any stock market or gangland war.

Because the Krugerrands were nice, it was hard not to slip the catalogue under my arm and take it with me. I guessed, in my own way, I was a money magpie, so I shoved my hands into my pockets and strode back to Tink who was still eying me like I had a contagious rash he didn't want to catch.

"You on your way out?"

We worked all hours, so my leaving at nine was pretty early. "Got a situation over in Brighton Beach."

"Need a hand?" he asked, straightening up, keying me into the fact that he was ready to have my back before I even asked for it.

I shook my head. "Nothing that bad. Just picking up a package."

He blinked, relaxed. "Oh."

Smiling a little, I murmured, "I won't be back in tonight. Need you at my apartment tomorrow at two-thirty."

Though he nodded, it didn't stop him from grousing, "Can't believe you picked me."

A laugh escaped me. "Consider yourself the lucky one."

"The one who's gonna get his balls dipped in molten shoe polish when your father finds out I'm the—"

Cocking a brow at him, I interrupted, "Loose lips sink ships."

"It's not 1942," he argued.

"No, this war is far deadlier," I rumbled with a sigh. "Be there. Make sure the other fuckers are as well."

"You sure you don't want your brothers around?"

"I don't want anyone trying to talk me out of it, and they might."

No 'might' about it. Especially when they found out Vasov was dead.

He heaved a sigh, making it clear to me that he was hoping my brothers would have the chance to talk some sense into me. No dice.

"See you tomorrow," he muttered.

I waved at him, then retreated to the foyer and out into the lot. Making my way through the puddles that were illuminated in the spotlights that were fixed to the roof, I climbed into my Maybach and made my way out of the dump that was The Hole after I checked exactly where Camille was going to be waiting on me.

It was pretty handy that I was still working, because if I'd been in Hell's Kitchen, it might have taken longer to get to Brighton Beach than I'd have liked.

I wasn't sure what I was going to find when I finally made it to Camille, but I had a feeling that I wasn't going to like it.

In my line of work, you either had the knack or you didn't. It was as clear cut as that. You knew when shit was about to drown you, or you were completely dumb to it. We worked hard to pair soldiers together who'd save each other's asses, because unlike the Russians and the Italians, we gave a fuck about our men.

In this day and age, people didn't feel like spending half their lives in a Supermax, taking dumps with a terrorist for a cellmate next door, and staring up at white walls with no natural light for decades on end. Neither did they want to die the second they made it through the ranks and earned a patch on the streets.

The Irish were the only ones who gave a fuck, and for all my father was a head case, that was one thing you could say about him—he cared for his people.

We had retirement slush funds for senior Pointers who were more useful sunning themselves in Florida than dragging shit down in the Big Apple, and the widows of soldiers who'd died on the job were well taken care of, and an integral part of the life.

I knew for a fact that we were the only family who had a safe place to lockdown our women when things really turned bad, and that said a lot about us. About who we were and what mattered to us the most.

But for all that, some soldiers were better than others, and in my instance, I had a knack for sniffing out trouble. That was why I'd gotten in touch with Maxim Lyanov a long time ago.

Something Eoghan had said, months back, when he'd gone to visit his father-in-law after the dumbfuck had been knee-capped had stuck with me. About how Maxim, though he was only young by comparison to Vasov's other guards, appeared to be higher up the ladder than Eoghan might have thought reasonable for a guy that age.

Guards had to be trusted, they had the responsibility of taking the bullet for their leaders, and that meant crafting a kind of loyalty that took years to build. The skills required to be a good guard were important too, but it was the trust that was the hardest thing to cultivate.

And it seemed that theory was right, too.

Maxim had sold out his Pakhan to me.

I wasn't happy about the cost, but I'd deal with it later. All transactions had a price and I understood why Maxim had demanded his payment in the form of Victoria Vasov.

The thought had me tightening my hands around the steering wheel.

It was a problem, but before that happened, the bastard might die. Whether or not that was at the end of my gun was another matter entirely. To keep my promise, I'd kill him, I'd just prefer not to have to.

At nine o'clock, the traffic down to Brighton Beach was just as busy as usual. With the rest of my crew back in The Hole, for the first time in a long while, I was alone and I took a moment to listen to the music that most of those fuckers would have mocked me for.

As Damien Rice belted out his favorite faded fantasies, I was stuck in the grind of gears and wheels as the cops did what they did best— traffic duty. Pulling out all the stops to get the roads churning in the aftermath of a car crash that was definitely going to make me late.

Checking my messages as we were at a standstill, I saw I had one from her.

Camille: *Is everything okay? Are you on your way?*

Me: *First time I could message. There's been a crash. Are you safe?*

I wasn't sure what had been the trigger, wasn't sure why tonight was the night when she'd shattered, especially when she was going to be free from her father's clutches tomorrow, but I saw no point in pouting over spilled milk.

She didn't need that shit from me.

She'd just killed her fucking sire—no bitch I knew would be okay with that. Even the ones who hated their folks didn't want their blood on their hands, and I couldn't blame them. My da hadn't exactly been a saint, and there were some days when he drove me to want to stab him in the neck to get him to shut up, but I never went through with it.

I knew exactly what he was. Knew his failings, and his weaknesses, and that I didn't kill him was a testament to the fact that I didn't want him dead.

I wasn't sure if that was a compliment or not, but on the days when he pissed me off, on the days where, at forty years of fucking age, I had to pull shady moves to keep my bride's identity from him—those were the moments when I could throttle him.

Vasov, on the other hand, was a different kind of monster.

Da celebrated family. At least, in his own way he did.

Vasov wasn't like that.

That had been clear to me every time Inessa was around us all. She looked like she was waiting for a time bomb to detonate, and when Da had his explosive bursts of temper, even now, after months of Eoghan's protection, she would always flinch like she expected him to hit her. That meant Camille would be the same way, which wasn't exactly something to look forward to. Maybe her time with the Sinners would have toughened her up some.

Ironically enough, she was the one who took a long time to reply to my message, which filled me with concern. I peered around, my foot tapping against the foot rest as I tried to figure out how long it was going to take for the pigs to get a move on, when finally she replied:

Camille: *I had to drive somewhere else. I recognized a group of boyeviks heading into a restaurant nearby.*

So, at least she had a fucking brain.

That was something.

Me: *Good thinking.*

I was about to ask her to send a live location, but she did that without me having to request it.

While she hadn't reinvented the goddamn wheel, in my world, some women had been raised to ask when they could go for a shit, so that she had some initiative gave me hope for the future.

Me: *Thanks.*

Another glance around the street provided me with the sight of a bunch of red lights flashing off up ahead as traffic finally began to shift.

Me: *On my way now. Hopefully I won't be long. If there's a problem, and you need to move again, send me another live location.*

Camille: *Will do.*

Short and sweet.

Just how I liked it.

Once traffic was underway, it didn't slow down again, so finally, I made it down the Beltway and toward the live location where she was hiding out—she hadn't sent me another, so I was glad to know she considered herself safe enough.

As safe as any woman could be in that fucking neighborhood.

Parked up on the border between Brighton Beach and Sheepshead Bay, I found the same SUV she'd driven this morning behind a small bakery that was closed now and a bar and sushi restaurant, both of which were teeming with patrons.

Thankfully, there was a lull in traffic, which, after what I'd just driven through, meant luck was on my side, and I pulled up next to it, giving her just enough space to open her door, lock it, then to climb into the passenger seat.

As she moved, I kept an eye on the bar and sushi restaurant, monitored the roads and the vicinity to make sure no one registered what was happening. For all that time, I didn't look at her once.

I wouldn't say I was nervous, because the butterflies of fear that existed in everyone's stomach had long since burned to ashes in mine, but when she was safely ensconced beside me, I'd admit to being relieved.

She'd had a close call.

Eying her purse, seeing it had some bulk to it, I asked, "What's in there?"

"T-The dress. It's bloodstained."

Jesus. "Okay. I'll deal with that later. Well done for bringing it with you."

She gulped. "I didn't want to leave it there to be used against me."

Smart thinking.

Christ, could she get hotter?

"Drop your cellphone out the window," I instructed her, pleased when she immediately obeyed. As I drove away from a phone that was probably hooked up with tracking devices, I took note of how few cars there were on the road. That put me more on edge than anything else.

It was quiet.

Too quiet.

"No one knows yet."

Her words were a whisper that wrapped around me like silk, making my dick hard and my body tense. I didn't like my reactiveness to her— her voice, her scent, her looks—but my cock apparently didn't agree.

Just the sweet perfume of her shampoo filled the small cabin of the Maybach, and the fact that I hadn't even glanced at her once pissed me off because her beauty should have me responding like this, not her goddamn smell.

That kiss had amped things up to a degree that put me on edge, but I couldn't find it in me to regret it.

Tension bracketed my neck, making my shoulders hunch up as I tightened my hands on the wheel.

"No one knows as far as you're aware. Maxim might have told one of his men by now."

"I doubt it. I think he's setting someone up." She cleared her throat. "I heard him on the phone. He didn't know I was listening."

So, she was sneaky.

It would be wise for me to remember that.

Of course, we all grew to be sneaky in this world. Listening in to information that people didn't want us to have was free, and it could keep our asses safe and sound. I didn't blame her, even as I registered that she had skills if a motherfucker like that *boyevik* cunt didn't hear her spying on him.

"Best to be safe," was all I said, and I didn't relax until we hit South Slope, allied territory, and made our way onto the Hamilton Avenue bridge.

Her tension was just as high, and her silence was just as loaded.

I knew we were both waiting for the shit to hit the fan, and though ordinarily I'd have done my level best for her to feel safe, in this instance, she wouldn't be that until we shared a last name.

When the Brooklyn Bridge was in the distance, Two Bridges, the Lower East Side, and Rose Hill all memories, I took a deeper breath because I was on home turf.

No one would touch her here.

They wouldn't fucking dare.

My reach was far, but when she was unclaimed, its power was dulled. Just not in my territory.

Everyone in this motherfucking city knew the O'Donnellys were rabid where family was concerned. They'd learned that hard lesson when the Aryans had kidnapped Ma.

Da had slaughtered so many of the fuckers that parts of the Bronx were still stained red. That was one of the bloodiest gang wars in the city's history. People had started to forget, but now Da knew we had rats, he was in exterminator mode.

God help NYC.

Da was about to make sure they knew just how deadly we were when our family was crossed.

Maybe she knew she was safer too, because her voice cracked as she asked, "Don't you want to know what happened?"

Was she nervous? Scared of me?

Was that the best way to handle this? To keep her on her toes?

It might well be, but truthfully, that would be fucking boring and would require a level of patience that I didn't possess.

I didn't require affection or tenderness from her, but I wanted her to be willing. I didn't want her to flinch when I walked in a room, and after we'd fucked, I didn't want her to be so scared that she couldn't sleep if I was beside her.

I was okay with a relationship that might be described as 'unusual,' but her fear wasn't something I wanted to cultivate.

So, even though I was pissed at having my evening plans disrupted, even though I didn't appreciate the SOS Lyanov had sent out on her behalf, I merely asked, "Do you want to tell me?"

I could literally feel her stress levels rise at my question, which had me rolling my eyes. There I was, trying to calm her the fuck down, and there she was, tensing the fuck up.

Talk about not being able to win.

"I—" She paused. "Victoria would never have been safe if he lived. He'd have done to her what he wanted to do to me. I had to protect her."

As we hit a stop light, I turned to her and murmured, "You did good."

She licked her lips; lips I wanted to bite. "I—It feels like a nightmare."

Softly, I murmured, "Camille, if sharing helps, then share. But if you don't want to tell me, you don't have to. Not tonight. At some point, I'll expect answers. Tonight, it's different. You saw some things I'd have spared you from if I could, but what's done is done. I'm not about to interrogate you when it's not necessary.

"As far as I'm concerned, I'm glad that cunt's dead. I'm glad he's no longer a threat to you or your sister. In my opinion," I repeated, "you did good."

"He's... *was* an ally," she whispered, her confusion clear, which clued me into the fact that she thought I'd be mad at her. Hence, I guessed, the hesitation and the nerves.

I snorted. "Allies aren't friends. They sure as fuck aren't family, either. In the Irish world, it's family that matters most. If anything sticks with you today, you should remember that one thing in particular."

Her gulp was audible, and over Midtown traffic, that was saying something. "He was family though."

I huffed under my breath. "That's a joke if ever I heard one. The bastard had your ma killed, Camille. He ain't no family of yours."

She was quiet a second, before she whispered, "Family first. That's how it's supposed to be."

"Well, in my world, that's exactly how it is. Just because your fucker of a father had different priorities doesn't mean we work the same way. You're about to become an O'Donnelly. That means something." I shrugged. "Anyway, your father was useful in the past, but he was turning into a liability."

"How?" she whispered, her voice soft. So soft, so goddamn silken again that I had no alternative but to turn to face her.

Jesus.

She was even more stunning than earlier on.

So fucking gorgeous that I knew keeping my hands off her tonight was going to be nearly impossible.

This woman was mine.

Tomorrow, it'd be official, but even as she sat here, both of us knowing exactly what she was, it was difficult accepting that I had to be a gentleman tonight.

Chivalry, in my opinion, wasn't dead, and the first night she slept under my roof, I didn't want her to have any negative associations with it. That home was going to be her haven, so I didn't want to spoil it for her, and fucking her when she probably still had tiny specks of blood under her nails after killing her father was a surefire way to achieve that.

I gritted my teeth against the need flourishing inside me, a need that made me want shit I had no business in wanting with my wife. That mouth was going to kiss my children, those hands were going to hold my babies, and that body was going to give life to my heirs... but all I could think of when I looked at her were things that made me want to wreck her.

She was dressed to impress, so fucking sleek with it that she could have been attending a gala. Only in the lights from the streets did I see that, in her eyes, she was devastated.

Tonight had affected her in a way that only someone who'd murdered another person could ever understand. But on the surface, she looked like elegance personified. Her make-up was delicate, understated, apart from the bright slash of red on her lips, and her eyes were smoky as she stared at me, her hair tousled in waves that were neat but made me think of how it'd be once it was rumpled on my pillow.

The dress was a rich red, short, exposing all her calves and her knees, nothing that risqué but everything about it was tactile, down to the short cashmere jacket she wore to offset the chill in the air as well.

I wanted my hands on her.

I wanted her to be mussed.

That hair a rat's nest, the slash of red on her lips to be marred and smudged from my kisses. I wanted panda eyes from her gagging on my dick, and I wanted those bounteous tits out, destroying the neckline of the dress forever as they provided a shelf for those mounds of heaven that I just wanted to fucking drown in.

Any other time, any other moment, I'd have had my hand up her skirt, my fingers in her pussy, making her ready for when we arrived home... and I actually disliked where my mind was taking me because I didn't want any of that shit with her.

She was supposed to be the kind of wife like Ma.

I didn't know if Da had a mistress, but I imagined he did. I didn't begrudge him for it either. A man had needs, after all. Knowing Da, he'd be as much of a sick fuck in bed as he was out of it, and I didn't want to think of my poor mother having to deal with his ass in the bedroom too.

My fingers tightened around the wheel as the urge to muss my fiancée up hit me, and the only way I could control it, the only way I could stop myself from doing something I shouldn't, was to answer her.

She'd asked how Vasov's usefulness had died a death, so I'd tell her. "You know what a Summit is?"

"When the four families get together."

I nodded. "Exactly. There was a meeting... it didn't end well."

"What happened?"

"This is one of the only times I'll ever discuss business with you," I warned gruffly. "You need to understand that now."

"I do," she said softly. "I understand, and I don't want to know anything that doesn't appertain to my father."

Well, that was a fancy word...

She wasn't as much of a doll as I thought.

In all honesty, I wasn't sure why I was surprised. Inessa had a voice, a brain in her head. Why shouldn't her elder sister?

I guessed it was Mariska's fault. She hadn't been the brightest spark in the fire, but I hadn't been interested in the stuff between her ears but the slit between her legs.

Grunting at her compliance, I murmured, "You know the Russians and Italians are at war?"

"I do."

"We joined in; we're at war with the Italians too, and so are some of our allies. The Don of the *Famiglia* died—" I didn't tell her that was at Eoghan's hands.

"There's a space at the top?" she guessed. "Just like there will be with the Russians now."

"Exactly. A power vacuum. Well, there's a larger vacuum now because something went down at the Summit, something that shouldn't technically have happened." I tried to hide my satisfaction, but I wasn't a miracle worker. I knew it leaked into my words because she shot me a look as I said, "Someone infiltrated the meeting and killed the potential leaders."

"Christ," she rasped, her eyes widening.

"Yeah. Anyway, in the subsequent discussions—"

She held up a hand. "Wait! This went on at the beginning of the meeting?"

"Yeah." At least, that was what Da had told me this afternoon.

"So, there were corpses in the meeting room with you while the discussions were ongoing?"

When you put it like that, I guessed it was a little creepy.

My lips twisted. "You're a child of the Bratva, Camille. I don't think now is the time to get squeamish."

My future bride gulped. "I suppose not."

"This is why you won't be hearing about business. This isn't something women need to hear."

"No," she confirmed, her head tilting down so that fucking hair of hers drifted around her ears.

I wanted to shove that golden curtain aside and plunder her throat, bite it and mark it.

Fuck.

What was wrong with me?

The sound of horns shattered my concentration, but I saw we could go, so I moved into 'Drive' and set off once more. A soft moan escaped her, one that had me shooting her a glance.

"What is it? What's wrong?"

She shook her head, making her hair whip from side to side, before she whispered, "Never mind. What did Father do?"

"He was belligerent and, to be frank, showed a distinct lack of understanding of how our streets are working at the moment."

Camille swallowed. "Maxim told me—" She broke off. Hesitated.

I didn't push her.

I hadn't expected any information from her, but I wasn't about to shove it aside. We needed all the intel we could get on our allies and enemies alike.

A shaky breath rushed from her lips, but I got the feeling my silence encouraged rather than discouraged her to speak up.

I'd have to work on her self-esteem.

This hesitation shit was going to drive me crazy.

"H-He told me that Father had cysts on his brain that were affecting his judgment. His vision too."

I hummed under my breath at what would have been very useful to know if she hadn't just killed him…

I didn't say that though, just murmured, "I think that fits with what went down."

The dumb fuck had insisted that his coke supply made him a king in the city, when everyone knew heroin was the gold dust of choice right now.

Thank you, Big Pharma.

You had to love when the legit corporations were the ones who brought a nation to its knees.

Ah, the American dream...

Then there was his refusal to believe in the very real Sparrows.

His level of asshole wasn't going to be missed.

As I rolled down the quieter streets of Carnegie Hill, finally back in my neighborhood, where the streets hummed with life thanks to expensive restaurants, where the brownstones didn't even have goddamn bars on the windows because it was *that* safe, and where I'd seen men wander down the sidewalks manicuring little flower arrangements on the roadside, a sense of warmth filled me.

My life was changing.

I didn't know if it was for the better, but I had a woman now. My safe neighborhood was going to shelter her, and our future kids.

With that in mind, I thought it best to ease her worries. "Liabilities don't live long in this world, Camille."

"No," she whispered, "I guess not."

The dark in the cabin encompassed us for a second as I drove down the tunnel into my parking garage, where only a few sidelights illuminated the way, and I murmured once more, "Cunts need to die. You don't have to tell me jack. But from this night on, remember what you are, and don't forget it, Camille. Tonight, you're a Vasov. Tomorrow, you're an O'Donnelly, and that makes you un-fucking-touchable."

TOMORROW WILL BE BETTER THAN TODAY.

FOURTEEN
CAMMIE

I STARED up at the ceiling of the guest bedroom, still unable to believe that he'd put me in here. Because I wasn't sure whether that was a good sign or a bad one, and because I kept thinking about that glass ornament digging into my father's skull, the wet splashes, the mushy sounds as the hard object collided with brain matter, I had yet to sleep.

Was it any wonder?

As such, I'd been staring into the void for what felt like forever, and what made it worse was the lack of a phone. There was no scrolling through Insta, no disappearing in vaguebooking. There was just me. And the hard facts of what I'd done.

I'd never hurt anyone before. Not really. When I'd joined the Sinners as a clubwhore, there'd been a few catfights, some behind the scenes, some in front of the brothers who got off on that stuff, but other than that, I'd never done anything worse than rake my nails down someone's cheek.

Tonight was what nightmares were made of, and I still couldn't believe I'd done it to be honest. But even as that disbelief filled me, I was aware that I'd do it again to stop Victoria from having to go through what I had.

It just disturbed me that, while I'd saved her from Abramovicz, I hadn't spared her from Maxim. And then there was how I was at the other side of the hall, right at the opposite end from where Brennan slept.

He'd said he wanted kids, so he meant to visit me at some point... if this was to be my permanent bedroom, that is.

My parents, by the time Victoria had come around, had both slept in separate rooms—

Christ. Both of them were dead now.

Gone.

We were orphaned.

The agony was constant where thoughts of my mother's death were concerned, and even though I was the direct reason behind my father's, the pain wasn't as acute. I didn't feel like someone was standing on my chest, compressing my lungs... I just felt a surreal sense of bewilderment. Like I wasn't sure how it happened. Like I didn't know how I could have done that.

Because I didn't.

I wasn't that person.

I wasn't.

Truly.

Tears burned my eyes, not for the first time, as my brain whirred in a cycle that seemed endless. I wanted to scream out my pain, my grief, but I didn't want to disturb Brennan. If I did, well, he seemed more than serious about claiming me as his, something that had resonated and filled me with relief when we'd discussed it on the journey to his building, but I didn't want to push my luck.

A lifetime of dancing on eggshells lay ahead of me, exactly like my mother. If I had a daughter, I wanted so much more than for her to be a pussy with a price tag. A womb for sale. A mother to future mobsters.

The tears fell at that, because I knew that was unlikely. Just because I wanted it, didn't make it so. Brennan would want his daughter to marry some Irish Mob general, and that was that.

What say would I have in anything?

I'd just give birth to the baby. I'd just raise it with love. I'd just make it a decent human being. Nothing important in the grand scheme of things.

Flinging myself onto my back, I stared some more at that goddamn ceiling which, thanks to the endless reel of thoughts, was now blurry and

I knew that if I carried on like this, I'd go insane. I'd literally lose my mind.

The walls were beginning to close in, and I just—God, I wished Victoria was here. Even though I never wanted her to know what I'd done, I wished she was here, just so I could hug her. Just so I could talk.

I had to, I realized.

Since Brennan had collected me like a lost wallet, he hadn't pressured me to talk about what had happened tonight, and while I'd been grateful at the time, I knew I had to or I'd go mad.

He'd deposited me in here, told me to make myself comfortable, and then had departed. I'd thought it was for the night, but he'd returned with a pair of his boxers and a shirt for me to sleep in. They scented of him, and I only just realized how nice that scent was.

We were strangers.

And we were going to get married tomorrow.

The day after I murdered my father.

God have mercy on my soul because I'd prefer to tie myself to this stranger for the rest of the days I was granted, than to be at his beck and call again.

I'd done the right thing, even though it was so beyond wrong.

Brennan had made out like, once we were wed, we'd become the underworld's Jackie-O and JFK, but even he couldn't protect me from a murder charge, could he? If it ever came out, I was screwed. Literally. I was putting everything on the line by trusting him, but the alternative was to run again. I had no place in West Orange anymore, which meant I'd have to start over, which further meant I'd have to leave Victoria behind which was something I wasn't willing to do.

In a flurry of movement, I surged out of the bed. My bare feet padded as I rushed out of the bedroom, and down the carpeted hall.

There was little to no illumination—this high up, there wasn't that much light pollution when you were peering down at humanity rather than looking up at it—and a burst of speed had my feet thudding against the carpet as I moved down the line of doors, shoving them open as I tried to find him.

He was in the middle, on the opposite side of the hall to the room he'd put me in, and I knew that because the scent of him overwhelmed the room.

Bergamot. Lemon.

Like my favorite tea—Russian Earl Grey.

I inhaled deeply, letting those grassy notes sink into me, and I had no idea why, but his essence calmed me.

For all that I felt alone, for all that he was a stranger, he was going to tie himself to me for life.

No divorce, he'd said.

We were stuck with each other.

Thank God.

His room was different than mine, which made sense because his was the master bedroom. There was a slim hall, and an open door revealed a connecting bath. When I made it to the end of that small corridor, I peered out onto his bed.

I couldn't see much in the dark, but it felt warmer in here than it did in mine. I could see the shadows of furniture, felt carpeting beneath my feet, and knew that my room was for guests and was anonymous, like a hotel room.

This was his place.

He'd bothered to fill his bedroom with home comforts.

"What are you doing, Camille?"

A sharp gasp escaped me at his question. He sounded drowsy, but also like he was aware. Had I awoken him? Maybe that made sense. I'd made some noise rushing through his apartment like a crazy person as I hunted him down, and I figured a guy of his stature would be used to having to sleep with one eye open, but those husky tones of his, dear lord. They sent shivers down my spine.

There was a rumble of warning, a slumberous drawl, and a genuine note of concern within those initial four words, but it was how he said my name.

Like my mother used to say it.

Not like Ca-Meel. But Ca-Me-Ull.

The difference might not seem that much, but to me, it was profound. He said it with a Russian accent, which told me she'd spoken of me. At least, by name.

But at that moment, the weirdness of how this was coming to pass wasn't what I needed to discuss. The desire to atone, to repent for my sins wasn't something I needed either.

Every single reason behind why I'd come here disappeared into the wind. I just needed to be in his arms.

To feel his warmth.

To be in this room where it felt cozy and lived in.

To be at his side.

I knew, right then and there, that I couldn't handle the kind of marriage my mother had. Having affairs that would result in my brutal murder. Being beaten and hiding those bruises. Dealing with jealous mistresses who would call and send photos to me. Being a broodmare until I had a son to take over the mantel before my womb gave out and my health with it.

No.

I needed to make him feel something for me.

I needed to make him need me.

And the only way I knew how to do that was with sex.

It hadn't worked with Nyx. I'd been and done everything he wanted, but it hadn't been enough. I had to pray that Brennan was different. That I could more than adequately satisfy him.

Our earlier kiss gave me courage where, before, I might not have dared approach him, but this was still me. I was still useless with my words, so I stayed silent. Instead, with my eyes now adjusted to the darkness, I saw the mound in the bed that told me he was on the right hand side, and I moved over to the left.

As I lifted the blanket and slipped underneath it, he asked, his tone more querulous than annoyed, "What are you doing?"

"I don't want to be alone."

"And I'll do because there's no one else?" He heaved a sigh as I moved under the sheet, making me feel doubly unwanted.

I wasn't sure what I'd expected in all honesty. I mean, I'd strong-armed the man into marriage. What more did I want from him?

But the truth was, he was the only person I had right now.

Which was so beyond depressing, so beyond illuminating that I huddled onto my side.

I'd chosen a life where I was a whore rather than work.

I'd chosen a life where I ran away from my responsibilities.

I'd chosen a life where my sisters didn't know me and only called me for gyno issues because it was too embarrassing to go to the ER.

And how did I fix all that?

By tying myself to a man in the most lowdown way possible.

Despair suffocated me as I reached for him, needing to fill the empty hole inside me—not the one that was between my legs, but the one in my chest cavity.

I needed to escape. I needed to be free from these thoughts.

I pressed my hand to his chest, encountering bare skin and more of that scent that seemed to seep from his sheets, but his fingers caught mine. He held me firmly, resolutely. In a way that told me not to press him.

But what alternative did I have?

I needed him more than he needed me, and that was a balance I had to rectify.

"Camille, it's late."

I swallowed. "So?"

"You just murdered your father," he said wryly. "This is reaction setting in, and I'm pretty sure that you're going to regret this in the morning."

"This time tomorrow night, you'll be my husband. Are you saying you won't consummate our marriage because of what I did?"

Another sigh gusted from his lips. "There's no right or wrong answer here, is there? If I take advantage of what you're offering, I'm a piece of shit. If I don't take advantage, you're probably going to think I'm not interested." His hand shoved mine deeper beneath the covers. "There, satisfied?" He was hard.

There *was* a god.

"I will be soon," I rasped, trying to sound seductive and failing. Could I do nothing right?

He grunted as I shaped him, my fingers sliding over his thick length. It was strange for him to be smooth, for his dick to be unlike Nyx's. I'd had precious little experience with anyone other than him, and his shaft was so studded with metal I was pretty sure he couldn't go anywhere near one of those detectors people used to find buried treasure in their backyards without setting off alarms.

"You don't want this," he said, his voice wooden. That wasn't what I needed.

I needed him to be desperate.

Hungry.

For me.

God, just for me.

As if that was even doable.

My eyes shuttered to a close as I moved nearer to him, not stopping until I shifted one leg over his hips, before I reared up, pinning him in place as I rocked onto my knees. When I was straddling him, I pressed my pussy against his hardness, wishing I was wet, wishing that I wanted this as I started to shimmy my hips, dragging his length along mine.

Most men would have lain back and taken what I was offering.

This was the first lesson Brennan gave me that taught me he was not like most men.

Though my sight had adjusted, the room was still couched in shadows, a thick gloom that made it hard to see anything other than a blur beneath me. I didn't expect his hands to snatch at mine, didn't anticipate him twisting us around so that he was on top of me and I beneath him.

For a second, relief soared inside me, like a firework display on July Fourth—my cup truly runneth over. Then, he moved off me. Shifting to the side so his weight no longer covered me.

A disappointed moan rushed from my lips, the mewling sound so piteous that it was no wonder he didn't want me.

Would he cancel the wedding now?

I needed him more than ever, but I'd fucked up by being the worst seductress.

I tried to reach for him, but before I could, he jerked my hands to the point of discomfort then raised them overhead. When he pinned them in place, he pressed his knee between mine then, with his spare hand, pinched the sparse flesh of my thigh and wordlessly encouraged me to part my legs.

A shaken breath escaped me, one loaded with hope until his hand pressed against my core, and he slipped his fingers through the boxer briefs I wore.

When he encountered dryness, chalky flesh that was proof I wasn't the least bit aroused, he rasped, "Just as I thought."

I imagined he'd back off, tell me to get out of his room, but he didn't. His fingers stayed exactly where they were, but his mouth whispered along my jaw as he trailed his lips up from my chin to my ear.

"W-What did you think?"

His tongue flickered out to lash at my earlobe, making me gulp as he whispered, "If you're not wet, then why are you in here, acting like a slut?"

The word, to anyone else, would have been an insult.

Years ago, it would have been to me too, but I'd been a clubwhore, and I'd been called names a thousand times worse than that.

"If you think you can tie me to you through your cunt, you need to learn that I'm not like most men." He patted my pussy. "You have a problem with sex?"

I blinked at that, shaking my head quickly. "N-No, of course not."

The tips of his fingers unerringly found my clit, which had tremors rushing down my spine as he didn't just rub it like it was a magic button he expected to press so that I'd miraculously orgasm, but he caressed it with a gentleness I didn't foresee.

He wasn't careful, just considerate. Touching it in a way that I would, that had memories of the few times I'd ever masturbated surging to the fore. My hips shifted down, my butt digging into the bed and I spread my legs a little wider so that I felt the pull of the muscles where thigh met groin. He carried on, and on. Fingering me like he didn't have a care about time slipping out of our grasp, but I felt his dick digging into me so I knew that wasn't true.

A part of me wanted to shout hosannas that he was hungry for pussy —if not mine in particular just a random hole he needed to fill. That was almost enough to have me sagging into the bed, arousal whispering through me. Later on, that other rational part of me would recognize how pathetic I was, but for now, his lips were on my ear lobe, and his breathing was all I could hear aside from my own heartbeat.

A shimmer of heat drifted over my body, making my insides feel heavy as everything seemed to turn inward. My focus, my thoughts, even my sight. It was like earlier, when I'd known he was taking me to heights I'd never reached before. I no longer thought about whether he was hard, no longer struggled against his grip on my wrists. I just let him pet me.

Because that was what he was doing.

Petting me.

And I loved it.

I couldn't hide from the fact that no man had ever given me this much attention. Had ever granted me so much focus that was fixed on me—on me and nothing else.

He touched me like he had all the time in the world, and I loved that too.

He hadn't even kissed me, but his fingers were touching the most intimate part of me like he was just holding my hand or something.

A whimper escaped me as a heavy fullness overtook my lower half. I writhed into him, pushing against his hold even though I didn't want him to let go, my legs slipping and sliding against the silky sheets as I tried to accept what he was gifting me—pleasure.

The whisper of his breath in my ear was like a serenade.

The heat of him against my side was like the warmest of hugs.

And the intensity of his focus was more seductive than a kiss to my damn clit.

He gave off a sense of immovability, like he was here for an endless amount of time. Like he had nowhere else better to be.

I had no idea where this had come from. Why the tides had turned and, when I'd tried to seduce him, instead, he was doing this to me. I had no room for thoughts, no space for anything other than the ecstasy his fingers gave me.

I could feel it. Hovering in the distance. I knew what it was, and wanted it so badly. So close... *so near...*

A keening cry escaped me as I peaked, my orgasm flowing through me, washing me clean while calming me down. I felt like I was dragged to an incredible height all while being grounded, and there was, I realized, nothing better than that.

To fly while being tethered—I wasn't sure I'd ever wanted anything else in my whole life.

The release and the relief tangled together, merging into one big ball of pleasure that imploded inside me, sending charges of sensation throughout my body. Kissing every limb and extremity with energy that both regenerated and relaxed.

When I sagged into the bed, when conscious thought returned to me, his fingers were tapping against my clit, and this time, as he did so, we were both aware of the difference from earlier. I was wet. So sticky wet that the noise was audible above my pounding heart. He moved, at last, so that his breath and mine mingled, and even though I couldn't see him, I was pretty sure these were the most intimate moments of my life. More than outweighing what we'd shared together in the stables.

I wasn't a hole.

A thing to fuck.

At least, I didn't think so—

Before insecurities, of which I had many, could overtake me, he pressed a simple kiss to my bottom lip, dragging it down as he moved his head, swaying slightly, like he wanted to see how dormant I could be. How docile.

Did he want me to move?

Or did he want me to just lie there?

Uncertainty had my nails digging into my palms as I curled my hands, and a soft moan escaped me as the bittersweet pain from that unintended caress mingled with the delight from before.

He stiffened, but even though I thought it was impossible that he registered the sound, he did.

He knew exactly what I'd done.

"Did you do that on purpose?" he rasped, and that he sounded genuinely angry was bewildering. What did he have to be angry about?

I stuttered the truth, not even thinking to lie, which was crazy because I had no intention of not being honest. "No, it was by accident."

"There are no accidents. No coincidences. Not in this room." My eyes flared wide at his certainty. "You clenched your hands. Why?"

My bottom lip quivered, the one that had just felt the delicate trace of his mouth against it. "I-I didn't know what you wanted me to do."

"You don't need to think with me, Camille. You just need to lie there. I'll tell you the rest."

Maybe, to another woman, that wouldn't be like a sweet serenade, but to me, it was bliss. It was like a kiss from God, because I needed that. I needed to be told. I needed not to think, and I felt like, even though the circumstances weren't ideal, even though it was probably so wrong considering his ties to my mother, maybe, just maybe, he was exactly what I needed.

A sullied savior, a life raft in a storm...

FIFTEEN
BRENNAN

IT WAS HARD NOT to pin her down, not to shove my knee against her cunt and to have her grind into me. It was hard not to sink between those too-thin thighs and to eat her out, to thrust my fingers inside her and make her work for her orgasm.

But what I wanted, tonight, was for her not to think. Was for her to sleep.

Just pinning her down, just getting her off had already taken away a lot of her tension, and had she not made that ecstatic sound, that faint clutch in her throat that reminded me of when she orgasmed, only not as powerful, I'd have let her rest.

If it was tomorrow, I'd have spun her face down and spanked her ass —exactly like I'd promised her I would this afternoon on the ride back to the stables.

But I wanted her to sleep.

More than I wanted her to bounce on my fucking cock.

Which was really saying something.

I could probably hammer nails into wood, that was how hard I was, but Camille wasn't just willing pussy. She wasn't a mistress.

She was going to be my wife.

The mother of my children.

And for all that I'd been led into this thanks to an association I wished I could forget, it occurred to me that she was so submissive I could guide her where I wanted her.

Mold her into what I craved.

The idea was enough to make me salivate. It hadn't been on my mind at any point while I'd been concocting this plan, but, and it was a massive but, it had been ever since she'd come barging into my room.

Everything about her, as she clumsily tried to seduce me—either into tying me to her or to help her forget, I wasn't sure which yet—had given off such strong vibes that it was like a magnetic call to the iron in my blood.

I could no more back away from that than I could stop being a fucking O'Donnelly.

Every inch of me responded, and the only way I could contain myself was to pin her down and to get her off. Anything else, any other movement, and I'd have found it impossible to stop myself from fucking her.

The second she moaned in pain, the second she admitted why she'd put pressure on those battered hands of hers, and the second that I'd told her she didn't have to think anymore—that I'd do that for her—she'd relaxed. Like I'd uttered her personal 'Open, Sesame,' she'd grown limp and lax, and when I'd made to move off her, to let go of her hands, that was when she'd grumbled, and started fidgeting.

I stayed where I was, unable to believe my future wife might potentially be... I didn't even want to think it.

But it began with K, ended in E, and was Superman's only weakness.

By no means was I an Irish Mobster version of Superman, but when a woman ticked every fucking box, it had to make you question things.

At least, it made a smart man question things...

And I was, if nothing else, smart. I wasn't saying I was like Conor, who crapped binary code every morning before breakfast, but I was definitely no dumbass. It would be impossible to juggle as many plates as I did if I was thick in the head, after all.

But this woman had the guts to kill—not just anyone, but a Pakhan— while clinging to me as sweetly, as softly as she was now. I knew she'd slay any fucker who tried to hurt our kids, would protect them just as she'd wanted to protect Victoria tonight, while blossoming under my variety of dominance as we made those future O'Donnellys together... How could that not give a man a hard-on?

Even though it pained me, I left her alone. Let her recover from the evening's violence, from the bloodshed, from the distressing truth of what she'd done.

This was a judgment-free zone because, in the long run, she'd done me a favor by ridding my world of a frenemy, but that didn't mean it wasn't hitting her hard, and that didn't mean that, if I fucked things up now, I wouldn't be paying for it for years to come.

See, smart. And selfish.

Sue me.

What stunned me the next morning was that I fell asleep in that position, and woke up with her arms around my throat, her face nuzzled against mine as we shared a pillow. My knee stayed between her thighs, pinning her to the mattress, shoving us flush against one another with my morning wood sandwiched between the pair of us.

Our skin was cleaved together from the shoulder down, and the scent of us was tangled amid the sheets. Oddly enough, though I hadn't drunk a drop of the hard stuff last night, I felt like I was hungover.

Groggy and drowsy, but comfortable.

This was going to be my future.

If I allowed it.

I could keep her at arms' length, maintain a strict distance between us, see her only perfectly made up at meal times and have her by my side at galas, or I could have her like *this*.

Raw.

Ripe.

Ready to plunder.

Almost shuddering at the thought, I looked her over, taking note that her hair wasn't as much of a rat's nest as I'd hoped. It was tangled and wavy around her head, a cloud of gold for me to breathe in.

I needed to work on that.

And I *wanted* to work on that.

That was the difference.

When Camille had come back onto the scene, a week or so after Inessa and Eoghan's wedding, I'd been reminded of that fucking promise I'd made. A few whispers here and there among my contacts, and I'd learned shit about the Vasovs that I'd always suspected but had never really wanted to know for certain.

Because he was the afore-mentioned frenemy, I wasn't going to kill the Bratva Pakhan, but I wasn't going to complain that she had.

If any fucker deserved it, it was Antoni Vasov.

The more I'd learned, the more I'd heard, the more that had been shared with me, I'd known I had to fulfill that promise to Mariska. She'd been a good mother, whose inability to bear a son and whose poor choices, of which I was dead center, meant her girls had to be raised by a fucking monster.

Camille had pushed all the right buttons yesterday when she'd tried to coerce me into this marriage, but she hadn't known that I'd been planning our union for longer than she'd even registered who Brennan O'Donnelly was to her family.

I'd thought of an anonymous union. Kids produced after rutting between the sheets. A family forged between strangers.

Yet, here and now, there was nothing strange about how perfectly her tit fit in my hand. There was nothing usual about how delicious she felt in my arms.

I just needed to fatten her up, and she'd be my dream girl.

Fate definitely had a way of fucking with a man...

Because she wasn't how I imagined she'd be, brazen after her time with the Sinners, and I had a feeling she'd be embarrassed, I was careful not to disturb her as I maneuvered away from her and made my way off the bed. We were so stuck together that it was impossible not to wake her, but she confirmed that incredible shyness that years with a goddamn MC hadn't managed to erase by waking up and pretending to be asleep.

My lips curved into a smile that was both amused and wry, because she was already proving to be a complication.

A man like me, with the various stressors I had in my life, didn't need complicated. If anything, I needed simple. Fuck, did I. But I liked how she had spunk in some things, then was innocent in others.

At least, I liked it for the moment.

After thirty fucking years, maybe I'd want to strangle her, but a lifetime married to me, married into the O'Donnelly clan, and I had to believe that she'd grow into her confidence.

I let her play pretend because I didn't particularly want to face facts this morning, at least, not with her watching on. Especially when, quite by chance, I saw some dirty smudges on the arm nearest to me.

Bruises.

That fucker had bruised her.

Christ, I wished I'd been the one to kill the bastard now.

Regret filled me, not just about Vasov's death. I also had to accept that I'd been a fool to do what I had last night, but it would have been impossible to stay away from her when she slipped beneath my sheets and offered herself to me the way she had.

The most I'd been able to manage was to pin her down and to give *her* pleasure, but my dick was already telling me I was a dumbass, even as I was relieved I'd managed to hold back.

I was going to have to accept that, for whatever reason, I'd been more than willing to give her pleasure without expecting any in return.

A sign of character growth?

Or just proof that she could tangle my balls into a knot?

I wasn't particularly impressed with either prospect as I left her, heading over to my bathroom and closing the door for some privacy while I used the toilet.

After, I stared at myself in the mirror, looked at the stubble I needed to shave, and deep in my eyes, I saw the strange resolve there.

For months, I'd known about Camille.

For months, that promise to her mother had been plaguing me.

Now it was coming to fruition, I didn't feel like a man being led to the guillotine. I didn't feel as if this was the end of my life as I knew it.

If anything, it was the beginning of another phase. The turning of a new leaf. And while the timing wasn't ideal, in my world, there was no perfect time to do anything.

We were always at war with someone—granted, not to this extent— and we were always involved in disputes with one gang or another, of the business variety if not the violent.

Sometimes, you just had to grab life by the balls or you never did anything. At forty years old, it was time.

Time for me to have something of what my baby brothers had.

Time for me to have a family.

I'd never have said I was a romantic, because I wasn't. You couldn't be in my line of work. But after last night, after how biddable she'd been... it made me wonder if I wanted her for real. Not just to fulfil a promise, but because she was a hot piece of ass and she'd managed to do what few had—killed a Pakhan in the Bratva.

That made her more interesting than the piece of fluff she came across as.

Deciding that I'd shower first because I wanted to jack off, I stripped down and pressed the button that triggered the waterfall shower head. As the water rained down, I pressed another button, one that had the wall of glass in front of me fading into a clear pane, and as I did, I saw she wasn't pretending anymore. Her eyes were open, her face tilted toward the ceiling.

Stepping under the fall, I let the water pound down on me before I grabbed my soap, let some pool into my palm, and then reached down and coated myself in the slippery liquid.

A hiss escaped me as my cock responded immediately, morning wood having made my earlier bout of chivalry seem even more stupid.

Hadn't she said it herself?

Tonight, I wasn't going to abstain, so why had waiting *last* night been so important to me?

I didn't know why, in all honesty. I knew the reasons I'd given her, but was aware that they were only half the truth.

As I shaped my cock, my jaw tensed as I pressed one hand to the glass, looking at a woman who was mine in a way... Hell, in a way that *no one* would ever be. *Could* ever be.

She'd be tied to me in every which way. Mine to protect, mine to shelter, mine to keep.

But as I looked at her, I had to accept that she was too hot for any of that.

Too fucking sexy, everything about her my idea of spankbank material, to just fuck her to get her pregnant.

Irony was, of course, that I accepted that just as she rocked her head down and her gaze drifted over mine. For a second, I saw her surprise, because she hadn't realized the piece of glass in front of me was a 'magic' window, and then, she registered what I was doing.

Her cheeks burned a bright red for the barest moments, before her gaze clashed with mine and she tipped her chin up, then declared war.

She licked her lips.

"Fuck," I muttered gutturally, the curse forming under my breath as I sped up, my fist flying as need rode me hard.

Her hand moved, roaming over the meager curve of her belly before she began to unfasten the buttons of my shirt.

That she was doing it to tie me to her, like she'd tried it on before, pissed me off, but I was too horny to complain.

Later on, I'd make her realize that if she was going to act like a slut for me, there'd be repercussions, but as it stood, I was willing to be a hypocrite because my cock ached like a fucker and we had too much to do this morning before Tink and my crew came around for the wedding service.

Few men would realize she was trying to pussywhip them, but I wasn't exactly 'few' men. She forgot I knew how she responded now. After last night and at the stables, I'd learned more about her than she probably knew.

The shirt buttons slowly parted beneath deft fingers, revealing creamy, golden skin that was begging to be licked, sucked, and bitten. Then her hands went straight to her tits, proof that I knew her body better than she did.

They weren't her hot spot. Her throat, neck, they were what got her hot. Her ear, too. She liked the sting of pain—which made sense—biting. Sucking.

My jaw clenched once more because the thought had shit ricocheting around inside my mind, shit that I wasn't even sure if I had the mental capacity to handle anymore.

I was no longer twenty-three. I had responsibilities and duties to my family and to the Points, and it wasn't like I had time to dance attendance on anyone.

The reason Ma was seeing a fucking shrink, I'd reasoned while I tried to get to sleep, was because I hadn't been doing my duty as a son to her.

Long ago, I'd promised her I'd never let her down again, and so, I visited, but I definitely wasn't around as much for her as I used to be... that was on me.

So how the fuck could I tame this little bitch in my bed?

Was she worthy of my time?

She was Bratva scum, but I'd seen Inessa flourish in the Irish camp. She'd gone through the same shit as Camille, but it was clear to me that Camille had seen a lot more than her younger sister had of their parents' relationship.

Something had fucked Camille up. Something had made her slice into her palms like she was peeling a fucking orange.

My fist tightened down on my cock as she circled the tips of her nipples with her fingers, and I slapped my free hand to the window, which made her jump. My jaw ached as badly as my cock with the need to tell her to get her ass in here and do something about my erection, but…

Fuck.

I was honorable now.

I had to be. I'd done too much shit in my life I was ashamed of. She was just proof of that. Even though I'd come to terms with being ready to marry, she'd be the last person on my list, what with her ties, but she'd said it herself—I'd made a promise to Mariska that might as well have been forged on her deathbed.

And the notion of Camille slicing her wrists or throwing herself down the stairs to avoid being Abramovicz's wife was enough to make me want to spank her for even allowing those thoughts to formulate.

When my little brain was in charge, there was no way I should be able to think as much as I was doing right now, but that she'd jerked me out of a lust-filled haze was testament to the volatile nature of my response to her.

I could jack off.

I could watch my cum swirl down the drain.

Or I could have her jack me off.

I could watch her fucking gargle my cum…

I could touch her pussy.

Punish her for trying to turn me into a cunt-slave…

My cock hardened, my brain switched off, and anything that was honorable disappeared.

I knew what I wanted, and it wasn't my fucking fist.

Rearing away from the window, I twisted around to turn off the shower once my soapy dick was clean, then I stalked out of the bathroom and into my bedroom.

She was sitting up, a frown on her brow, confusion and concern in her eyes as she watched me, but all I saw were those tits concealed by the two flaps of my shirt, playing peekaboo with the fabric now she'd covered herself up.

And there she went again...

Ms. Modesty.

Time she learned there was no such place for that in here.

She shouldn't have pushed me.

Shouldn't have tried to tie me to her that way.

Now, she was going to get something she hadn't expected.

Something *I* hadn't expected.

And she'd have no one to blame but herself.

"Take off the shirt and the underwear."

Her eyes widened, but she was quick to obey.

Good.

From my tone, she discerned I didn't want a striptease either.

That clever little mind of hers picking up nuances that made me hope for the future and how smart our kids would be.

A hiss escaped me as she flung the fabric aside then rocked back so that her weight was on her spine and the balls of her feet so she could make a bridge with her hips dancing in the air. She shoved down the elastic waistband, letting the white cotton ripple and ruffle against her thighs as she wiggled out of them. They pooled around her ankles and that was where I took over.

"Leave them, and put your hands behind your head," I commanded, moving closer to the bed as she obeyed.

I grabbed one leg and then the other, making sure the briefs stayed banded around her ankles, before I grabbed the fabric, tightened them in my fist and looped the underwear around her feet once more to make a binding.

Bondage wasn't my thing, but tying this little minx down was becoming imperative.

With her legs spread, her pussy revealed to me in the gloomy light of morning, I stared down at her and watched as the blush surged from her tits and up to her cheeks.

I'd never seen someone blush so hard before, almost as though she were a wallflower, for God's sake, when I knew she'd been a club-fucking-whore.

"How many faces do you have, Camille?" I rasped, half-expecting her to frown up at me, to not understand what I was asking.

I wasn't sure if either of us realized the power her answer would have.

If she'd given me a different one, I might have backed away.

Might have stopped, reverted to the original plan of banging her until she was knocked up, and then keeping my distance.

Instead, she drew me in closer, tying me to her with the siren's call that was exacerbated by the sight of the crumpled Band-Aids on her palms and the boniness of her ribs and collarbone.

"Two," she whispered, her voice thick with tears that made her green eyes morph into precious gemstones. "Camille and Cammie." Her mouth wobbled. "I don't even know which one is the real me."

"Cammie's the slut and Camille is the little ingenue who can blush like she's a Regency heroine?"

She blinked at me. "A Regency heroine?"

I wafted a hand. "Your sister and soon-to-be sister-in-law talk about romance novels a lot at Sunday lunch."

Her eyes widened, before she whispered, "Oh." Then she licked her lips, with none of the show of earlier, making me growl under my breath at the sight. "I-I don't know if they're both just facades." Her smile turned sad. "Or maybe they're as much depth as I have."

"And maybe we need to work on that," I told her gruffly.

With her legs forming the shape of a diamond, and her arms doing the same, just inverted, I stared at her tits, and seeing the lack of jiggle, and the way they remained very firmly at the front, not even by an inch sagging into her armpits, had my hands craving to squeeze them.

I was a tit man, through and through.

"You'd better learn," I told her gruffly, "that you can't control me through sex, Camille."

She swallowed. "I never intended to—"

I moved my hand to between her legs, and upon stroking my fingers over her pussy and finding her dry, I told her, "Another lesson, don't lie to me. Because that was bullshit. If it was the truth, you'd be wet, but you're not."

"I-I—"

"Y-You," I mocked, and I tapped her there, a flat clap to the pussy. "Only honesty in here, or I'll be pissed, Camille. You don't want to see me angry."

Her cheeks flushed again—with temper this time. "You can't be any worse than my father."

"And that's one way to kill a boner," I said dryly, even though my cock refused to listen and stayed as hard as ever.

Deciding that I was done talking, before I talked myself out of this, I acted. Doing exactly what I'd wanted but denied myself last night.

Grabbing the briefs that cuffed her ankles, I moved her legs high, so high that her thighs pressed against her chest, leaving her pussy exposed to me in a whole different way.

She groaned and rasped, "Please, Brennan," which detonated something in my mind.

I climbed onto the bed, pressing her ankles above her head so she was pinned in place, her ass rocking up to the perfect angle that meant I could drop my dick onto her cunt like it was a ledge.

The sweetest, pale pink ledge there ever fucking was.

My mouth watered with the need to taste her, but that wasn't what this was about.

I'd admit to acting on instinct here, but the second I started to rock my hips, I decided that words were important after all.

"See that pretty pink pussy?" I rasped at her, encouraging her to look down, to look at us.

I wasn't going to deny that it was awkward for her, because it was. She was pink again but from lack of air and from my turning her into a human pretzel, but she didn't argue. In fact, she did as I asked, and though we meant nothing to each other than a means to an end, even she responded to the visceral sight of that beautiful cunt of hers and my cock soaring over the quivering, frilly flesh that I was determined would be sopping wet with my cum in a few minutes.

"I-I see it."

"I'm going to come all over it," I told her gruffly. "And because you teased me, you're going to walk around all morning covered in my cum."

Beneath my dick, I felt her sex contract in response to my order.

A cocky smile twisted my lips as I murmured, "Someone likes the sound of that."

She gulped, shook her head. "N-No, I mean, that's gross. I have to shower."

"You smell as good as you did last night," I argued. "And if you keep on lying to me, I'll make you marry me not only with your pussy covered in my cum but your tits too after I fuck them before the ceremony."

Eyes flaring wide, that goddamn cunt of hers clenching down again—so goddamn hard that my dick could feel it—she whispered, "I won't lie to you again."

"Good girl," I purred, before I leaned one hand on her thigh and then placed the other above my cock so that as I rocked against her, the friction was even better, especially now some of her pussy juices eased the way. "Although," I told her softly, "I think you like the idea of being covered in my cum. Why is that, Camille?"

SOMEONE WILL LOVE ME. HE'S OUT THERE. WAITING FOR ME TO LOVE HIM EXACTLY HOW HE NEEDS TO BE LOVED TOO.

SIXTEEN
CAMILLE

HE WASN'T WRONG.

God, he *wasn't* wrong which had to mean I was some kind of freak.

Even in a sham marriage, who the hell wanted to attend their wedding covered in a man's release?

The idea should revolt me, but it didn't. If anything, it had my hips tilting back, the muscles in my thighs tightening. With the way he positioned me, it was a little hard to breathe, but I got into it as he started to thrust against me, and my heart began to pound, sending tidal waves of adrenaline through my blood.

A moan escaped me when he put pressure on his dick as it nudged my clit, and I pressed my head back into the pillow, my body tensing and releasing as I felt the heat surge through me, much as it had done last night.

He followed through, moving down the length of my cunt, not stopping until the tip surged into my pussy, just the barest half-inch, enough to coat him with more cream that magically appeared from out of nowhere.

Well, not nowhere, but in comparison to the Sahara of before, I felt like the Hoover Dam, for Christ's sake.

My hands clenched into fists behind my head, and the sweet whisper of pain from that move had my moan morphing into a groan.

At the sound, he paused, and I blinked up at him, feeling dazed and hazy but also so bewilderingly close to climaxing that I wanted to tell him to hurry up, but Brennan wasn't the kind of man you ordered around.

A fact I liked.

A fact that reminded me of Nyx.

I knew I shouldn't think of him at a moment such as this, but he was my only comparison, what else was I supposed to do?

Right now, Nyx fell short.

A gasp escaped me when Brennan tilted forward, pushing more weight on my chest. I shouldn't like that, I really shouldn't, but I loved how he got in my face. Loved how he didn't let me hide.

It had been a day, a single day, and already I felt as if he'd seen more of me than most people ever had.

The thought had anxiety whispering through me, anguish too. Thank God his plan was still to get married today. If I had to wait, I knew I'd turn into a nervous wreck. Trying to please him only to piss him off—I'd thought showing him my tits would get him hot. Instead, it had triggered this.

And now, with him looming over me, I wasn't sure what I'd done wrong, but as oxygen sluggishly filtered into my system because he was damn heavy and compressed my lungs like I was a set of bellows for the fireplace, I just knew I wanted to please him because that orgasm?

I wanted it again.

"I told you not to do that," he rumbled, and with all his weight on me as he pressed me into the bed, he reached up and dragged my hands down. "Hold them flat to the bed. If you want pain, I'll give you pain, but you're going to let those heal. If they bleed again, you'll regret it," he warned, and the flash of anger didn't scare me. I was too used to feeling a man's wrath aimed my way, but it was the reason for his anger that had my heart skipping a beat.

Which was pretty unfortunate with my current position.

Dark spots began dancing around the edges of my vision, and instead of asking him to get off me, I did as he asked, pressed my hands to the sheets, and let them lay flat.

With all that pressure, he had to work harder to thrust against my pussy, but he did it, and it felt like heaven and hell especially when he tilted his head to the side, pressed his teeth to the meat of my calf and bit down.

Not a love bite.

Not a nip.

A full on bite.

So hard that I wasn't sure if he was going to break the skin. So full on that the agony of it had me howling and bucking against him in response.

But he ignored me, just carried on doing what he was doing, and I felt it.

It.

The shameful gush of cream.

The fucking geyser he triggered that coated him like he'd just dropped a bottle of lube onto us both.

He pulled back, a smirk on his face as he looked at me, the promise of sin in his eyes that might have been an hallucination thanks to how hard it was to breathe, and he did it again.

He moved, took another meaty part of my calf and bit down once more.

It was then the doorbell rang, and though we both heard it, he didn't stop clenching down or moving. He didn't push off me and hurry over to the door, he just sent that sweet pain whistling through my system before he released my skin and against my leg, murmured, "That might be your sister. I arranged with my men to have her brought here this morning."

My eyes flared wide when I heard a pinging sound that told me the elevator had been activated, one I'd heard yesterday evening as the doors opened into the main hall. Before I could protest, he pressed a hand to my mouth, covering both it and my nose, then he bit me for the third and final time.

And that was it.

Lights out.

Explosion not just imminent but detonated.

As the lack of oxygen turned my vision dark, a thread of golden light illuminated the world as my orgasm shot through me, ricocheting inside my body like it was a bullet shot wide.

There was no air to scream with, no way I could even wail.

I stared up at him blindly as the delirium of what he forced me to experience made me see things with a clarity that had always escaped me.

Brennan, at that moment, was the most beautiful man I'd ever seen.

Had ever wanted.

His nostrils were flared, his eyes wide, and his mouth a snarl as he chased his own end, and when I felt the tension in him reach fever pitch, he bit me one last time to stop himself from crying out.

I accepted the pain, savoring it as his hips rocked with wild abandon, as his movements became jagged and jittery, no longer dancing to that same rhythm of before as the heat of his seed drenched us both.

With his last thrusts, he rubbed it into me, and then he let go, and rasped, "You're going to sign your life away today, Camille. You're going to be mine." Tension hit me, as exquisitely as my climax of before, then he broke it by rasping, "You'll have my protection, your sister too, but this is your last chance to walk away."

I shook my head as he moved, freeing my chest from the pressure of before, enough for me to cry out, "No—"

He raised a hand to stop me, but his focus wasn't on me but my sticky pussy. His jaw worked, the muscles visibly clenching before he ground out, "You've done it now. This'll be it. Every fucking time. If you don't want what we just had, if it scares you, if *I* scare you, then, when I've finished, you'll get into that shower, you'll clean up, and we'll pretend like this never happened." His gaze trapped mine before I could even squeak out a response. "If you're ready for more, if you're prepared for worse, then you'll get dressed, covered in me, knowing fully what you're walking into—a lifetime of this—and you'll fucking love it." He growled under his breath. "One last chance, Camille, that's all I'll give you."

"I don't want it," I whispered, meaning it, choking out the words as he pulled back.

Pulled away.

And suddenly, I didn't want that.

I never wanted him to pull away again.

There were shadows in his eyes as he growled, "You got me here on a promise. Well, I'm warning you that you might *wish* you were married to Abramovicz."

My head whipped from side to side on the pillows. "Never."

"I'll be on you so much you won't goddamn know where I begin and you end—"

"That's...fine," I whispered. *Fine?* More like bliss.

His mouth firmed. "Then you know what to do."

And with one final lingering look to my cunt, like he was taking a mental snapshot, like he seriously thought this might be the last time he saw it, he climbed off the bed.

Bare-assed naked, he walked to the corridor lined with closets, where I heard a door opening, the rattling of coat hangers, before I heard another final door which he closed. Leaving me in here to slowly lower my legs, to feel the ache in my muscles, to take a deep inhalation at long last which triggered a bout of coughing, to accept a sorry, despicable, delicious truth.

I wanted more.

Of this.

Of him.

Of *Camille*. Not Cammie.

SEVENTEEN
BRENNAN

KNOWING that Forrest would have taken Victoria straight to the living room, I pulled on my jeans in the hall and felt like a fucking teenager when I had to hop and jump to get into them.

I had weak knees, and it had nothing to do with my daily ten-mile runs and everything to do with that mind-bending orgasm back there.

Fuck.

How I hadn't pushed into her, taken her—I deserved a fucking medal.

Or that sainthood Baggy and me had been talking about yesterday.

Yeah, I should definitely be canonized because pulling away from that sweet cunt made me want to punch myself in the face.

Growling under my breath as I finally got my jeans on, then shoved on a tee, I decided that I wouldn't get too close to my future sister-in-law because I stank of soap and sex. Personally, they were my most favorite of scents, but they had no place outside of the bedroom I'd just left. A bedroom I *hadn't* wanted to leave, in all honesty.

Grateful that my apartment was a duplex, and that Victoria could live downstairs because her sister was definitely a screamer, I tried not to listen to the bedroom to hear if she was heading into the shower. Tried not to listen for the sound of water as I stormed down the hall and toward the upper living area of the penthouse.

When I saw Forrest standing awkwardly by the window, I arched a brow and watched him flare his eyes in warning. Turning to face the youngest of the Vasov sisters, I found her scowling up at me.

"Where's my sister?" she growled at me, but her arms were held tightly at her waist and even as she was glaring, I saw the fear in them. A fear she was trying to hide with a ballsy attitude.

Whatever the hell that fucker of a father had done to her, he'd had more time to do worse to Camille...

"Which sister?" I asked instead, and without waiting for her to reply, I moved over to the other end of the room.

It was unorthodox, but my living area was one big open-planned space, mostly because it had been that way when I was a kid and I liked it. I liked the kitchen leading onto the dining room table and I liked being able to see the TV while eating at the breakfast bar.

With two floors, I had enough room for three other living rooms, each more formal than this one, but this was my favorite. It reminded me of simpler times, before I was a killer.

Before Brennan O'Donnelly inspired fear in people.

Before hearing that name had men running the other way...

Moving over to the kitchen, I peered inside and found a jar of overnight oats my housekeeper prepared for me before she left. When I pulled it out, Victoria was there, at my heels, and I asked, "Do you want some? Mary leaves me two jars."

She blinked. "Who's Mary?"

"She's my housekeeper."

"Oh." Her gaze drifted to the jar. "What is it?"

"Oatmeal."

"With chocolate?" She peered at it suspiciously. "For breakfast?"

"I have a sweet tooth," I said wryly, shoving the one with berries at her. "If you want to be healthy—"

As my voice waned off, she grabbed the one with chocolate then demanded, "I meant Cammie. I know where Inessa is."

"Where's that?"

"JFK, probably," was her reply. "She's on her way back from Texas. But that's the sister I know about. Where's Cammie? And why wasn't Maxim the one who picked me up? And why can't I go home?"

I arched a brow at her. "With all those questions, I'm surprised you got in the car with Forrest."

"Trust me, we had an argument first," my buddy grumbled.

"Never heard of stranger danger?" Victoria retorted, making Forrest roll his eyes.

"She has a point. That's how you know where Inessa is, right?" I asked, smiling as I pulled open a drawer, grabbed two spoons and shoved one at her.

"Where's mine?" Forrest groused as he moved over to the kitchen.

"You don't like oatmeal," I pointed out.

"I meant, *breakfast*."

I shrugged. "You know where the fridge is."

Victoria frowned at our conversation, before she confirmed, "Eoghan told me I could trust Forrest. That's why I came. He said he was on your crew. Whatever that means."

"It means he's a friend. And it means I trust him with you."

Forrest heaved a sigh. "God help me."

I smirked at him, then turned back to my sister-in-law. "Camille is just getting ready."

"Ready for what?" she asked warily.

I didn't have an answer to that. I might have been listening to the plumbing as I dealt with both Victoria and Forrest, and I might not have heard the sounds of a shower, but it wasn't my job to explain what had happened with her cunt of a father.

Victoria didn't know me. I'd danced with her once at Eoghan's wedding, just like she'd danced with all my brothers, but she'd been pink-cheeked, and I'd been trying to stop Da from losing his shit with Eoghan who'd just dislocated Vasov's shoulder after their church service.

Heaving a sigh, I just said, "Eat your oatmeal. She'll be along soon."

I took a seat at the breakfast bar, hooked my feet around the stool, then opened the mason jar. By the time I was digging my spoon in, she took a suspicious step closer to my side, and took a seat at the other end, which I was grateful for. I really didn't want her sitting close to me, just in case. Camille would probably stink worse, which had me reconsidering a whole host of things...

Shit.

That was going to spoil my fun. Big time.

Heaving a sigh, I began eating, but I stopped when I heard the padding of footsteps down the hall. When she made it to the door, I was watching for her, and our eyes caught and held as she stepped deeper into the room, her cheeks flushed again, but there was something different about her.

A buoyancy I hadn't noticed before.

She smiled at me, which was, I realized, the first time I'd seen her do that, and it packed a real punch. Megawatts of energy were aimed my way, but it didn't knock me off my stool, just made me wish I could bend her over the counter.

In last night's dress, she shouldn't look so hot, but she did. Mostly, I regretted the stockings she wore because it hid my bite marks on her calf.

What a shame.

"Camille?"

Victoria's soft, scared voice broke into my lust-filled thoughts, and it also jarred Camille into looking away from me and hunting for her sister.

"Vicky," she said with a sigh, her smile toning down, her energy changing as guilt began to ride her.

She'd forgotten.

That was clear to see.

She'd forgotten about the blood she'd spilled, about whatever it was that made her cut herself, that made her seem so sad.

For those moments, she'd been Camille, and she'd been fascinating with it.

I rubbed a hand over my jaw, wondering if I was getting more than I bargained for, but if that was the case, then that would only be proof that the luck of the Irish really was a thing. It'd be just my luck that I did something out of charity, taking in a rough stone, and with a bit of polish, I'd find out I had a diamond...

"What is it? What's going on? Why didn't Maxim take me home?" Victoria darted over to her older sister, her hands grabbing at Camille's arms. "Is it Papa? What's wrong?"

Camille reached out, dislodging Victoria's grip on her arms and tugged her into a hug. "I'm so sorry, Vicky. I-I didn't mean to—"

When she broke off, I cut Forrest a look. He dipped his chin and faded away. By the time I heard the elevator ping its farewell, Camille still hadn't explained what happened. Not that I could blame her, was, in fact, curious if she'd lie or tell her the truth about the role she'd played.

It'd be easier if she lied, but it wasn't my place to direct her otherwise. Complications could arise if Victoria—

"Father's dead, Victoria," Camille rasped, her eyes clashing with mine once more over her sister's head, and I watched the panic in her fade as she took comfort in me, prompting her to whisper, "W-We're not safe at home anymore."

"What about Svetlana?" That that was Victoria's first question told me there was little to no love lost between father and daughter.

Unsurprising.

Because she'd had the chance to explain what had really happened, I decided to tell her the truth as Maxim had spun it in a text he'd sent me before I'd climbed into bed.

"Svetlana killed him, Victoria. She was having an affair with one of his *boyeviks* and he found out about it, confronted her, and she defended herself."

Victoria gasped, and twisted around to stare at me. "You can't be serious! She killed him?"

That she focused on the murder and not the cheating was interesting, but I just cleared my throat. "Sadly, I am." God could strike me down for that particular lie, and I wouldn't complain. *Sadly?* My ass.

She whipped back around to look at Camille, who was still staring at me like I was a script she needed to read. "Who told you that?"

"Maxim." I answered for her, then returned my attention to my breakfast. "Just as I told him our happy news."

From the corner of my eye, I saw Camille wince, before she clutched at Victoria's hands and rasped, "You know Father and me didn't see eye to eye..."

Vicky frowned, her youthful brow puckering even as her eyes remained clear. I thought it was likelier that she thought she *had* to cry because her dad had just died and that was why she looked so torn.

I could have told her that tears only fell for those who deserved them... and that bastard of a father of hers didn't deserve even a single one.

Still, it wasn't my place, and I stayed quiet as Camille rasped, "I know the timing is terrible, Vicky, darling, but... I hope you'll be there this afternoon when Brennan and I get married."

"Wait, you're getting married? *Today?*"

Camille shot me a weak smile. "We've been dating a while. Ever since I got back." When I didn't correct her lies, she grew a little braver. "We were going to do it in secret, but then... last night happened." She blinked. "I was there when he accused her, Vicky. It was terrible. I saw it all."

Her younger sister gasped. "You saw him die?"

Camille nodded, then wrapped her arms around Victoria again. "I did."

Victoria allowed Camille to hug her for a short while, before she twisted back to glare at me. "What kind of man would let his fiancée be treated as badly as my father treated Cammie?" She tipped up her chin. "He was so mean to her. All the time. He called her names, and he was going to make her marry that creep." She pointed her finger at me. "I don't know if you deserve Camille, Brennan. Eoghan would never have let Father do what he's done to Inessa."

"No, he wouldn't. He'd have broken both the bastard's shoulders and his legs too." My smile was tight. "But a man can only protect his woman from what he knows about."

Camille winced, before she admitted, "I didn't want him to know, Vicky. It was too embarrassing."

I almost laughed when Victoria sighed and patted Camille on the shoulder as if that news didn't come as much of a shock. Apparently, the eldest Vasov daughter was secretive... go figure. "Is it terrible that I'm glad he's dead?"

Camille shook her head. "No. I am too."

"It's quite liberating, isn't it?" was her reply, the words coming out in an embarrassed rush, to which Camille sighed.

"It is."

"Where will I live?"

"Here. With Inessa." She hitched a shoulder. "It's your choice."

"I can't live at home?"

"*Malyshka,*" Camille whispered, "that was never your home. The second Mama died, it stopped being that." She reached for Victoria's hands, squeezed them. "You know it as well as I do."

Victoria blinked up at her. "I-I guess." Then she frowned. "What about my things?"

"Maxim is going to arrange for them to be brought here. Or to Inessa's," I said gruffly, feeling selfish for hoping she'd prefer to live with Eoghan.

How long did the bastard need for a honeymoon anyway?

And I had plans for my bride... unintended and unexpected plans, but they were there nonetheless.

Victoria bit her lip. "Do you mind if I stay with Inessa for a little while, Cammie?"

Sorrow lit her features, but I had to admire her for shaking it off, and doing it damn well.

"Of course not," she told her, and when I saw her squeeze Victoria's hands a little harder than before, I knew it had nothing to do with imbuing the sentiment by touch, but to experience that whisper of masochistic pleasure I was going to cure her of.

I stared at her long enough so that when she raised her head and happened to glance at me, she couldn't miss my narrowed focus on her, before I dropped the look to her hands. Immediately, she let go of her hold on her younger sister.

"You might have to stay with us tonight. I don't know when Inessa's coming back—"

"They're flying in from Texas now," Victoria told her, which let me know that Inessa hadn't kept Camille in the loop.

It was easy to see that there was a chasm between Camille and her sisters, that, even though she loved them, I wasn't sure if that love was returned. Or at least, not as much. If love could even be quantified. Favoritism was one thing, but to this extent?

Aidan drove me more insane than Conor did, but that didn't mean I wouldn't go to the ends of the earth for both of the fuckers. Hell, I loved Aidan enough to save his ass from Da, picking up the slack for him when few other brothers would do the same. Letting him bottom out so that he'd know he had to clean up on his own terms.

Adding the reasons behind the chasm between the sisters to the questions I needed to ask my future bride, I merely said, "Victoria, we were going to have a small, private service with just a few friends—"

"But Cammie doesn't have any friends."

Camille's cheeks turned pink. "Don't say that, Vicky."

"Well, you don't. Not anymore, do you?" was the grumbled retort, one that anyone with younger siblings had heard way too many times to count.

Not anymore?

What had she done to piss off both her family and friends?

"Shut up," she hissed, nudging her arm.

"Anyway, you can't mean there'll be no family here." Victoria scowled. "What's a wedding without family?"

"Peaceful?" was my wry reply. "I'm not going to put either of us through what Eoghan and Inessa dealt with."

Victoria crinkled her nose. "I think it was romantic."

"Well, it might be, but even though no one else who's family is attending... would you like to be there?"

"Duh," Victoria muttered. "Of course."

My lips twisted into a smile. "Of course," I repeated, which was how, six hours later, I ended up getting married in front of my sister-in-law and three of my best friends in my living room.

It wasn't ideal, but it was done.

And for our purposes, that was what mattered the most.

As I pressed my lips to hers, I let my mouth whisper along to Camille's ear, and I murmured, "Feel any different now you're Mrs. Brennan O'Donnelly?"

"Yes." She tipped up her chin. "You were right. I finally feel untouchable."

"By anyone but me," I rasped, letting my teeth nip her earlobe as I pressed my hand between her shoulders and held her close. Feeling her shiver, I whispered, "You had the choice to walk away."

She tipped her head back, brave enough to meet me stare for stare before she murmured, "What makes you think I want to be anywhere but here?"

FILTHY SEX   195

HAVE FAITH. YOU DESERVE TO BE SOMEONE'S NUMBER ONE.

EIGHTEEN
CAMILLE

WAS it the wedding a little girl dreamed of?

No.

There was no wedding dress, no cake, no family, no party, no games, no gifts, and no big meal.

Nothing.

I wore what I'd arrived in last night, with another borrowed pair of boxers and a cum-covered pussy that was decidedly uncomfortable by this point in the day.

I stood in a living room that, while pleasant enough, was no church, and certainly had no atmosphere—neither grave and serious, nor joyous or otherwise.

But for all that, I was glad. I was even happy because the relief was so acute, I couldn't be anything other than incandescent with it.

Truly.

In the grand scheme of things, I'd prefer a small non-affair for an occasion that tied me to a man who'd keep me safe than a massive reception that celebrated my marriage to a sadistic bastard who'd rape me until the day his cock stopped working.

What I got were three guys showing up at the door at three that afternoon, two of whom I recognized, the other I didn't. That one had a discussion with Brennan, while the others drifted into the living room, settling down to watch a show Victoria had on as she stared blindly into the ether. I couldn't blame her—in the space of an evening, her entire life had changed.

Because of me.

After Brennan's conversation with the one man on his crew I didn't know, he'd tugged me into the kitchen and placed a ring on my finger.

"With this ring, I thee wed," he'd murmured, with the dirty oatmeal dishes still on the counter, a mocking twist to his lips as I stared down in surprise at the large ruby I was now wearing. Shaped into a princess cut, it was elegant and sharp, like blood. Too like it, if I were being honest.

Still, it hadn't stopped me from retorting, "With this body, I thee worship," and satisfaction had filled me to see that gleam in his eyes once more. A gleam that had chills running up and down my spine, that made me think of the mess he'd left me in this morning.

He'd reached up, cupped my cheek, and with his thumb against my bottom lip, he'd murmured, "Be careful what you promise. That's what got us into this mess in the first place."

I'd never know what made me do it, but I let my tongue flutter out to rub over the tip of his thumb. An expletive escaped him, bursting free from him like it was beyond his control, but it didn't make him move back, didn't make him drop his hand.

The promise in his eyes told me that the second this apartment was empty, I'd be a married woman in all the ways the law required.

Maybe that sense of security gave me the balls to do it, to whisper, "You have no reason to believe me, Brennan, no reason whatsoever. You've been a gentleman, and you've gone above and beyond whatever my mother could possibly have expected, but..." I'd sucked in a breath. "I'll do my best to be a good wife to you. To make you not regret what you're doing. To change this 'mess' into something good, great, even."

His mouth curved into a smile that might have been cynical, but equally, might have been genuine. "Don't worry, Camille. I'll lead the way."

As I promised myself to him, and as he did the same to me, with a man called Tinker overseeing the vows, those words haunted me.

'I'll lead the way.'

He was bossy, dominant. A little too like my father. By reputation, I knew he was quick to temper, and was aware that he was even quicker to commit violence. But he'd been kind to Victoria this morning. He'd been patient as the hours passed and she watched cartoons on the TV, little sniffles escaping her every now and then that I knew came not from grief but from a selfish concern for herself—who could blame her?

But she didn't have to worry.

I'd protect her, and I knew, *now*, that Brennan would too.

I'd seen his relief when she'd said that she wanted to live with Inessa, which had told me one very important thing—he'd have let her live here if she'd wished it.

Which led me to another important fact—family really was everything to him.

And that meant *I* had to become family. Not just in name, but in deed.

I'd find out over the upcoming weeks if being married to him was enough to join that lofty group, or if it required something else of me, but it gave me hope.

Brennan might seem like my father on the surface, but he *wasn't* in the ways that mattered.

Thank God.

When Victoria got a text from Inessa telling her she was back in the city, that seemed to be the trigger for a mass exodus.

Eoghan and Brennan must have discussed the situation at some point because the second she received that text, his crew got to their feet, and Brennan informed me, "Forrest will drop off Victoria at Eoghan's apartment." Then, to Victoria, he'd said, "Eoghan will introduce you to a new guard. It's down to you if you want him or Forrest."

Victoria blinked. "I get a choice?"

Brennan's smile was soft, but somehow all the more dangerous because of it. "The Irish do things differently."

She bit her lip, sending a cautious look Forrest's way. "Do you mind, Forrest?"

"Nah." He'd winked. "Driving you around the place will be fun."

"Will it?" Her eyes rounded. "I only go to school. That's not fun."

Brennan snorted. "Let's keep it that way." He raised a hand. "Meet Eoghan's guy first. We want you to be comfortable."

Her eyes turned into silver pennies, and I got it. Comfort, choice...

these were like curse words for us. Neither was an option. We got what we were given and we were grateful for it.

"Thank you, Brennan," Victoria said, but it wasn't parroted. Words trotted out of politeness. There was a heartfelt gratitude to them, and it made me realize that somehow, amid the weeds growing in my father's household, he'd managed to cultivate a hothouse flower.

Victoria, now she was free of his poison, would be the best of all of us.

After some flustered goodbyes, awkward congratulations and bewildered, grief-stricken smiles, I'd watched her get into the elevator and had stayed there until the doors closed on us both.

That was when Brennan asked me, "Why are things strained between you?"

I turned around and found him leaning against the door to the living room.

My husband.

It had happened so fast, so much faster than I had imagined, and in circumstances a thousand times deadlier than I could have foreseen.

Mama had somehow predicted that her daughters would need a man like this, would need a protector and a guardian, and she'd tied him to us. She'd had no way of knowing that he'd be honorable enough to respect that promise, but her faith hadn't been wasted.

That was why I told him the truth.

I'd never lie to him. I'd do what I could to be the perfect wife in thanks for what he'd done for me.

"Because I left."

He arched a brow. "That's it? Older siblings often leave."

My smile was sad. "I cut myself off entirely."

"Inessa knew where you were. Eoghan told me as much."

"It comes as no surprise that Father had my whereabouts investigated." I pulled a face. "It's why I went where I did."

"From one wolf's lair to another?"

I hummed. "Truthfully, if he'd wanted me back, nothing would have stopped him... I didn't go to the MC for a long time."

"No?" He folded his arms across his chest. "What changed?"

"Poverty," I told him shortly. "It sucks."

"That it does."

I sniffed. "As if you even know what it feels like to be poor." I raised my hands, encompassing the massive apartment that was as big as my father's mansion, just in the sky instead of on the ground.

"I can imagine."

"You can't. Not knowing where the next cent is going to come from, working so hard you cry yourself to sleep at night from exhaustion, but even though you spend every hour you're awake working, it's never enough." I grimaced at the memories. "I did it for four years—"

"So long?"

I nodded. "Better that than the life Father wanted for me." I tipped my chin up. "I'd gone to quite a few parties at the MC over the years, but only to check things out. I knew, if Father ever sniffed around, I had to look as though I was one of them, but Nyx..." I cleared my throat, trying not to show the pain that speared me in two at just thinking of him. "...he's the MC's Enforcer, well, he was back then—"

"I know who he is," Brennan rumbled.

"He's very protective of women. You could dance naked on the snooker table and every court and jury in the land might tell you that you deserved to be attacked, but on his watch, you were safe. I went to two other clubhouses while I was with the Sinners, and I saw how they treated the women, like they were animals." I shook my head. "I was fortunate."

"That's one way of looking at it."

"Maybe," I conceded.

"What made you turn to them in the end?"

"A roommate who ran off with her boyfriend and that month's rent, then a further two late payments. I was on my ass. I could either go back to Father or I could try something new."

"You say that like it was a different recipe for cookies."

"Maybe it was. You think in those four years I had much of a life?" I sneered at him. "I was working every moment I had awake. When I..." I straightened my shoulders, ready and waiting for him to mock me or, worse, to call me a liar. "When I went to the MC, I was a virgin."

For a moment, I wasn't sure if he'd heard me. His expression of bland interest didn't change until something flared in his eyes. "They should be shot."

Surprise had me flinching. "Why?"

"Passing around a virgin—no wonder you're frigid at first."

"Ouch," I bit off.

He wafted a hand. "You make chalk look slick, Camille. There's no denying it. You have issues with sex."

"I don't," I denied.

"You're an ex-clubwhore. You're used to spreading them for any two-bit fucking biker—"

I growled at that. "Whether or not that was how I spent the past few years, they were my choice. For the first time in my life, I was free." I didn't tell the prim bastard that that wasn't how I'd spent my years at the clubhouse. For over eighteen months, I'd been Nyx's girl, which meant I was hands' off.

"Nobody is free," Brennan countered. "And lying on your back and spreading your legs to pay for your rent isn't what I call free. Sounds more like prostitution."

"Thinking of getting an annulment?" I snapped, but the second I dropped the words, I regretted them. I clapped a hand to my mouth, wishing them back, dreading his answer because why wouldn't he say no when he thought I'd gone through a chapter of bikers faster than Chlamydia?

Fire danced in his eyes, which was ironic because shadows seemed to crawl over his face. It sounded like something from a nightmare, but instead, that darkness called to me.

I was used to the dark.

The light was what frightened me.

He strode forward, not stopping when he met me, pushing me backward, further and further until I bumped into the nearest wall. He collided with me, his body against mine, his hardness against the little softness on my frame. My hands automatically went up to stop him, to push him away, but he was like a Mack truck. Intent on one thing, and one thing only.

Making a point.

He grabbed my hands but before he could raise them high, I threaded my fingers through his. It derailed him, my acceptance of his desires flashing him out of his mood for a split second before he lifted our joined hands and pinned me to the wall, binding me in place for the fourth time since we'd met.

We all had our kinks, was this his?

He bowed his head and, in my ear, whispered, "You're many things, Camille, but destined to be a clubwhore? No." He pulled back to glower at me. "That you could degrade yourself like that fucks me up, and I have no right to feel that way. You should mean shit to me. You're a duty, a favor called in. This entire thing should mean nothing, and yet, the fact that you slice your palms angers me like nothing else. That you spread your legs for a battalion of bikers to make rent makes me want to kill your father, and makes me pissed at you because you took that opportunity away from me.

"You're okay with marrying a man your mother screwed because you're desperate, and that pisses me off too." His mouth curved up into a mean snarl, but before he could carry on slaying me with his words, his cell phone rang, vibrating between us in a way that had me jerking with surprise because it was low down against my pelvis.

He noticed.

Of course.

"Keep your hands above your head," he commanded, his snarl transforming into a smirk as he reached down to get his phone.

He proceeded to stun the hell out of me by sliding his hand over my hip and snagging the skirt of my dress, tugging it higher so skin could touch skin.

My gaze was glued to his as he pressed the phone between my legs, over the second pair of his briefs I wore, and slotted the thin device along the length of my pussy.

For whatever reason, the caller didn't give up, if anything, they refused because the pulsing of the vibrations carried on for just long enough to get me wet. For that delicious twinge in my belly to stir to life, for my pussy to contract around the emptiness inside it. All the while, we stayed locked together, our eyes tangled, until the ringing stopped.

I thought he'd move away, pull back, ring whoever it was that found it important enough to stay on the line for that long, but he didn't. He angled the phone so just the corner was pressed against my clit, after he used that handy split seam to slide his fingers through the gap and to find their way to my slit.

He thrust two thick fingers into me without even testing if I was ready, and though I was wet, the act had me surging onto my tiptoes and my pussy clenching down around him.

"Your mouth tells me one thing," he snarled into my ear, just as the phone started to ring again and that goddamn pulsation recommenced, "but this cunt tells me another. There's no way in fuck you've serviced an MC."

"I-I—" I sputtered wordlessly, my head rocking back against the wall as the thick fullness of his fingers combined with the vibrations that seemed to be even more powerful now he'd angled the phone directly on my clit had me gasping for air.

"Y-You?" he mocked, so hatefully I wanted to slap him, but I didn't. *Couldn't.*

He was being a jerk but, God help me, this felt so good. *Too* good to spoil, to let the glimmer of an orgasm in the distance go to waste.

Shamefully, I lifted my leg, hooking it on his and curling my foot around his calf so I could arch my hips. The moment I did, the relief was exquisite, and he knew, because he pulled out, then thrust into me with three fingers.

He scissored them open and closed for a second, then started to thrust into me in time to the pulses. The phone stopped and started again, and within thirty seconds, I wasn't just climbing the way toward an orgasm, I was there.

A hoarse shout escaped me, one loaded with my surprise and my glee as I rocked into him as fast as he thrust into me, riding the waves of pleasure as they hit me square in the face.

Gasping, I pushed my forehead against his chest, dragging it from side to side as he carried on, raking his fingers down the front wall of my cunt, hitting some secret spot that had a scream splitting my ears as I cried out, howling with the pleasure/pain that had me reaching around, my fingers digging into his back as he bombarded me with the most acute ecstasy I'd ever experienced in my life.

When his cell rang off for the final time, I was left a panting mess in his arms. Unsure of what to expect, and my brain fried, I let him prop me up. Then, I heard the dull thud of the device colliding with the carpet and groaned when his hand grabbed me by the hair and he dragged my head back so there was no hiding from him.

No evading that gimlet stare that was starting to make me feel as if he could see into my very soul.

How did he know me so little and know me so well at the same time?

And what would he come to learn after we spent years together?

Before fear could overcome me, he tightened his grip on my hair, tugging so that I felt the pain of it, then simultaneously withdrew his fingers from my still-twitching pussy. I knew what he wanted, so I opened my mouth to give it to him.

The shadows retreated for a second, just a second, as he looked at my lips, stared at them and the round 'O' I made before I took his offering, sliding my tongue around the digits to lick them clean, before they returned full blast when he murmured, "You could have walked away, but it's too late now. For both of us."

Why did he keep on saying that? Was it a taunt?

I half expected him to leave me there, with that dire warning ringing in my ears, but he didn't. Still with his hold on my hair, he forced me to turn around, and I complied, pressing my hands flat to the wall and resting my forehead against it too when he let go of me and moved to shape my ass with those hard fingers of his.

The tips bit into the meager curves, hard enough to bruise before he started dragging my skirt all the way up, not stopping until it was around my waist, then he pulled my borrowed underwear down, using his foot to slide them to the floor, leaving me naked from the butt down.

Brennan shoved one leg between mine, slipped his fingers around my stomach and hauling me back into him. "Grind down on my leg."

I blinked at the wall. "I'll get your pants dirty."

"I can afford another pair of pants," he growled, before his hand arched downwards, pressing against my pubic bone in a way that did strange things to my insides.

Doing as he asked, I swayed my hips from side to side, trying to grind on him like he wanted, and while it didn't rub my clit at all, it made me incredibly aware of just how wet I was. Of how pleasure could exist without a peak.

Groaning when he reached up to palm one of my breasts, I listened as he whispered in my ear, his breath brushing my earlobe as he communicated with me in what I was coming to learn was one of his most favorite ways, "You're not going to come like this. You're just going to be hyper aware of that pussy. It isn't greedy right now. If anything, it's been starved and doesn't recognize what it needs. But soon, when it gets a sniff of my hands or my dick or my mouth, it's going to get hungry. You're going to be desperate for my dick, Camille. Absolutely fucking desperate for it."

My eyelids fluttered at his words. "Why do you want that?"

"Because that way I'll erase every other son of a bitch who's been inside you." He nipped on my earlobe. "That phone call will have been important. All my calls are. But I shoved it aside, for you." He squeezed on my nipple. "I'll have to go out soon. I want you to make an appointment with a clinic."

Hurt washed through me, extinguishing some of the liquid pleasure I'd felt in my core. "W-Why? I already showed you my clean bill of health."

"Because I want you on birth control. I'm not ready for you to have my kids yet."

Was that a compliment or an insult?

Wasn't I good enough now that he supposedly knew how many guys I'd fucked?

He bit down on my earlobe, harder than before, harder than ever. "Unfurl those fucking hands of yours."

I hadn't even realized I'd done that. Unaware of the gesture that was second nature to me, I blinked and found my hands were, in fact, curled into tight fists that I'd rested against the wall. Carefully doing as he asked, and trying not to moan as I did so because I didn't want to anger an already pissed off beast, I whispered, "You said you wanted children."

"And I do. And we will. Just not yet. I told you, Camille, you should have walked away when you had the chance." He squeezed me in his hold in a kind of reverse hug that somehow let me feel every part of him. "Get the pill, the shot, whatever. I'll decide when we're ready for kids, and it won't be when their mother is still strung up on slicing her hands open and her cunt isn't gagging for my cock."

He made a disgusted sound at the back of his throat, before he let go, dipped down, then hauled me into his arms, carrying me like a real husband carried his bride over the threshold.

Bewildered, I looked up at him, aghast and astounded, as he carried me down the hall, toward the farthest end where I'd started off last night.

Disappointment filled me, before he walked in and said, "Take one last look at this bedroom, Camille. If I find you in here, I'll spank your ass until you can't sit down for a week." His eyes leveled on mine. "There's no running from this. Not now."

My mouth worked, confusion filling me. He was acting like I was a woman he'd been craving for a lifetime, like I hadn't twisted his arm into marrying me.

He was...

Possessive.

And as I registered the fire in his eyes for what it was, I melted.

I absolutely, one-hundred-percent melted into him.

My bones turning molten, my being just disintegrating into a goo that clung to him as he hauled me out of the room and down toward his.

"You're not going to like everything I do. You're going to hate some of it, and sometimes, you might hate me, but that's fine. I can deal with your hatred—I'm more than used to that," he said grimly, prompting me to blink up at him.

What was he talking about?

Hate?

Hate a man who barely knew me, but who looked at me like he'd set the world on fire if I dared self-harm again?

Hate a man who told me he wanted my cunt to be gagging for his dick?

None of this was anticipated, but then, I thought Brennan felt the exact same way.

He didn't look particularly happy, just resolved.

Like something had clicked on in his mind, and when a man like him made a decision, it wasn't often he went back on it.

There was only one thought that whispered through my mind at that...

Thank God for bullheaded monsters...

NINETEEN
BRENNAN

I WASN'T sure what was going on in my head, was well aware that the brain between my legs was taking control, and because it had been too long since I'd allowed that to happen, and because she was my wife, I saw no harm in it.

She knew why she was here.

I'd given her the chance to leave.

She hadn't taken it.

Whether she'd come to regret it would be another matter entirely, and something I'd deal with in the future.

I meant it when I'd uttered my vows.

There would be no breaking them.

This was it.

For the both of us.

Having recognized Conor's ringtone, I knew I didn't really have time to dick around. He didn't call unless it was strictly necessary, preferring to text over speaking on the phone, but for the moment, he could wait.

I'd been my family's fixer for too long if they thought I'd drop everything just because they rang at the drop of a hat.

When I maneuvered her into my, *our* bedroom, I was well aware that nothing was going as I'd planned.

I was going to have sex with her to get her with child.

Now?

I wanted the exact opposite.

Just the thought of this woman, this fucking *Queen*, degrading herself with a bunch of dirty bikers fucked me up like little else could.

What the hell had her father done to her to make that seem like the best option out there?

It made no sense to me, but it didn't have to. I was the one who'd have to revert ingrained behaviors, and luckily for her, I was man enough for the task.

I took her straight into the bathroom, and told her, "Press both those switches."

She did as I asked, which had the magic window turning on, clearing the glass like it was a smokescreen so we could see straight into the bedroom. Mostly, I just wanted the extra light, because I hated how bright it was in here with the lights on. Next, the waterfall shower turned on. I placed her on the ground, let her get her balance before I started to strip her down.

The evening dress clung to every inch of her too-thin body, and prying it off was like how it would be in a few months whenever she tried to get me off her.

Impossible.

I was going to be in her every which way I could. She didn't really know what she'd triggered in me, and I couldn't even tell you what the fuck it was in particular.

The pathetic misery in her eyes when she spoke of her sisters, the fact she'd killed her father with a pyramid souvenir—something I'd gleaned from Maxim—that I had a blood-soaked dress in a shopping bag to take to The Hole, the way she constantly sought relief in pain by squeezing her hands into fists...

Tick them all, tick none.

It could have been that I wanted in her cunt like I'd wanted no other pussy for a while.

It could be that I was fulfilling a promise while also making it my own.

Or it could just be that she was mine.

Mine, like no one else ever had been.

Eoghan had it right—the possessive fucker.

Shit changed when they took on your last name, and even though I'd known her for barely any time at all, I'd known of her for a good long while. I'd seen her pictures when she was a kid. I'd seen her similarities to her mother, and that had been something I imagined would be off-putting. Instead, it showed me the truth.

Mariska was quartz, masquerading as a precious gem, aware of her powers, unashamed of her ability to seduce.

Camille was a diamond masquerading as quartz, unaware of her powers, ashamed of her body, ill-at-ease with it.

I'd been a project to Mariska.

Camille was *my* project. Except, this project would last until death did us part, which I couldn't deny shoved shit up a notch.

Still, if there was a woman to lose your head over, it was your wife, wasn't it?

Dragging off the dress and the boxer briefs she'd borrowed, I stripped her down until she was bare, then I undressed myself too.

Moving with her so that we were both under the spray, I grabbed the bottle of soap and began to clean her. Making suds with it, I smoothed it along each of her limbs, letting her feel my touch everywhere. Her head stayed bowed, from shyness or appreciation, I didn't know, but she acquiesced to my touch.

When I cleaned her tits, she peered up at me through a mop of wet gold hair, and when I slid my hand between her legs, she bit her lip, her fingers moving over my chest, the tips and the edges of her nails digging into my pecs.

It was the wrong thing to do.

Feeling those nails against my skin, I realized she shaped them in a way that would turn them into pincers against her cut palms, and the red mist that overcame me was something that ashamed me just as it pissed me off that she could do this to herself.

When she was cleaned up from the cum I'd drenched her in this morning, I grabbed the chrome accessory that was the detachable shower head, turned it on, then I pressed it between her legs.

She leaped up onto tiptoe, her eyes flaring wide as they caught mine.

"When you were a teenager, did you have a boyfriend?"

She'd said she was a virgin until she chose to whore herself out to the

MC who I had to force myself to remember were fucking allies, but had she fooled around any?

"No. Father wouldn't allow it. Didn't want to risk my sale price," she said bitterly.

"Did you sneak around?"

Shadows of the fear she'd felt back then drifted into her gaze. "Are you being serious? And get him killed and me whipped? No way." Her mouth twisted into a sad smile. "Anyway, I was a bitch back then. No guy wanted me."

I snorted at that. "Guys don't care if you're a bitch. They just look at your ass and want between your legs."

"Well, evidently not. I didn't have to fight them off." She shrugged. "I had small tits."

"So? Not everyone's a tit man."

She peered up at me. "Are you?" Before I could answer, a sharp gasp escaped her. "Oh, God!"

My grin, I'd admit, was smug. "Just started to feel it, huh?"

Her nails dug into my chest once more. "Christ, yes."

The pain of her touch had me seeing red again. I watched as her focus started to drift to what was going on between her legs, and just when she started to rock her hips, I moved the flow of the water away.

She peered up at me, and her beseeching glance, however faint, had me pressing a kiss to her temple.

"You're clean now," I rumbled. "Don't get dirty today."

"What's that supposed to mean?" she rasped.

"It means, keep your hands away from your pussy. And while you're at it, I want you to file your nails down or cut them off, or whatever the hell it is you do with them. I want them flat."

She scowled at me. "Are you being serious?"

My lips curved into a smirk. "You'll find I'm *never* not serious." With that, I tapped her on the ass and said, "Dry off. I need to shower and change."

Her mouth worked, and I watched her gaze drift down to my dick. "But—"

"But nothing." I started to wash myself, and when she just stood there, watching, I murmured, "What is it?"

"Are you—" When her cheeks tinged pink, I arched a brow at her, and that turned the pink into red. Christ, I loved how she reacted. How the hell had she stayed like this after living at the MC compound?

I refused to believe this was all an act. I'd seen her at her lowest now—killing your father tended to do that to a person... so I had faith that she was as sensitive as I'd come to believe. Still, she wasn't a kid.

Thank fuck for that.

"Am I, what?" I replied, grabbing my dick, washing it, and watching as she licked her lips.

This time, I almost dragged her to her knees and told her to suck it, because it was without artifice. She wasn't trying to entice me. If anything, she just stood there, dripping wet.

That was the power of her though.

Which made her dangerous.

"You're not going to—" She winced. "I'll gladly... I don't want..."

"Spit it out," I rasped, even though I knew what she was asking.

"I'm not unwilling," she blurted out. "You don't have to see your mistress today."

"I'm not going to," I informed her briskly. "I've got business. Our little situation got in the way of that." She blanched, but I ignored that. "I have shit to do. I'll be back when it's done. That's one thing you need to get used to, fast."

"I've spent a lifetime in training, Brennan," she whispered. "I know how to blend in with the furniture."

I scoffed. "Nothing about you blends in with the furniture." I reached over and cupped her tit. "Nothing. Now, I told you to dry off." The last thing I wanted was her coming down with a chill.

Her mouth tightened, but she nodded, twisted around and stepped out of the shower.

The stall was a long one, with a stone base and no curtain or separator, so I had an unimpeded view of that delicious ass of hers. When she reached for a towel, I watched the play of her muscles, the way she stretched, the plump curve of her tit bouncing as she dried off, but I also saw her ribs. The narrow indent of her waist.

"Camille?"

She stilled, but peered at me over her shoulder. "Yes, Brennan?"

"Eat something today. I'll be pissed if you forget."

Her mouth tightened. "I don't need to be told to eat. I'm not a kid."

"No? Then you've been starving yourself for fashion, have you?" I retorted.

"Eat, don't masturbate, cut my nails... anything else you want me to do today?"

I wanted to laugh, but managed not to, just in time to tell her, "Yeah, the doctor's appointment, remember?"

Her eyes narrowed at me as she clenched her jaw, pissed at being ordered around just not brave enough to counter those orders with sass, but before she stormed out of the bathroom, she nodded.

And that was all I needed from her.

Compliance.

STAY STRONG. JUST BECAUSE IT'S HARD TODAY, DOESN'T MEAN THAT NEXT WEEK IT WON'T GET EASIER.

TWENTY
CAMILLE

SINCE MY TEEN YEARS, I'd never touched myself before, not without it being a sex thing. As in, Nyx asked me to do it while he was fucking me. That was pretty much it.

It had just never interested me after I'd tried it a few times when I was still in high school, which had always made me wonder if that unoriginal 'Ice Princess' title was actually more apt than I'd have liked.

Frigid, Brennan had described me.

After my childhood, who'd blame me?

But after this morning, after the way he'd made me aware of my pussy, I wasn't going to lie—my attention was very much centered between my thighs, and it wasn't helping that I'd managed to squeeze in an emergency appointment with my doctor.

One shot later and I was protected for three months. One pill later and I was protected from pregnancy. Even though he hadn't come inside me today, I'd been drenched in his cum. I figured it was prudent to take the morning after pill just to be on the safe side.

I wasn't ready to be a mother yet, not with a man I knew so little. Who knew me so little too.

We were stuck together; there was no evading that, and I didn't want to. I was quite happy to be stuck with Brennan.

First off, I'd never had an orgasm before, for God's sake, so that made me be pretty taken with him. Not only that but he hadn't forced me to do things I wasn't comfortable with—hadn't forced me to do anything, period, other than climax. Who was going to complain about that?

He'd come to my rescue, and he'd let me sleep with him, had held me too... as far as I was concerned, he was Prince goddamn Charming.

Still, I was glad he'd made this suggestion. I'd never have had the balls to take this step without his say so—and yes, I needed to grow a spine worse than a worm did—so now, I didn't have to worry about it.

We had time.

That was what mattered.

Even if he was only interested in fucking me for a month before he went to his regular mistress, that would be more of a relationship than I'd ever had before. When he lost interest, that was when we'd probably try for a child, and that was when I'd focus on them. I'd be happy. I'd be a mother, and I'd be with a man who would protect us all, who wouldn't hurt us, and who thought family came first.

Heaven.

So even though my attention kept veering off to the nagging ache at my core, my day brightened up further once the appointment with the doctor was over.

With one thing off my to-do list, I decided to be brave and texted Inessa over the next task at hand:

Me: *I'm going for a manicure. Do you want to come?*
Inessa: *Which nail salon?*
Me: *The one on West 46th St. and 11th Avenue.*
Inessa: *What time?*
Me: *Now.*
Inessa: *Great. Google says there's a coffee shop next door. Want to meet there for a coffee first? I'd like to talk about Victoria.*
Me: *Sure. Is she okay?*
Inessa: *As well as she can be.*
Me: *Figures. I'm a few minutes away so I'll wait for you in the coffee shop.*
Inessa: *See you there.*

Sending her a thumbs up, I turned my attention to the road. Not unlike my father, Brennan had assigned me a guard. Bagpipes. I wasn't sure if he was happy to be doing the guarding, but I knew how men like Brennan worked.

Even if my father hadn't given a shit about his daughters, in our world, treasures were protected. If they weren't, then they were no longer treasures, which wouldn't do as it lowered our value.

We were commodities, after all.

Always had been, and always would have been.

Even after we left the nest and made our own, because escaping the Bratva was impossible.

It was shameful, really, how happy I was the day after I'd murdered him. The day *after* I'd spilled blood, but if anything, I just felt free.

Liberated.

And now I was Brennan's wife, that sensation was compounded to the point where it was like I could breathe again. All my life, I'd felt much as I had this morning, when he'd rested his weight on my chest. As Bagpipes drove me toward the Upper East Side, I felt lighter. So much lighter that a smile kept popping up from nowhere.

I was safe from everyone apart from him.

But I could deal with that. Would gladly deal with that.

For the moment, anyway.

I hadn't just left one cage to be trapped in another with a more wicked beast than the one I'd clawed my way free of.

Speaking of which... if Brennan was going to take away my *real* claws, then I needed to start finding other ways to defend myself. And having access to a set of car keys was the first step in that plan.

"Bagpipes?"

"Yeah?"

"When we return to Brennan's building, I need to drive."

He arched a brow at me. "Why?"

"Because I get car sick."

As we pulled up at a stop light, he shot me a dubious look. "You ain't puked yet."

"Yet being the operative word," I told him just as dubiously. I knew an expensive car when I was sitting in one. "If you want to be the one cleaning up vomit from between the creases in the leather, well, that's on you."

He scowled. "You bullshitting me?"

"Why would I?" I groused back. "You think I want to drive in wall-to-wall traffic?"

Staring ahead at the traffic jam we found ourselves in, he heaved a sigh. "True. I wondered why you always drove, not your guards." He tapped his hands on the steering wheel. "He'll kill you if you scratch it."

"I won't scratch it," I muttered, even as my mind was still fixated on the fact that he'd used the word 'always.'

Brennan never had told me why he'd turned up at the stables yesterday, had he?

Yet here Bagpipes was, implying that he'd been watching me for a while.

Why?

I'd sensed a tail, but how long had I driven around without knowing someone was watching me?

The thought was unnerving enough for me to glance into the wing mirror to check out who was driving behind us.

"In fact, if you scratch it, it won't just be you he'll be killing, so you'd better be careful because it's both our asses on the line if you drive," Bagpipes muttered, evidently unaware that he'd just dropped a bombshell.

At least, what felt like a bombshell to me.

Perplexed to say the least, I replied, "I'm a good driver. When I was younger, I took a defensive driving course."

"You did? Why?"

"Because Father got tired of me being sick in his cars. Some smells you just can't wash out of upholstery." My smile was tight. "I even learned how to drive if I was in a situation where I was being held at gunpoint or being taken hostage."

Bagpipes grunted. "Your father was a weird fuck."

"You won't hear me argue," I muttered.

"Hasn't he ever heard of Dramamine?"

"Oh yeah, but it got embarrassing when I kept falling asleep everywhere."

Bagpipes chuckled. "Made you sleepy?"

"Like I had narcolepsy," I confirmed wryly, my hands pleating the skirt of my dress. "I wonder if there'll be time to go shopping after the nail place—"

Bagpipes shook his head. "Brennan wants you back by seven."

"Why? Will he be there?"

"Doubt it." He snorted. "But you'll figure out soon enough, he might look mild, but he's fucking particular."

"In what way?"

He shrugged. "Likes what he likes, loathes what he loathes. Ain't afraid to point it out, either."

Hadn't I had a trial by fire of *that* this morning?

Warily, *cautiously*, because this man was Brennan's and owed me no loyalty, I queried, "Is he—well, do you think I need to watch myself around him, Bagpipes?"

"I think a smart woman like yourself would always watch herself around a stranger. This marriage is going to cause trouble within the family, Camille. There's no hiding from it. But ride it out and everything will be okay eventually. Brennan inherited a lot more from his da than he realizes. He won't take shit from them."

Words to inspire a flock.

Jeez. Everyone knew how insane Aidan O'Donnelly Sr. was. My father had been wary of him too.

"What did he inherit?" I asked gruffly.

"He's temperamental. Volatile. But he ain't fickle. You get on his good side, he'll be loyal to you until the day you die." He shot me a look. "I know what you're asking, Camille. Will he beat you? Will he mistreat you?" He shook his head. "Never seen him with a woman longer than a couple of months so I can't tell you what he's like after a while.

"Everyone who's married knows that what goes on behind closed doors is a whole other ballgame to what that couple shows the world, but I've known Brennan all my life. He's a prick at times, capable of cruelty and spite, just like his da, but for women, he's a sucker."

"What do you mean? He's a manwhore?" I asked quietly, wanting to know, but not wanting to discourage Bagpipes from being so candid either. I hadn't expected such honesty, so I was grateful for it.

"Nah, I mean he's a sucker. It's to do with his ma. He ain't a Momma's boy, not really. Not more than any of those boys are. He just... he's protective. That's what all this is about, ain't it? Him protecting you?"

Surprise filled me. "He told you?"

Bagpipes shrugged. "Not a lot he don't share with his crew."

"That's unusual, isn't it?"

He grinned. "Brennan's unusual. You'll see. I won't talk shit about him, won't tell you secrets. He's my friend. More like a brother to me than anything else, but I just wanted you to know that with a good woman, he'll be a good man. And..." His mouth tightened. "If you betray us, if you betray the O'Donnellys, I'll slice you from throat to belly before he even gets a chance to."

The threat meant nothing, not when I'd faced worse over the years. "I'd expect nothing less, Bagpipes."

"Baggy, Camille. I'd like to think if I gotta sit bitch while you drive me around the city, we can be a little less formal."

"I'd like that too, and I appreciate the advice."

He shrugged. "Don't cost nothing."

"I suppose not." My lips twitched. "You mind me asking why you're called Bagpipes?"

The guard heaved a sigh like I was the most wearisome thing in the world, but I didn't mind, especially when he replied, "When I got married, my wife insisted on walking down the aisle to bagpipes. The piper stuck around for the reception. I got a little drunk, me and him got into a small fight when I saw him eying up my bride like she was a T-bone, and he whacked me over the head with it. The name stuck with me ever since, especially when Kerry-Louise started learning how the oven worked." He patted his belly. "Got the gut to prove she's a brilliant cook."

Laughing, I asked, "Does she call you Bagpipes?"

He arched a brow. "No. Would you call Brennan that?"

"True. What's your real name?"

"Donal."

"Thank you for telling me, Baggy," I murmured.

He just shrugged, and a few minutes later, he dropped me about twenty yards from the coffee shop thanks to a pedestrian crossing, handing me a burner cell with instructions to call him when I was done at the nail salon.

As I climbed out, it felt strange to be wearing an evening dress for coffee when I was in such a nice part of the city. Couldn't be helped, though. I'd had to leave everything behind apart from the bare minimum like a tub of Vaseline that could fit into my purse alongside the dress that needed destroying.

Before he'd left on business, Brennan had asked for it, and I'd felt nothing about leaving it with him, even though I knew he could hold it against me for life.

But I preferred it that way.

It was a means of showing him I was willing to have faith in him, and I wanted him to know that more than I cared about my freedom.

That rested with him anyway, so what was another piece of leverage in the grand scheme of things?

As I walked toward the coffee shop, there was a used coffee cup on the ground and a dirty sleeping bag with someone huddled underneath it.

It wasn't that cold, *yet*, but I didn't know how miserable it would be later on. Too miserable to stay in a damn sleeping bag, that was for damn sure.

Since my return from New Jersey, I'd noticed there were so many more homeless people on the streets, and though I couldn't help them all, I tried to do what I could.

At the same time he'd asked for my dress, Brennan had given me a wad of cash. I had to assume that was supposed to last me a while, but I couldn't, in good conscience, go into the nail salon to have my nails filed while this poor guy was sleeping rough outside it.

Dipping into my purse, I pulled out a couple of hundred dollar notes, and placed them into the cup. As I straightened, I saw Inessa was outside the coffee shop, watching me, and a few yards away, her guard hovered, watching me as well.

My cheeks turned pink as I strode toward them. As always, I wanted to reach out to Inessa, to have her hug me, but there might as well have been a 'back off' sign hanging around her neck. I respected her boundaries and just shot her a wary smile.

There was a lot I had to say to her, a lot I *couldn't* say to her, but I needed to kill two birds with one stone and eating before I got back to the apartment would accomplish that.

"Shall we go in?" I asked her, pushing the door open before she could question what she'd just seen.

She'd painted me as a bitch for leaving them a long time ago, but that didn't make me one. If I'd shaken that belief with human decency, then so be it. I hadn't set out to do that.

The coffee shop was quiet, because it was a weird time to grab a drink and a snack, so I strode straight over to the counter without waiting on her, and placed an order for an open-faced chicken cobb salad sandwich and a latte.

After I'd paid, I left Inessa to make her own order and took a seat in the corner. It was a little cold out, especially with my meager outfit, but it was toasty warm in here.

A quick glance around told me we could talk in privacy, as the only patrons were at the other side of the storefront, clustered around a bunch of armchairs and sofas.

It reminded me of *Friends*, to be honest. There were three girls, three guys, all smiling and hanging out.

God, how simple their lives were.

Did they appreciate the freedom they had?

Just to hang out, for the sake of it? With no guards questioning their location, just striving to stay afloat?

As a teenager, I'd been an envious person. I'd coveted the freedoms that I thought regular people had, but as I grew up, and as I saw the MC and the families of the brothers who were more normal than anyone I'd ever known, I realized everyone had their stresses, their strains. Nothing was ever easy.

There was just less bloodshed.

And striving to stay afloat sucked. *Hard.*

I curled my hands in on themselves, feeling the sting of pain and reveling in it. A shaky sigh escaped me, much like it would when a junkie took a hit and the feelings of that drug-induced ecstasy slowly started to take over everything else...

This was my crack.

My acid.

I understood why Brennan wanted me to change the way I did my nails, and oddly enough, I didn't resent it.

He was the first person to notice.

The first person to *care*.

My heart was in my throat as I registered that, but before I could get maudlin, Inessa appeared at my side.

She sported a frown that marred her perfectly made-up face as she slipped into a seat. "It's not like you to eat through the day."

"Is that an accusation?"

Her mouth turned down at the corners. "No. Of course not. I was just making a statement."

I shrugged. "I'm hungry."

"Good. You're too thin. I can see your collarbones."

"I can see yours," I retorted waspishly.

"Yeah, but mine aren't so prominent." Her frown made another reappearance. "Are you sick or something? You've lost a lot of weight."

I heaved a sigh. "Hence the sandwich. Look, I'm okay. Are you?" I asked pointedly, my gaze drifting to her stomach. It wasn't like I could gawk at her between her legs, was it?

"The treatment's working."

"Glad to hear it."

I caught sight of the server making his way toward us, and I let my focus shift to him until he placed our drinks on the table and returned to the counter, before I asked, "How's Victoria doing?"

"She's freaked out, and I can't blame her." Inessa doctored her coffee with a bottle of Stevia sweetener she pulled out of her purse, then leaned into me. "What the hell happened last night? Everything was normal as far as I could tell."

"Nothing was ever normal in our household, was it?" I retorted dully, making a little hole in the foam so I could tip some sugar into my latte. As I stirred my drink, I murmured, "You know how everything derails, Inessa, and you can't turn back the hands of time. I suppose that's what happened last night."

"Victoria says you were there."

"Is that another accusation?" I snapped. "Are you sure they sorted out that rash? Is that why you're so irritable today? Because I know as well as you do that you won't be shedding a tear for that bastard. If anything, I'm grateful for what happened, and I'm pretty certain you are too."

She pursed her lips. "Considering the circumstances, I don't suppose there'll be a funeral."

I shrugged. "Off topic, but who knows?"

"I won't be sad if there isn't one. I'd prefer to toss dog crap on his casket than dirt."

I grinned. "Well, that would definitely set the tone for the event."

She didn't smile, just narrowed her eyes on me, before she leaned into me and rasped, "Is it true?"

"Is what true?"

"Victoria said you told her not to say anything... she said she watched you and Brennan get married today?"

I winced. "Dammit." Grabbing her hand, I squeezed her fingers and told her, "You mustn't tell Eoghan. Brennan doesn't want his brothers to know yet."

Inessa blinked. "Why not?"

"I don't know."

"Is he ashamed of you?"

I snorted. "I don't think so."

Uneasiness crossed her expression, and slowly, she turned her hand in mine. "You've been riding too much again."

The statement, as far as I could see, came out of the blue. "What do you mean?"

"I mean your hands are wrecked. I never did understand what happened at those stables to make them like that."

She tried to flip my fingers around so she could look at my palm, but I resisted. "It can be hard work. I get a lot of blisters," was all I told her, and I could tell that she believed me.

So, Inessa *had* noticed but had mistaken where the scars and cuts came from.

Was that her being naive? Or had everyone else known too and I hadn't hidden my hands as well as I thought I had?

My younger sister hummed at my reply before she took a sip of her coffee and slouched back in her seat. She wore a bright pink Polo sweater that clung to her curves, and dark navy skinny jeans she paired with a set of gold ballet pumps.

She looked natural and at ease, like she was running errands.

Me, in my evening dress and cashmere jacket, well, I looked as if I was doing the walk of shame hours after I woke up.

"I haven't told Eoghan," she said with a sigh.

Relief filled me. "Thank God for that."

"I don't understand how any of this happened. Do you even know Brennan?"

"Apparently. I wouldn't have married him otherwise," I remarked.

"You were scared about Abramovicz—"

"Yes, wouldn't you be?" I shook my head. "I knew Father wouldn't agree to Brennan and me getting together. Why would he waste one of his pawns on the Irish again? He didn't need to strengthen their alliance, did he? One sacrificial lamb was enough."

Inessa grimaced. "True. Is that why Brennan didn't want his family there today?"

"I think so. It's highly likely Aidan Sr. won't be thrilled either."

"I guess... although, he's not as bad as Father."

"Words to live up to," I said dryly, making her laugh.

"You're not wrong," she agreed. "He's... I mean, I won't lie, he's a headcase, and he does things that are scary. I wouldn't be surprised if he's bipolar or something, and the dude seriously needs lithium, but, for all that, he loves his kids.

"It's weird but true. You'll see what I mean when it's time for Sunday lunch. They dote on them, it's just not a regular way of doting."

"And what's that? Wasn't like we were doted on either."

She wafted a hand. "You know, what you see in shows and things. It's not like that. But they're a devoted family. Dedicated to each other. It's—" Her smile was sheepish. "It's nice. I'm glad you get to experience that if nothing else."

"Does it make a difference?"

"Knowing that people care about you?" Inessa nodded. "They were kind to me even before they knew me, even before they could see I'd fallen for Eoghan, and that he'd fallen for me... That takes good men. I'm happy for you, *ma sœur*."

"Thank you, Inessa. That means a lot to me." I smiled at her, seeing her sincerity and appreciating it wholeheartedly.

Her lips twisted a touch, before she whispered, "Maybe it's a chance for us to get closer again?"

"I'd like to think so." I didn't reach over to grab her hand, just in case she tried to look at my palms, but I said, "I've always hated the distance between us. Physically and emotionally. Sisters should come first—even before husbands."

Inessa blinked, then surprised me by nodding. "I'm still mad at you for leaving."

"I know. I deserve that."

"But," she conceded with a wince, "after how I got married, I can't really blame you."

"What happened?"

She pursed her lips when the server popped up with our orders—my sandwich, her salad. As she stabbed a couple of lettuce leaves on a fork, she muttered, "I tried to back out of it, Father beat the shit out of me. Eoghan saw that I'd been beaten and... let's just say, things didn't get better after that." She shrugged. "The upside was that I knew he was just crazy enough to take on a Pakhan because I belonged to him." She shook her head. "It was surreal, but I knew I could trust him with my safety. If nothing else."

"He beat you before the wedding?"

"He did." Her jaw clenched. "You're right. I'm glad he's dead."

"Me too," I rasped, staring into her crystalline eyes and seeing the truth there—she didn't believe the story Victoria had been fed.

"Did he hurt you?" she asked simply.

"He was going to," I replied, just as simply.

"Well then... I'm sure he deserved his fate."

I took a bite of my sandwich, swallowed it even though it felt like a lead weight, and nodded. "I'm sure he did." I cut her a look. "Truly, is everything better? What happened after we spoke yesterday?"

Her nose crinkled. "He took me to the ER, terrified a bunch of innocent doctors, wouldn't let any men look at me, then when I got a shot to calm things down—" she cleared her throat, "—and a prescription, and we went back to the hotel, wouldn't speak to me for the rest of the night."

"He's annoyed at you for not telling him?"

She sighed, but there was misery in her eyes that gave me my answer without her having to utter a word.

"Eoghan's very protective," I told her. "That's obvious even from a distance."

"He said I was supposed to tell him stuff like this. Pretty much what you told me."

"He was pissed you waited that long?"

She nodded, then started twirling her fork amid the lettuce leaves. "It was just mortifying." Her brow furrowed. "He didn't seem to get it."

"Why would he? He's not a woman, and he's a lot older than you, Inessa." Shoving my concerns about my hands aside, I pressed my fingers to her arm and reassured her, "You're only eighteen. That changes things more than you know, but even so, I'm older than you and I wouldn't like having to tell Brennan that. It's..." I sighed. "While we're married to them, we don't know them that well. Neither of us have deep foundations for our relationships, do we? That doesn't mean they're bad or wrong or weak, it just means we need time." I shot her a smile. "Time is something we all have in abundance."

"I guess." She pulled a face. "When did you get to be so wise, huh?"

I snorted at that. "Me? Wise? Yeah, right." I hesitated a second, before I decided it was better to give her my take on it than for her to keep on worrying. "He'll get over his anger with you. He loves you, Inessa. He just wants you to be safe and healthy and happy is all."

"Doesn't exactly make me happy when he's mean to me," she groused.

"Mad or mean?" I asked, wanting to make sure Eoghan wasn't mistreating her or anything.

"Mad, I guess."

"Is it so bad if he's looking after you when you're not looking after yourself?"

"That doesn't make it okay. This isn't 1980."

"No, it isn't, but men don't change. Not that much." I hitched a shoulder. "He'll probably be sorry tonight. You'll see."

"I hope you're right." Then, she frowned at me. "Is there a reason you're wearing an evening dress?"

Sisters... always cutting to the heart of everything. From genital rashes to fashion. I'd forgotten about that part of sisterhood.

TWENTY-ONE
BRENNAN

BY THE TIME my prick of a younger brother let me into his apartment, I was already regretting leaving things the way I had with Camille.

Mostly because my dick was aching, but also because she wasn't my fucking lap dog and I'd just bossed her about like she was a prize poodle.

If that made me grouchier than I usually was, then, sue me.

One of Conor's crew, a friend of the family, Callum O'Reilly opened the door for me, which told me he was on his way out.

We bumped fists as *noxxious*, Kid's favorite band, bellowed through the speakers—Conor had a real boner for 80's hair bands.

Grimacing because I hated this kind of shit, I yelled over the music, "You doing okay, man? Haven't seen you in fucking ages."

"Couldn't be better." Callum shot me a grin. "Priestley's pregnant."

"Congrats." I shoved his shoulder. "Who the fuck would have imagined you as a dad?"

"Trust me, Conor's giving me enough shit about it." His grin turned from pleased to wry. "I can't believe it myself to be fair." He cast a look at the door. "Then, you see shit like this, and you remember the crap we got up to when we were kids. That part I'm not looking forward to."

"What's happened?"

Callum's nose wrinkled. "You'll find out soon enough. I'd stick around for the fireworks, but Priestley's got her first ultrasound. Had to pay her bitch of a doctor a fucking fortune to see us this late at night."

"Give her my best, Cal, won't ya?"

"Cheers, Bren. I will." He clapped me on the shoulder and said, "We need to catch up. You're right, it's been ages." He pulled a face. "Moving to Staten Island has really messed with my social life."

"Lucky you." I grinned. "Message me when my prick of a brother gives you some time off, and we'll meet up for drinks."

"Sounds great." He waved at me, and left me to lock up behind him.

Being forewarned, in my family, wasn't necessarily forearmed, so I girded my goddamn loins as I headed down the corridor, toward Conor's living room.

The second I breached the doorway, I hollered, "Turn this fucking shit down."

Conor accommodated me quickly, meaning I could hear myself think, but when I entered the room, I found Shay, our nephew, standing there awkwardly, sporting two shiners, and my thoughts jammed to a halt.

"What the fuck?" I demanded, watching as Shay straightened his shoulders while Conor slumped back on one of his sofas. Striding over to him, I grabbed his chin, tipped his head up and snapped, "Who do I need to kill?"

Conor hummed. "Let's not frighten the kid just yet, hmm?"

"Little man's seen more shit than most his age," I disregarded, seeing Shay's fear and nerves unlocking before my eyes. "He has to know he's an O'Donnelly now. That means we'll fight his battles for him."

"But I don't want you to!" Shay snapped, his hands balling into fists.

After a day, barely even that, it was almost second nature to snap at him to unfurl his fingers like I was doing with Camille whenever I saw her do that, but Shay wasn't self-harming.

Thank Christ.

"Dude wants to protect himself," Conor told me, lifting his legs and crossing them at the ankle as he rested them on this weird cat ornament he'd bought a while ago. It was five feet tall, two feet wide, studded in diamantes, and was enough to give any bastard nightmares if they stubbed their toe on it in the middle of the night.

"Yeah, I do. Conor said if I wanted that then you'd be the one to teach me."

I shook my head. "Declan's a nasty fighter."

"You're nastier." Conor smirked. "Plus, he's a dad now. He can't be teaching his kid that kind of shit, can he?"

"Why not? I'd teach mine," I retorted, folding my arms across my chest.

"Yeah, but you're not cultured like our Dec." Conor shot Shay a look. "Brennan thinks ballet is boring."

"So do you, dickwad," I retorted, scowling at him for stirring shit with me. The whole family knew Shay had been taught to appreciate the arts.

"Ballet isn't for everyone," Shay dismissed, but his gaze was fixed on mine even if I kept on casting glances at my brother to glower at him. "But I need to know how to protect myself."

"From what?"

"People."

I frowned. "People? In general? Or bullies?"

His mouth tightened, and at that moment, he looked so much like my younger brother it was uncanny. Seriously, no paternity test was required where Seamus O'Neill O'Donnelly was concerned. He had the same scowl as his father, and the same brooding stare that was more apt for that prick who threw himself off the hill—that Heathcliff fucker—than a mobster.

"Bullies," he confirmed.

"Who the fuck would be insane enough to bully you?" I rumbled, shooting Conor a stare.

"Idiots?" he confirmed. "They're everywhere. Not as bad as ants but almost."

"What?"

"Did you know that the total weight of ants on this planet is more than the weight of humans?"

"No, I didn't know that, and I could have lived a long time without knowing it either." At Conor's shrug, I reached up to pinch the bridge of my nose. "Let's start at the beginning. Do your parents know you're with Conor?"

Shay nodded. "I told Mom I was coming here."

"Good."

"That's not the beginning," Conor pointed out. "The beginning is that some assholes thought they could mess with our little dude." He cracked his knuckles. "I'm not having it, so I called in the heavy hitter."

I scowled at that. "I'm not a prized bull."

"Now you know how it feels to be objectified," Conor said dryly. "But you are. You're the fixer." He wafted his hands, somehow managing to look both pissed off and supremely at ease as he slouched against the sofa, directing the troops from his seat. "So fix this."

"I haven't fought in years. That's not how I work now."

Conor and I shared a look, but we didn't verbalize what I was talking about. Other people grabbed the fuckers who were unfortunate—read, stupid—enough to come to my attention. I didn't do any of the heavy lifting now. I just made the bastards regret they were born.

"Like you don't train anyway."

"Declan won't like this," I argued.

"Stop worrying about that. Kid's already going to have to explain the shiners."

"Isn't that school of yours like sixty grand a term?" I asked. "Why the hell didn't they call your ma in for fighting?"

"Because the—" Shay clenched his jaw, his hands turning white from the pressure he put on his knuckles.

"You can swear here, Shay. We're the cool uncles. Your mom and dad have to turn you into a semi-decent human being. We're not obliged to do the same."

Making a mental note that, when I did have kids, not to leave them alone with Conor—ever—I rolled my eyes at him. "Neither are we *obliged* to turn him into a psycho." I squeezed Shay's shoulder. "Tell me what happened. With swear words or not."

"The bastards attacked me during Phys Ed. It looked like it was just a part of training."

My brow puckered. "They should still have told your parents."

"Maybe they have." Shay shrugged. "Mom never said anything when I texted her about Uncle Conor. Anyway, she's used to me coming back home a little bruised up."

Conor straightened up at that. "You were bullied in your old school?"

"No. From training. I fight hard on the field." He winced. "I don't know why. I guess I just get angry sometimes."

"Because you're an O'Donnelly," I drawled. "That's all we bastards know how to do—fight hard or fuck off home." With a final squeeze to his shoulder, I pulled back. "I ain't doing shit without Declan's approval. Conor, you can be the cool uncle, or you can be the castrated one when he finds out you're teaching Shay to fight."

Conor grimaced, sending Shay an apologetic glance before mournfully telling him, "I do like my dick where it is."

My nephew heaved a sigh. "Dad might want to stop me."

"Why would he want that? We all grew up the same way—using our fists." I scraped a hand over my jaw. "What started the fight? And don't BS me, there's always a trigger."

He ducked his head. "They were talking smack about the family."

Conor and I shared a look. "People always talk smack about the family," I informed him softly. "You'll just have to get used to that."

"Until you're old enough to beat the fuck out of anyone who dares without the threat of being grounded," Conor chimed in.

"I wasn't having them saying that my mom was an Irish mob slut," he retorted heatedly. "Those pricks are barracudas. When they scent blood, that's it, they're in for the kill. I had to nip it in the bud."

"I thought you were all excited about the place?" I questioned, taking a seat on Conor's coffee table. "Thought you were all about making connections so you can be President one day. You can't do that if you beat up every fucker who talks shit about us. They're all up each other's asses for a reason."

"He has a point, Shay," Conor confirmed. "We gotta think of the White House."

My lips twitched at Conor—we all humored Shay, knowing the kid didn't have a snowball in hell's chance of becoming President with his ties to the Irish Mob, but Conor? Nope. He wasn't about to let our nephew think he couldn't have everything his heart desired.

Conor rubbed his chin as Shay shot us both a defeated look. "We could drain their trust funds."

Shay's eyes widened. "You can do that?"

"Con," I muttered, a warning note in my voice.

"It'd only be for a little while," was his defensive reply. "I wouldn't spend any of it. It's not technically stealing if you give it back."

The mental note to never let my kids anywhere near cool uncle Con became a permanent fixture in my memory banks...

And that was how I spent the afternoon of my wedding day, plotting how to 'redistribute' the trust funds of the bastards who'd been talking smack about our family.

It was about seven when I finally got Shay to come back home with me. It was evident he wasn't looking forward to telling Aela that he'd gotten into a fight, but I figured Declan would come to his defense. I'd already shot him off a couple of messages, explaining the status quo, and while he wasn't happy about encouraging his kid to engage in illegal online activity, he hadn't said no.

In Manhattan, the O'Donnellys were both revered and feared. It was a strange mixture, really. A delicate balance. Socialites wanted to wed us for our cash and our power, but their fathers were more aware of who and what we were. What we did.

That didn't mean they weren't in business with us, because that would be bullshit.

They were.

We were all up to our necks in it; we just weren't hypocrites is all and married among our own.

"It'll be all right, kid," I told Shay after we pulled up outside his building.

"Will it?" He shot me a look as he reached for the door handle. "If they talk smack about Mom again, I won't—"

I reached over to clap him on the back. "Every son should defend his ma. That's right. The natural order of things."

He frowned. "Is it? One second they were dissing her, the next they were calling me a momma's boy."

"Nothing wrong with that either," I said gruffly. "To them, being a momma's boy means that a kid actually gets attention from their mother. They ain't being shoved off to a nanny, and only get a kiss and a gift at Christmas before their cun—" I cleared my throat. "Before their egg donors tail off to Aspen for the winter." I winked at him. "The next time they call you that, hit 'em where it hurts."

"Where's that?"

My dash lit up with a call, and though it was Da and you never ignored one of his calls without knowing you were about to get a kick to the head, this was too important.

"Just tell them that their egg donors don't give enough of a fuck about them to know more about them than their names. Tell them that if anyone's gonna need decades of therapy, it ain't you." Then, realizing what I'd said, I winced. "Sorry, Shay. I didn't mean—"

Kid already *was* in therapy, thanks to seeing a woman being murdered. We'd only just learned who that was—the sister of the ex-VP of the Satan's Sinners' MC West Orange Chapter.

"I know what you meant. But that's different. I'm not fucked up because of what the family does or how my mom treated me. She's the best mom. Everything she did, she did it with me in mind. She loves me. That's a good thing, not a bad thing like they try to make out." He tipped his chin up. "Thanks, Uncle Bren. I really appreciate the way you dropped everything for me tonight."

"It's what family does, kid. And you wanna remember that the next time they talk smack. They're lonely little bastards. They don't mean dick to their people."

His smile was tight. "So I should pity them?"

I winked at him. "Nah." I answered the call because I knew Da would give me shit otherwise, but before he could gripe at me, I greeted, "Da, Shay's in the car with me."

"My boy Shay!" Da declared, like he hadn't seen him last Sunday. "How's my little man?"

We'd all started calling him 'little' and so far, he hadn't given us crap over it.

"I'm great thanks, Granddad."

I nudged him in the side. "He'll be proud of you. You should tell him. Just don't let your ma know he was happy, yeah?" That'd only cause shit down the line.

"Tell me what?"

"I got into a fight today, Granddad."

Da was silent a second, then his smugness shone through as he said,

"Apple doesn't fall far from the tree. Come on, Seamus. Give me the details."

I shot Shay an encouraging grin, but saw he didn't need to be encouraged. He knew his grandfather wasn't about to give him any crap, was, in fact, going to applaud him for his actions.

"They were calling Mom names, saying things about us, how we were mobsters."

"And did you tell them they were right and that they should be careful because your grandda has an itchy trigger finger?" was my father's insane retort.

Shay choked a little. "No, I just punched them."

"Well, tell them that next time. Any little bastard who comes at my grandson comes at us all."

I elbowed him again. "See? Told ya."

"What's the damage?"

"Two shiners," I informed him. "They'd make you proud."

"Will they still be there on Sunday, Bren?"

"Should be."

"Mom will go crazy," he groaned.

"Probably, that's what good mothers do. But when you go to bed tonight, Aela, like the good Irish girl she is, will turn to Declan and say, 'The boy did good.'"

I wasn't sure how true that was, but it had Shay straightening his shoulders for the first time, which was interesting because I didn't think Shay actually liked Da.

Aidan Sr. wasn't exactly woke, and Shay most definitely *was*.

I guessed that was just positive proof as to how acceptance mattered.

"What's the damage to the bastards?"

"A couple of black eyes. But there were three of them and only one of me."

Silence fell at that, and then Da growled, "Bren, you're dealing with it?"

"Conor and me are. Yeah." Only knowing they'd ganged up on him had made me agree to the insanity of reappropriating three little shits' trust funds.

He grunted his approval. "Shay, I'm telling you—you did good."

"Thanks, Grandda," he said gruffly, and I knew I wouldn't be the only one to take note of him dropping the 'd' on Da's title.

I smiled at Shay and told him, "Go on, kid. Get. Face the music, give her the apologies, take whatever punishment she gives you on the chin, but know we're all proud as fuck of you."

His smile was sheepish, but he nodded. "Night, Uncle Bren, Grandda."

"Night, kid."

"Night, Seamus."

As the door closed behind him, and I watched him head into the foyer of Dec's building, Da said, "Did you hear that, Bren? He called me Grandda."

"I heard, Da. I heard. Little man's not used to getting into fights. He's a bit shaken."

"He's a good boy," Da agreed. "Not ideal really."

I snorted. "It *is* ideal. Remember, he wants to get into politics." Even though I knew it was a pipe dream, I wasn't about to encourage Da to start tainting Seamus with mob bullshit.

"True." He hummed under his breath. "That might come in useful. A few legitimate O'Donnellys along the way. I know *your* grandda would have fucking loved to have one of his descendants in the White House."

I rolled my eyes but said, "Yeah, he sure would."

My grandfather wasn't as insane as Da, but he still was a bit mentally unstable. Not that I could judge. You had to be in this line of work.

The difference between me and my father, though, was enjoyment. To me, it was a job. All the shit I did, all the moves I made, all the blood I spilled, it wasn't for pleasure. Da liked it. The entirety of NY-fucking-C knew that.

I scrubbed a hand over my chin as I watched Shay from the side of the road, not pulling away until he got into the elevator and was whirled up to Declan's high rise.

As I drove into the heavy traffic, I asked, "What's wrong, Da? Did you need something?"

"Can't a man just call to shoot the shit with his son?"

Some men might, but not this one.

Wryly, I said, "It's unlikely."

Da huffed. "Well, what's with these fucking snakes you've sent my way?"

"I didn't send the snakes to you. Just the task of finding them. You know I ain't got contacts in the right departments. Plus, I got enough to handle thanks to those fucking Sparrows."

That had Da falling silent. "You figured something out?"

"A couple of things." I cleared my throat and decided to dodge a bullet. "You and Ma got plans for tomorrow?"

"No. Not as far as I'm aware, anyway."

"Can I come around for dinner?"

"You don't have to ask."

My lips twisted. "Cheers, Da."

"No need to thank me, son." He hummed. "This for business?"

"No. Everything's under control for the moment. I have news though."

"Spill."

I explained about Coullson and how we'd found him in a compromising position, and I could just imagine his eyes sparkling as he roared with laughter.

"That fucking prick. He was the one who tried to block us buying the Andersen lot, wasn't he?"

"Yeah. That was him. Coullson got in with donations from the Hannegan Corp. He's their bitch."

"Not anymore," Da said gleefully. "Well fucking done, Bren. What's the game plan?"

"You still got that invitation to the Davison's Hudson River Clean-Up Gala?"

"Yeah. Want it?"

"The bastard knows we have him on a string, but I think we need to show him how much we can make him dance."

Da hooted. "You go for it, kiddo. It's next Friday."

"Thought so." As I headed over to Linden Blvd, making my way to my pit, AKA The Hole, I told him, "I'd really appreciate it if you could deal with the snakes, Da. Got a lot on my plate at the minute. Those fuckers raided another of Hummel's jewelry stores the other night, and I need to get cracking with figuring out who they are."

"Understood, son. He pays a lot in protection money so you're right, he's the priority. I'll get my people in Customs to deal with the snakes and help get them where they need to be. Consider it done."

I arched a brow. "You're in a good mood today." What I meant was an 'amenable' mood, but I didn't say that. I didn't feel like turning his proverbial smile upside down.

He'd been on a rampage ever since we'd found out we had a lot of rats in our midst. The Sparrows had infiltrated the Points in more ways than we'd have liked. Sniffing them all out was at the top of Da and Aidan Jr.'s agendas.

I knew Da was dedicating himself to the job with the zeal of a missionary in uncharted waters. Whether or not Aidan was pulling his weight was another matter entirely.

"Got a reason to be in a good mood," he murmured, "my boy just called me Grandda, you just told me we have the mayor in our pocket, and I trapped some rats today."

Wincing, I asked, "How many?"

"Six."

"Jesus. So many?"

Da hummed. "I'd be pissed if I hadn't had fun."

"Who?"

"They were on Junior and Finn's crews."

"Figures. Money and the direct line to you... the Sparrows aren't messing around."

"No, but we knew that already. If they wanted us in jail, we'd already be there. So they want something else."

"What do you think that is?"

"My guess would be information. Or, they might want to make the same deal with us as they did with those Italian cunts."

"Would you go for it?"

Da snorted. "Brennan, when have I ever been anyone's bitch?"

"Well, when you put it like that..."

"That's exactly how I'm putting it. I ain't about to be fucked in the ass by these bastards. If anyone's doing the fucking, it's me. We're going to get them right where we want them, turn them on their heads, and bury them upright. Fuckers think they can mess with us? They can think again."

For a second, I didn't reply, just let the silence hover, before I said, "Might have some leads on a couple more rats."

"Damn. I keep hoping that's the last of them, and we flush out some more." He sighed. "How did you hear about these?"

"Caroline Dunbar."

He grunted. "At least she's keeping to her end of the deal."

I snorted. "What? The 'tell us everything or you die' deal?"

"Yeah," was his gruff reply, but he laughed a little. "That sounds about right. Good thing too. Don't mind getting into shit, but prefer to leave the federales alone if I can. When they turn up dead, it always causes such a fucking stink."

"What happens when a bunch of pigs get together to mourn another pig's death, I guess."

"True, true." He sighed again. "You got it under control or need some input?"

"I can manage. If I can't, I'll bring Declan and Eoghan into it."

"Okay." Da hummed. "I understand *why* they turned. What concerns me is preventing it in the days ahead."

Reaching into the cup holder where I had a pack of money mints, I popped a couple in my mouth, unable to believe I was about to make the suggestion at the forefront of my mind: "How about a *céilidh*? That's a good excuse for all the ranks to mingle. Shore up ties while maybe seeing if anyone is on edge? Acting suspiciously, you know?"

The *céilidh* was a traditional Gaelic dance. I hated the fucking things. The music, with all the bodhráns and the fiddles, was a migraine waiting to happen. I chomped down on the mints at the prospect.

"Thanksgiving *is* approaching," he mused, his voice introspective. "Might be a good idea."

"I have them sometimes," I said wryly, popping a couple more mints into my mouth. "Anyway, I'll see you tomorrow night, Da."

"That you will, Bren. You're a good boy, son. Thank you for all you're doing."

Though I was about to choke on his gratitude, because he'd never thanked me once for the shit I did in his name, I didn't have the chance to reply before he cut off.

Peering up at the sky then glancing down at the ground, I saw that pigs weren't flying and hell hadn't frozen over, which meant Da had thanked me for something without Armageddon breathing down his neck.

"Jesus Christ," I muttered, and for the first time in my life, I said the Lord's Prayer without being instructed to by Father fucking Doyle.

If Da was thanking *me*... of all people, well, I didn't know what to think.

INESSA HAS TO FORGIVE ME FIRST.

TWENTY-TWO
CAMILLE

MY APPOINTMENT with the nail tech had been awkward to say the least. She'd kept peering at my palms, and I'd remembered why I'd stopped going to a nail salon before—questions. Even if they weren't voiced, they were there. In someone's mind.

With Inessa lurking on the opposite bench, the last thing I wanted was for her to see my hands so I'd been glad for the simple manicure, and had gone for a full out pedi instead.

Inessa elected to have both, but we'd still managed to chat over the treatment, and while it wasn't, and probably never would be, as comfortable as it had been in the past, that wasn't to say that we couldn't start afresh and make something better.

I hoped so.

I hoped that my adolescent fears wouldn't wreck ties that should be concrete.

If that meant making an effort, I would.

So when Inessa asked me, shyly, "Would you come with me to church on Saturday? For Vespers?"

What was I supposed to say?

Tell her that I'd prefer to stick pins down my nails than listen to a bunch of pious pricks spout nonsense at me?

That would go down like a lead balloon.

"Of course. That would be great. Does Victoria go?"

"She will if I tell her to," Inessa said with a sniff, then, her lips curved. "Just wait for Sunday."

"Why? What happens then?"

"They're religious. The whole family. We have to go to church and everything. I only go to Vespers every month or so. For Mama, mostly. But with Aidan Sr., there's trouble if you don't go every week, and the men *have* to go to confession."

For a second, I wanted to gag.

Church—*twice*? In the same week? Hell, in the same year was two times too many, never mind within the latter half of this already shitty week.

Maybe I had something to confess, but I wasn't religious. Had stopped believing in that stuff when I found Mama bleeding out, covered in Italian cum...

My jaw clenched at the thought, but I just said, "That's really going to be fun." Poor Brennan... I couldn't imagine him on his knees in a confessional. It just didn't fit his personality.

"Yeah, Father Doyle is a real prick. He makes the new priest at the Orthodox Church look liberal."

Rolling my eyes, I told her, "Can't wait."

She grinned at me. "I'll bet."

Which keyed me into the fact she knew I'd prefer to overdose on Swedish Fish rather than go to church but was making me go anyway...

Why did I want to be friends with her again?

Still, aside from the prospect of that particular torture, it had been quite nice to clear the air.

She knew I'd had something to do with Father's death, even if she didn't know what, but rather than cast stones at me, we both concurred we were going to have a better life without him.

Which was, all told, pretty horrendous. Talk about a testament to how shitty a parent he'd been.

After we parted ways, with a promise to meet tomorrow for the early service, I headed out and found Bagpipes moving around the vehicle so he could climb into the passenger seat.

Thankful he'd remembered, I rushed over to him because traffic was on the rise, jumped behind the wheel, then, when there was an opening, pulled out onto the road.

"Hey," I greeted him as I settled in, unable to deny that this SUV was so much more comfortable than my own. I rocked back into the plush seat, placed one arm on the rest, and let the car drive me.

He grunted at me in reply—charming. "Go straight ahead. I'll tell you when to turn off."

"Okay." I cleared my throat. "You were fast. Thanks for picking me up so quickly."

"Was twiddling my thumbs when you texted me."

I shot him a quick look at the unusual turn of phrase. "Are you originally from New York?"

"Nah. Irish. Moved over when I was eight."

"Why?"

"Why not? People immigrate, don't they?"

"They do, I was just curious is all," I told him, unruffled as I started back toward Hell's Kitchen.

In the distance, the majestic lines of the Empire State Building made an appearance, twisting in and out of sight like a mirage as massive skyscrapers stole it from view. All around me, the buildings loomed, but I liked it. I'd missed the city. New Jersey had granted me shelter, sure; that didn't make it home.

Baggy broke into my musings by grousing, "Curiosity is dangerous. You know that as well as I do."

"I do, but we're going to spend a lot of time together, aren't we? You should take it as a compliment. I never wanted to know anything about my Russian guards."

"Why not?"

"Because I knew they'd die soon." I shrugged. "My father wasn't as cautious with his men as the Irish."

"Ain't that the feckin' truth." He grunted. "Shit general was your father. Too short-sighted."

"You won't hear me arguing. I know nothing about how he handled business, just know there were a lot of miserable *boyeviks*."

"You told Brennan that?"

"No. Haven't had the chance." I shrugged.

"He'll be interested to hear morale is low."

"Morale was always low, but Father ruled with an iron fist."

"Aidan O'Donnelly Sr. does too," he pointed out.

"Maybe, but everyone knows the Irish care for a man's family. In the Bratva world, it's different."

"For someone who knows nothing about business, you know more than I do."

His grousing had me scowling at him. "This isn't business. This is people. That's different."

"How is it?"

"Because *boyeviks* aren't just soldiers, they're men too. The Bratva likes to tear families apart, make people rely on the Brotherhood for everything. They gain strength that way. The Irish do the opposite. I think that makes them stronger, no matter what Moscow believes."

"Bet the Bratva wouldn't agree."

"Well, they wouldn't, of course, because it's just how it's done. Doesn't mean it's right though. Doesn't mean it creates loyalty."

"Agreed." He sighed, conceding, "We immigrated because my da got into trouble with the *Garda*—the Irish cops. Aidan Sr. brought us here to save his bollocks from jail."

"Bollocks?" I asked, turning to him with a frown.

"Balls." He grunted.

"Thanks for telling me."

"You're right. We're going to be stuck together, might as well get to know you. Although Kerry-Louise will probably get jealous and make my life a living hell when she claps eyes on you."

"She's your—" A quick glance at his ring finger confirmed my belief. "Wife?"

He hummed. "Capable of making a man more miserable than a TSA agent with a pair of gloves and a bottle of lube."

I blinked. "Huh?"

"Never mind." He pointed at the road ahead. "Take the next left."

I did as he asked, following his instructions until we got back to Brennan's building.

My new home.

Bagpipes instructed me that the garage would open its doors when it scanned the plates, and as we maneuvered through the levels, finding the spot Brennan had parked in last night, he said, "Lyanov sent some of your stuff over."

"He did?" I asked, surprised that Maxim had been so thoughtful.

"Yeah. Your sister's things to Inessa's place too. Forrest delivered both while you were busy."

"Thank him for me?"

Bagpipes shrugged. "Will do." He pointed to the elevator. "Conor, Brennan's brother, will set you up with security clearance once the family knows about you and Bren. As it stands, I'll come up with you because I have a pass."

"Thanks, Bagpipes."

"Just doing my job."

We were quiet on the way up to the apartment, and even though I asked if he wanted a coffee or something before he left, he refused, saying there was still work to be done before the night was over. Considering it was past seven, our version of 'night' was evidently different. Still, I didn't expect to see Brennan for a good couple of hours so I decided to check out the apartment.

My new gilded cage.

I knew the living room already. With its open plan layout, it was a comfortable space and that was where Forrest had dumped a lot of black bags—my stuff. All jumbled together like it was trash.

To Maxim or whichever *boyevik* he'd had gather my things, it probably was.

Still, I was grateful that I wouldn't have to wear the same dress tomorrow for church, so that was something.

Before I bothered sorting everything out, I decided that I preferred to explore the place without Brennan around. I wasn't at ease with him—only natural as I didn't know him, even if relying on him for my security and safety meant a part of me *had* to be at ease with him—so it would be more comfortable to discover my new home alone.

I liked the open plan kitchen/living area. It was a space I would spend a lot of time in. With the kitchen separated by the dining table, there were a few squashy armchairs that were centered around the windows. Not only so you could look at the view, but also because there was a TV on a bracket on the wall between them.

That you could watch Netflix while checking out the grandness of the city skyline, be it night or day, was definitely a luxury.

It was all very simple in design, block colors, no patterns, but everything was rich—rubies and emeralds instead of standard reds and green. It made up for the plainness of everything, and created a warmth that was pleasant considering the season.

Deciding to explore the rest of the place, I took off empty-handed. Finding four bedrooms on this level, two of them containing nothing more than minimum furniture, a third with gym equipment, it was the fourth, and what it contained, that had me backing away.

Most Bratva leaders were like Brennan. Housing basic medical equipment for any soldier who needed it. I.e. who'd been shot on the streets and couldn't go to a hospital.

Not wanting to see that, and hoping it wasn't going to happen often —having men traipsing in and out of my home who were bleeding everywhere—the only other room I evaded was the one I'd slept in last night. Obeying Brennan might annoy another woman, but I was used to being given strictures I had to comply with. It didn't bother me, and if it kept him from getting mad at me, why wouldn't I do as he asked?

A no brainer in my opinion.

Not only that, but I wouldn't put it past him to have security feeds in here. The last thing I needed was him being able to watch me sneak around the place.

What did come as a surprise were two doors at the end of the corridor.

One led to a massive terrace with a hot tub, some sleek loungers, a grill, and a view that was enough to give me vertigo. The railings were glass, and over six feet high, but every screw and bolt could work its way loose over time. I didn't go anywhere near the edge, even though I loved the seating area which made me feel like I was on top of the world, while safe in my little bubble.

There was a dining area and a kind of ultra-sized hammock that was more of a swinging, king-sized bed than anything else. I knew, come summer, I'd be glued to it, and if I could get some of those outdoor patio heaters and a couple of heavy duty blankets, I'd be spending a lot of time out here now.

At home, even in the yard, I'd felt unsafe. A theory that was proven to be a fact when my father had his kneecaps shot out by a sniper. I had a feeling the glass around the perimeter was bulletproof, so without a doubt, I knew I was protected up here.

After I explored the terrace, I found my way back to that other door which revealed a set of stairs that led to another level below. I came across two more living rooms, one with a massive screen and which was evidently a home theater, and another that was for the 'boys.' It had a full-sized snooker table—not pool, it was too big, too wide—a poker table surrounded by comfortable leather armchairs, and various other games that made me realize Brennan had to be a big kid. Why else would he have old school arcade games like *Pac-Man* in here if he wasn't?

There were two more guest bedrooms, and a final door that was locked. I'd bet my left boob that was his office, but I wasn't offended. My father had always locked his office door too, and Brennan had no reason to trust me.

Not yet.

I'd work on that.

If Inessa could fall for Eoghan, and vice versa, there was no reason deeper feelings couldn't flourish between Brennan and me. I still had no desire for him to love me, but trust was more important than love. At least, it was to me.

I'd loved Nyx. What did that get me? Nothing. I'd felt like a stranger in the home I'd made in the compound, to the point where turning to my dick of a father felt like my only option.

No, I wanted nothing to do with love.

Trust was what I was aiming for.

Retreating to the upper floor, appreciating how much space there was here, and knowing that I could take over one of the bedrooms and make it into something for myself, some personal space that could be a crafting room if I wanted it to be, I felt a little brighter when I returned to the living area and started to sort through my things.

I had a mixture of designer clothes that Father had bought for me, stuff that was from my childhood, and then the gear I'd brought back from West Orange. Most of that was Target stuff to be honest, nothing as fancy as the Gucci dresses, the LV purses, and Prada shoes he'd used to decorate his sacrificial lamb.

I'd have tossed them out if I didn't need them. I didn't have any money of my own, not unless Father had left a will for us, which I doubted. Most of his ill-gotten gains would probably sink into one of the Brotherhood's fronts. God only knew who he'd deigned to assign Victoria's guardianship to—a matter I'd have to ask Brennan to look into. Like he didn't have enough on his plate.

My lack of funds, however, meant I'd be beholden to Brennan for cash, so wasting good clothes wasn't sensible. Didn't mean I had to like it, though, did it?

He'd told me not to go into the bedroom, but would he be okay with my storing my things in his closet?

And what of my toiletries? Would he be annoyed if I put them in his bathroom?

It was when I found my self-harm kit that I knew I'd take over another bedroom tonight without asking. If Brennan saw it, he'd throw it out, and even though its contents were destructive... I couldn't bear to part with it.

Not yet.

Maybe not ever.

Brennan couldn't remove every knife in the house, could he? It wasn't like tossing this out would do much, but I had a lot of memories in the box that was decorated with stickers. Glittery ones, Vans ones, some Roxy Girl ones... my teenage years were in them, as well as the doodles I'd drawn on there.

What I didn't find in the bags was probably the one thing I needed the most: Mama's journals.

Had Maxim mistaken them for regular books? I supposed it was easily done. None of my fiction or crafting books were here, either. He'd obviously emptied my drawers and wardrobe, but not cleared my bookshelves.

I tried not to get upset about the diaries but it definitely dampened my mood.

It was hard to move past the loss of them when those were the only things that you had of your mother which reflected her as a woman, as a person.

All of the other 'stuff,' I dumped back into the black bags so I could heft them downstairs. Toiletries, a box with my crafts in, yarn, my jewelry box, they went in there. I laid a pile of dresses over my other arm and carried them to the lower level.

Deciding I'd take the guest room at the head of the hall, the opposite end of Brennan's office so he wouldn't think I was spying on him, I started to unpack my stuff. It took about four more trips before I brought everything down, and when I looked around, I made a list of what I'd like Bagpipes to help me do in the morning.

Moving the bed and nightstands into storage was top of the agenda, and I'd make do with working at the dinner table until I built up the courage to ask Brennan for a desk and other pieces of furniture that would make this room mine.

For now, with its plain white walls, and rose pink carpet—proof that Brennan had hired a decorator, because I couldn't imagine him choosing pink *anything*—it would do. I could deal with a Barbie carpet for the moment.

Maxim wasn't exactly a considerate man so, knowing that Brennan was the only reason I had any of my possessions back, I used the burner cell Baggy had given me, one that had two numbers programmed into the contacts—his and Brennan's—to send my husband a text message.

Me: *My things are here. Thank you for arranging that.*

Brennan: *As much as I like your ass, it's not practical to keep you naked all the time.*

He liked my ass?

God, I was too pathetic to live when that simple statement made my heart skip a beat.

I knew I had image issues, but this pretty much confirmed it.

Me: *Well, thanks.*

Brennan: *You're welcome. Is everything there?*

Me: *No books, but everything else, yes.*

He was quiet a few minutes, so I started to make my way to the upper level.

Then: **Brennan:** *What about your ma's journals? You were going to tell me what she said about me.*

I bit my lip. **Me:** *Just that she loved you.*

When he didn't reply again, and I was treated to radio silence, I understood that he didn't want Mama's love. Considering how she'd adored him, that hurt me, but it also filled me with relief, which just made me feel guilty. It meant I wasn't diving into my mother's place, and afforded me the chance to be me and not be compared to her all the time.

Because I had no idea when he'd be back, and I had no desire to text him and ask him, I retreated to the kitchen, made myself another sandwich from fixins in the fridge, then when I saw it was going on twelve, I went for a shower, undressed, tugged on one of his shirts from his closet, and got into bed.

As I stared up at the ceiling, at the end of one long and very bizarre day, covered in his shirt when I'd prefer to be covered in him, the desire to touch myself was strong.

An act of rebellion? My way of snubbing him like he was snubbing me on our wedding night?

I wasn't sure.

I'd purposely not brought any panties or sleepwear up from downstairs before my shower, so I was naked apart from the silk of his shirt.

Perhaps it was because I was in *his* bed, in *his* bedroom, but it made me hyper aware in a way I'd never been before.

Four hours ago, he'd teased me in the shower.

Four hours ago, he'd given me a list of orders he expected me to obey...

The desire to be a brat to spite him was at the forefront of my mind, but it was overtaken by a simple thought.

Downstairs, I'd thought about how I wanted him to trust me.

That had to begin somewhere, didn't it?

Masturbating when he expressly asked me not to, even if he'd never really know the truth, wasn't the way to start things as I meant to go on.

So even though I was pretty sure I was more aware of my clit than I was of the chill in the air outside the covers, I rolled onto my side, curved into a fetal ball, and told myself to get some sleep.

TWENTY-THREE
BRENNAN

WITH A YAWN, I strode into the back office at the warehouse in The Hole, and stared at the three guys who were strung up on hooks.

It was too early for this shit, but I couldn't fault my crew. They'd found the fuckers, and I had to make them regret the day they were born. I just wished they'd found them a couple hours later, when I'd had a chance to get some more sleep.

I'd gotten in late last night and had found my place as quiet as a graveyard. So quiet, in fact, that I wasn't even sure if I was alone or not.

I was used to the silence—liked it, in fact. But I'd expected there to be a TV on, or some signs of life now that I was sharing my space.

When I'd found her in my bedroom, my wife, by Christ, I'd been satisfied. When I'd climbed into bed, her clean scent perfuming the covers, and my shirt the only thing between us, I'd been hard pressed not to drag her into me, to wake her up and to start something. The only reason I didn't was because Bagpipes and Forrest had kept me in the loop.

With the living room empty, I knew she'd unpacked all her things, and I also knew that she'd done as I asked—gone to the doctor's office, had something to eat, and had a manicure at the nail salon. Pleased she'd obeyed, relief settled inside me. Letting her sleep was a kindness that both of us would reap, and when I'd awoken to the buzzing of my cellphone, taking note of the fact she was still asleep, I knew I'd been right to let her rest.

After showering, shaving, and dressing, she'd remained sleeping, and I knew when someone was playing pretend. The dark shadows under her eyes said it all, as did her thin frame, and that general air she had around her—like she was too exhausted to live.

My brain couldn't seem to process that she was a stranger who was now married to me, whereas my body found it too easy to accept that she was mine.

All mine.

Which made it even more annoying that I had to wake up and head on out before I could do anything about that.

I wanted to ask her if she touched herself before she fell asleep.

Wanted to know if she'd been tempted.

If that dry little pussy of hers had been hungry for her fingers or my dick.

Those thoughts did exactly what I needed them to do—switched my brain into 'on' mode, because I wanted to get back to my apartment as soon as possible so I could fuck my wife.

If that made me a little more aggressive, then that would ramp things up nicely.

The back office was loaded up with old hooks we'd found in an abattoir in Tribeca that we'd bought to flip. Now, in its place, was a trendy apartment complex where each unit sold for over four million dollars a piece, making my perennially displeased father a very rich man. Especially as that was just one of the buildings on his portfolio.

Swinging from those hooks were three shivering whelps. They'd been stripped down to their boxers because Da might be willing to cut off another dude's dick, but I wasn't that cruel, and one of the men had doused them in water. It was cold back here anyway, but I knew they'd also turned on the AC because I felt the chill in the air too.

Grateful for my woolen overcoat, I took the three bastards in.

One was the brains, and probably the in, one was the heavy, and one was the driver. At least, that was how things tended to work in my experience.

The driver and heavy were of no importance to me, but the brains—he'd be the one who'd have come up with the job, and he'd be the one with the contacts. I needed the fence they were using to sell their stolen goods so I could go and torture his purchases out of them.

The heavy was easy to pick out. Chrissakes, the bastard's neck was thicker than my thigh. But for all his biceps were as thick as tree branches, it hadn't stopped my guys from being able to incapacitate the bastard. Which meant I had to pick between the two scrawny cunts, one of whom was already sniveling for his ma.

Picking up the cattle prod, I set it to stun, prompting their attention to shift to me as I moved deeper into the room.

"I have better things to be doing today than shocking you motherfuckers. Tell me who's fencing your haul and I'll only beat the shit out of you."

The guy who wasn't sniveling growled, "Like you're going to let us walk out of here alive. Why the fuck should we tell you anything?"

I smiled at him. "Ever thought about how you were going to die? Would you like it to be quick? A knife to the throat? Or a cattle prod shoved up your ass until you fry from the inside out?"

He gulped. "That's impossible."

"You do anything long enough and it'll work out just fine. You might want to be a human fry but trust me, I have no desire for this place to stink of bacon. You can choose how you want to die. Cleanly." I turned on the cattle prod, and the electric snapped into the air, making the three of them jump like I'd already hit them with its charge. "Or gnarly."

The heavy raised his head to stare at me. "I don't know shit, man. I was just paid to make sure we didn't get roughed up during a gig."

"Shut up," the ballsy guy threatened. "Keep your fucking mouth closed. They ain't got shit on us."

"Ain't got shit on you?" I laughed. "You think my guys are in the habit of waking me up at four in the fucking morning for shits and giggles? You think I'd be here if I didn't know for certain you were the fuckers who took down three jewelry stores under our protection?"

"Some fucking protection," he snarled.

By way of reply, I raised the cattle prod, pressed it to his armpit and hit it.

When the fucker screamed, juddering in place like he was on the electric chair, I switched it off again. Direct contact to the chest would only trigger a cardiac arrest, and I didn't want him dead.

Not yet anyway.

The shock had the bastard slumping, his body turning lax as he not only pissed himself, but hung like a dead weight from the hook. Only by the faintest movements on his chest did I know he was alive, and so did the others.

I turned to look at them. "That was on a low setting."

The heavy gulped. "I-I don't know anything, man. I swear."

"What about you?" I asked softly, snapping the button on and off again, just long enough for the sizzle to whip along the air waves.

"I-I don't know who the fence is, but I know his number is on Justin's burner."

I twisted around and found Tink leaning against the back wall, watching me work. "You find a burner on Justin?"

He nodded. "Password protected."

The scrawny sniveler whispered, "The pin's his birthday."

I rolled my eyes—maybe the guy wasn't as smart as I thought. Although he'd managed to breach three Thomson 0235 alarms so he wasn't completely a fry short of a Happy Meal.

"You know what that is?" I asked, and when the heavy fed me the digits, I heard Tink moving around behind me, and knew he was getting the burner out of the pile of clothes for me.

"Here." He passed me the phone, I input the code, and when it worked, I scrolled through the contacts.

Finding thirty names, none of them suspicious or titled, 'The Fence,' because that'd be too fucking easy, I shoved the phone back at Tink, grunting, "Recognize anyone on there?"

"I'll check it out."

I nodded as he backed off, leaving me with the three Stooges.

Sometimes, getting information out of people was easy. Then, others, you had to set them up with a trans hooker and catch them *in flagrante delicto*. One thing I could say about my job—it was varied and rarely dull.

"You're lucky you're dealing with me today," I told the two conscious guys. "If it was my da, he'd be getting off on causing you pain. As it stands, I'm a man of my word. Don't fuck me around, and you won't suffer before you die."

The sniveler started wailing. "W-We didn't mean to piss off the

Points. We swear we didn't. We didn't even fucking know, man. Why would we? Everyone knows Aidan Sr.'s fucking insane—"

"Then why did you? No one forced you to raid one of our storefronts."

"Justin said—"

When the sniveling fucker's voice waned, I arched a brow at him. "Treat me like your confessor, kid. It's one way not to die in agony."

"H-He had inside knowledge."

Now, *that* was interesting. I narrowed my eyes at him. "From the jewelry stores?"

"N-No. From the Five Points. Someone told him that the store owners weren't under your protection anymore."

Carefully, I placed the cattle prod on the same table I'd picked it up from, and folded my arms against my chest. After my conversation with Da, and knowing we had more fucking rats than our sinking ship could hold, it didn't take a genius to work out what had happened.

"Who'd do an insane thing like that?" I rasped. "And I need a name, kid."

The heavy and the sniveler shared a wary look, and surprisingly, it was the heavy who whispered, "Guy called Callum O'Reilly. He's a drinking buddy of Justin's."

Reaching up, I rubbed my chin as I contemplated that particular news, trying not to show that this pair of bastards had just speared me in the belly with a verbal knife.

Da was *not* going to be pleased.

Neither was Mark O'Reilly—one of Da's best friends.

Bowing my head to hide my expression, I felt the betrayal whip through me. I'd only just seen Callum at Conor's last night. Which had me second guessing if I'd missed the word 'nark' carved into his forehead.

I'd known him since I was a fucking kid... I had to give the Sparrows some credit, though. They'd done their jobs. They'd done it too goddamn well.

Callum wasn't just on one of Da's son's crews, he was like family to us.

Conor had gone to school with the bastard, they'd spent holidays at our home, and Ma and Callum's ma were friends. From way back.

Any traitor hurt. That was the nature of the Five Points. We weren't an army, even if we were set up like one. We had ties that bound us together, making the fuckfest of what we had to do on a daily basis that much more bearable because we had each other's backs.

Even the new recruits that we'd been integrating into the ranks were personally known to my Da. Most of us brothers too. Only people who had a link to the Motherland were welcome among us, because being Irish bound us together, but the family was what made us strive for more.

When a runner died, a penny-ante no one who'd only worked for us for three weeks, no one important in the grand scheme of things—Da paid for their funeral, and every O'Donnelly had to turn up.

This was going to devastate the family in more ways than one.

Thinking about earlier, about him being so fucking psyched about Priestley... Jesus.

None of this was going to be pleasant. None.

The ramifications of what I'd just learned were enough to have me turning my back on the thieves. I was more generous than Da, not as 'Old Testament' in my nature, and because they didn't want a cattle prod up their asses, I got the feeling they weren't going to lie to me about this shit. That made me want to grant them leniency. If they'd been told by a fucking Five Pointer, a high-ranking cunt at that, that those stores weren't under our protection, why wouldn't they believe it? Why wouldn't they take that as Gospel? But their survival depended on my next steps, steps which, unfortunately for them, might require their eternal silence.

This was a conundrum I hadn't wanted the day after my fucking wedding and the morning of the initial meet between my family and my wife.

I'd have liked a distraction, something to take the heat off my getting married without telling any of the clan, but this was disastrous. So goddamn disastrous that, for a couple of minutes, I just stood there, staring at nothing, trying to figure out what to do, to say, and even worse, *how* to do it and say it.

Because I needed out of this fucking place, I stormed off. Tink had yet to make a reappearance, but I caught up with him heading out of his office on my way out.

He grabbed my arm when I didn't stop, demanding, "What's going on?"

I shook my head. "You don't want to fucking know," I rumbled.

"Bullshit. Course I do. Tell me."

I'd have trusted Tink and Forrest and Bagpipes with my life... but if Callum could be gotten to, then so could any fucker. Even the men who were like brothers to me, who I treated like they were kin.

"Don't kill them yet," I rumbled. "Just leave them there. I'll have further instructions before the day's out."

Tink frowned but nodded. "Sure thing, Bren."

Because I didn't know if he deserved my distrust, and because it was more than likely he hadn't betrayed the Pointers, I clapped him on the shoulder and asked, "Did you pick a coin yet?"

He shook his head. "Nah. Not yet."

If money was how the Sparrows got to our men, I'd take that as a sign of innocence. A sign that the man was trustworthy, but the NWS played dirty. They didn't use money, the regular means of placing pressure on people. Nah, they played hardcore and used a man's freedom against him.

I wasn't even certain if I could blame the cunts who'd turned on us for that. When you were faced with life in prison for a crime you truly hadn't committed, why wouldn't you do anything in your power to avoid that fate?

"Well, make your choice. Did you tell the others to pick one as well?"

"Yeah, I think Bagpipes's picked one. That bitch wife of his wants new curtains."

Despite the situation and the yawning pit in my stomach where Callum's betrayal was creating a new ulcer, I laughed. "God help him then. Who the fuck knows what kind of drapes Kerry-Louise will end up picking."

Tink grimaced. "Puke on pink."

We snickered because we both knew she was more than capable of decorating their apartment that way, and he was whipped enough to take it.

"See you later, Tink," I told him mid-snicker.

"Okay, Bren. Just let me know what to do with the fuckers."

"Will do."

Heading out of the warehouse, I stared around my miserable domain.

The view wasn't exactly picturesque but it sure as fuck fitted my mood.

A mood that was only going to get worse once I spoke with Da.

Because I'd never been the kind of guy who borrowed trouble, I opened the door to my Maybach and pulled out the device Conor used to scan for bugs and other monitoring tech. As clever as the Alphabets were getting at hiding that kind of gear, my brother was smarter.

Each of us had a sweeper, and we were supposed to use it every morning before we got into the car. It was a force of habit now, and I'd done it before I went to the warehouse today.

With what I'd just learned, however, I used it again, and was relieved to find that my car hadn't been tampered with while I'd been dealing with the thieves.

The sweep now complete, I jumped into the Maybach, roared out of the yard, and the second I was on the right track for home, I called Da.

It wasn't even seven AM yet, but I knew he kept early hours. I didn't think he had nightmares, but if anyone deserved them, it was my father. I just knew that he didn't sleep a lot, never had done.

"You canceling this early, son? Your ma will be disappointed."

My hands tightened around the wheel before I murmured, "I'm not canceling. I just have news."

"This early?"

"Yeah. I got a call… those jewelry heists, I picked up the bastards who pulled them."

He clapped his hands together. "Well done, Bren. That was fast."

"Yeah. I set Forrest onto it."

"Good kid, Forrest. Smart."

"He is." I stared at the shitty road ahead of me, wondering how I could make this easier to swallow, wondering if that was even fucking possible—

"Everything okay, Bren?"

Well, that was definitely a segue.

Scrubbing a hand over my face, I rasped, "Not really, Da. No."

His jovial tone disappeared, the one I was more accustomed to hearing bled into his voice as he demanded, "What's going on?"

Hands back on the wheel, I tightened them to the point of pain as I did something only a fucking idiot would do—I lied to him.

The insane leader of the Irish Mob loathed liars, stacked them up in a special place in hell where he tormented them worse than the Devil himself could. But, and it was a massive but, I had to investigate this some more. Had to make sure what those dumbfucks back there had said was correct before I condemned Callum to a gruesome death that made perishing by being fried inside out seem like child's play.

"Nothing, Da, nothing. Just been a long fucking night…"

I HAVE TO MAKE SURE VICTORIA
REMEMBERS MAMA BEFORE I DIE.

TWENTY-FOUR
CAMILLE

I WOKE up to find Brennan sitting beside me in bed.

He was fully dressed, wearing his shoes even, and he was staring straight ahead like the back wall held the Mona Lisa.

I peered at it to make sure that *La Gioconda* hadn't made an appearance while I slept, before I murmured, "Is everything okay?"

He didn't stir, didn't even blink, just carried on staring straight ahead. I wasn't sure what was wrong, but it was like someone had died. Those moments of incredulity, when you didn't know what the hell was happening, how the world could carry on turning while you were lost in the labyrinthine maze of grief.

I'd felt that way when Mama died. Like the hands of the clock should stop spinning, like everything should freeze when, in fact, the world seemed to move faster than ever before.

It made the difference between my response to my father's death all the more acute.

I felt no grief, no shame, no distress—even though he'd died at my hand.

But I knew this kind of pain, had embraced it a long time ago, and I couldn't just let him deal with whatever had happened alone.

I had no idea how he'd react to my touch, to my comfort, but I reached out nonetheless and placed my hand on his leg. It was easy considering I was on my side and he was just there—a few inches away.

Was his proximity on purpose?

The bed was massive. We could sleep on our sides of the mattress without ever having to touch if we didn't want to, so for him to be there, within reach, had to be intentional. Surely?

He didn't respond to my touch, but I let my fingers flatten out against his thigh. It was tense, the thick muscles bunched like every part of him was straining against whatever had happened, like he could deny it physically.

What kind of confidence, of self-assurance did he possess if he thought he could push grief away like it was a boulder in his path?

"Brennan?" I whispered, concerned when he didn't make a move, when he just carried on sitting there. "What's happened? Has someone died?"

"Someone will die soon enough," he rumbled, his voice like chalk against a blackboard.

"Who?" I questioned, his ominous words prompting me to sit up.

"Someone you don't know. Someone you'll never know now," he replied, his gaze drifting my way at long last. It danced down, over my face, touching me here and there with an intangible caress, before moving over my body, over the shirt I wore to cover me up, over the tangle of my hair around my shoulders. "You look like an angel," he said gruffly.

My eyes flared wide at that. "Angels don't usually have blood on their hands."

He shrugged. "They do in my world. Angels avenge, don't they?"

"I-I suppose. It depends on which religion you aspire to."

His lips twisted. "True. Are you like Inessa? Russian Orthodox?"

"No. But I was going to the chapel today with her." I cleared my throat. "She asked me to attend, and because it means something to her, I thought it would be a step forward for us both."

His only reaction was to blink.

"I'm not really religious," I tacked on awkwardly. "I don't believe in that stuff."

"Me either."

"Inessa said you go to church every Sunday."

"Because Da insists. Says we have to repent or we'll never end up in heaven." His mouth twisted into a snarl. "Like that exists for any of us after what we've done." He surprised me by moving his hand and covering mine with it. "Never thought about how strange it would be to marry and to have someone be in your home, in your bed. It's quite..." He cleared his throat. "Pleasant."

Because I thought he'd say the opposite, I hesitated over my next words. Still, curiosity drove me, and I just hoped it wouldn't bite me in the butt. "You never lived with anyone before?" I asked warily.

He shook his head, the lines either side of his mouth tightening a second before he rasped, "Not since I moved out of the family home."

"Why?"

"Because I didn't want to be tied down."

I winced and started to pull away but his fingers tangled with mine and kept me in place. "I'm sorry, Brennan."

He pursed his lips. "Don't be."

"Don't be?" I queried, bewildered. "I forced you—"

"You'll learn fast enough, Camille, that no O'Donnelly is forced to do anything they don't want to do already." He stared at me, and I knew he saw my concern, because a smirk appeared, one that filled me with confusion.

I was the spider who trapped the fly.

So why was I feeling suddenly as if I was the one who'd grown wings?

"You were on my radar long before I was on yours."

"What does that mean?"

"You think I forgot that promise to your ma? Do you know how many promises I've made in my life, Camille?" His hand snapped out, and though I flinched, he ignored it and settled his fingers around my chin. "Take a guess."

I shook my head. "I don't know."

"Take a guess," he repeated, and I tried not to shiver as his thumb whispered along the line of my jaw. He was capable of stirring something in me with the softest of touches, something that had never been stirred before.

Was that chemistry?

I knew we had it.

Had known when he'd pushed me up against the stables and, instead of crying or being filled with fear, I'd just felt his solid presence against me and had wanted more. Had wanted the heat of him to sink into my very bones.

After a lifetime of being cold, to feel the embers of banked fire was enough to draw sensations out of me I'd never experienced before.

"People make promises all the time," I rasped. "And they break them as easily as they made them."

He tutted. "And there you go again with your generalized assumptions, Camille. I'm not most people."

"Neither am I," I admitted. "Promises mean something to me."

"That was why you thought you had leverage over me, I know. To you, you'd act to make sure a promise wasn't broken, wouldn't you?"

"I would," I agreed, but shame filled me, and he saw it because his head tipped to the side. "I have broken one though."

"To your sisters?"

It was a good guess, but he was right nonetheless.

"Yes."

He nodded slowly. "What did you promise them?"

"To protect them from Father."

"After Mariska died?"

"Yes."

"You were a child," he comforted softly, *sorrowfully*. The tone had me on edge, because I'd thought he'd condemn me, not defend me. "And your circumstances were different."

"Not according to them. I know they'll never forgive me."

"Then they don't deserve you," he said simply, further surprising me. "You didn't do it out of malice, just out of self-preservation."

"At their expense," I whispered.

"If you'd been there, if you'd been Abramovicz's wife... would you have been able to stop Inessa having to marry Eoghan?"

"You know I wouldn't."

"Exactly. So what's the point of punishing yourself, hating yourself over that?"

"Because I shouldn't have left them, but even knowing what I do, I'd do it again. I meant what I said—I'd have killed myself before I married him."

"I know. I saw your resolve. I like a woman who knows her own mind." He tapped the corner of my mouth with his thumb. "I've made three promises in my life."

My eyes widened. "Just three?"

"Just three," he confirmed. "To my mother, to *your* mother, and to you."

Mouth gaping, I whispered, "No way."

"Yes way." His smirk disappeared, fading as he stared at my still parted lips. "I never forgot what I promised Mariska. How could I? There wasn't much I could do when we were on opposite sides, but when we were on the same, and when Inessa became family, I knew I had to monitor you."

"Bagpipes said something yesterday..." My mind whispered back to the car ride home. "It made me wonder if you'd been having me followed for longer than I first thought."

"I had. You've been under surveillance since you got back to the city."

"Why?"

He shrugged. "You were more at risk than Victoria. She was too young to be of any use to Vasov, and when Mariska wanted me to protect her daughters, I knew it was from Vasov."

"Do you want to know something sad?"

"Why not? It's a day for sad news."

Though his words were dismissive, I knew he meant each and every one of them. Intending on asking him what had happened after, I replied, "I think, for a while, Inessa and Victoria thought Mama and Papa were happy together. I think they thought that was how a marriage should be."

"I saw her bruises," he rasped. "They were *not* happy together."

"I know." I swallowed down my sorrow.

"The second I knew about Abramovicz, Camille, the second I knew your father was about to flog the same dead horse, you were always going to be my wife."

My throat felt like he'd shoved an orange down it, but I still managed to choke out, "That's not possible."

"It is. I was going to get in touch with you a lot sooner, date you, even. But that didn't work out. My family was involved with some shit that..." He blew out a breath. "Well, we're still dealing with the same BS. It's just a different fucking day."

"Brennan?"

"Yes?"

"Why are you telling me this?"

His jaw clenched. "Because I'm an asshole. Because I'm going to do shit that pisses you off, and even if it does, I'll still expect you to obey me if I ask you to do something... but that's just who I am. I might only be the spare heir to the O'Donnelly throne, but I was born with power, Camille. I know who I am, know what I'm capable of, and know that now you're my wife, there are going to be some days you hate me.

"And, in all honesty, I'm okay with that. I'm not a prick for fun, Camille. If I tell you to do something, it's for a reason. Not because I'm a boring cunt with nothing else better to do with my time than make you miserable.

"If I tell you to stay in, then that's because it's not safe outside. If I tell you to stand in the fucking corner and face the wall, it's because you've done something stupid and you need to think about your actions—"

I had no idea, *no idea whatsoever*, why that had heat whipping through me.

Stand in the corner?

Like I was a little girl?

I'd seen them do that in old movies. Seen kids who'd had to wear paper cones on their heads with a massive letter 'D' for dunce on it.

That should *not* be a turn on, but tell that to my body.

Unaware that my mind had just gone down a decidedly deviant route, Brennan continued, "—for all that, I want your loyalty. Your trust. And I'm aware I need to earn it."

Of the million things I could have woken up to today, of the many things he could have said or done, whatever I might have anticipated, *this* was not it.

But then, I took a second to look at him, to take every inch of him in and process.

He was fully dressed, and his shoes were dirty. I had no idea who polished those Italian Oxfords, but someone did, and I'd seen them all lined up in his closet. The dirt on them, that tracked mud onto the gazillion-thread count sheets, meant that he'd gone out.

Everything Russian in me cringed at the sight. In my culture, it was rude to wear shoes inside the home, and filthy ones? In *bed?*

Still, there were more important things to concern myself with...

A glance outside the windows let anyone know that it was barely morning, but something had evidently happened. Something that put shadows in the eyes of this frightening man I called husband.

But for all that I'd been thinking of ways to tie him to me, he'd clearly been wanting the same thing in return.

I could have been coy, could have milked this situation for all it was worth, could have kept him hanging—but that wasn't me.

I wasn't, and never would be, like that.

So I was honest with him, and I hoped he didn't fuck me over because I didn't want to play games with him.

"You saved me from my family," I intoned softly, lifting my legs so that I could wrap my arms around my knees. "From the Bratva," I tacked on. "You spun deals to keep me safe. Without speaking to Maxim, without making that happen, I have no idea where I'd be right now."

"Brennan, we don't know each other that well, so you don't know if you can trust me or not. If anything, you know what I'll do to survive, so I understand if that doesn't mean that much to you. I'm here, my father's blood on my hands, with no guilt in my heart, no grief weighing me down, but I'm telling you now—I'll never betray you." When his face remained a blank slate, I whispered, "I told Maxim that too. If he ever tried to use what I did to Father against me, to manipulate me into spilling secrets about the Five Points, I told him I wouldn't, and I meant it."

His mouth twisted into a skewed line as he sat up, his elbows coming to his thighs as he propped himself up. He shoved his face into his hands like he was going to cry, but he rubbed his palms over his eyes, digging in as if he was trying to rid them of sleep.

I wasn't sure what that meant. If he believed me or not, and just as a whisper of hurt tried to flare inside me, he rasped, "There's some shit you're not supposed to tell anyone. You're just supposed to lock it up inside, and you have to deal with it. Usually I can do that, usually, it's just another day on the fucking job. But..."

"Today's different. Why?" I asked softly.

"You've been betrayed, Camille. I guess you didn't know that at the time, but your father betrayed you, didn't he?"

"He did. Not just with Mama but when he wouldn't change his mind about who he wanted me to marry. I had no alternative but to run."

"What if you can't run? And what if, you know something that could destroy a family, but they're going to destroy your world—does that make it okay to retaliate? To act first before they have the chance to?" He shook his head. "This is fucked up."

"It sounds it," I whispered, surprised he was telling me this even though I was also glad. Tentatively, I pressed my hand to his leg. The silk suit didn't crease beneath my grasp, but I was reminded of just how dressed he was and how dressed I wasn't. "Brennan? What can I do to help?"

"No one can help, Camille. This is one of those Catch 22 situations, and the bitch of it is that I'm not supposed to be talking about this kind of crap with you but—" He shook his head again. "Ain't got no one else who won't fly off the handle when they hear this news."

Cautiously, I questioned, "Are you in danger? Is that the kind of betrayal you're talking about?"

He cast me a look. "We're always in danger." His mouth twisted. "Didn't you know?"

"I did, but this sounds more urgent."

"It is." He grunted under his breath. "What time did you agree to meet with Inessa?"

I blinked at the abrupt change of subject. "Six. For Vespers."

He shook his head. "I'm sorry but you have to cancel. I need to intro you to the parents before Sunday lunch tomorrow, otherwise that will just be a whole mess that I can't deal with on top of this."

"I understand," I told him calmly, and I did. "Inessa will get it."

She might not, but once I explained why Brennan needed me, I figured she'd forgive me, and we could reschedule for next week.

After clearing my throat, I asked, "So, tonight's the night?"

"It is." He gritted his teeth. "I'll be speaking with Da after the meal so that you can get to know them both without him being on edge. Well," he said with a sigh, "more on edge than usual."

"I understand." I patted his leg, wanting to help but knowing that was probably impossible. "Is it really that bad?" I asked cautiously. This world we lived in, caution didn't favor the brave. It favored the smart—and that meant keeping your nose out of things that didn't concern you. He probably didn't realize the trust I showed in him by even bothering to ask.

He didn't answer for the longest time. Long enough for me to think I should just get off the bed. I had things to do if I was going to meet his parents today—I needed to find them a gift to take to their house, and I had to plan what I was going to wear. We also needed to discuss whether we were selling our marriage as a love match or something of convenience.

Just as I started to cringe inside at having the head of the Irish Mob peer down at me like I was a dog turd he'd trod in tonight, Brennan rasped, "We've been having issues with people who've been betraying the Points, Camille.

"This isn't something I should share with you, but the people closest to the O'Donnellys might have been compromised so I need you to listen to me when I tell you to watch yourself."

"You think someone on your personal guard might be compromised?" I asked on an exhalation, easily picking up on what he meant.

He shrugged, but I saw his hurt, registered it in the miserable slant to his mouth as he grimaced. "I—" Brennan released a breath. "No one is what they seem. Not anymore. I promised to protect you. Not just to Mariska, but yesterday... my vows meant something to me. I might not be the good Catholic boy my da wishes I was, but vows matter.

"I want your trust. Your loyalty. But sometimes, I'm going to test both. I can't tell you why I ask you to do something, or why I ask you not to, you just have to know that I won't do it unnecessarily." I stared at him long enough for him to sigh and mutter, "I know that's a big ask."

"It is considering we don't know each other well enough for me to understand your judgment calls, but..." I sighed, and even though I knew any feminist around would want to strangle me, I saw a light at the end of the tunnel here. A light that hadn't been there before.

Sex was temporary.

I knew that from Nyx.

Sex would keep a man interested only for so long before the promise of some other pussy, another pretty ass and a good set of tits had them sniffing around like the horn dogs they were.

This was tangible.

This offered more than I could have hoped for.

"But?" Brennan prompted, his hands balling into fists.

"But we both went into this with open eyes, and eventually, when we want children, I would like for us to seem happy, to be a team when it comes to raising them. I'll trust you, Brennan, if you'll show me the same esteem in return."

His eyes narrowed on me. "So, you're going to do this for the kids we haven't had yet. For kids we may never have?"

"Why wouldn't we?" I questioned warily.

"Life happens. Biology and health aren't always on our side."

Everything inside me clenched down with horror at the thought of being sterile or having issues like Mama. In this world, my worth depended on my ability to have children. I wasn't a regular woman. IVF or adoption weren't routes made men were willing to traverse.

Feeling sick to my stomach with fear for something I had no control over, and wishing I could just be normal, miserably I whispered, "I suppose not... but yes. For those future children, I'll do this."

"You're a lot more generous than I am."

The twist of my lips was rueful. "I didn't grow up with parents who loved each other."

"You think my folks were like the Von Trapps?" He snorted. "They loved each other for sure, but I grew up with clipped ears and—" A breath gusted from him. "Never mind."

"Isn't the role of a parent to want better for their children than they had?"

Our eyes caught and held. "You're right," he agreed.

I shot him a gentle smile, and feeling brave, I let my hand slip higher, higher and higher until mine covered his fist. "I need to buy your parents a gift."

He nodded. "Call Bagpipes."

"I will."

"Inessa..." Brennan pulled a face. "Inessa bought them a set of slippers each. Ma liked that."

"Yes, it's custom in our culture not to wear shoes in the house." I cast a look at Brennan's dirty footwear. "It's rude."

"It's rude in every culture to wear filthy shoes in bed," he said dryly.

"Then why did you do it?"

"Because it never mattered before. I could do whatever the fuck I wanted."

Could?

Past tense?

I'd take that as a glimmer of hope.

"I'll be more mindful in future, but this morning was not an ordinary morning."

"I can see that," I whispered, then, squeezed his hand. "I'm sorry, Brennan. I won't let you down. I promise."

"No one can make that particular promise," he rasped, turning his face away.

Maybe I was a fool, maybe I was borrowing trouble, because he was right—it was a promise, in our world, that would be difficult to keep, but, voice husky, I repeated, "I can and I do, Brennan. I won't let you down."

He turned back to me, stared at me for what felt like endless seconds, then rasped, "Call Bagpipes." Inside, I deflated. I didn't know what I'd been waiting for, but I didn't get it. "I need you to be ready by four, okay?"

"We'll be leaving that early?"

"It takes ninety minutes in good traffic to get to their place." He reached into his inside pocket and slipped something out. A credit card. He passed it over to me. "We should have discussed this before, but this is yours. Use it however you want. I'll top it up once a month."

My throat tightened at the financial freedom he was giving me. "You don't have to do that."

"No, maybe I don't," he muttered, "but... for those future kids of ours, yeah? We'll trust one another."

I sent him a soft smile. "We will."

TWENTY-FIVE
BRENNAN

"CALLUM," I greeted, my smile wide as I held out my hand for him. When our fingers collided, I tugged him into me so I could slap him on the back. "Thanks for coming over."

"No worries. Is everything okay?"

"Sure is. I just need your help with something." I held out my arm, indicating he should go down the corridor. "It's in my office."

"Never been to your place before," he said sheepishly.

"Shit, I'm sorry. I should have invited you over once the decorator had finished. I didn't really have a housewarming. Just my brothers came over and trashed the place."

He grinned. "Sounds about right."

I ran down the steps, hearing his thudding footsteps behind me and I pointed to my game room. "You have to see this. It's my seven-year-old self's version of heaven."

Callum chuckled as I guided him inside, showing off a collection of arcade games I was pretty proud of—they'd cost me a fucking fortune to hunt down.

"Shit!" He ran over and gaped at my favorite cabinets.

"They're all mint condition."

"I can't believe you have *Galaga*. Holy fuck, is that *1942*?"

"Sure is." I smirked at him. "We should have realized back then the fuck ups we'd be when all we loved were the shoot-'em-up games. Have at it," I told him, waving a hand as he immediately booted up the sci-fi classic that was *Galaga*.

I walked toward the snooker table, and started to set up the balls for a game.

Now he was here, that was half the battle.

The other half was me not ramming a snooker cue down his fucking throat.

My jaw worked at the thought, but I maintained a placid expression as I set up a triangle on the green baize, then placed the red balls inside it. Setting the colored balls on the grid, I moved over to grab two cues, leaned one against the table, and then started chalking up my tip.

When he'd finished, he was grinning from ear to ear. "I swear, if I have a boy, I need to get them hooked on that. I loved that shit when I was a kid."

"Who didn't?" I knew my smile would be reflected in my eyes. "Simpler times back then, Cal."

"Tell me about it. I'm still freaking out about Priestley pissing on a stick and it turning blue." He pulled a face, but something about his words had me tipping my head to the side.

Was he trying to remind me he was about to be a family man? To deflect from the situation? I knew he had to be wondering why the hell I'd invited him here. Deflection might be his first line of defense.

I scrubbed my chin as I murmured, "Might as well have a game of snooker."

He shrugged. "Don't play. And I really need to get back when we've done. Priestley wants to go shopping. She wants to get the nursery ready ASAP."

"Similar principles to pool. You pot a red, then you go for a colored ball. Don't worry, I'll tell you the order as we go," I instructed, ignoring the rest of his BS.

"Why not?" His smile was tight when he realized I wasn't going to let this go.

"I'll break," I told him, leaning over the head of the table and tapping the white ball. It connected hard with the 2D red pyramid, sending balls shooting over the green surface. When I potted one, I murmured, "Next, you have to pot a color in ascending order of points. Yellow, green, brown, blue, pink, then black."

I tapped the yellow into the top corner pocket, then aimed for another red and missed.

"Your turn."

He leaned over the table, made his aim and tapped the white. He potted a red, a green, and another red. I saw the flush in his eyes as he grinned at me. "Beginner's luck."

"Must be."

I hitched my leg onto the side of the table, watching as he moved around, potting balls left, right, and center, before I asked, "You know we'll always look after Priestley, and your kid, if anything ever happens to you, don't you, Cal?"

He missed his next shot. "Huh?"

I shrugged. "In our line of work, anything could happen. But you know the Five Points will look after your kid and your woman if anything *should* go wrong."

He blinked at me. "That's pretty fucking grim, Bren, but yeah, I guess I knew that."

"Good." I smiled as I got to my feet so I could take my shot.

"What did you call me over here for, Bren?"

I didn't answer, but I purposely let the white ball drift into the pocket nearest him. "Shit," I murmured, strolling around to that side, watching, waiting until he tucked his hand into it.

When he dug deep for the ball, I grabbed his forearm and dragged it back against the side of the pocket. As he howled, I didn't stop until the dual cracks of his ulna and radius splintering ricocheted through the room, which was when I gripped the back of his neck and rammed his face into the wooden panel that lined the edge of the pool table.

I moved so fast that he didn't really have time to defend himself and, dazed, he flopped forward, but before he could get blood on the green, which was a bitch to replace, expensive to boot, and would raise questions I didn't want to answer, I pulled him back, grabbed his arm out of the pocket, then kicked him behind his knees.

When he dropped onto the floor like a sack of shit, I hooked my hands around his ankles and started to drag him out of the room and toward my office.

With each step I took, he struggled, his one good arm clinging to the door, his body curling around it like I couldn't beat the crap out of him wherever I was.

When he did the same thing again with my office door, I bent over and jabbed him in the face, before I stomped on his abdomen. That shut him the hell up.

Closing the door behind me, I moved over to my desk, pulled out a reel of duct tape and pushed it onto my wrist like it was a bracelet, then wheeled my chair toward him. Hauling him into the seat was hard when he was a deadweight, but I managed.

When he was in place, I started to bind him with the tape. First things first, I wrapped him up like he was a mummy, from shoulder to calf, then I covered the bottom half of his face with it, which had him waking up as he couldn't breathe.

His body wriggled from side to side, the chair moving with him as he struggled to find air. Watching him plead silently with his eyes, his desperate moans doing nothing more than amping up my annoyance, I said, "You get air if you'll talk."

His head started bobbing like one of those toy dogs you saw on a dashboard, so I snagged a pen from my desk, moved over to him, grabbed him by the hair and let gravity tilt him back in the rocking desk chair.

His eyes were wide with desperation, as I ordered, "Stay very still, Callum."

A grunt escaped him as I pressed the pen to the canopy of tape that covered each nostril, then punctured it.

Immediately, the plastic quivered inward, squeaking as he sucked down air.

When I pushed the tip of the pen to the second one, he froze, then let out a few mumbles as he started straining to breathe through the tiny holes.

They wouldn't sustain him for long, but I didn't need them to.

What I *needed* was answers.

Lifting my arm, I took note of the time, and said, "Six hours until the wife's due home. Oh, I forgot, you didn't know I was married. It's a family secret right now. I know how much you love secrets, Callum." I moved over to my door and turned the key in the lock. "We can have plenty of fun in that time, though, can't we?"

Turning back, I saw the terror in his eyes, even worse, I saw the guilt. With that, he sealed his fate, because I knew the thieves had spoken the truth—he'd betrayed us.

"Yeah, *brother*," I mocked. "I know what you've been up to. Know about the secrets you've been spilling. Who's been a bad boy? One guess..." I sneered. "You."

SHE DIED KNOWING THAT THE MAN WHO PROMISED TO PROTECT HER PUT HER IN HARM'S WAY. YOU NEED TO AVENGE THAT. EVEN IF YOU'RE TOO CHICKEN SHIT NOW, MAYBE TOMORROW, YOU'LL BE STRONG ENOUGH TO MAKE FATHER PAY.

TWENTY-SIX
CAMILLE

HE DISAPPEARED to his office shortly after our conversation, and once I'd called Bagpipes and told him I needed to run some errands, I followed Brennan downstairs to the room I'd claimed as my own and grabbed the clothes I wanted to wear today.

All the while I was rifling through my newly organized closet, two problems plagued me.

One: what had really happened to instigate that conversation in bed? Would I ever know? Did I *want* to know? Those were questions that pinged to mind every time I heard him snarling at someone on the phone in his study.

Two: I knew what his promise to my mother had been, and to me, but he'd said that he'd made one to his mom too—what was that? It wasn't just curiosity that had me wondering either. It was concern.

My thoughts were tangled, snagging like my callused palms on my silk stockings as I bustled around, but eventually, I got my outfit set out and started getting ready for the day ahead of me.

When I returned upstairs, I rifled through the drawers, and found some fresh bed linen so I changed the sheets before showering and quickly dressing in the yoga pants and sweater I'd set out, and teamed them with some comfy UGGs. Not bothering with make-up, I left the bedroom and headed for the kitchen.

Filled with all kinds of goodies, from a food fairy I'd yet to meet and maybe by the nature of her magic I never would, I grabbed what appeared to be an oat bran muffin and a banana, just in time for a buzzer to sound by the elevator.

Thinking that was the warning someone was on the way up, I just waited, but then it came again, and I darted over there, not wanting to disturb Brennan, and found Bagpipes peering at me on a screen.

"Come on down," he told me as a greeting.

"Be there in a second. How cold is it out?"

"It's okay. Sweater weather."

Considering myself dressed enough, I headed for the elevator without a backward glance and pressed the button for the basement.

Bagpipes was waiting by the door, his back to it, one foot kicked up against the wall, and with his focus on his phone, he murmured, "Pick whichever car you want."

We were within a kind of compartment of ten cars, partitioned off with windows. I'd figured that this was special parking for the penthouse apartments, but I guessed I was wrong.

Seeing a Ferrari, a couple of Porsches, a very nice Bugatti and a couple of Bentleys that all apparently belonged to my husband, I whistled under my breath, but selected the Merc I'd driven yesterday.

Comfort, in Manhattan traffic, mattered to me more than anything else.

He grunted at my choice, and collected the keys from a compartment beside the elevator. He pulled out a kind of stick too, black and shiny with a couple of LED lights that flashed to life when he turned it on. Before my bewildered eyes, he headed to the car, opened the door and started doing *something* with the stick.

When he was done, he tossed the keys at me, explaining only, "Sweeping for bugs."

"Oh." *God, this life...*

Shoving that thought aside because this was it until I died, I climbed behind the wheel, hooked up my phone to the dash, then immediately called Inessa.

Knowing that Bagpipes would tell Brennan I spoke in French with her, I chose to speak in English, because I didn't want them to think we were hiding anything from the O'Donnellys. Especially when we were only going to be discussing the heads of said family and what to gift them—nothing important enough to require accusations of espionage.

"Camille? God, it's early."

My lips twitched at her groan, but I just said, "Brennan told me we're having dinner with his parents tonight."

Bagpipes' interest shifted to me, but I ignored him and focused on Inessa as she gasped. "Oh, dear."

"Yeah," I said dryly.

"No church for us then, I guess," she grumbled, but didn't sound angry at me, more unsurprised. I guessed we mob wives had to learn to be accommodating or go mad. "Okay, well, Lena loves lilies. You could get her some of those. Aidan's a sucker for the Knicks."

Appreciation swirled inside me. That she was willing to help me felt like a massive virtual hug. I wasn't sure why, but I'd really needed that this morning.

I cleared my throat, feeling stupid for the tears of gratitude that were gathering there, and rasped, "Brennan said you gave them slippers. Maybe I should do the same?"

She hummed. "Well, they understand that practice now, so that would be nice, but you could get them and gift them tomorrow? I mean, you *are* coming to Sunday lunch."

"I think it depends on how bad tonight goes," I said dryly, prompting Bagpipes to snort.

"We all go to church. Even if we're at death's door, there's no escaping that. Just like Sunday lunch is never missed. You'll be going, whether or not Aidan Sr. beats the fuck out of Brennan for marrying you without his permission."

I frowned at that, then asked, "He'd really do that?"

"He would," Inessa confirmed. "I know he beat up Eoghan when he tried to get out of marrying me."

"You always going to hold that against me?" I heard Eoghan grumble in the background.

My eyes flared wide. "Eoghan's there?" I burst out, concern whirling inside me. "You weren't supposed to say anything, Inessa!"

"Sorry, Cammie," was her immediate, *sheepish* reply. "I didn't mean to."

I closed my eyes, worried about what Brennan would say about that. "Dammit, Inessa."

"Don't worry about it," Bagpipes mumbled around a yawn. "He'd have found out tomorrow anyway. Bren was more concerned about them stopping him from marrying you. What's done is done."

True.

Relief whispered inside me.

I was an O'Donnelly now.

I was untouchable.

Still, I cleared my throat and asked miserably, "Aidan Sr.'s like Father then."

"No," Inessa countered immediately, but I heard the contrition in her voice. Making a mental note that she couldn't keep her trap shut around her husband, I focused on her next words as she explained, "He's nuts, but like I told you yesterday, he's oddly family-centric. It's strange. It's like his heart is in the right place but his head just isn't."

Bagpipes snorted again but didn't comment which told me he was in agreement with Inessa's opinion.

"He's like the gossips say? Unstable?"

Inessa laughed. "Yes."

Confused because she didn't sound disturbed by that, I just plowed on, "Okay, so something from the Knicks and some lilies?"

"She'll think you're arse-licking if you get her the lilies," Bagpipes said, his focus on his phone. "Lena's not like your average mother-in-law."

Inessa hummed. "That's your guard, right?"

"It's Bren's man, Bagpipes," he called out.

Inessa, amused, murmured, "Eoghan says good morning."

"Tell him he has the right of it being in bed at this godawful time."

"It isn't my fault!" I excused, feeling guilty. "Brennan was the one who told me I had to move fast. And it's Saturday. If I don't get to the stores early then it'll be chaos."

Bagpipes just grunted, which had me rolling my eyes as I headed for Fifth Avenue.

"So, slippers for tomorrow, ask Eoghan if his father mentioned something he'd like—"

"Just get him a bottle of Glenrothes," Eoghan groused, his voice clearer which told me Inessa had placed us on speaker.

"Whiskey?"

"Single malt." He hummed. "The best. The older the better if you have about five grand to spare."

I had no idea what I had on my card but if it meant currying favor with the in-laws, I'd spend every cent I had.

"Okay, I'll head to—"

"Bagpipes, take her to Vinny's."

"Will do, Eoghan."

"Thanks for the rec," I murmured, encompassing Bagpipes in that with a smile he sniffed at. "What about your mom?"

"She's more difficult. The slippers, definitely. She'll like that. Even if she doesn't like you, she'll appreciate that you're saying she's welcome at your place all the time."

I winced. "Does she come over a lot?"

"No. I thought she would," Inessa answered. "But I think the drive is too much for her."

"She's been in a funny headspace the past few months," Eoghan agreed. "I don't really know what she'd like. Even if it means sucking up to her, maybe that's the way to go—lilies. Inessa's right. She does—oh. Wait. Bagpipes, that chocolatier on 11th."

"Girani's?"

"Yeah. That one. Is it still open?"

"Just." He cleared his throat, which, because men were dumb, instantly made me realize that some kind of business was going down either in that area or with the owner of the chocolatier.

"Ma used to love that place. She doesn't get to go so often anymore. Maybe you can buy her some chocolates from there."

"Chocolates it is," I said, smiling because now that was settled, I felt a lot more comfortable about tonight. He'd thrown this meeting at me, but it was more of a battle than anything else. And showing up to a war without a weapon, even if it was just a gift meant to disarm, was stupidity itself. "Inessa, what slippers did you buy them?"

"Louis Vuitton. I'll message you with their sizes."

I hummed. "Okay. Right, I'll see you both tomorrow at church then. Sorry about canceling later."

"No worries. I know what these O'Donnellys are like, remember?" she teased, which had Eoghan responding in a way that made her giggle again.

Relieved that the post-depilatory disaster hadn't put a dampener on things, I murmured, "You'll have to show me the ropes."

"I will, definitely." Her laughter faded. "Sorry about telling Eoghan, sis. I really didn't mean to."

It was worth it just for her to call me that. "Don't worry—"

"You shouldn't keep secrets from your husbands," Eoghan interrupted, but he sounded like he was on the brink of sleep again.

Bagpipes snorted. "You're newlyweds. The longer you're married, the more you hope they'll keep shit secret."

Grinning, I just said, "Bye, *malyshka*. See you tomorrow."

"Speak later, Cammie," she replied as I cut the call.

"You wanna go to the chocolate place first or the bodega?" he groused.

"Whichever's closest."

And that was how I spent most of my morning. Buying gifts for my in-laws and hooking myself up with a new phone so I could return the burner to Bagpipes.

Once it was set up, I sent out my new number to the only people who really mattered to me, Inessa, Victoria, and Brennan. It took way longer than I hoped, but as the hours passed, the city just got busier. I was lucky to get back to the apartment by three.

Knowing he'd given me until four, I was in a rush as I grabbed the gifts, left Bagpipes to his own devices, and ran to the elevator.

When I arrived, I dropped the packages by the door, and rushed past the bedroom and to the stairs so I could go pick out what I was wearing tonight.

It wasn't stupid to be nervous, not when meeting the heads of the Irish Mob, but I just wished that I had more time to make myself presentable. Less than an hour to shower, change, and get ready wasn't much in the scheme of things—not when I was meeting the parents for the first time.

A skirt and blouse in hand, a bandeau, and a pair of stockings and some lacy underwear too, I draped them over my forearm and dashed out into the hall.

I almost didn't hear it.

That was how faint it was.

A slight cry. A choked sound that had me twisting around, trying to find it.

"Brennan?" I called out, concern hitting me.

Had he fallen? Hurt himself?

I rushed down to his office and twisted the doorknob. Finding it locked, I started to tap on the door when I heard another soft whimper.

"Brennan!" I called out again, banging my fist on the office door before I pressed my ear to it, trying to figure out if the noise *was*, in fact, coming from in there.

Hearing a louder mewl this time, something twisted in my head because it had sounded like someone was in pain at first, but what if—

No.

He wouldn't have brought a mistress here, would he?

So soon?

Not after what we'd been talking about earlier.

Rage and hurt flushed through me as I made to bang on the door again, but this time, my fist never collided with it. Fingers coiled around my wrist, prompting me to shriek. I twisted around, my other hand forming a fist too as I punched out at my attacker. My clothes and underwear went flying, but I didn't care. Just as my other hand was ensnared, I found myself staring up at a glowering Brennan.

The relief was instantaneous.

A sharp gasp escaped me, one loaded with panic and relief and... God, *gratitude*.

He wasn't having sex in there.

I had no right to feel possessive over him, but I'd just... what we'd talked about made me hope for more.

And, for a woman like me, *more* was as unattainable as love.

There was a storm cloud in his eyes as he stared down at me, but I ignored that to take him in in all his glory.

Jesus, Mary and Joseph.

I'd seen him naked, but somehow he was even more impressive looming over me the way he was. Dressed in nothing but a towel, one that was so white, so clean against his skin, it seemed to emphasize every single muscle he possessed. And trust me, there were muscles on top of muscles on top of muscles.

It was only now that I registered that even if he looked phenomenal in a suit, the suit certainly didn't do the man justice.

Hell's bells.

There were tiny droplets of water on his chest, between his pecs. I ached to feel one such drop against my tongue, because my mouth was suddenly parched.

From the tiny bubbles around his ears, I knew he'd been shaving when I'd come in, which was probably why I hadn't heard him upstairs. But that didn't explain what was happening in his office.

Or *who* was in there.

I blinked up at him. "I thought you were injured."

His gaze darted to the office door for the barest second, which told me I hadn't been imagining things—someone *was* in there, and someone *was* injured. Maybe another person wouldn't have spotted the tell, but I'd been raised to suspect everything and nothing.

"Go upstairs. You're late."

"Traffic was crazy, and the stores were packed," I informed him absently. "What's happening, Brennan?"

"Now's one of those times you don't need to be questioning me, Camille," he rumbled, his words setting off a wave of vibrations that I felt in my core.

Business.

Some poor schmuck had gone against the O'Donnellys and was being served his fate just behind this door.

"Did you have to bring it home with you?" I whispered.

"*It?* Like a lost puppy?" He arched a brow at me. "Go upstairs. Get changed. We need to go soon."

"You can't just leave—"

"Can't I?" He narrowed his eyes at me. "I've asked you twice now, Camille. Nicely. Please, go upstairs before you piss me off."

I should have just left. Done as he asked. He *had*, after all, been polite about it. But this was my home. *Our* home. I understood the need for medical care, that was one thing. But this? It was completely different.

"You can't bring—"

He swooped down, his face coming so close to me that mine almost banged into the door as I jerked backward to avoid it—what stopped the collision? His hand. He grabbed me by the nape, just in time, and he hauled me into him even as he used his grip on me to tip my head back.

"You really trying to piss me off today, Camille?"

I swallowed. "N-No, of course not, Brennan."

"Then why are you questioning me?" His nostrils flared for a second, and he rumbled, "This is business. I wouldn't bring it here if I didn't have to." He clenched his jaw. "Pick up your clothes, get your ass upstairs, and wait for me."

"I'll go and get showered," I tried to appease.

"No. Just wait for me." With his hold on my nape still, he maneuvered us around so that his back was to the office door and mine was to the hall.

The air was almost incandescent with his agitation, and I had the feeling that, whatever had happened this morning, was tied to this. Tied to whoever was in his office.

Heart in my throat, I dropped down to my knees the second he released me, grabbed my clothes, and rushed over to the stairs.

My lungs were burning even though I didn't run that far when I made it to the bedroom, and I laid out my things over the dresser in the corner.

As I twisted around, trying to figure out where to sit, I took in the large space.

The bed was massive and sat right in the center. On a raised platform, it overlooked the picture windows which opened up onto the Manhattan sky. To the left of it, there was a dresser, to the right, a vanity area that I couldn't see him using all that much, even if he had a Louis Vuitton watch case on there.

At the foot of the bed, there was a bench, brown leather so dark it was nearly black and that matched the headboard. Beyond, there were two armchairs, a rich cream velvet with gold undertones that added a hint of warmth to the space.

I could sit on the bed, the bench or the armchairs, but I didn't want to sit down. Nerves filled me, making my agitation worse.

Would he hit me?

I couldn't see it.

But why didn't he want me to get showered? To start getting ready?

Though I thought he was going to punish me, his actions and words didn't correlate.

I'd pissed him off, but even though he'd loomed over me like Hades himself, he'd been the one to stop me from hurting my head when I'd nearly collided with the door.

My fingers twitched as I dug them into my palms, and the exquisite pain had me closing my eyes, the relief so intense it was almost pleasurable. As I released a shaky breath, I took measure of my options.

I shouldn't have questioned him, but this was my home now. I didn't want him bringing people to be tortured into it, and I didn't think that was a lot to damn well ask. God, didn't they have places for that express purpose? Did he really have to bring it home?

He'd said it was to do with this morning, but because he hadn't clued me in on what had actually happened, I was still in the dark, and I was okay with that. I preferred the darkness. Call me a coward, but I didn't *want* to know. There was no remaining in that darkness, however, when he brought it under my roof too.

The longer I thought about this, the more my fingers burrowed into my palms. It was so second nature to me that I didn't even realize it. Not until I felt the Band-Aids sliding around now the flesh was slick with blood.

Wincing at the mess I'd made, I peered down at the carpeted floor, grateful that I hadn't dripped any blood onto it, then I made my way to the bathroom to clean up. Only, as I did, I heard him. I had no idea how long he'd taken down there, but the sound of his thudding steps on the stairs, then the padding of his bare feet as he moved down the corridor had my heart taking residence in my throat.

With time running out, I did the only thing that was sensible. The one thing that my mind had clung to this morning when he'd said it.

I rushed to the nearest corner, one that was part wall, part window, turned my face to it, and tried not to wonder why, when my body barely reacted to direct stimuli, a ball of heat had formed in my core as I pushed my nose against the wall, hoping that would be enough to quell his anger...

TWENTY-SEVEN
BRENNAN

USING my elbow to knock the door open, my focus was on not getting blood everywhere as I maneuvered into my bedroom. Upon straightening up, I caught sight of her, face to the wall, tucked in the corner directly opposite the doorway.

Rather than acknowledge her, I moved into the bathroom. The sink was still full of soapy water from when I'd been shaving, so I plunged my hands into the liquid, then focused on cleaning them up. Using a nail brush, I made sure there were no crevices in my skin where blood could gather.

Maybe I took extra care because I knew she was waiting out there.

Maybe I was both pleased and annoyed that she'd taken it upon herself to shove her face in the corner...

Funny how I'd mentioned that this morning and here she was, topping from the bottom.

Lips pursing at the thought, I pulled the plug, releasing the vat of pink-tinged water, then turned on the faucet to clean up the sink, before I gave my hands one final wash.

That done, I dried them off on a towel, then strode into my bedroom.

"Place your hands on the glass, take a step back, and bend over at a ninety-degree angle," I ordered her.

A whisper of breath escaped her, but she didn't argue. Her compliance was immediate.

Shaking my head at her character's strange mixture of gutsy and submissive, I ignored her again, and made my way to the closet. With great care, I picked out the items I was going to wear tonight.

I wasn't known for my fastidiousness, but she'd chosen this path, so I wasn't going to disappoint her. I selected my jeans first, and when I'd made my choice, I moved over to her side and draped them over her back. She tensed but didn't argue.

Then I did the same with my shirt and sweater. Even my socks and boxer briefs were carefully picked and laid over her like she was a clotheshorse.

The position, though simple, required a lot of core strength, and I witnessed a faint tremble that rushed down her spine and along her thighs as she maintained the hold.

Spying that, I moved to her side, and asked, "If I touched your cunt, would it be wet or dry?"

A shocked gasp escaped her, and she jerked up slightly, which made her hands slide against the glass. Seeing the blood trails left from her palms had anger whipping through me.

"I-I don't know," she said after a few seconds.

"Bullshit."

Heading over to my nightstand, I pulled open the top drawer. There was a secret ledge built into it, so I checked that my gun was still in place, and that she hadn't taken it, before I pulled out my knife.

Returning to her side, I repeated, "Is your pussy wet or dry?"

"How would I know?" she rasped. "I can't touch it."

Did she know bupkis about her body?

Jesus Christ.

I wasn't sure what infuriated me the most in all honesty. The blood which meant she had opened her wounds again—at least, that had better be what that meant, and not that she'd self-harmed while I'd been dealing with business downstairs—or the fact she was in the dark about her body.

Were there any other twenty-four-year-olds this naive in the fucking country—never mind the city—or was she just trying me?

With her ass poking out the way it was, I saw the seam that ran down the peachy curve to between her legs. The yoga pants gave her a camel toe that was almost too perfect to wreck, but I had plans, and I was pretty sure she'd own a couple dozen more pairs of yoga pants so I'd get to see that plenty more times in the future.

Pressing the tip of the knife to that seam, I sliced it open. It parted like butter against the sharp blade, and because she'd pissed me off, I continued down that seam until I reached her cunt.

Resting the knife at the base of her back, using her like a stand again, I grabbed both halves of her pants and tore them wider open.

With that done, I plucked at the gusset of her panties, pulling it away from her pussy lips which, as I'd suspected, were drenched with her arousal, and keeping it that way, I reached for my knife and slashed through that fabric too.

"You're trying to tell me you don't know if you're wet or not?" I demanded.

A whimper escaped her. "I-I really don't."

"For fuck's sake," I groused under my breath. This time, I twisted around and tossed the knife on the top of the dresser.

When I turned back around, I couldn't deny that she made a stunning picture.

Her legs were pushed together, so her pussy lips were sandwiched between them. Her golden skin was creamy against the black fabric of her pants, which made the bright red flush of her cunt, slick with translucent juices, seem all the more shocking.

In the best possible way, of course.

Licking my lips at the sight, I reached down and traced my finger over her slit. A groan escaped her as she surged onto her tiptoes, and her back bowed, dipping in at the bottom as she responded to the caress.

As she did, the clothes shifted slightly, so I told her, "Those clothes stay where they are. You let them fall, there'll be consequences."

In all honesty, I had no idea what those consequences would be. I wasn't into punishing where sex was concerned, but if it got her this fucking hot, maybe I'd have to come up with some alternatives.

Punishments were for life and death situations.

Even though she'd questioned me downstairs, I'd never have shoved her in the fucking corner the way she'd elected.

I should be pissed, but how could I be when her cunt was this ready for me?

A mewl escaped her at my words, like the whisper of a consequence was enough to get her off.

Shaking my head at her, I let my fingers fondle her slit, moving them around her clit, rubbing it and taking my time with it so that she knew I was playing with her.

Every shudder, every groan, every whimper was enough consequence for me, but still, seeing how fucking ready she was had my dick close to bursting.

The trouble was, we had to shift our asses. All I wanted to do was fuck her, take my time with her, but my day had gone to shit already, and I knew Da would give me crap if I was late.

Unable to stop myself, I thrust a finger into her. The tight, clinging walls were a sweet torture of their own, and I closed my eyes as my dick throbbed in time to the way her pussy pulsed around the digit.

The moans she made weren't helping either. They were sweet agony too.

Slipping a second, then a third into her, I gritted my teeth against the need to fuck her. She wasn't going to lead me around by my cock, even if she thought she could...

"Don't come," I told her coldly, my voice hoarse as I battled my own needs.

"Huh?" she replied on a sharp intake of air.

"Don't come," I repeated as I started to thrust into her faster.

Just like I thought—the second I said that, her pussy clenched down on my fingers, hard enough to cut off the circulation to them. Okay, slight exaggeration but still, fucking tight.

A soft, keening sound escaped her, one that was loaded with a desperation I almost felt as she fought my retreat and invasion, trying to cling to me, to keep me in place.

Seconds before I knew she was about to get off, I pulled out of her, and damning the fucking time, I threw my towel to the floor, pushed the tip of my cock to her slit, and thrust home.

Her cunt fought me for every inch I claimed, making a liar out of her —no way in fuck had she serviced a whole chapter of the Sinners—but when I was all the way in, it treated me to a little Mexican wave as she exploded around me.

"What did I tell you?" I snarled at her, even though it felt like bliss.

That soft, keening sound became a wail. A long constant sound of agonized bliss as I fucked her through her orgasm. Reaching between her legs, I bent over slightly and began to rub her clit again as I fucked her from behind. The wail made my ears ring but though my thrusts were hard and fast, furious, she took it like a trooper.

With each thud of my thighs to her ass, of skin bouncing against skin, her fingers squeaked against the glass, and when her cunt clutched at my cock with more ferocity than before, I closed my eyes, reveling in the tight squeeze as she came again.

When she crumpled, falling forward, the clothes tumbling with her, tangling around her, I stopped rubbing her clit and instead, grabbed her hips. Continuing to fuck her as she tried to gain some balance, her hands flailing to straighten up, I stopped thrusting and, instead, rocked her back and forth, pivoting her off my dick and letting her fuck me back.

Like a rag doll, she let me, and when she came again, without any help from me, she sucked my cum right out of my fucking balls.

Head thrown back, throat straining as I roared out my release, I let the day's stresses, and the upcoming ones the evening ahead promised, float away, because at that moment, she was the only thing that grounded me. And fuck, I needed to be grounded.

A series of low grunts escaped me as I screwed her until she milked me of every drop. My legs felt like they were made out of Jell-O as I came back down to earth.

It took an ungodly amount of time, but when I was done, I stared down at the mess she'd made, at the clothes which were everywhere, and I leaned over her, rumbling, "I should make you meet the folks with cum dripping out of your cunt." No surprise, that dirty little pussy of hers squeezed my softening dick hard. Though I maintained my grip on her, supporting her, I pushed her forward and said, "Use your hands to walk your way back into a standing position."

Limp like spaghetti, it took her way too fucking long to do as I asked, but I wasn't about to complain. My grip on her kept my cock inside that tight heat, and when she was back upright, I moved one arm, banding it about her hips, then used the other to angle her so her back was to my chest.

I rested my head on her shoulder, and whispered, "You'd like that, wouldn't you?"

"N-No," she moaned, her head dragging from side to side.

"Your cunt tells me otherwise. You want to eat at the dining room table, with my folks there, my cum all over you, making those pretty little thighs sticky with my seed. You want to be thinking about tonight, when I fuck you again—" I paused. "Did you like your first time with me, Camille? Your first time as my woman. My wife. *Mine*."

She didn't answer. She didn't have to.

Her cunt was more communicative than she was.

But I forced her to reply, demanding, "Camille! Did you like your first time as my woman?"

"Y-Yes," she breathed, and as the sun drifted a little lower in the sky, at that second, I saw her reflection in the glass. Her eyes were dazed, her face relaxed, everything about her looked like she was coming down from a high.

Good.

I'd keep her like that for a lifetime if I could.

Fuck, if she'd been beautiful before, that was nothing to now when she was hungover from my cock.

"What about at dinner? You want to be sticky with my seed?"

She gulped. "I-I s-shouldn't."

"No, you shouldn't want that, you dirty little slut," I whispered, but I pressed a kiss to her cheek, letting my tongue trail out to lessen the sting behind the insult. "But, do you?"

"Y-Yes," she hiccupped, confirming what I suspected. "I do want that. I don't know why, but I do." The latter half came out on a confused sob as she twisted her head to the side, shoving her face against mine, hiding from herself rather than me.

Humming under my breath, I told her, "You let the clothes drop. You didn't obey me when I told you to come up here, you made us late leaving, and you opened the cuts on your hands again... so, instead, you're going to get cleaned up."

I wasn't sure how bad a consequence that'd be. Most women I'd fucked would be *happy* to shower away a load of cum—saying that, I had to figure they would. I'd never fucked a woman without a rubber before —but she pushed her forehead against me.

"No, please, Brennan. Please."

Inwardly, I'd admit to being stunned, but who the fuck was I to question what got her hot?

Every time I'd fingered her up to now, she always started off as dry as a bone. I wasn't concerned about her being frigid, but I couldn't help but think she might be.

Maybe she'd just never found her kink.

To be a cum slut.

Well... *my* cum slut.

Her pussy wasn't the only thing doing the twitching. My cock did as well as that thought whispered through my mind.

"You disobeyed, Camille," I rumbled. "I told you there'd be consequences."

A shaky sigh escaped her, but I heard the pout in her words as she whispered, "No fair."

I smirked. "Who said life was fair?" She clucked her tongue at me, but I shut her up by asking, "You ready for me to pull out?" Pressing another kiss to her cheek, where I could reach thanks to the way she was hiding against me, I felt and tasted her pout.

"No," she admitted, which had me sighing and reaching down to cup us both where she still held me in place.

Another shaky sigh whispered from her lips, and it had me promising, "Later, Camille. Later."

And it had me being grateful that I never made a promise I couldn't and wouldn't keep...

NOT EVERYONE HAS TO LIKE YOU.
JUST BE YOU. YOU'LL FIND YOUR
PEOPLE.

TWENTY-EIGHT
CAMILLE

I KNEW Brennan's father by looks alone.

Even in his late sixties, Aidan Sr. was an undeniably handsome man.

It was almost perverse that he could be so attractive, that Brennan and his other sons could be too, considering their work.

They had blood on their hands, on their hearts and their souls, but their faces were angelic. At least, if angels had the kind of faces that you wanted to kiss.

Not that Aidan Sr.'s made me want to get kissy with it, but it certainly made it easier for me to understand how Inessa had fallen for Eoghan so fast, and why, with Brennan, all of these bewildering desires were flooding me to the point of being overwhelmed.

How could any mortal resist a fallen angel?

His grin of welcome morphed into a frown of confusion as he looked me over, his eyes narrowed. From that in-depth scan, I was aware that he knew who I was. He recognized me and he didn't approve of my presence here and what it might mean that Brennan would bring me here on a Saturday night for a meal with his folks.

For all that he was insane, he was evidently shrewd.

"None of that, Da," Brennan rumbled, his voice low and deep. The warning clear, and all the more soothing to me for that.

I peered up at him, finding comfort in his proximity. Finding comfort in him, truth be told. In this, the land of my father's enemies, it was nice to have a friendly face close by.

"None of what? Why's she here?"

"Aidan? Are you interrogating our Bren on the doorstep? What's the matter with you?"

The waspish grumble had me tilting my head so that I could see around Aidan better. When I found a woman, all curves and red hair, a face that would have been pretty when she was younger but was stunning now, I knew this was the famous Magdalena O'Donnelly.

The woman Aidan Sr. had gone to war over.

God only knew how many men were dead because of this man's love for his wife.

It would be romantic if it wasn't also depressing.

"The matter is he's brought someone with him," was Aidan's retort.

Lena frowned, but her gaze drifted to mine. "Oh."

"*Oh?* That's all you've got to say, Ma?" Brennan chided, but his tone was softer. Gentler.

With his father, he was brisk and to the point. Not necessarily argumentative, but borderline aggressive.

It was quite apparent that my husband loved his mother.

"You should have told me you were bringing company." She barked at Aidan, "Let them in, man. What do you want them to do? Camp out on the doorstep? They'll catch their deaths in this cold."

Aidan grunted but shuffled backward, his unwillingness clear even as his hands went to my shoulders to help me out of my coat.

I turned to look up at him, and whispered, "Thank you."

I'd learned over the years to face a predator with strength so I looked him right in the eye until he arched his brow, seeming to understand what I was doing.

He broke eye contact first, but that was less to do with how impressed he was by my ballsiness, and more to do with Lena calling out, "Aidan, give the girl room to breathe."

Though he backed up, taking my coat with him, with his other hand, he reached for mine, twisted it around, and pursed his lips as he cast my Band-Aid-covered palms a sharp look.

"Da, leave it alone," Brennan rumbled, making me wonder if these O'Donnelly men were some kind of mentalists. After all, I'd gone through an adolescence with no one in my family recognizing what I was doing, yet they'd learned the truth in a shocking amount of time.

Aidan grunted under his breath, but backed away, moving toward a closet in the hallway where he placed my coat.

Brennan passed the bag he'd been carrying over to me, and I smiled a little awkwardly at the gimlet stare Lena cast my way.

"Let me introduce Camille to you, Ma," Brennan said gruffly, his hand entwining with mine as he tugged me into his side.

The instant I collided with his heat, a strange welter of relief filled me.

Like I was safe.

Like, even though I was with two of New York's most dangerous clan leaders, he'd protect me.

I wasn't sure he'd ever know how much gratitude filled me at that moment. How, in those seconds, where he could have tossed me to the lions, he earned something that couldn't be bought.

He'd wanted my trust.

He'd said he wanted my loyalty.

But in that simple move, he earned them.

Or the seedlings of them, at any rate.

He broke the union of our hands and instead, covered my shoulder with his arm, tucking me even deeper into his hold.

I didn't know where he ended and I began as I faced his mother, who merely pursed her lips and said, "Brennan, son, if you didn't think I figured that out the second she crossed the threshold, you must think I'm going senile." She tipped her head to the side. "What I'd like to know is why you brought Inessa's sister for dinner with your parents?"

"If you're so smart," he jeered, but there was a grin on his face, "then I'm sure you can figure it out."

"What I'm figuring out is that you've done something damn foolish," was her waspish retort, as her gaze drifted over to her husband who was somewhere behind us.

"I hate it when you do this," Aidan grumbled. "It's like the two of you speak your own language."

Lena snorted. "Not our fault you can't keep up."

Aidan heaved a sigh as he passed us in the wide hall, then moved to

Lena's side. In a way that mimicked Brennan's hold on me, he slipped his arm around her waist and tucked her into his side.

His mouth brushed over her crown as he kissed her, his eyelids fluttering closed as he did so. It was strange to meet the man the city both revered and feared, and to see him so evidently in love with his wife after all these years. He breathed her in as he held her close, like he never wanted to let her go.

Touched, I bit my lip, both charmed and a little awestruck by the sight of such devotion.

They knew I was Russian. Knew I was Bratva. Yet Aidan still showed me that side of himself, of their relationship.

In my world, that was a weakness. Something to be exploited.

And while I was sure Aidan Sr.'s world worked the exact same way, he didn't care.

That strength—or insanity—made me relax some.

During the ride upstate, Brennan had told me he was going to paint us as a love match to his parents, and I realized that was the smartest way to go. If Aidan could look and hold and touch his wife the way he did, then surely he had the closet heart of a romantic?

"What's going on, son?" Aidan asked after he focused on us again.

"I'd like you to meet my wife."

A wave of emotion flashed over Lena's face, but Aidan's scowl would have had me backing up if Brennan hadn't tightened his hold on me.

I peeped up at him, saw he wasn't frightened of that scowl, and I was overawed by how in control he was, how unafraid. It wasn't an act, he wasn't faking it until he made it. He wasn't scared. Genuinely.

If anyone knew what the man was capable of, I had to reason it was his sons, but Brennan stood there, uncowering as he murmured, "We met at the Jupiter Wells party. The one you forced me to go to because Aidan was sick."

Aidan's scowl darkened. "Meaning it's my fault?"

Brennan smirked. "I guess. Not my fault, is it? Look at her, would you? An angel come to Earth. How couldn't I make her mine?"

How was it that he called me an angel when I'd just likened him to a fallen one?

As I peered up at him, I saw that smirk, but deep in his eyes, a glimmer of *something* stole my breath, because it made me think he wasn't bullshitting them. That he really meant what he was saying.

Wishful thinking?

Or serendipity?

His words, however, triggered more silence until Aidan snapped, "She can't be your wife."

"Why can't she? Got the marriage certificate to prove it."

Before my eyes, Brennan pulled a piece of paper out of his pocket and passed it to his father.

Aidan scanned it like it was a ten-thousand line contract when, really, it was barely anything at all. I was the one who'd know—I'd read the damn thing before I signed it.

"There's no fine print, Da," Brennan said wryly, seeming to think as I had—that he was looking for an out. "It is what it is. Camille's mine now."

Three words.

Three.

Not the ones most women wanted to hear—*I love you.*

But a possession of ownership all the same.

Inside, something tightened and then relaxed. Like, at long last, I'd found exactly where I was supposed to be.

I'd found someone who'd call me *his*.

I settled deeper into his hold, moving into his side like we were meant to be, and I tilted my face against the thick cable knit sweater he wore, nuzzling my nose against it and inhaling his purely masculine scent.

At that moment, I knew I'd found my place.

A man who declared to his parents I was his? A man like *this*, with a family like *his*?

Like he'd told me...

There were no take-backs.

No divorce.

This was forever.

I was *his*, forever.

Until death did us part.

Those vows... they meant nothing to some people, but not to Brennan O'Donnelly.

Thank God.

"We need to discuss this. My office. Now."

The command might have had a lesser man tensing up, but Brennan merely shook his head. "No, Da. No discussion. This is my life. My choice. My decision. I made it knowing that it'd piss the family off, but it didn't stop me."

"Why?" Lena asked, the question soft, her disappointment clear.

I didn't think that was because *I* was the disappointment, but because he'd made his choices without conferring with the family.

"Because I'm a man, Ma. I can pick my own feckin' wife." He grunted. "I'll admit things were sped up a little by certain circumstances that happened recently but Da's the one always going on about us getting married, settling down. Well, consider me settled."

Aidan, whose scowl had been growing darker and darker as his son spoke, rasped, "What 'things?'"

Unsure what Brennan was about to say, whether he was about to blend the truth with fiction, I tensed up, just waiting for his next words:

"Vasov's been murdered."

He was going to lie. *For me.*

"What?" Aidan straightened up. "I've heard none of that chatter."

I licked my lips. "He died the other night."

Brennan squeezed my arm, a noiseless command that told me to shut up. "They're keeping it under wraps." He reached up, scratching his jaw with his free hand like the stubble I knew he'd shaved off earlier was already growing back in. "Looks like some mess up with that bitch of a wife of his."

"Svetlana's pregnant," I murmured, being careful with my tenses.

"With another man's baby, apparently." Brennan shrugged. "I only heard more of the tale this afternoon from my in with the Bratva. The second I know more, you'll hear it first.

"But I wanted Camille out of that place, so I did it the one way I knew would give her the permanent security she deserves. Whether you like it or not, Da, she's an O'Donnelly now."

"Not by my say so she isn't," he growled.

"So, you'll give Inessa the family's protection because you forced her on Eoghan, but the woman I *choose* to be mine, you'll cast out?" Brennan scoffed. "That makes sense."

Lena tugged on Aidan's hand. "He's right."

"No, he isn't. Inessa was—" An explosive snarl escaped Aidan as he pulled away from Lena and ran a hand through his hair. "Inessa was an olive branch between us and the man you tell me is dead now. What fucking use are either Vasov daughters if they're not tied to the Pakhan anymore?"

His words should have meant nothing to me, but they made me want to scream. An endless, eternal scream that was like falling into a black hole, one I'd never escape from, one that would reclaim me time and time again.

I was worthless to another father.

A womb, a defective olive branch, never a woman.

Never someone to love—

Unaware of my anguish, Brennan merely snorted, stunning me with how brave he was. Where Aidan Sr. shoved me down that black hole, Brennan leaned into it to help pull me out.

"If you don't know what use a good woman is to a man like me, then there's no hope for you. I thought you of all people would get it." He cast a look at his mother who flinched. "Anyway, don't worry, Da. You've still got two sons left who aren't married. I'm sure you can shove the next Pakhan's daughters on Con and Junior."

When Aidan spun around, I didn't tense up, didn't show I was scared because I recognized that inherent, brewing violence that was simmering beneath the surface.

Just like my father.

God, Brennan had been raised exactly as I had.

I reached for his free hand and tangled my fingers with his, squeezing them, putting pressure on them as I tried to give him some of my meager strength. He'd saved me from that black hole which was still trying to grasp a hold of me, clinging tendrils escaping the pit, swirling about my feet as the mist pulled me deeper...

I knew he wasn't frightened of his father now, but that didn't mean the young Brennan hadn't been. What had he suffered as this man's spare heir?

"Calm down, Aidan," Lena snapped, wading into things in a way that surprised me.

Mama would never have dared get in the way of Father when he was in this mood, but Lena did it with ease, which gave me hope for Brennan and made me wonder if this was why she had his devotion. Why she'd earned that *promise* of his, whatever it might be.

She turned her back on us, her hands going to her husband's shoulders as she stared up at him.

"Calm down," she repeated. "There's no point in crying over spilled milk." Whatever she saw in his eyes had her reaching up, grabbing his jaw and forcing him to look at her. "You're going to go take a walk in the garden, and you're going to take a second to calm down." When he didn't budge, she shoved him, pushing him away. "Go on, *now*."

His nostrils flared like an angry dog's, but with a malevolent glance at Brennan, he stormed off, heading away from us with heavy, pounding footsteps.

A door opened then slammed and only then did Lena release a heavy breath and turn back to look at us.

In the dim light of the corridor, with its walls that were covered in family photos, she didn't look like a woman who was nearing retirement age.

With her gleaming red hair, creamy skin, the slim figure and straight shoulders of a woman much younger than her, she looked like the powerhouse she was.

The one person who kept Aidan O'Donnelly Sr. on a leash.

It was almost surreal that, directly behind where he'd been standing just seconds before, there was a picture of a much younger Aidan with a man who had to be his brother at his side.

I recognized Coney Island in the background, a rickety Ferris wheel and a colorful merry-go-round churning forever onward while they stood directly in front of 'Petey's Famous.' The pair of them were dressed in sharp suits, at least, sharp for the 70s, but they were both grinning around hot dogs like big kids, not the hardened killers they must have been at that time.

Not everyone had two faces like me—but it was clear that Aidan Sr. did. Brennan, too. Was it because of how we'd been raised? Though, I doubted Inessa was like this, and Victoria didn't seem that way either. Was it about an aptitude to kill?

Uneasily, I switched focus, taking note of a picture beside the hotdog one, which showed a man I recognized from the society pages.

Finn O'Grady with his wife and their newborn son. My brow puckered as I let my gaze drift between the two photos—

Lena growled under her breath, shattering my focus as she snapped, "There wasn't a better way you could think of doing that, Bren?" It was a rhetorical question because she shook her head at us both. "You'd best go. Give him time to calm down."

Brennan shrugged. "If you say so, Ma."

"I do say so," was her bitter retort.

The gift bag hung redundant in my hands, a silent reminder that I needed to give it to her. Facing her, I cleared my throat, wanting her to know that even if I'd been shaken on Brennan's behalf by what I'd seen, I wasn't afraid. Which I wasn't. Not with a father like mine. But a woman like this appreciated strength.

If I was scared, she'd sense my weakness and I'd never earn her respect. And that mattered. Brennan cared for his mother. Cultivating a relationship with her was smart.

"Lena, we'll leave, but I'd still like you to have this."

She held out her hand for the bag. "Thank you, Camille." Her lips pursed but, a tad resentfully, she continued, "I'll look forward to getting to know you."

The ominous tone made that more of a threat than a greeting, but I'd take it.

She'd just offered me acceptance, after all. Begrudging though it might have been, that was what she gave me nonetheless.

Brennan urged me around, his hold on me as absolute as it had been before while he guided us to the closet.

For the first time, he let go of me, and only then, to get my coat and help me into it. Then, he shrugged his on, turned back to look at his mother and said, "She's my choice, Ma."

"None of us have choices, Bren," was Lena's reply, but rather than be belligerent, it was almost sad.

"That's just it. We do. Da's going to struggle getting the rest of us to comply. Eoghan did because Da got Louie and goddamn Niall to hold him down so he could beat the shit out of him to get him to marry Inessa—"

Lena gasped at that, prompting me to look back at her; her horror was clear. As was her surprise. I doubted the surprise was for the beating, but for how Aidan Sr. had gone about it.

Holding Eoghan down to be beaten? It reminded me too much of a dog being chained to the wall and whipped.

Brennan either didn't care his mother was startled or didn't realize, because he stormed on, "Declan's got the woman he wants, now me. Why should Junior and Conor settle for less? Why would you want them to?"

Lena reached up to cover her mouth, but, for the first time, she appeared fragile. She looked her age.

Her shoulders stooped.

The whisper of wrinkles on her brow and around her eyes made a telltale appearance.

And she looked... *tired*.

I couldn't blame her.

This world we inhabited had a tendency to make us feel a damn sight older than we actually were. A lot more exhausted, too.

"I'll see you tomorrow, Ma." He turned away, until she called out:

"Bren?"

"Yeah?"

"Did he really get Louie and Niall to hold Eoghan down?"

"He did."

A swift intake of breath whirred through the hall like she had the force of a hurricane behind her.

"I didn't know."

Brennan just peered at her over his shoulder. "In the end, he was lucky. The marriage worked out. She's his choice now. Luck isn't something men like us often get though."

She shook her head, but I could see the tears welling in her eyes. Brennan did too, because he hesitated, and I knew he wanted to go to her. Wanted to make this better, but how could he?

Lena, seeing the internal war, just whispered, "I'll see you tomorrow, son." She turned her attention on me. "And you, Camille." She licked her lips. "Thank you again for the gifts. I'm sure we'll cherish them."

The inclusive pronoun had me sending her a soft smile.

We were women, born into this underworld, and we knew we weren't often the ones who had a say in these matters...

Maybe that shot between us like lightning bolts that united us together. Both from different camps but still existing in this half place where we were second class citizens with our men.

Unless we claimed our territory.

Unless we made it ours.

And now I saw Lena, now I could see her interactions with Aidan, and the force inherent in her, I knew Brennan would never respect any woman who wasn't like that.

Who didn't have power, meager though it might be, behind her.

I'd just been given a life lesson, did mother and son but know it, and I wasn't a slow learner.

TWENTY-NINE
BRENNAN

THAT DEFINITELY HADN'T GONE AS PLANNED.

While I could have prevaricated over who Camille was to me, the second he'd opened the door, when I'd seen Da's reaction to her, I'd known that wasn't possible.

In all honesty, I'd thought it more likely that I'd walk out of their place with a full belly than a shiner, because Da was not only getting old, he wouldn't have pulled that move in front of Ma. But I'd been wrong on both counts.

None of Ma's roast had been consumed, and I wasn't rocking a black eye.

It was a close won thing though. The more shit he spewed, the more I wanted to beat him, but my week had already taken a twist, I didn't want to end it with sending my da to the ICU.

With years' worth of bitterness building up, there was no way in fuck I could do anything other than make him pay for what he'd done to us. I never allowed myself to feel resentment for the path I'd taken, and I wasn't about to start now, but when it boiled down to a fight? I'd let my fists do the fucking talking.

The journey back to the city was quiet. I appreciated that. I knew we were both deep in our thoughts, so I set a playlist on low that suited my mood—Jose Gonzalez. I appreciated the soft, twinkling notes of his guitar and dulcet voice as I tried to figure out my next move.

Not just with Da, or Ma, but with the NWS. As well as all the other crap that was coming home to roost.

Rats, rats everywhere. It was starting to feel like this was a ship that was about to sink from the weight of them.

When we made it back to Manhattan, I broke the silence to ask, "What do you want to eat?"

I half expected her to dither or to ask me what I wanted first, but she surprised me by immediately answering, "Sushi."

Though I didn't feel like eating out, she was all dressed up, and even though she'd rushed through her make-up thanks to our fuck before leaving, she looked like a million dollars. I was prick enough to want to show her off.

Though respectable, with the skirt running at mid-length, it clung to her ass and thighs in a way that should be illegal.

The blouse she wore had a deep V-neck and she'd placed some kind of bandeau there to make it less racy. It revealed toned arms, strong and lean, and shoulders that were made to be marked by my bites.

The thought had me grunting under my breath as I directed us through Midtown toward my favorite sushi place.

It was packed, like always, but when I gave the valet my car keys, I saw the guy manning the valet stand pick up his radio to warn the owners I was here.

"Wait here," I ordered her as I jumped out and rounded the fender to open the door for her.

Helping her out, I tucked her arm in mine, and together we walked down the carpeted sidewalk toward the entrance.

The maître d' opened the door for us, all beaming smiles and ass-licking words of greeting as we were guided to my regular table.

A couple shot me a glower, which told me they'd been the unlucky ones to get moved so I could eat here, but I ignored them, knowing they'd get a free meal from the tab that I'd be picking up later. Akemi, the maître d', knew how I rolled.

When he took Camille's coat, I arched a brow when I saw the skirt had magically drifted up a few inches, and the bandeau that made her tits look respectable had disappeared too.

My jaw cracked as I pulled back the seat for her. When she slipped into it, I leaned over and, in her ear, rasped, "Feel like playing with fire tonight, do you, Camille?"

"I don't know what you mean," she whispered, tilting her head to look up at me.

Her eyelashes weren't false, they were just fucking long, and I felt the brush of them against my cheek.

The slight tickle shouldn't have turned me on even more, but it did. I straightened up, shoved my coat at Akemi, then grabbed my chair and rather than sitting opposite her, moved it to her side so we were sitting at 12 o'clock and quarter past.

Taking my place, I rocked back as a server appeared to whisk our coats away from Akemi, who beamed a smile at me, acting as if I hadn't just fucked up his service for the night.

"I'll have my usual," I told him gruffly, planting my hand on Camille's thigh and glowering around me as I saw a couple of the guys in our perimeter staring at her tits.

Akemi bowed, before he gave his attention to Camille, handing her the menu and asking her what she'd like to drink.

When she chose a glass of house rosé and a bottle of sparkling water, he disappeared to give her some time to select her food.

My fingers spread wide to cover a large part of her thigh, before I asked, "What happened to the Mary Tyler Moore look?"

"That was to impress your parents, not you."

The candid answer had me grinning. "So, I just needed to fuck you to get you to let your hair down, huh?"

"Takes a stick to remove a stick."

"Out of your ass?" I arched my brow at her again. "I'll be more than willing to shove something up there later on."

"That a promise?" Camille questioned, her gaze meeting mine over the menu.

My hand clamped down on her thigh again. "You want to tease me by wearing short skirts, and skimpy tops," I rasped, sitting up and whispering the words against her cheek, "go for it. I can take it. But you don't dress like this when I'm not with you. Understood?" I kissed her there, where I'd let my words make their brand.

"Seeing as you're the one I want to tease, where would the fun be in dressing like a slut if you're not around?"

Heat sparked inside me, not just at her words, but at the fact she wasn't cowering at mine, but fighting fire with fire.

Maybe it really had just taken a good fuck to get her to chill out?

Who the hell knew how a woman's mind worked?

"Good point," I rumbled, and maybe I was dumb to let her words appease me, but they did.

When a guy, evidently returning from the restroom, caught sight of Camille, I let him take his fill of her, before shooting him a death stare when he shot me a glance too.

Let him *try* to take his fucking measure of me.

Asshole.

I couldn't stop myself from pressing my lips to her shoulder, from letting my tongue peek out to trace a shape on the bony joint, before I murmured, "I can call you that, Camille, you can even think it, but no one will ever think that about you. Do you hear me?" She wasn't a slut outside of our bedroom, and I'd kill any cunt who said otherwise. Because if she was, then so was I.

"You're very bossy tonight," she said breathily.

"I'm always bossy," I rumbled. "Always."

"Well, more so than usual," she acquiesced, tensing up as I let my fingers trace the same shape my tongue had on her shoulder, but on her thigh instead.

If this was the human male version of pissing on my territory, then so be it.

And I'd do it every fucking time if it meant that I got to peer down that blouse of hers and to see those luscious tits while I ate Michelin-starred sushi.

Mine.

The word wouldn't stop reverberating around my head.

Mine.

Maybe saying it out loud to Da changed shit for me—I'd never know for sure. But I'd already been feeling the pull of it, the sneaky tendrils of possessiveness that came when a woman wasn't something just to bang but to keep too.

Akemi appeared again, a waiter at his back with her sparkling water and an iced tumbler, a frosted bottle of Shochu—Japanese vodka—with two shot glasses and a chilled rosé on a tray, his smile still in place as the server placed both on the table while the maître d' waited on Camille's order.

"That's not enough," I told her as she made her selections, knocking back a shot of vodka to take the edge off. That was all I'd be having of that seeing as I was driving, but Akemi would package up the bottle for me to take home.

The server took it away, and within seconds, a glass of Anahi, Japanese beer, replaced it.

"It's plenty," she argued, her gaze irritated as she shot me a look.

It wasn't.

I didn't think she was on a diet, but it made sense that months' worth of misery while she lived under her father's roof was enough to cut her appetite in half.

"If you're going to keep up with me, you need the energy."

Her lips moved into a mutinous pout, but she conceded by adding a couple more dishes to her order.

That we shared an appreciation of sushi pleased me. I didn't know her, she didn't know me, but what I was coming to learn was a good sign.

Whether we argued every day of the fucking week or not, we could always eat sushi on Saturdays.

The thought amused me enough to have me sinking back into my seat. Peering around the restaurant, I took note of everyone and anyone in here. Spotting a few familiar faces, not just from the Points either. Some politicians, a couple of celebrities. Akemi's place was popular with the rich and famous of New York.

"I'm surprised you want to sit here."

"Why?" I asked, letting my attention drift to her.

"We're in the middle," she pointed out, like I didn't know that already. "You're surrounded."

"Better than being at the window." I tapped my nose. "Drive-bys still happen."

She winced. "Yes, I know."

She wasn't surprised when our orders started to pour out almost immediately, because there was no hiding from the preferential treatment I got. Not only was Akemi's restaurant under the Five Points' protection, but we also helped him with his imports, which saved his profits from the greedy-fingered IRS.

As an array of dishes started to make an appearance, cast iron plates and chopstick holders did too. A special ceramic bottle of Tengumai did as well, along with small clay pots tinted with gold for the sake, followed by steaming bowls of tempura vegetables and a vintage bottle of fermented soy sauce, Goyogura *shoyu*, that Akemi knew was my favorite. As well as the Imperial Household's. Few soy sauces were given warrants from the Emperor, but this bad boy was, and it tasted like fucking nectar. Akemi knew to always have some in stock for me.

As the staff retreated with bows, the maître d' included, we were left to our own devices.

"Everyone's wondering who we are," she declared, her tone amused as she picked up her chopsticks.

"Let them wonder," I retorted, grabbing mine as well and making a start on the food. It wasn't one of Ma's roasts, but this was a fond favorite too.

For a few minutes, neither of us talked much, just enjoying the food. I almost thought she'd be too nervous to speak, but I should have known otherwise.

"I'll have to bring Inessa here."

"She likes sushi?"

"Well, it wouldn't make sense to bring her here if she didn't, would it?" Camille teased, her grin cheeky. "I wonder if she's still friends with Lisandra—that girl could eat more raw tuna than a sumo wrestler."

"Lisandra?"

"They went to school together. Used to be best friends."

"I think Eoghan's mentioned her." My brow puckered. "In fact, I know he did. She's a nightmare, isn't she? Always getting into trouble?"

"Oh dear, I was hoping she'd have grown out of that."

"Apparently not. She moved away for college though. At least, I think so."

"I'm surprised you remember."

My lips curved. "She came back for Fall break, and she and Inessa went to a club together."

Eyes round, she asked, "Did something happen?"

I shook my head, but I thought by my deepening smile she knew that was a lie.

She leaned into me, bringing with her the scent of chamomile, and whispered, "What happened?"

"Eoghan followed them to the club to make sure everything was going to stay copacetic for them—he's a control freak. Anyway, he broke two guys' arms..." I rubbed my chin. "I remember because it was one of my clubs and I had to pay the bastards off."

"You mean it's not out of the ordinary for him to break random people's arms?" Camille questioned with a laugh.

I arched a brow. "What do you think?"

She chuckled, then murmured, "By the way, I claimed one of the lower bedrooms as mine. I hope that's okay?"

I just shrugged. "Fine with me. You won't be sleeping in there though," I tacked on, a warning throbbing through the words.

"I never said I would be," she pointed out. "In fact, I was going to ask Bagpipes to move the bed. I'd like to buy a desk and a few other things."

"Go for it. I'm sure Bagpipes will have a blast as your furniture mover. Although, tell him in advance because he'll bring Forrest to help out if you want to shift a large piece like the bed."

I already knew which she'd claimed for her own, because I'd been in there to check things out.

"Okay, will do." She took a sip of water, then asked, "Mind if I serve myself some sake?"

"Knock yourself out."

Her delicate hand reached out to cup the bottle, the short nails catching my eye as she poured us both some, as well as the polished stone bracelets she wore. They were pretty, in moonstone, but they didn't fit her outfit. They were all uniform in size, but for one. It was as large as a piece of bubblegum.

When she saw me looking at it, she grimaced. "It's for motion sickness. If I'm not driving, I get nauseated."

"Do they work?" I asked, surprised.

"It's pretty effective if you get the right spot. It works on acupressure points." Her smile turned cheeky. "Don't tell Bagpipes though."

"Why not?"

"I told him I have to drive or I'll puke all over your car seats."

Amused, I chuckled, but I pointed out, "You should let him drive. He has a lot of experience."

"I had a defensive driving course when I was younger," she informed me. "I was even trained how to respond in hostage situations."

I arched a brow. "I'm surprised your father cared enough."

"Me too," she said wryly, "but remember, I was an item to sell. You can't sell it if it's damaged goods."

A thought occurred to me. "Camille?"

"Yes?"

"I know it's not exactly dinner talk but..." I rested the polished ebony chopsticks on their small perch. "Why did you wait to lose your virginity?"

She blinked. "Well, a part of me was scared, but mostly it was because I was a romantic."

"*Was?*"

"Yes. Was." The word was firm. "I waited even though I'd have been safer sleeping around, but I tried to perpetuate the belief that I was a whore by hanging out with the brothers and at the MC clubhouse when I had time. That must have protected me because he never came for me.

"To be honest, I was surprised Abramovicz still wanted me after my past." She shrugged. "He must have pissed Father off, and it was a favor or something."

My brow puckered as I took her in—she truly believed that. I shook my head. "What do you see when you look in the mirror?"

"Umm, me?"

Her blonde hair was like spun gold, her skin so pure it made porcelain look marred. In fact, her face was so perfect, it was like a china doll's. With the make-up she wore, she was the most flawless woman I'd ever seen. She was too skinny, and she definitely needed to eat more, but with her tits, she was a clotheshorse so she looked phenomenal in everything.

Didn't she realize that Abramovicz wouldn't have been doing Vasov a favor?

He'd have been drooling over her since she'd first been promised to him. Maybe even before, the perverted bastard. And now she had those tits, sweet Lord.

She must have realized where I was looking, because a smile danced on her mouth. It pissed me off that one of the Sinners must have paid for them, but hell, they were mine to play with forever now.

"You're beautiful, Camille. I'm glad you weren't wasted on that cunt."

Her smile was like the sun appearing on a darkened horizon. The stars, the moon, the sky itself had no choice but to fade away under its beaming power.

I found myself staring at her a moment too long, before she murmured, "I've only ever had cold sake before."

Clearing my throat, I decided she was wise to change the topic. Picking up my chopsticks again, I popped a salmon nigiri into some soy sauce, explaining, "Declan, my brother, told me chilled sake was for wannabes." I grinned then popped the sushi into my mouth and savored the bite. "He said that premium sake should be enjoyed at room temperature, not chilled like everyone says. I tried it with him, and I've never gone back."

"He's younger than you, isn't he?"

"He is. They're all younger than me apart from Aidan Jr," I told her. "You'll meet them all tomorrow."

Another smile danced on her lips. "Oh, you're all in alphabetical order. How did I only just realize that?"

My nose crinkled. "Original, right?"

"Well, it makes it easier for me." She hesitated, then asked, "Finn O'Grady's Aidan's age, isn't he? I, just, well, I mean, he looks older than Eoghan, you know?"

"I'm surprised you know him."

"He's in the society pages, plus, Inessa mentioned his wife and their son to me a few times. I saw his picture in the hall too."

I shrugged. "Yeah, there's a couple of months' age gap between him and Aidan. But he isn't blood, don't forget. He's a brother, but more like an adoptive one."

Her eyes rounded. "Oh."

"He moved in with us when he was a teenager," I explained. "Ma and Da are like his adopted parents. They treat Jake as if he's their grandkid and everything."

"Right. Good to know." Her smile was genuine, but something in her expression had me frowning. Before I could ask what the problem was, she questioned, "So, Declan knows everything about sake but isn't a wannabe?"

Snickering at that, I explained, "Declan's a poser, sure, but he's obsessed with all things Asia. He's got me hooked on quite a few things over the years."

She turned a little in her seat, moving into me like this was an intimate meal. Like we were dating. Instead, we'd bypassed all that shit and were married.

I'd come to see if I'd regret that in time, but I'd have regretted letting her loose and not living up to the honor I vowed to live by. Sure, my honor code was a little more skewed than most, but I had standards.

Either way, I liked that she moved into me. She didn't have to do that. She could have stayed where she was, only allowing the bridge of my hand on her thigh to connect us. But she didn't.

She charged things up a notch.

"What like? What did he introduce you to?"

"Pho? Some Thai dishes. But I prefer sushi. That's my favorite." I wrinkled my nose. "This is exotic by comparison to the kind of food we grew up eating. Da likes nothing that he considers 'foreign.'"

"That rules out a lot of food."

"Having met him now, do you think he cares about that?" I said wryly. "The man's a walking '-ist.'"

"Is that why he doesn't approve of me?"

"Because you're Russian? Nah. It's because there's no deal to be had or to make. I told you, there's no divorce with us. No matter how hard he huffs or puffs, this is it."

"No offense, Brennan, but you're not exactly twenty-five anymore—"

My lips twisted. "Thank you."

Her cheeks turned a charming shade of pink. "I just mean, well, he can't think you'd let him lead you around? Wouldn't he have done that already if that were the case?"

"He's tried to get me and Aidan to marry in the past, but we never bit, and we always managed to get out of it."

"He must have let you."

"I think..." I pursed my lips. "This is a deep conversation for a public restaurant."

"Oh, I'm sorry." She grimaced. "I thought it was open season for questions."

I shrugged, because she wasn't wrong. I *had* just asked her about her virginity over sashimi. "No need to apologize. Most things where the family is concerned are deep unfortunately." I heaved a sigh. "Anyway, I'm the one who's sorry. I didn't expect tonight to go well, but I didn't think we'd be leaving as soon as we got there."

"Everyone knows his reputation," she pointed out gently. "He's renowned for being volatile."

"And he's getting worse," I muttered, squeezing her thigh. "I mean it though, Camille. I'm sorry."

Her smile was gentle as she caught my eye. "Thank you, Brennan. It's not your fault though."

No, it wasn't, but I'd spent a lifetime paying for my father's mistakes and his volatile temper. It was second nature to apologize for it, and even more important that I did so to the woman I'd be stuck with for the rest of my life.

ONE DAY, YOU'LL LOOK BACK ON TODAY, ON HOW HARD IT WAS, AND YOU'LL SMILE. YOU'LL BE GRATEFUL YOU MADE IT.

THIRTY
CAMILLE

THAT HE WAS chivalrous shouldn't have come as a surprise to me, but it did.

He opened doors for me, helped me out of the car. When I went to use the restroom, he got to his feet as well and aided me back into my seat.

The advantage of dating an older man, I supposed.

I'd never dated a younger man who'd do that, and Nyx, well, he'd never think to treat me like a lady.

Brennan did, though.

Even better, he acted as if I was a fire hydrant he had to piss on.

Most women might have disliked that, but I adored it. I loved the glares he shot at male patrons in the restaurant, I loved how he moved his chair so that we were in each other's private space. I loved the hand he clamped to my thigh, and the way he stuck close to my side as if I was precious to him.

I loved it all.

And I wanted more.

I felt like a flower who'd been left to grow in a shady part of the garden, and who'd just been repotted in a sunny spot. As if, at long last, I could grow massive blooms, blossom how nature intended.

The best part?

This was now.

When he barely knew me.

What would he be like when we'd been together a while?

I almost shivered at the thought.

Of course, he noticed.

"Are you cold?"

I shook my head, watching him watch me in the mirror lining the elevator.

"Then why the shiver?" A filthy smirk creased his lips as he turned to me. "Thinking dirty thoughts?"

"Maybe," I whispered, peering up at him, aware that I was encouraging him and wanting nothing more.

Somehow, I'd triggered this caveman-like response in him and I wasn't about to stop.

With that in mind, I let my coat fall open, revealing the deep V of my blouse and the skirt I'd rucked up slightly so that it was short enough to raise eyebrows, never mind dicks.

I'd walked bare-assed naked, or almost, amid a crowd of rowdy bikers, so I wasn't nervous or embarrassed, but I hadn't known him long enough to be able to read him, or to predict his responses.

When his gaze dropped to my tits, I knew that I'd be wearing low necklines for the foreseeable future, if not forever. His nostrils flared at the sight, the bag the maître d' handed him as we were leaving fell to the floor with a dull thunk, and he reached over, cupping one of them even as he was charging forward, tangling our legs together as he pushed me into the back wall.

His other hand dropped down to my thigh, and his fingers, callused and rough, snagged on the silk stockings I wore, before he found gold in the form of actual flesh.

"I didn't realize you were wearing thigh-highs," he rumbled, his eyes on my tits still.

His fingers worked the lacy top of the stockings as I told him, "I'm not."

He froze, then his gaze drifted to mine. "You're wearing garters?"

My smile was wicked. "You'll have to find out, won't you?"

A growl escaped him as he moved back so he could grab the hem of my skirt and drag it up to my hips. His nostrils flared again when he saw

I wasn't wearing panties, and when his gaze caught on the belt around my waist, that shaped my slim curves, and kept the silk fripperies from tumbling down, I felt the disturbance in the air—like a thunderstorm was rumbling overhead.

He was a constant surprise, so I should have expected him not to react how I thought he would, but when he dropped to his knees and urged my thighs apart, a shocked breath escaped me even as I complied with his wishes.

One hand went to my calf, and he encouraged me to prop my heel on his shoulder, which gave him more room as he went to work on me. His lips unerringly sought my clit, and I didn't bother staring down at him, just watched him in the mirrors as he ate me out like he hadn't just eaten.

Like he was starving.

And God, so was I.

In barely no time at all, I went from being as dry as a bone to slick with arousal.

I hadn't a clue what it was about him, just knew that he could get me this hot with a glance.

My body was accustomed to being used for sex, but I'd never been an active part of the event. My mind skipped out on things as if it was self-preservation. I was used to being fucked, but fucking in return was a treat.

While I'd dressed with respectability in mind, I'd also picked clothes I knew would turn him on, never expecting that he'd turn the cards on *me*.

He tongue-fucked me, thrusting into my wet pussy, groaning as he did so. Plying my clit with the tip before sucking down on it, he teased me and tormented me, giving me what I needed, making me revel in his caresses as much as I looked forward to what was coming.

In no time at all, he'd trained me to expect orgasms. Lots of them. So many that it was like Christmas morning every time I knew sex was on the horizon.

And why shouldn't it be that way?

Just because I'd been treated like a cum dumpster before, didn't mean I couldn't be cherished and appreciated by someone else where sex was concerned.

My head rolled back against the glass as he ate me out, savoring me like a fine wine, and I let him, unashamed to have him enjoy me as an appetizer for the main course.

One of my hands slipped through the short locks of his hair, and I tugged at it, feeling the silk sliding not only against the palms of my hands but my thighs too.

When the doors pinged, my heart leaped as I half expected someone to be standing there, waiting on the other side, but of course, this was a private elevator and the only thing that happened was it opened onto the front hall of his apartment.

My stupid body didn't put two and two together, though, and I cried out, hoarse and husky as the climax powered through me like a champion.

Back arching, hips pumping, I rode his mouth as I eked out every last morsel of pleasure, adrenaline making it surge through my veins like the very purest of drugs. A sharp cry burst from my parted lips, and I clenched my eyes closed. Lifting an arm, I tucked my face into the nook of my elbow, needing to hide from how devastating the orgasm was, needing to hide from what this man, of all men, could do to me.

It was probably luck that he seemed to fit into me like a key to a lock, but it was bewildering too.

Knees buckling as they gave out under my weight, I almost fell but he was there, ready to catch me. His lips scented of me as he raised my arm, pressing it against the glass, not letting me hide, not letting me do anything other than face him as our mouths brushed together, and he ate at me much like he had moments earlier.

I shuddered as his fingers found my core once more, and he played with me there, continuing to drive me higher and higher, until I knew I could come again. So fast. Just like that.

A shriek escaped me as I tore my lips from his and I burrowed my face in his throat as I rode his hand. Mewls and whimpers tangled together in my throat as I tried to fight it, tried to fight the ecstasy but it wasn't possible. It was just... *inevitable*.

I heard the sounds of a zipper opening, that unmistakable noise of the tines unfastening, and I knew what that meant and I embraced it.

His hand moved away, slick fingers trailing over my thighs as he hefted me up, lifting me against the glass. I raised my arms to hook around his neck, just in time for him to press the tip of his dick against my slickness.

My eyes clenched closed again as the ricocheting delight of his thickness filling me took control of my senses. I screamed when gravity did the rest, impaling me on his shaft, and he let me hover there, my weight doing the work for him as I was forced to deal with just how big he was, how he filled me to perfection.

Arms tightening around his neck, I clung to him, crawling up him almost to ease some of the pressure, but as I did so, he grunted, and I knew why.

It was hard work—God, was it—but I started to rock against him. Crossing my feet at the ankles and digging them into his ass, I tightened my thighs and pulled upward. Each time I did that, he grunted into my ear, and he planted his hands against the mirrors, so that everything was on me.

Every time my muscles gave way, I sank down onto him, so heavily a keening cry was wrung from me, but whenever I almost reached his tip, a high whine escaped me because I felt so empty.

My pussy clung to him throughout, and when he burrowed his face in my throat and bit down, hard, enough to bruise, to mark, I screamed again, unable to stop myself, unable to stop the barrage of pleasure that filled me to the brim.

It was no surprise that his hoarse cries ricocheted around the elevator alongside mine, and our panting breaths merged into one delicious soundtrack as I took a second to savor the magic we made together.

When one of his hands cupped my ass, I thought he was going to lower me to the ground, but he didn't. He held me closer, one arm sliding to the center of my back, as he directed, "Push the 'Open Doors' button."

I peeked over his shoulder, and found we were by the console. I did as he asked, and the doors whirred open. He strode through, straight down the hall, and carried on to the bedroom. Only when we were standing by the bed did he urge me back, and when he did, he pressed a kiss to my lips, murmuring, "Thank you."

I didn't know what to say to that, so I just bowed my head, feeling unbelievably shy as he helped me to my feet. When I was standing there, shaky on my high heels, he supported me as he looked me over.

When I peeped up at him, wondering what he was thinking, I saw the glint in his eyes and basked in it. Once again feeling like that flower which was finally allowed to be in the sun.

There was heat and, even better, possessiveness.

I could see him stamping it all over me.

HIS.

I might as well have flashing lights over my head, and I was more than okay with that.

More than okay.

He reached down and tugged at my skirt, not stopping until it was pooling around my knees and then sinking to the floor. He traced his fingers over the garter belt, then murmured, "You may have just created a problem."

Concern whipped at me, but I modulated my tone, asking, "What kind of problem?"

"You wear panties again and I might have to make you stand in the corner."

My lips twitched as relief battered me. "Oh, well, that's something I can keep up."

He hummed, his fingers tracing my bare pussy, and I knew he could see the cum starting to seep out, making my inner thighs sticky. His fingers swirled in it and he asked, "Does this bother you?"

Was it comfortable? Not really.

Did it bother me?

"No."

He narrowed his eyes as he lifted those sticky, filthy fingers and pressed them to my lips. I parted them instantly, letting him stick them in my mouth, cleaning them up as expected. When he went a little too deep and I gagged, that heat flickered into a fire, but I didn't pull back, just let him fuck my mouth with his cum-soaked digits until he was happy.

A grunt escaped him when he stopped, but I could see from the tension in his jaw that he was ready for round two.

Eagerness filled me, but before I could get too excited, he murmured, "Get into bed. I'll join you later."

I blinked at him. "It's only eleven."

"You need your sleep."

I frowned, about to argue, but he tapped my bottom lip. "I'll join you in a little while."

My mouth parted, not to accept his fingers, but to argue, "Are you going out?"

"No. I have work to do downstairs." His eyes darkened. "Rest. I won't be long." He pulled back, jaw clenching as he looked me over. I thought he'd go, but he didn't. His hand grabbed my ass and he squeezed it, dragging me against his chest, rumbling, "Mine, Camille. No other fucker's."

Heart in my throat, I whispered, "Yours. No one else's."

He grunted again, then let go, only I never wanted him to let me go. I wanted him to hold onto me forever.

Brennan O'Donnelly had started out as a life raft. A last, desperate chance at a future that was of my own making. Now? He was turning into something else. Something far more dangerous than Abramovicz could ever be...

Something I didn't dare put a name to.

Couldn't put a name to.

A shaky sigh escaped me as I watched him leave, and call me a fool, but I didn't go against his wishes. Like a good girl, I undressed and slipped into bed.

I didn't sleep though. I wasn't nine years old.

Instead, I stared up at the ceiling, uninterested even in checking out my phone. The day's events were more than entertaining as I thought back to everything that had happened. From the way he'd taken me against the window, to the elevator, my still-sticky thighs and the slight ache were enough to make my cheeks burn, to how we'd been treated like royalty at the sushi restaurant, and then to his parents' reactions to our marriage...

Mostly, I was astonished by the attitude of the staff at Akemi's restaurant. Whenever my father dined out, people were scared of him. They didn't treat him with deference, but with fear. The O'Donnellys clearly inspired a different kind of response, one that was just as powerful but meant we really had been waited on as if we were the underworld Jackie-O and JFK.

That butted heads with what I'd gleaned from meeting Aidan Sr. for the first time today. He was a fearful man, after all. Terrifying if the hell promised in his eyes was anything to go by...

Uneasy, I turned on my side. The O'Donnellys weren't Bratva, but that didn't mean they weren't still mobsters. A thought that was confirmed when noises started bleeding from the lower level to this one. Pain-filled, scared, violent... hearing them prompted me to close my eyes.

Whoever was in his office... I was glad I wasn't them, and it made me vow never to turn my back on the O'Donnellys. Not just in action, but in deed.

THIRTY-ONE
BRENNAN

I STARED BLINDLY AHEAD as Father Doyle preached to us about the Sermon on the Mount, one of his go-to sermons for when the old fucker had drunk too much the night before. I'd heard this bullshit time and time again over the years, to the point where I could probably preach it to him.

Unlike most Sunday mornings, my head wasn't aching from too much Japanese vodka. This time, instead, I had a wife at my side, and my knuckles were bruised to hell, and my wrist was aching like a fucker. Well, the latter wasn't unusual, but the wife? Definitely new.

This was the first time my brothers, my family, and the Five Points in general, had ever seen me with a woman.

It wasn't like we brought our dates to church, was it? But aside from Eoghan, the rest of my brothers kept shooting her glances, curious as to who *she* was. I couldn't blame them. This latest bit of family intrigue was a hell of a lot more exciting than Doyle's lecture. Even Da, who usually ate up every word the old bastard spouted, stared down at his lap, the brooding scowl keying me into the fact that he wasn't happy and still hadn't gotten over last night.

I had two words to say to that—tough shit.

Although, an hour later, when Ma pulled me aside after we made it out of the church and that agonizingly long sermon, I wouldn't deny I was surprised by her words.

"It might be best if you skip Sunday lunch this week, son," she murmured, sending Camille an apologetic glance.

"It's okay, Lena. I understand that our marriage comes as a shock to your family," Camille replied, smiling softly as she patted Ma's arm like my wife hadn't just been grossly disrespected by my parents.

How was it that rat bastard, Vasov, had managed to breed such genuinely sweet daughters?

In her position, I wasn't sure I'd have been so goddamn polite.

"This is bullshit," I told Ma stonily.

She bit her lip, but reached up to cup Camille's hand, ignoring me as she told her, "Thank you for being so understanding, dear." She squeezed her fingers. "It's been a long time since I had any chocolates from Girani's, so that was a real treat. And the slippers are beautiful."

The smile didn't hit her eyes, even if I sensed her genuine pleasure with Camille's gifts. I arched a brow at that, wondering what was going on with my mother. Something clearly was. And I wasn't just overreacting because of the shrink stuff, either.

Ma, showing weakness in front of a crowd? Biting her lip? Hovering and dithering by our side as we were cut off from the pack? Not tearing off Da's head instead of uninviting us from a family ritual?

No, something was definitely going on with her.

Pressing one hand to her arm, I squeezed softly as I leaned down and pressed a kiss to her cheek. She moved closer, slipping her arms around my waist before she murmured, "Speak soon, son."

"We will," I confirmed, eying her as she scuttled away to Da's car.

"You know where Callum is?"

I blinked at Conor who strolled over, squinting at Camille like she was a logic problem he wanted to solve, even if his mind was elsewhere. "Callum?"

"Yeah. Priestley said he went out on business for you. She ain't seen him since."

I shrugged. "Don't know where he is." I felt Camille's tension, but ignored it, even as I dropped her a glance and saw that, not by a single flutter of her eyelashes, did she give a damn thing away.

I figured that she knew who was making the noise behind my office door now...

"Well, I don't know where he is. I sent him out on a job, and I ain't heard from him either."

"Not like him." Conor heaved a sigh. "I'll ping his cell."

"Surprised you didn't do that already."

He shrugged. "Wasn't a priority." Tipping his chin to the side as he took me and Camille in, he frowned, then when I didn't say anything, prompted, "Shouldn't you introduce us?"

When, in less than two minutes, all my brothers, their wives, and Finn and Aoife were gathered around us, I heaved a sigh, aware that this was how I was going to introduce Camille to the family—in front of St. Patrick's church, with the Five Points' Mob milling around the vicinity.

Perfect. *Not.*

"Camille is Inessa's sister," I told them, just in case they were blind and couldn't see the family resemblance. "Babe, this is Aidan, Conor, Declan, Finn, and you already know Eoghan, don't you?" I said with a smirk before I pointed to my nephew who appeared to be flirting, albeit shyly, with Jericho Mills' kid, and murmured, "That's Declan's son, Shay. Aela is Dec's wife, and Aoife is Finn's."

"Pleasure to meet you all," she said shyly, her cheeks pink enough to stir some very unwarranted emotions in me.

I'd watched her deal with my mother like a champ, but here she was, becoming all pink and shy... Fuck. She was turning me into a caveman. I wanted to haul her over my shoulder and take her home where she didn't have to be shy again.

Those pink cheeks were mine.

To slowly morph from embarrassed timidity to dawning fire as I turned her onto the path of temptation.

Before I could get any ideas, Inessa moved over to Camille's side, and slipped her hand into her big sister's. I almost smiled at the sisterly comradery, before I informed the pack of vultures, "This is Camille. She's my wife."

"Your wife?" Conor questioned skeptically.

I nodded.

"This was fast," he replied. "Too fast—"

"Shotgun wedding?" Declan demanded, earning himself a hissed, "Declan!" from Aela.

"Dec has a point," Aidan confirmed. "Is it?"

"No," I said with a laugh. "She ain't pregnant."

"Then what was the rush?" Finn asked, his hand tucked in Aoife's while Jacob, their son, was hitched onto his side, peering at us like we were the most fascinating thing in the city.

We weren't that impressive—the kid was still in awe of dogs and all things fluffy.

Aoife snorted. "Like you can ask anyone that?"

He grinned down at her before he pinned me in place with a look again.

"The rush was Da," I told him with a shrug.

Eoghan, folding his arms over his chest, frowned. "What do you mean?"

"Because he wanted to forge another dynastic marriage, one worthy of Charles and Di?" was my droll retort as I slipped my arm around Camille's waist. It didn't escape me that she huddled into my side.

I had no idea why I liked that, but I did.

She turned to me, not her sister... after barely any time as my wife. It should have saddened me that she did that, but it didn't. If anything, I *liked* it. I wanted her to turn to me—every fucking time.

Scowling, Conor narrowed his eyes at me. "You mean, that's why he's got a hard on today? Over this?"

"Yeah. Well, that and Vasov's dead." My brothers tensed up, which told me Da hadn't let them know that salient fact. It was also a testament to how tightly the Bratva were keeping a lid on their Pakhan's murder if my brothers hadn't heard any whispers about that yet. Because we couldn't talk business, I carried on, "We've been uninvited from Sunday lunch too."

Accepting the change of topic, Aidan tipped his chin forward. "You mean, Camille hasn't been made welcome?"

"No," I told them, wondering what their reaction would be.

Conor pursed his lips. "Well, I didn't feel like Ma's roast dinner today anyway."

My brows rose. "You love her food."

"We all do," he countered, "but Da can't keep pulling this BS over us. We're not six any fucking more."

"Language," Finn rumbled. "Little ears."

"Jake can't wipe his ass yet. I don't think he knows what the word 'fuck' means," Conor argued.

"If he starts dropping F-bombs," Aoife told him, her sweet voice like a song, "then we'll bring him to you to reprogram."

"If only kids could be coded," Conor said with a sigh, but he stared at Jacob the way most of us did.

Like he was an alien.

He was more of a toddler now, but we all remembered the days where he pissed and shat and cried all at the same time.

"Speaking of coding, I need you to give Camille access to the penthouse."

Conor nodded. "I'll sort that out when I get home."

"Thanks, Con."

"No worries."

"Let's get back to the matter at hand, eh?" Aidan rumbled, his brow puckered in a way we'd all come to recognize—he was coming down off a high.

"What matter? That Da's a prick?" Conor chirped.

"Yeah. That matter," Aidan groused. "Look, it's all right for you fuckers, Conor and me are the sitting ducks now."

"Fuck you, Aidan. I really saw you coming to my defense when I had to get married and Da beat the shit out of me," Eoghan groused, his glare morphing into an apologetic glance at his wife.

Inessa's lips twitched, so I figured we hadn't started a Baltic War on that front.

"Yeah, well, that was different."

"Why was it?" Eoghan snapped.

"It just was, okay?" Aidan blew out a breath. "Conor, do you feel like being fitted up with some Italian snatch? Because the *Famiglia* is where he'll make his next deal. You just watch."

Conor pursed his lips. "Is Italian snatch hairy?"

Aoife groaned. "Don't be gross. Italians have heard of Brazilian waxes too."

He blinked. "Oh, it's the French who are supposed to be hairy, isn't it?"

"Back in the sixties," I said wryly. "Get back to this decade, Con."

"Why? It's so much more pleasant in the past," he said with a smirk. "But you're not wrong, Aidan. If we don't take a stand, we'll find ourselves married to any bitch Da wants to make a deal with." He wagged a finger at me. "You know what, Bren, this was smart of you. Taking the matter out of Da's hands."

Aidan muttered, "This is going to turbo-charge things with him. Just you watch us being married off to terrified cu—"

"Aidan!" Aoife snapped. "Language!"

He shot her a glare, but Finn smirked and said, "The 'C' word is a bit much for church, Aid."

My elder brother grunted but, shoving his hands in his pockets, muttered, "Maybe."

"No maybe about it," Aela warned as Shay started shuffling toward us. She slung her arm around his shoulders and asked, "You okay, Shay?"

He hummed, cast us all a glance and frowned. "What's going on? You talking about me?"

Conor snorted. "Your shiners are old news, kiddo."

Shay grinned. "Really? The way Mom keeps going on about them, you'd think it was front page material."

Aela reached up and scrubbed her hand over his hair. "First and last time, Shay. I warned you—you come back with more black eyes, you'll be grounded until you're eighteen. Minimum."

Shay shot me a sheepish look, which had me winking at him.

Of course, Aela saw. "Don't encourage him, Brennan!"

I just shrugged. "What's a man to do? Let himself be cornered and not come out swinging?"

She heaved a sigh. "Not get into corners in the first place."

Aoife cleared her throat. "Can we get a move on? It's freezing out here."

She wasn't wrong. It was unseasonably cold, with the dew on the grass around us gleaming like the fronds were coated in glitter because they'd turned frosty at the tips.

I shuffled my shoulders together inside my coat, then tucked

Camille closer, because she had to be colder as her jacket was only waist high.

"We're going home seeing as we don't have Ma's roast to look forward to."

Conor wagged his finger. "I think we should all cancel. Make a stand. Let Da know we're not ten anymore and aren't okay with being bossed around."

"Why's Grandda bossing you around?" Shay asked, his curiosity evident.

"Never you mind," Aela mumbled, ruffling his hair up again. "I agree with Conor. You all let them have too much sway."

"Isn't that what good sons do?" Shay asked again, the question innocent but I saw the twinkle of laughter in his eyes.

"They do until they're eighteen," Declan confirmed with a laugh.

Aela crinkled her nose. "Okay, maybe twenty-five."

Shay grinned, while the rest of us chuckled.

Well, apart from Aidan. Apparently, he could see his freedom coming to an end.

I didn't blame him for being pissed off. Just because Da didn't have any plans at the moment, that wasn't to say they weren't in the making. You never knew with him. One second, all could be well, and the next, there'd be some backdoor deal going down.

"I agree," Aidan said with a grumble. "I think we should all skip this Sunday lunch. Anyway, Da'll be in a pisspoor mood. It won't be fun."

"That's hardly fair to Lena!" Aoife argued.

While she wasn't wrong, the rest of us just shrugged.

"She's used to his moods," Conor pointed out. "Plus, he'd never hurt her." He cut off his sentence right there for Shay's benefit. Because we all knew he'd hurt *us* given the chance.

I rubbed my chin. "You don't have to do this for our sake. Skip the meal to take a stand or don't. It's no skin off my nose."

"No, just skin off ours," Conor said with a huff. He rubbed his hands together. "If I don't see you through the week, I'll see you through the window," he declared, before clapping Shay on the shoulder and strolling off to his car.

Finn and Aoife grinned at each other, which told me exactly how they planned to spend the rest of their Sunday, before waving at us and pulling a disappearing act.

Aidan wandered off as well, Inessa kissed Camille goodbye before she and Eoghan headed for their car, and Shay and Aela began to drift off too.

Before Declan could join them, I grabbed his arm and asked, "They look good... is it just for show?"

Dec shook his head. "No. Shay's still having nightmares, but that's to be expected. Aela's a bit shaken up but she's doing okay."

"I'm glad."

His lips twisted into a smile that was the opposite of cheerful. "Me too. We're getting there. Thanks for being there for Shay. I meant to call you about it, but shit got busy."

I shrugged. "No need to thank me."

"Conor said the same thing." Declan shook his head. "Last thing we need is him getting into fights to cope with things."

"Just talk to him. Maybe get him into something organized. Wrestling or whatever?"

"I've been taking him to the shooting range."

"Good idea. When can he be armed?"

"Not for a long while, but he can be ready for it," Declan said with a deadly grin. "Anyway, none of us said it to you, but, congratulations." He cast Camille a warm look. "I don't know what's going on with you two, but knowing Brennan, there's something brewing... When are you throwing a reception?"

"I wasn't planning to."

Declan snorted. "Ever the romantic." To Camille, he said, "You arrange it, honey, and we'll be there. Welcome to the family." He leaned down and pressed a kiss to her cheek, before he waved at us and started off toward his wife and son.

I leaned down and whispered into her ear, "My brothers will be the only men who'll ever kiss you again. And even then, only on the fucking cheek."

She shivered, just like I knew she would. I didn't know if she was aware of it, but she was putty in my hands the second I showed any sign of possessiveness. Any other woman would bitch slap me. Camille? Got wet. I didn't need to slip my hand between her thighs to know it either.

She turned to me, all big eyes and angelic countenance, rasping, "Good."

I hummed. "Our Sunday has suddenly opened up. Want to go riding?"

Her excited gasp had me grinning down at her. I didn't have a clue why I'd made that offer, especially when I hadn't gone riding in a good four years, but for that smile? For the buzz of joy around her?

Worth it.

And that was the first clue I had, the first sign of change... when her pleasure became more important than my own.

THIRTY-TWO
BRENNAN

I YAWNED as I climbed out of the Maybach and headed into my building at The Hole. My breath frosted in front of me, which told me that if it was this cold this Fall, then winter was going to be a fucker.

I was too young to be a snowbird, but sweet fuck, I was getting sick of the winters here.

Grumbling under my breath, I headed inside, found Tink itemizing his stock, and yelled, "Morning, bro."

He twisted around to look at me, two bags of coke in his hands, and nodded. "Morning, Bren. You can take the catalogues now. We've picked our coins."

My eyes lit up. "Oh, good." I rubbed my hands together in delight at being able to take those bad boys home with me.

Striding into the warehouse, I asked, "Everything okay? Good weekend?"

Tink snorted. "There ain't no good weekends when you've got kids, Bren. Remember that before you get Camille in the family way."

"You're the one who wanted to be a young dad," I teased.

"Yeah, well, if I could turn back time and keep them all seven, I would. Noisy little fuckers. I thought they were bad then, but Jesus, they're worse now. This fucking TikTok shit's driving me insane. They keep jumping up and doing all these weird dances. Ashleigh asked me to film one." He shook his head. "My eyes almost popped out my fucking head. She only starts twerking in front of me. *In front of me*, Bren."

I smirked at him. "Nipped that in the bud, I hope?"

"Bet your ass I did. She's bitching at me now because she wants to be a TikTok star. Some of those fuckers are on millions." He grumbled, "We're in the wrong job."

"Either that or we should start filming our work. That'd get views," I joked.

"And our asses in the pokey." He grunted. "Fucking twerking. Never thought I'd see the day when I had to watch my baby girl grinding in front of me."

Cringing, I muttered, "Didn't she think it was weird?"

"She was more concerned about the views." He rolled his eyes. "Anyway, life lesson. Only have kids if they'll stay seven forever."

My lips twitched as I hefted the collection into my greedy paws, telling him, "I'll remember that, Tink."

"Do."

He waved me off, going back to the solace of his eternal counting, and I headed on out and up to my office.

When I made it there, I heard a few mutters behind the door and only my brothers or my da would have the audacity to go in there without me in it. Praying it was my brothers though, because I wasn't in the mood for my prick of a father who'd be 'holier than thou' with me about Camille, I nudged the door open with my foot and came face to face with them all.

Every single one of the feckers.

Heaving a sigh, I muttered, "Should have known you'd be in here today. Was hoping you'd leave me in peace."

"You think you can get married without any of your brothers there and we won't be pissed?" Aidan grumbled.

"Didn't think you were on planet Earth, Aid," I snapped, "so wasn't sure if you were open to invitations."

He glared at me, but Finn placed a hand on his shoulder. "Bren, watch it, bro."

I barged past him and dumped the catalogues on the desk.

"What have you got there?" Declan asked, wandering over from the window where he'd been standing to look at the folder. He was a collector like me so his interest was more than just piqued.

"Coins. Little gift from the Yakuza." I rubbed my hands together. "They say 'thank you' in the nicest ways."

"What did you do for them?"

"Got one of their boys out of a pinch of trouble."

"Why?" Conor asked, his brow puckering.

"Because they asked me to. I was in one of their sushi joints and the fucking oyabun only walks out like he owns the place."

"Which he does," Eoghan said with a grin.

I grinned back. "Yeah, technically. Not sure if the owners of that fine establishment would agree though." I elbowed Dec. "That place over on 55th Street. Their unakyu is to die for."

"I'll remember that and go visit. Wonder if the Yakuza'll ask me to do something. I feel like getting a trinket from the homeland."

Laughing, I said, "I doubt it. The staff looked as if they were going to piss themselves with him at one of their tables."

"Why were you in their territory?"

"Didn't you hear me? Their unakyu is to die for."

"Worth braving Yakuza land? Jesus," Conor muttered, before demanding, "How did he know you were dining there anyway?"

"I don't know, Conor," I retorted grumpily. "I just know that the head wondered if he could join me and when I agreed, quite civilly, asked me to get one of his boys an alibi."

"Why did you agree?"

"I was feeling charitable," I lied.

"Bullshit. You ain't the charitable sort," Aidan muttered, staring at his expensive leather Brionis.

I flipped him a bird he didn't see. "There might have been *some* incentive."

"What like?"

"What the fuck is this? Twenty Questions? I told Da before I did anything like a good little boy. He told me to go ahead because he wanted to cultivate a relationship with them."

"Would have been nice to know that," Declan groused.

"None of you could handle the shit I gotta deal with," I rumbled. "Ever since dipshit over there started getting high all the time, my workload has tripled. Shit's been getting worse too now we know about these Sparrow fuckers. Dunbar's been in here, bitching about getting a tail, and I know Da's been pulling the slack for you, Aidan. We've got more rats than a graveyard."

Conor's lips twitched. "About as many as in the library in The Last Crusade?"

I shook my head. "Now ain't the time for Indiana Jones, bro."

"There's always time for Indy." He grinned. "We need to watch a marathon over Thanksgiving weekend."

We all snorted, but none of us bitched about his request. The 'Indiana Jones' series had been our favorite movies when we were kids, back when we'd been filled with fucking hope instead of the quagmire of misery we were steeped in now like some noxious tea.

"Anyways, I got a wife now," I told them, getting back to the heart of the matter. "Something's gotta give."

We'd all been pussyfooting around my elder brother since the drive-by, but things were changing. We needed all hands on deck now.

"Speaking of," Eoghan murmured, "since when were you and Cammie a thing?"

"What's it got to do with you?" I folded my arms across my chest, not liking being interrogated, and not liking that Declan was nosing through my coin collection.

The majority of the coins were South African Krugerrands, but I'd bet my fucking ass there'd be an Asian one in there that he'd just have to have.

Younger brothers—couldn't have jack without them wanting a piece of the action too.

"Everything. She's my sister-in-law. Inessa's concerned."

"Fuck off," I said with a laugh. "She'd prefer her to be stuck at home, huh? At the Bratva compound? Without any protection? Do me a favor." I sniffed. "Look, I liked her, she liked me. She wants protection, I wanted to give her protection. She's got a great set of tits, I'm a tit man."

Conor frowned. "You know she was a clubwhore for the Sinners, don't you?"

"You repeat that to anyone outside of this fucking room and I'll string you up in the back, Conor. The fuck has that got to do with anything? I never needed a virgin sacrifice—"

"Good thing," he retorted, triggering my anger as I stormed forward and grabbed him by the collar, jerking him onto his feet.

The second I did, Declan and Eoghan were there, dragging me back but Conor just grinned at me. "Boys, he loves her."

"Fuck you," I growled at him. "That was a shitty move, raking up her past."

"It was, actually," Finn said wryly. "Still, Kid's capable of worse."

Conor took a bow before he smoothed down his collar, tie, and lapels. "I'll take that as a compliment."

"Don't bring it up again," I warned.

He raised his hands in surrender but his grin made me want to wipe it off his face.

Eoghan slapped me on the back. "If you love her, that's different."

I glowered at him, feeling trapped with my words and actions. "Fuck off."

He grinned. "Bro, take a chill pill. Love's supposed to make you feel like you're walking on air."

"Or like you've sniffed too much helium," Conor inserted.

I glared at him, prodding a finger his way. "One day, fuckface, I'm gonna fuck you up."

His smirk deepened. "I can take it."

"You're the one who was all, 'Brennan, you have to teach Shay because you're the best fighter ever,'" I mocked.

"Well, you are."

"Now who's the dipshit?" Eoghan asked with a laugh. "You really picking a fight with him?"

Conor shrugged. "I could take him."

As one, all my brothers, apart from Conor and me, howled with laughter—nice to know they knew which side to pick in a bet.

He glared at each of them, then shrugged. "You ain't seen me fight since I was twenty."

I leaned into him. "Baby bro, I can guarantee, you still don't defend your left side. You never did."

His mouth turned down at the corners, but before he could whine, Declan murmured, "Speaking of, thanks for dealing with Shay the other day. I know he was feeling all kinds of messed up."

Shrugging, I cast him a look. "It was our pleasure. Wasn't it, fuckface?"

Conor flipped me the bird. "It was. I like Shay. He's cool."

Declan grinned. "He is, isn't he?"

I laughed a little because that grin was dopey as hell and loaded down with pride. "You should have heard Da when he called him 'Grandda' on the phone. You'd think his Lotto numbers had come in."

Dec sheepishly scrubbed his jaw. "Yeah, Aela's not best pleased about that."

"Probably because she doesn't like the prick," I said wryly. "Who the fuck could blame her?"

As a unit, we all pulled a face.

Da was definitely an acquired taste. Forty years into knowing him, I still wasn't sure if I'd acquired it.

"I think it's more to do with encouraging him to get into fights," Declan murmured. "At least, right now, anyway. She's still smarting over Da's monologue on why artists are a drain on society over Ma's topside of beef the other week."

"I'm sure he does it to wind us up," Finn grumbled.

"He probably gets a kick out of it," Conor agreed, throwing himself back onto the seat I'd forcibly vacated him from.

"Sick fuck," I muttered, before I shrugged back my shoulders and smoothed my jacket down. "Anyway, dipshits, the interrogation over? Some of us have work to do."

"Because you're the only one who's working right now, huh?"

I smirked at Dec and said, "Feels like it sometimes."

He rolled his eyes, but asked, "You think you can get married without a massive bachelor party beforehand?"

My mouth turned down at the corners. "If I wanted one, I'd have asked."

Conor grinned. "Don't worry. We're going to have a belated one."

"When's that going to be?"

He tapped his nose. "It's being handled."

I scowled at him. "Conor, if you think I've got time for this bullshit—"

Con waved a hand. "Look, chill out. You'll have a blast."

"If you say so," I said wryly, before I took a seat behind my desk.

"Don't make solid arrangements, fuckface. You know what it's like with the Sparrows right now. We're all on borrowed time."

A collective sigh seemed to wend its way among us. But I felt their pain. As if we didn't have enough plates to keep spinning without those bastards getting in our way.

"Any news from the Mayor?" Aidan asked, which meant Da had been speaking with him. That he'd shared that, but not news of Vasov's death, didn't shock me. He wasn't exactly forthcoming.

"No. I'm going to put some pressure on him at the gala on Friday."

Conor smirked. "Am I going to see you on page 6?"

"I'll dress up nice just for you," I taunted.

He grinned. "I'm going to start making a scrapbook of cuttings from magazines you guys feature in. Ma will love that. Now we've got women in the family, you're all turning nice and respectable, going to galas and the ballet—I think it's going to be my Christmas present to her."

Declan wrinkled his nose. "Fuck, that's a good idea. She'll love that."

"Probably more than that ugly plant you got her last year, Dec," Eoghan agreed, laughing when Declan moved to punch him in the shoulder.

Thinking about what Tink had said downstairs, I shook my head as he started chasing him around the office… seven, fourteen, or thirty-fucking-four, kids were always goddamn noisy.

ONE DAY, YOU'LL FIND A MAN WHO'LL DANCE UNTIL DAWN WITH YOU JUST BECAUSE HE CAN. JUST BECAUSE HE WANTS YOU IN HIS ARMS. DON'T YOU WANT TO HANG AROUND FOR THAT DAY?

THIRTY-THREE
CAMILLE

I FELT like I could burst.

Each pore in my body ached with how happy I felt as I tipped my head back and let the sun warm me, the sky made my eyes sting with how bright it was, all while Terry plodded down the trail.

I was in my most favorite place.

But it was better today.

Brennan was here.

The thought had me casting him a look, and immediately, arousal and amusement danced together inside me.

Arousal because he was hot. Simple as. He also looked like he'd been born to ride, which came as no real surprise. My husband was the most competent man I'd ever met. I wasn't sure if there wasn't anything he couldn't do if he set his mind to it.

This clearly wasn't his first time on a horse, though. The way he sat in a saddle, how he held the reins, the ease with which he directed Princess Plum—all of it spoke of experience.

Which made me want to drool.

He looked like a warrior on horseback. I could easily imagine him with a sword strapped to his back as he charged into battle, which made him even hotter.

The amusement stemmed from his lack of a riding hat. I always wore one, mostly because I was a scaredy cat, but Brennan didn't. The prospect of him in one, though, made me hide a grin. As if a horse would dare buck under his command.

As if.

"What are you grinning at?" Brennan grumbled, our eyes tangling for a flash before he returned his focus to the trail.

I thought he'd been appreciating nature, instead, he'd been watching me hide my amusement...

Ugh, why did that fill me with warmth?

I loved that he watched me. Loved. It.

"I was just imagining you wearing a riding hat."

"And it made you grin?"

"It did," I said, reaching forward to pet Terry. "I don't think Princess Plum would dare toss you off her back."

He snorted. "It's happened a time or two."

"It has? When?"

Brennan shrugged. "When I was learning to ride. Hobbled around for a week each time." His lips twitched. "But it was always my ass that hurt, not my head. Anyway, helmets are uncomfortable."

"They're protective."

"We all die. I'd prefer to die from falling off a horse than with a gun to the temple."

The ease of his words had me biting my lip. We both knew that second option was more likely, so when he put it like that, I thought I'd prefer for him to die that way too.

Of course, that had turned this cheerful outing into a depressing one.

I cleared my throat. "I'm surprised you want to do this again so soon after Sunday."

"Had a shitty day," he grumbled, twisting his neck to ease the strain there. "But the weather's good, and I figured, why the fuck not spend some time with my wife and get some fresh air out here?"

When he said stuff like that, how was I not supposed to fall for him? I knew this was an arrangement, but riding together hadn't been a part of that. Him making sure I got the New York Times in the mail every morning wasn't a part of it. Then there was his whole, 'three orgasms a day keeps the doctor away,' mantra. I was pretty sure that had never been a part of the program, either.

"Well, I'm glad you called."

"Me too." He clucked his tongue when Princess Plum decided to get sassy and veer off course. Not unsurprisingly, that and a soft squeeze of his knees was enough to elicit her compliance. For me, she was a real bitch. For Brennan, not so much. "We'll have to take a trip somewhere, a dude ranch or something. Don't you get sick of the same trails?"

"Not really. But we can. I'd like that." I peeped at him. "For our honeymoon, maybe?"

He scratched his chin, flashing his watch at me as he did so. "Sounds good."

It did? Excitement filled me, but I dampened it down, curious now about something else. "Your watch..." My voice waned a second before I decided to stop being a wuss. "Where did you get it from?"

He blinked. "This old thing? From my uncle. He bequeathed it to me when he died."

That was my kind of gift. I'd never heard of Vacheron Constantin before, but when I'd googled them, out of curiosity, my mind had been blown.

"When we were at your parents' place, I saw a picture of your dad with someone who had to be his brother. They were at Coney Island."

His lips twitched. "Eating hot dogs, right?"

"Yeah, that's the one."

He nodded. "That's one of Da's favorite pictures. He doesn't have many pictures of Frank."

"He's the one who gave you the watch?"

"No, that was Patrick." He pursed his lips. "Patrick was the wild card, Frank was strong and steady."

"He's dead too?"

Brennan pursed his lips. "Yeah. They both died when they were real young."

"Do you have any cousins?"

"Only two. Do you?"

"Unfortunately, a few. I don't want anything to do with them though. They're from Father's side of the family and just as bad as him.

Mama had two brothers but they died when they were children." My lips twitched as something occurred to me. "I think our children will have a lot of cousins."

He snickered. "I think so too."

"Well, there's already Shay," I pointed out softly.

"Jake as well." He cracked his knuckles. "Little fucker is going to be a brilliant fighter by the time I'm done with him."

"How did the training go last night?"

He grinned. "Got two good punches to the gut. Nearly got kneed in the balls too."

"You're teaching Shay how to fight dirty!" I accused. "You shouldn't do that. You'll get him into trouble."

Brennan snorted. "That's the only way to fight. Never leave a mark on your opponent if you don't have to, Camille." He tapped his nose after he winked at me. "That'll stop the bastards from going to the teachers."

"Will you teach Jake too?"

"If Finn asks. He used to be a nasty fighter though. He's getting soft, but he might want to handle that himself."

I thought about the man I'd seen at church the other day and arched a brow at him. "He didn't look soft to me."

Brennan scowled at me. "You shouldn't be looking."

I snorted. "What would you like me to do? Study the floor when someone introduces me?"

My husband grunted. "Fucking Finn. The ladies always love him."

I could see why...

Not that I said that, even if it was nice to know his jealousy and possessiveness worked in that way too.

If I could inspire nothing else in him but that, I'd be happy.

"Finn isn't related to you, is he?" I asked softly, *cautiously*. That photo in their parents' hallway wouldn't stop nagging at me. I guessed it was because I loved a puzzle, but I knew I had to tread carefully

"No. He's an O'Grady." His nose wrinkled. "For what that's worth, which ain't much. His father was a bastard."

"I wasn't sure if he was a second cousin or something."

"Why? Because we took him in?"

"Well, that, and he looks very much like your uncle. The one in the picture? Frank?"

Brennan frowned. "He does?"

I shrugged. "Yeah. But if he isn't a second cousin, then..." Casting a look around us, I changed the subject quickly, murmuring, "When you're here, it's hard to believe that the city is so close. It's like being in the middle of nowhere, isn't it? No people, no crowds, no traffic. No noise."

"You like it quiet?" he asked, his surprise evident, but I could see I'd set the cogs grinding in his mind.

"Why does that shock you?"

"Because you're sixteen years younger than me, not older."

Laughing, I just hitched a shoulder. "I like it noisy when I like it noisy. But for the most part, I appreciate the quiet. You don't get much of it in our world, so I think that's why." I sighed. "Your terrace is peaceful too, that's why I love it out there."

"*Our* terrace," he corrected gruffly, drawing my attention his way.

That ratcheted up my joy a smidge. "Our terrace," I agreed.

"I barely sit out there to be honest," he admitted.

"You should try to. I've been going out there after I wake up."

"Isn't it getting cold?"

"I guess, but nothing too unmanageable. I just take a blanket out with me."

"I'll get Forrest to bring up some of those patio heaters."

Though the idea had occurred to me as well, I just said, "You don't have to do that."

"It's New York, Camille," he said dryly. "It's gonna be freezing soon. We won't be able to do this for much longer."

"The younger horses don't mind the snow. Terry hates it." He'd hated it back before I'd left New York, now in his twenties, I knew he'd loathe being out in the cold. My lips curved into a smile. "Vicky used to love the snow. She'd play in it for hours at a time, would even toss snowballs at the *boyeviks*."

"I bet they loved that."

"They didn't," I said with a laugh. "But they never complained. Most of them were from Moscow though so they were used to it. Their temperatures make ours look balmy." I chuckled. "I remember this one time she got a bucket and shoved it full of snow, then she went upstairs to the upper hall, rushing so it wouldn't melt, and waited, dangling out of the window until someone left the house by that exit, and she poured it on their heads. Then she did it all over again."

He snorted. "Sounds like a charmer."

I grinned at him. "When you get to know her, she is."

A frown had his brow puckering. "You're not going to ride if it snows, are you?"

"If the mood takes me." The weather wouldn't stop me from coming to the stables. I wouldn't ride in bad conditions, but that didn't mean I couldn't hang out with the horses. I'd missed too much of them already. I wasn't going to miss anymore.

His frown darkened. "If you want to go riding, we'll ride together. Okay?"

"How will that work?" I countered, but there was no heat to my words. "Do I make an appointment with you three weeks before?"

Brennan pulled a face. "Well, no."

"Bagpipes will be with me, won't he?"

"Yeah, but not on the trail. He can't ride."

"I'll be fine."

"You might not be." He shook his head. "No, give me a day's notice. I'll figure something out. Or pick a day every week, and I'll make sure I have free time."

I bit my lip, and let my eyes drift down to the pommel. "You don't have to do that, Brennan."

"I know I don't," was his gruff reply.

Neither of us said anything after that, letting the silence fall between us. It was surprisingly comfortable. Just the two of us, the horses, the quiet, and the trail.

It shouldn't have felt intimate, but it did. We were alone, together, and it felt like we were advancing. Taking steps forward that would bring us closer, not just figuratively either.

I wasn't sure if I'd ever feel comfortable asking him for things, because I didn't want to be a burden. Maybe that would change when we were ready for kids. For myself, I couldn't ask him to drop everything to go horseback riding, but for them? I would in a heartbeat.

That he was willing to make time for me meant more than he probably knew.

When we were on our way back, he asked, "Camille?"

I hummed. "Yes?"

"You know I'll keep you safe, don't you?"

My mouth curved into a smile. "I do, Brennan, I do."

THIRTY-FOUR
BRENNAN

"YOU'LL NEVER GUESS where the fuck I am."

From my vantage point, I frowned down at a pool of blood that was gathering on the floor below me. "Are you fucking messing with me right now?"

"No. I'm not."

"You pulled me out of an interrogation to bitch at me?"

"Guess where I am, Brennan. Guess where your wife has brought me."

Using my forearm to wipe away the sweat on my brow, I grumbled, "If you're moaning about her going shopping—"

"No, I'd prefer that. We're in a goddamn soup kitchen."

Surprise had me straightening up. "You're shitting me."

"I ain't," he countered. "I'm in a fucking soup kitchen, and she's elbow deep in carrot peelings."

"Why?"

"Why what?"

"Why is she elbow deep in carrot peelings?"

"Because she's peeling carrots, dumbfuck," Bagpipes grumbled.

"Why though?"

"She's volunteering. Just signed up today."

My brow creased. "My wife has volunteered to work in a soup kitchen?"

"Do you have soap in your ears or something?"

"Maybe." I grunted. "Well, that'll get Father Doyle off my back."

"Why would her volunteering at a soup kitchen that's not attached to St. Patrick's get him off your back?"

"Shit!" I groused. "She ain't at St. Patrick's Community Center?"

"Nope. I'm guessing you guys don't talk about this shit?"

"When the fuck am I supposed to talk to her about stuff like this?"

"In bed." Bagpipes laughed. "Ya know, before you fuck her. Then there's after the fuck. Never heard of pillow talk?"

The second my head hit that pillow, I was fast asleep. But we talked when we were together. She wasn't a bit of fluff, actually had something going on between her ears. Listening to her discuss horses, the sisterly anecdotes she dropped from time to time, and conversing about what was happening on the news had told me that much.

That she'd whored herself out still boggled my fucking mind. She must have had an education, so why the hell she'd taken that route was beyond me. Unless, of course, it was down to that masochistic side of her personality...

Aware Bagpipes was waiting on me to reply, I grumbled, "I ain't working you hard enough if you've got time to talk to Kerry-Louise."

Bagpipes snickered. "Oh, please, sir, just add another six hours' work to my twenty-hour shift."

My lips twitched. "Shut up."

"Well, if anyone could make a twenty-six-hour day, I'm pretty sure it's an O'Donnelly."

"You picked that fucking coin yet?" I demanded, knowing full well he had.

Bagpipes snorted. "Never said you didn't pay us well. Just said that you can't make extra minutes in a day."

Wasn't that the goddamn truth.

Pulling a face, I muttered, "Is she safe there?"

"Give her some credit, Bren. She's Bratva. She knows how this stuff rolls. She's as safe as she can be. She's in the kitchen, not serving or anything."

"How many days did she sign up for?"

"Five mornings a week."

My brow crumpled at that. "Think this is some kind of penance?"

"Maybe, but I doubt it. It ain't like she's going around lashing herself over her da, is she? If anything, she's happy the fucker's dead."

I thought about the hands that had given me a handjob this morning—there'd been no Band-Aids on them, so he was right. She wasn't going through with her version of lashing herself. Neither had she asked about a funeral. The only request she'd made about her family was regarding the legalities of Victoria's guardianship. I was looking into it even though Vasov's death hadn't exactly been made official, so it wasn't like the State of New York even knew she was an orphan now.

Mouth turning down at the corners, I muttered, "It ain't right her working there."

"Why? Because it ain't Doyle's church?"

"I don't know. She's a—" She was a queen. Why the fuck didn't she get that?

"Maybe she's just a nice person. I mean, if you talk to her for more than five minutes, I'm sure you'd pick up on that."

"We talk," I muttered. "Just not about this. Mostly about the family and—" A thought occurred to me. "You remember my Uncle Frank?"

"How couldn't I? Remember that time he filled your da's office with those rubber snakes?"

I grinned. "Thought he was gonna kill Frank."

"Probably strangled him a bit. You know, like Bart and Homer Simpson?"

Chuckling, I agreed, "You're probably right."

"What about him?"

"Do you think Finn looks like him?"

Bagpipes fell silent. "I mean, I've never thought about it, but I guess so. It's been a long time since I've seen Frank's picture though."

I just hummed. "I wondered if Finn was one of Frank's by blows. You know what he was like with the ladies."

"A legend," was the wry retort. "Aidan Sr. would know though. He'd have said something."

"True." I frowned, then turned back around and stared down at the factory floor from the office I was using at this depot we'd overtaken in Bed-Stuy. There, I faced Callum who was hanging from a meat hook. His head was lolling on his chest, but I could tell he was starting to stir. His shoulders were no longer straining under the deadweight of his body and that was jolting him awake as agony splintered down his arm.

"Why do you ask?"

"Just something that occurred to me is all." I cleared my throat. "Anyway, you get off."

"He spoken yet? I can't believe I'm stuck here while you're breaking that fucker."

My lips curved into a grin. "You're guarding treasure, Bagpipes. That's important to me."

"You and your treasure. I can just see you sitting in your office, surrounded by piles of coins like King Midas, jacking off to it."

I grinned, but corrected, "Nah, everything he touched turned to gold. He didn't have a thing about coins."

Bagpipes grunted. "Ali fucking Baba, then."

"If all you've got to do with your time is bitch at me, instead of watching my wife peel carrots, go and fucking help her."

"Knew I should have kept my trap shut."

"Roll up your sleeves," I joked.

He hesitated a second, then said, "Donny messaged me today. Conor's been asking for Callum. Donny wondered if we knew what was up because Aidan Jr. didn't have a clue."

I grimaced. "Since he asked on Sunday, Con ain't mentioned him again."

"Why would he, though?"

"Why's Donny called you, then?"

"Curiosity." He sighed. "It gets better. Mark's been on the phone too. Asked me to keep an eye out for his kid."

Clenching my jaw a second, I muttered, "Fuck."

That meant Da would be getting involved soon.

"About sums it up," he agreed. "You gotta make a decision about what you're going to do with the fucker, Bren."

"I know." I heaved a sigh. "Speak to you later."

Bagpipes' answer was another grunt and feeling the urgency biting at my ankles like a Pomeranian on steroids, I headed out of the office and down the stairs.

Once there, I murmured as I shot off a text, "I know you're awake, Callum."

Me: *Couldn't you have volunteered at St. Patrick's soup kitchen?*

I didn't expect a reply, not with her being busy, so I placed my phone on the table and turned my focus to the matter at hand.

"He must think having a nap will delay the inevitable," Tink murmured.

I cut my other man a look, saw he was leaning against the wall, watching the state of play like it was a show on TV. Forrest was bouncing on his heels, pissed at having to stop because Callum had passed out.

"The inevitable is fucking dying," Callum rasped, finally raising his head and spitting out a globule of saliva that was drenched in blood.

"How else do you think we should handle traitors?"

"What would you have me do, Bren?" he rasped. "Go to jail for something I didn't fucking do?"

"Don't cut that bullshit with us," Tink retorted. "You could have gone to Conor. If any fucker pulled those kinds of moves with me, that'd be the first thing I'd do."

His disgust was so tangible that I believed him. I actually fucking believed him. That was a massive weight off my shoulders, and he didn't even know it.

"Conor ain't like Bren. You know he's on another planet most of the bastard time." He spat out some more blood, his beat up face puckering with pain as he wriggled on the meat hook, his skin blanched and a wail escaped him as his broken forearm made itself known. When he got himself under control, he gasped out, "He ain't interested in this world, just his fucking computers and that goddamn Lodestar. She's all he can talk about now."

Forrest and I shared a look.

"You could have come to any of us. You didn't have to deal with the NWS," I told him, siding with Tink.

"I haven't done much dealing with them," he muttered. "They just told me to tell some people *some* things."

Well, at least we were getting somewhere.

Four days into having the fucker hung up like a side of beef and the bastard was finally starting to talk about the shit I was interested in.

"What like?"

"Let me down? My shoulders are knackered, Bren, and my fucking arm, I'm pretty sure it's going to need surgery." Callum begged.

My mouth turned up at the corners as Tink hooted and Forrest chuckled. Methodically, I tightened the Ace bandage around my weak wrist.

Wrapping it so that it would support me as I beat the fuck out of him. "That's the point, Callum. Torture's supposed to hurt. And I wouldn't worry about the surgery, my man. Where you're going, St. Peter's the best plastic surgeon around. He'll fix you right up."

He registered that truth then swallowed, before reasoning, "I'm gonna talk though, ain't I? You can see that."

"Why, because you think talking will spare you from dying sooner?"

"Maybe." He shot me a pleading look.

"You know that if I'd told Da what you'd done, he wouldn't have strung you up by your hands."

"Knowing Aidan Sr., he'd have him hanging by his dick," Forrest joked, his smile mean as Callum winced.

Rage filled me. On Conor's behalf. On my behalf. On Da's. I'd never liked Mark O'Reilly, thought he was a dumb piece of shit, but the bastard hadn't raised a traitor. This was going to kill him as well.

"You're fucking family," I snapped. "How the fuck could you eat at our table and fuck us over like this?"

"I didn't have a choice," he yelled. "I told you Priestley's pregnant. What was I supposed to do?"

"Not betray your family," Tink said stonily. "Lead by example. What kind of fucking kid are you going to raise when, at the first sign of trouble, you double deal the people who'd kill for you?"

"That's bullshit, anyway," Forrest muttered. "Priestley ain't exactly been carrying for a couple of years."

"True, although, we don't know how long the bastard has been double dealing us, do we?" I almost hoped that it was a recent thing. It wouldn't make it better, but it would feel less like we'd had a sniveling rat sneaking out onto our table to rummage through our leftovers for material to nark on.

Callum's head bowed, which pulled the muscles in his shoulders and chest into sharp relief. His right arm was bent at an odd angle, which was one of the principle reasons he kept passing out whenever he put too much of a burden on it. We had him strung up so that he could lever his weight on his tiptoes.

As for the rest of him, he was bruised and bloodied, battered all over from the various beatings me and Forrest had put him through.

I stared at the cuts, the seeping wounds and shook my head, unable to countenance that I'd done this to *Callum*.

His betrayal slashed at my insides, but it didn't take away from my feeling like I was betraying him. I'd hurt him, hurt a man I thought of as family—the correlation wasn't easy. My brain knew the truth but my heart couldn't accept it.

"He's not wrong, though. What kind of kid would you raise if even basic loyalty is beyond you?" I rasped, cracking my knuckles and clicking my wrist by twisting it slightly.

For the first time, I got why Camille dug her nails into her palms. With the split skin on my knuckles, cracking them added to the discomfort, throw in my messed-up wrist, the pain made me feel a burn that eased the cacophony going down in my ears.

"I'm sorry, Bren. Truly, I'm sorry," he whispered, staring down at the ground, not up at me.

"He's not Bren to you, anymore," Forrest spat.

I swallowed down that particular truth because he wasn't wrong.

But I was stuck between a rock and a hard place on so many fronts here.

If I told Da, the pain I felt at Callum's treachery would be nothing in comparison to what he experienced.

If I didn't tell him, just buried Callum, then there'd be a manhunt for the prick who didn't deserve for anyone to give a fuck about him.

"You can't kill me without your da's permission," Callum whispered, finally peering over at me, like he was reading my thoughts.

Like he knew I was at a crossroads.

My father didn't care about hurting my feelings, thought nothing of dismissing my wife because he hadn't chosen her, but the ramifications of Callum's actions would be long-lasting. *That* was what I couldn't handle, and Ma would be the one who bore the brunt of it simply because she had to live with him.

"You're really asking to have your cock lobbed off, ain't you?" Forrest mocked.

"Shut up the lot of you," I snapped. Rubbing a hand over my face, knowing I needed to get this underway, I bit out, "Callum, who was your point of contact?"

He hesitated a second, then rasped, "Just some detective in the 42nd Precinct."

I frowned and cast Forrest a look, who muttered, "Let me guess. Craig Lacey?"

Callum blinked. "How the fuck did you know that?"

Lacey's was a name that kept popping up. We'd first heard it from the Sinners, who told us the cop had set up one of their men who was currently serving time in Rikers.

Rex, the Prez, had petitioned the family to get the guy out early, and Da, being unusually accommodating—but then, Rex had just slaughtered some Italians which always put him in a good mood—had hopped onto the phone to make it so. Within the week, Quin should be a free man.

"Never mind," I grunted. "Tell me what the NWS wanted you to do."

He licked his lips. "Let me down, Bren, please?"

"Tell me what they wanted," I bit off, hands bunching at my sides.

"Just to mess with commands, cause dissent."

"Oh, just little things like that?" I rasped. "What was with the jewelry store robberies?"

Callum chewed on his bottom lip. "I think Hummel's involved in something they want to muscle in on."

"Like what? Blood diamonds?"

Callum shrugged, then groaned as his body responded to the movement. "I don't know, Bren. I just know what they told me to do."

"Give me specifics," I demanded, even as I pointed at Tink. He nodded, so I knew he'd stored that piece of info in his mental computer to check it out later. Hummel's were supposed to be respectable, and I'd never heard of their name and blood diamonds being mentioned in the same breath, but I could never have imagined beating the fuck out of Callum either.

"They said to get in touch with a thief with experience breaking into vaults and safes. To tell them that Hummel's Diamonds was no longer under Points' protection."

My brow puckered at that as Tink, Forrest and I all darted glances at one another.

"How long have you been their patsy?"

"Three years, but they've only been in touch three times total." He winced. "I wasn't about to complain, was I?"

"What else have they asked you to do?" Tink inquired.

"It was in the early days, and the first time they just wanted to know if Lena had a routine, and what it was, where she went. Shit like that."

"Why?" I asked, my temper bubbling now Ma was involved.

"They don't tell me, Bren. They just want to know something so you give them that info. It was harmless. Back then, she only went to her shop and that little tea place over in Hell's Kitchen."

"What tea place?"

Callum blinked. "The one... Fuck."

"What is it?" I snapped.

"The one Finn bought from Aoife. They just entered the final phase of development on the new skyscraper where her place was located, that Acuig Heights' project."

Uneased whittled away at my insides. "Ma went there? Why did neither of them ever say anything?"

"Aoife's a baker," Tink pointed out, his voice calm. "She was probably in the back, baking."

True.

"Pretty odd coincidence," Forrest rumbled.

He wasn't wrong.

"What else did they ask you?"

Callum's shoulders hunched. "If a rumor was true."

"What rumor?"

"That Finn and Aoife were going to get married at St. Patrick's. I mean, they asked, but it was public knowledge. Father Doyle would have called the banns—"

"There wasn't time for the banns to be called," I whispered, my busted knuckles breaking like the Hoover dam as I clenched them tight, blood seeping through my fingers as the ramifications of what he was telling me hit home. "They either told the Colombians, or they triggered that drive-by shooting, Callum. On your word. That rumor they wanted clarifying was their way of scheduling what could have been a mass murder."

"No! Fuck no," Callum growled, his shoulders straining again as he straightened up. His arm buckled, but he stood strong, terror on his face as if he knew this was it. He'd done it now. "That ain't got nothing to do with me. I would never have—" But his pleading fell on deaf ears.

My control snapped.

I rushed for him, fists flying, blood spurting, bones colliding until Callum O'Reilly was no more, and I had another soul on my conscience.

REMEMBER—YOU WERE LOVED. YOU
KNOW WHAT THAT FEELS LIKE.
DON'T SETTLE FOR LESS.

THIRTY-FIVE
CAMILLE

"THIS ONE?" I heaved a sigh when Brennan didn't look up from his phone. "Brennan? You wanted to be here, remember? I could have gone shopping with Inessa."

He scowled at his cell, then peered over at me, and then at the dress.

This morning, pretty much seconds after he'd pulled out of me, then fallen back against the sheets, he'd informed me we were attending a gala tonight, and that I needed a new dress worthy of a ball.

He'd also informed me that we'd spend the morning looking for said dress before he had to head off and work.

Which was why he was here. Darkening the waiting area with his scowls. It was clear he had other things to do, which didn't involve him *doing* me. At least... not with the dresses the attendant had picked out.

I thought he'd been interested in getting a free show, but I had to admit, she'd dressed me like I was about to turn fifty.

"You look like a pigeon. And with your tits and ass, Camille, the only thing you should look is hot. Not like a sky rat."

Even though I agreed, I only let my lips twitch once before I demurred, "I don't look like a pigeon. This is a ten-thousand dollar dress."

He shrugged. "So? You look like a black dove then."

I hid a grin as the flounces of tulle bobbed and swayed with every movement I made as I returned to the cubicle.

After his announcement, I'd almost expected him to join me in the changing room, had even been looking forward to it, but he hadn't. Not that it came as that much of a surprise, this past week, I'd come to learn that my husband had a disarming ability to compartmentalize his life.

The second one face switched on, the other switched off.

I knew how that worked, how it felt, so I didn't begrudge him that shield. I also knew that it took someone like that to even register the difference. Another sign we were well suited, I supposed.

When my phone lit up, I smiled, seeing Inessa had sent a meme. It was of Squidward, sheathed in bandages, sitting in a wheelchair, all gussied up with a big pink bow and gold hoops, with the caption, *"When the deep dicking damn near broke you in half but you show up the next day ready for round 2 because Mama didn't raise no bitch."*

Snickering, I replied: **Me:** *Is that me or you?*

Inessa: *Both of us now.*

Me: *LOL. You're the one with the 'No Access' pussy.*

Inessa: *True, but that doesn't count. When I'm back in action, it'll be me though.*

Me: *Looking forward to it?*

Inessa: *Mebbe. >..< I mean... you have seen my husband. >..>*

Me: *I have. Prefer mine though. :P*

Inessa: *Good. Don't wanna get into a cat fight with you.*

Me: *Because you know I'd win?*

Inessa: *Meooow.*

Me: *LOL.*

Inessa: *TTYL xoxo*

Me: *xoxo*

Quickly switching to the chat I had with Victoria, I spied that she'd read all the messages I'd sent her this past week, everything from telling her this was my new number to asking if she was okay at Inessa's place, but hadn't replied.

Trying not to be disheartened, I took a snapshot of the gowns the attendant had suggested, gowns I knew Brennan wouldn't like either because there were a lot of frills and a lot of taffeta for some reason, and sent it to her.

Me: *Brennan and I are going to a gala. Look at what the store attendants have hooked me up with. They must think I'm 80.*

The ticks appeared, so I knew she'd read it, but she didn't reply.

"Damn," I muttered under my breath, trying not to be disheartened when staring at the screen didn't miraculously make a text from her appear.

Heaving a sigh, I stripped out of the taffeta dress Brennan hadn't approved of, then bent over to pick it up and to place it back on the hanger.

As I did, I saw the curtain move and sway, and peered over to find him standing there, his eyes on my ass, his head peeking through a gap he'd made between the curtain and the wall.

"Thought you were busy," I told him huskily.

"I am," he rumbled, in a voice I was coming to recognize easily now. "That's why I decided to speed things up. Those attendants apparently have no taste, because why they want to cover those tits and your legs up..." He shook his head, then in a lower voice, muttered, "People think *I'm* the criminal."

My cheeks flushed—he made no bones about the pleasure he found in my body, but it still came as a shock to me to be praised.

Dolls weren't rewarded with praise, after all. They were just fucked. Used.

Brennan didn't treat me like a doll. I couldn't say he treated me like a wife, either.

"Here." He shoved his way through the curtain, armed with two dresses, and said, "Two steps out of the waiting room and I found these. They should suit you, but try them on first."

I licked my lips. "Are you going to help me into them?"

He smirked. "No. I'm going to watch you get dressed though."

Pouting a little as he moved over to the low armchair and took a seat, I focused on the ridge of his dick which made a prominent bulge against his tailored slacks as he settled down. The dresses he draped over his lap, seeming to bring his erection further to my attention.

After crossing his legs, one ankle staying propped up on his knee, he rested his hands on his belly as he tipped his head back, declaring, "Try them on."

Leaning over to grab the first one, I let temptation strike me as my fingers drifted over his cock, brushing him with just the tips.

He growled. "If you don't want to drop to your knees and suck me off in here, Camille, you'll get changed fast."

I smirked at him. "Who says that'd be a punishment?"

His lips gathered into a tight purse before he heaved a sigh. "I don't have time for this." His hand ruffled through his hair as he stared at me impatiently. "Get changed, Camille."

I heard the warning, the low throb that ran through the words too, and shivered inside. Not out of fear, but a complex mixture of trepidation and excitement.

I wanted him to pull me by the hair and drag me to my knees, and I half expected him to do that, but he didn't. Instead, he watched me, with burning eyes as I slipped into the black gown first.

My disappointment was real, but the dress was perfect. Inky-black crêpe, it gathered at the waist with thin bands of crystal that accentuated my slenderness while creating a sweeping silhouette. It had a V-neckline that showed off my breasts, and which, after tugging at the skirt, was deep enough to require tit tape as they popped out to say hello when I straightened back up again.

I cast him a look, saw he was still sitting upright, but his dick made even more of a bulge against his zipper...

Was it strange that my mouth watered?

In the shortest imaginable time, I'd come to associate all things sex with orgasms. Which might seem the logical route, but it hadn't been for me this far.

"Every man at tonight's event will be thinking of fucking those tits," he said succinctly, his gaze on the swells.

After the sushi restaurant, and three more trips out this week, to a Thai place, a Michelin-starred Italian eatery, and a dessert bar, I'd come to realize that he liked that other men wanted me.

They could look, but only he could touch.

Which didn't thrill just him, but me too.

It made me be brave, and I wasn't sure I'd ever been brave in the past, just resilient.

It didn't take bravery to walk naked through a bar full of men. Just a thick skin.

But to go to high-end restaurants, to still retain some elegance, all while showing off skin that made a man's cock hard? That was a lot more difficult.

Good thing I liked a challenge.

And a good thing that the only man whose dick I wanted hard was this one's.

"Only you can fuck them though," I whispered, watching his eyes light up at my words.

"Maybe I'll fuck them before the event, on the ride over." His top lip quirked up into a smirk. "Come all over them. People will think it's that sparkly stuff, what do you call it?"

I laughed a little as my hand traced over my breasts, deep between them. "Highlighter."

"That's it." He clicked his fingers. "Instead, it'd be my cum. What do you think?"

"A new trend," I purred.

He settled back in the armchair again. "You really do get off on this shit, don't you?"

I blinked. "Yes." There was no point in denying it. *I did.* I wasn't sure why, but I did. Concern filtered through me though, as my insecurities flared white hot. "Don't you?"

"Never could trust bitches with my cum. I didn't want any kids until recently." He shrugged. "I think we both know I get off on it, Camille. Been waiting a lifetime to claim a woman in as many ways as I've claimed you." Before I could wheeze out a response, he commanded, "Try on the red one."

I obeyed even as my heart rate picked up.

Been waiting a lifetime to claim a woman in as many ways as I've claimed you.

Those words would be imprinted on my soul until the day I died.

Tugging on the dress momentarily shielded my expression, but my game face was back on a few seconds later. The minute I looked in the mirror, I knew he'd pick this one.

The color of blood, it had padded shoulders that gave a deeper slant to the neckline, which somehow revealed more of my chest while exposing less. There was a high slit to the skirt with a ruffle that was lined in silk. It made the skirt drape as I moved, revealing all of my legs with each step I took. It had long blouson cuffs, and made me think of Hollywood glamor back in the thirties.

It also augmented the golden hue of my skin and my blonde hair in a way the black one didn't.

He crossed his legs at the ankle. "I think we have our winner."

I smiled, satisfied I'd guessed right.

Satisfied, even more, by his words, *'Been waiting a lifetime to claim a woman in as many ways as I've claimed you.'*

Unaware I was still on Cloud Nine, he twirled his hand in a circle, and I followed, turning around too, before he beckoned me forward with his fingers.

A shocked gasp escaped me as he plunged those fingers straight between my legs as he peered at my skirt.

"They'll see you're not wearing panties at the gala," he murmured, raking his fingers over the gusset of the set I had on now. A set he'd only permitted me to wear this morning because I was trying on clothes.

"I-Is that a problem?" I asked shakily, stepping up onto tiptoe as he pushed down, pressing into the folds of my sex in a way that made me wish he'd rub higher up.

"More of a perk of the dress," he confirmed softly. "Camille?"

"Y-Yes," I stuttered, my eyes falling closed as he found my clit and started to rub it.

"You're wet."

I licked my lips. "I know." And I did. I was getting more comfortable with my body now he spent so much time focused on it.

His fingers withdrew, prompting my eyes to pop open. I gaped at him as he got to his feet and traced his sticky fingers—God, had I made my panties wet?—between my breasts.

"Buy both of them." He leaned down and pressed a kiss to my lips, his tongue tracing over the bottom one before he thrust into my mouth and claimed my breath right from my very lungs. When I was sagging into him, he pulled back. "Bagpipes is waiting outside on you. I'll see you tonight."

As he started out of the changing room, I choked out, "Brennan?"

He peered back at me. "Don't get off. I'll deal with you before the gala."

I chomped down on my bottom lip, trying not to be even more aroused at that command than I already was.

He knew.

Dammit.

He knew what those orders did to me, making me aware that in barely no time at all he knew my body better than Nyx ever had.

A shaky sigh escaped me as he left the cubicle, and it was only by chance that I heard Bagpipes mutter, "Bren, we've got a problem."

"What kind of problem?" His voice was fainter, like he'd moved away.

"That Quin kid. He's just got shivved."

I knew what 'shivved' meant. In jail, prisoners made makeshift weapons out of the most banal of items. Spoons, for example, were weaponized by sharpening them into hard points, turning it into a dagger that could kill.

As concerning as that was, it was the name that registered.

Quinn. Or maybe, Quin.

Double 'n' or just the one?

I worried my bottom lip between my teeth, because I knew a Quin in prison—Nyx's brother was in Rikers.

"Is he alive?" Brennan asked, his voice grim. "Or did the bastards kill him?"

The few instances I'd heard him talk about business, I knew that his voice was oddly without inflection. Like nothing surprised him, nothing worried him. I doubted that was always the way as I'd yet to hear him be angry, but still, that he sounded anything at all told me this was not a good development.

And not just for the poor guy who'd been shivved.

"No, he's alive. Barely."

"Fuckers," Brennan growled, and I heard a sound that made me think he was pounding his fist into his palm. "The kid must know more than Rex let on."

A sharp gasp escaped me as I had my confirmation.

It *was* Nyx's brother.

Quin had just been stabbed in prison!

Heart in my throat, my shoulders hunched in on themselves as I tried to process that horrifying news.

The Sinners had been feeling a world of hurt lately. What with their clubhouse being blasted, and God only knew what else. I'd only stayed in touch with Jingles but she'd died in the bombing, and because I hated the other clubwhores and knew that by staying in contact I was only doing so to hear news about Nyx, I'd gone cold turkey and had no idea what had happened since the compound's destruction.

But hearing this raked up all the old pain, all the longing and the need for more than Nyx was ever willing to give me. What he'd only ever given to Giulia, his Old Lady.

I bet he cared if she came.

Hell, I bet *Giulia* cared if she came. I bet she made demands on him, not just where sex was concerned but in life too.

I hadn't been good enough for Nyx, but Giulia, who'd been dragged up, *had*.

When she'd made an appearance at the clubhouse, I hadn't realized that my life was about to change. That I was about to be usurped.

I'd thought Nyx loved me, but when he and Giulia had grown entangled, I'd come to see that I was the fool. He'd never promised me anything, but I'd gone chasing rainbows with the desire for protection. With the need for security.

As I stared at myself in the mirror, wearing a bright red Gucci dress that wouldn't fit in at the Sinners' compound in West Orange, it was so easy to see me in the barely there gear I'd worn before.

Only through Nyx and his particular proclivities had I not been passed around. If it weren't for him being a possessive bastard, I'd have been whored around the brothers...

When Brennan teased me, taunted me, called me a slut, I knew that I wasn't. I also knew that *he* knew I wasn't, but with him, the label turned me on. *He* turned me on. Everything he did, the way he talked, the way he walked. What he wore, how he carried himself... The way he touched me, kissed me, sucked me, licked me...

I would never have known sex like this was real if it weren't for him.

Brennan, in a week of marriage, had disproven my self-belief that I was frigid.

I wasn't.

I just needed the right man.

He was that right man—my body had made that decision for me. And maybe his had made that decision for him too...

Been waiting a lifetime to claim a woman in as many ways as I've claimed you.

My heart was still pounding, the past and present blurring, my heartache for a man who'd never wanted me fading away as I realized that it wasn't Nyx's fault I'd pinned all my hopes on him. It wasn't Nyx's fault that I'd fallen for him when he hadn't fallen for me.

Ever since I'd shoved my way into Brennan's life, thoughts of Nyx hadn't been as constant as before and that feeling of being heartsick had disappeared. I'd been so stupidly in love with him that I'd been pining, but Brennan didn't give me room to pine.

If anything, I only thought about Nyx now to compare him to Brennan, and my husband always won.

Always.

How was it that hearing about his kid brother being injured was a slap in the face that proved to me how over Nyx I was?

The curtains parted, and I jerked when I saw Brennan watching me. "Everything okay?" he asked, frowning when he saw I was still wearing the red dress.

I blinked at him, feeling dazed with my revelations. "Huh?"

A rueful smile creased his lips as he looked me over—his awareness of me was incredible, as I came to realize he'd heard my gasp so was checking in with me.

Swaggering in, he hauled me against him before he lowered his head and let our mouths collide. Relieved that he'd mistaken my mood, I raised my arms and tucked them around his neck, clinging to him as he pressed me against the wall of the changing room.

His tongue thrust against mine, eating into me as he tipped my head to the side for better access. When I was breathing his air and he was breathing mine, I rippled against him, needing to get closer as I raised my leg and cocked it against his hip.

A grunt escaped him, prompting him to pull back before he muttered, "Fuck, I knew I liked this dress. Easy access."

His hand slipped between my thighs and he rubbed along the gusset of my panties again before he prodded beneath, letting bare flesh connect with bare flesh. I shuddered against him, my back arching as he let out a hiss.

"I swear to fuck, you make me remember what it was like to be twenty." His dick was thick and hard against my thigh, before he muttered, "Goddammit." His mouth burrowed against my throat, where he pressed a soft kiss, mumbling, "I have..." Another kiss anointed my collarbone. "To..." Another to the divot between my breasts. "Go."

I smirked up at the ceiling, letting my head tip to the side so I could see us both in the mirror, and as heat flared inside me, acceptance did too.

Nyx was the past.

Brennan was the present.

But, more importantly, he was my future.

I let my nails rake over his head, ruffling up his hair, before I purred, "There's always later."

"There always is with you," he said dryly, pushing his forehead against my chest, smothering himself in my cleavage.

After a good minute passed, with him suffocating between my tits, he straightened up, stared at me, then shook his head like...

With any other man, I'd think he was disappointed in me.

That he thought me lesser.

But Brennan, when he looked at me like that, I knew he was thinking, 'How am I supposed to keep my hands off her?'

Beneath his gaze, I actually felt *desirable*. Not just for who I was or what was between my thighs, but me. As a whole.

I'd never realized how deconstructed I felt and what that did to my self image, something I'd even perpetuated when I'd had breast augmentation surgery that had nearly bankrupted me at the time. I was a womb, a pussy, tits, ass. I'd never been *Camille*.

Until now.

And the craziest thing of all?

I liked Camille.

A smile curved my lips, one I didn't even register, one that came with a contentment that I hoped would only grow with time, getting deeper and deeper the longer we were together. I was taking every day as it came, would continue to do so with the weeks and months ahead, but for now, I was happy.

I knew, where regular dating was concerned, we were in the first flush, but this wasn't a regular relationship. Nothing about us was.

I just hoped that we continued in this vein.

He clucked his tongue as he reached up, his thumb smoothing along my smile. "I'll see you later, Camille."

Nodding, I whispered, "Can't wait."

That wasn't a lie, either.

I couldn't.

THIRTY-SIX
AIDAN JR.

"HI. I'M ASHER." The guy in front of me hesitated, his head bobbing as he hunched his shoulders. "I've been sober for fourteen years and three months."

"Hi, Asher," the room intoned apart from me.

I was in the corner. At the back. Just not as far back in the corner as I'd thought because this guy was in front of me, and everyone was shooting him looks which meant I might be in their line of sight.

I never spoke at NA meetings, but attending them was cathartic.

Every day, I'd say to myself that it was going to be the last day I took some Oxy, but it just never fucking worked out that way.

The men and women in this room were a hell of a lot braver than I was. They might not own as much as I did, might not command fear or loyalty in people, might be average Joes and Josephinas, but they had the balls to do what I couldn't.

They were clean.

The guy, Asher, didn't speak after he was greeted, not until the group leader, a guy called Christopher, prompted, "Is everything okay, Asher?"

It was a testament to how long the guy let the silence last that Christopher said anything, period. This was, after all, a safe space.

People were never pressured into talking. Like me. I'd been coming here for a month, and I'd said dick.

Asher was new, though. From what I'd seen of him, he had shaggy blond hair in need of a trim, his arms were covered in inked sleeves, and he had what I thought was an MC cut, just worn inside out so none of the insignia was showing.

To anyone else, it'd just look like a leather vest, but I knew differently.

I was the second-in-command of the Five Points' Mob—this kind of shit had been fed to me along with sweet potato mash when I was a brat.

"Not really," Asher replied eventually. "Everything isn't okay. The drugs... I got them under control a long time ago, but what replaced it is much worse. It's destroyed my life. Ruined my marriage. It's wrecking my kid's life too. I—" He sucked in a breath. "My name's Asher and I'm a sex addict."

My brows rose at that admission. I mean, come on. What guy wasn't addicted to sex?

The thought was instinctual, but when I thought about the last time I'd gotten laid, when I'd started preferring popping Oxy to orgasms... Jesus.

Reaching up to rub at my eyes, I realized how fucking low I'd sunk.

The only reason I wasn't shooting up heroin was because I could afford the Oxy. Only my position saved me from tacking on a 'yet' to the end of that.

Heroin was a lot fucking easier to score, and were I anyone else, there'd only be so many doctors I could call on for prescriptions... As it stood, I was a prescription junkie, one up from a regular hood rat because I was an O'Donnelly.

Go figure.

"When I got off the drugs, I switched to fucking everything that moved. My lifestyle isn't regular. There's a lot of easy pussy around—" Talk about a confirmation that the guy was in an MC. "—it was okay until I met my wife. I tried to stay faithful to her, but when she got pregnant, she was... she couldn't have sex." He gulped, and the sound was audible. A quick glance around the room told me the guys were sympathetic and the women, if they had a desire to get locked up, would have stabbed him on his wife's behalf. "I tried. I fucking tried so hard. I was jacking off twenty, fucking twenty-five times a day. So much I was getting goddamn wrist strain, but then a bit— I mean, a chick came onto me. She... offered herself, and I was desperate. I hated myself after, and every time I cheated on her, it was like a knife to the heart." He shook his head. "I hate myself now. Every time I have sex with someone who isn't her, I hate how weak I am.

"I had to leave town... and I promised myself that I'd do everything in my power to get a handle on my addiction. I want her back, want them both back in my life, full time... Hell, all the time. But to do that, I have to get this under control." He sucked in a breath, straightened his shoulders, and declared, "It's been seven weeks since I had sex. F-Five since I jacked off." He clenched his hands into fists at his sides. "It's difficult. Some days, it's impossible. It's harder than the drugs, because what I'm chasing is as easy to grab as a donut." He tightened his fists some more. "For my kid, for my woman, I have to do it. If I don't, I'll lose her, maybe both of them, and I know I'll deserve it."

With that, he plunked himself down on his seat, abruptly ending his monologue and prompting Christopher to lead into a round of applause that most of the women in the room begrudgingly took part in.

I stretched out my legs, wincing as the agony in my knee ricocheted through me. That bastard was why I had to attend these fucking meetings.

Until the drive-by shooting on my best friend's wedding day, one that had destroyed my fucking patella and had nearly killed Finn's bride, I'd been fine. A little heavy handed with the whiskey, okay, a lot when it was hard to sleep at night, but nothing like this with the Oxy.

I glared at it, a part of me wishing that they'd just chopped the fucking thing off, but instead, it was plaguing me. Killing me as I chased a way to escape the pain.

Wasn't that what we were all doing here?

Chasing a way to escape the pain?

And didn't addiction lead to other addictions? Just like that schmuck in front of me?

A month, I'd been coming here.

Four, fucking, weeks.

I'd never had any desire to say a word, mostly because I didn't have the right.

The Oxy was already starting to wear off, and I'd only sank some back two hours ago. The pain was like a monster, gnawing at my nerve endings like Da gnawed on a turkey leg at the end of the Thanksgiving meal.

The sweats would come next.

The jitters.

The vomiting.

Christ, I was so fucking sick of this life. So fucking sick of trying to escape, but how—

I closed my eyes when the room burst into applause after Sandra, a housewife from Queens, finished her speech about being clean for three months, and I darted onto my feet as fast as my bum knee would let me.

"Aidan, you wish to speak?" Christopher asked, his surprise and pleasure clear.

I'd had no intention of speaking. I'd just wanted to get the hell out of this grimy community hall that stank of bleach, disinfectant, and sweaty socks. But... Asher had just admitted to jacking off twenty fucking times a day. And I was so tired of my life. The pain was here, like a physical entity in the room. I might as well have been punching my knee for the past forty minutes instead of just taking it easy...

I needed it to stop.

I needed a way to make everything stop.

"Aidan?" Christopher queried softly, his pleasure fading into unease.

I lifted my head to face the room, saw the expectant faces, scented the shitty coffee and the sugary tang of donuts that were only marginally more bearable than that tar they served, and... *Asher had just admitted to jacking off twenty times a day.*

I could admit to this.

"My name's Aidan," I rasped, "and I've been clean for one-hundred and twenty-three minutes..."

THIRTY-SEVEN
BRENNAN

I CRACKED my knuckles as we rolled up to the hospital. Da had managed to pull some strings, get shit rolling so that Quin kid wasn't in a prison butcher shop but a decent clinic. But it didn't take away from the fact that the fuckers had gotten to him inside.

Unsurprised to find a half-dozen bikes outside the clinic, I made my way in and saw Forrest was waiting on me at the end of the corridor.

Heading for him, I asked, "What went down?"

"It's hard finding out because they're on lockdown now. The guys who have phones probably don't want to risk losing them so it's all quiet for the moment."

I grunted. "We need answers. We must have a couple of guards on payroll—"

"We have four. None of them were on shift."

We shared a look.

"That can't be a coincidence," I rumbled as our shoes squeaked against the linoleum.

"I don't think it is."

"Fucking Sparrows," I snapped under my breath as Forrest guided me down a couple more corridors, taking us to the ICU unit where I saw a few brothers gathered around in a waiting room. A couple of chicks too.

I recognized Nyx from the few times I'd met him, and saw that one of the women was his spitting image, so I took her to be a sister. As for the other one, the way she was clinging to him and he to her, I reckoned she was the infamous Giulia.

Rumor had it she'd set fire to a pedo over in Ohio... I wasn't sure how true that was, especially when rumors spread like that Chinese whispers game, where one elephant turned into a menagerie of unicorns, but she looked like a spitfire. Enough for me to eye her warily as I approached.

Nyx, on his own, was volatile.

With his woman and sister to protect, and his baby brother in a hospital bed?

I wasn't about to get my dick cut off for something that wasn't my fault.

The sound of Crocs and boots were evidently different than the snap-snap of our Oxfords against the linoleum because the second we arrived, we were at the center of everyone's attention.

Knowing Nyx was VP now, I arched a brow at him, and asked, "Can I speak freely?"

Nyx's eyes turned stormy, but he shook his head. "Giulia, Indy? I need you to step outside for a minute. Just until we figure shit out." He cast a look at one of the guys, saying, "Hawk? Follow them, yeah?"

Hawk nodded, traipsing after Giulia as she growled under her breath, storming off with a glance that promised she'd make Nyx pay for making her leave, but Indy, the one I thought was his sister, merely cast me a look, then squeezed the inked hand of the man holding her close.

Declan would know who was who, as he usually liaised with the Sinners, but Da had called Bagpipes to inform him of the stabbing, which meant he was assigning this crapshoot to me to sort out.

He was a big fucking baby sometimes, but if this was his idea of a punishment, I'd take it. I preferred this to being picked up by his crew, pinned in place, and having the shit kicked out of me.

I didn't mind pissing blood for a few days, but I had an insatiable wife to feed my dick to now. That changed things.

When the women had gone, I demanded, "What does Quin know that you haven't told us? Why the fuck would they try to target him when we'd arranged for his release?"

It was clear that they hadn't expected me to go on the attack. None of this shit was our fault, and we'd been doing the Sinners a favor by getting Quin out early, but I knew how wars started—this was enough for an alliance to turn deadly.

Nyx scowled at me. "I thought you told Rex you'd have people on him."

"We did. There must have been a problem. As it stands, communication is zero right now. His unit is on lockdown," Forrest chimed in.

Nyx pursed his lips, but I merely repeated, "You told us he was a kid who'd been shafted by the authorities because he was Native American and he had a racist judge.

"If the NWS thought he was worthy of targeting before he got out, then there's something missing from that story, Nyx. What the fuck didn't you tell us?"

Nyx clenched his jaw before he lifted his hands and scrubbed them over his face. "Rex told you everything we know. About Craig Lacey, the cop who framed Quin. How he's the son of a guy who's running for Mayor in West Orange... there's nothing else, man. Nothing else we know about anyway."

Gritting my teeth because I believed him, I strolled into the den of lions and took a seat next to Nyx. I felt the tension edge up in the bikers, almost like they expected me to pull some kind of stunt, but that wasn't my intention.

Instead, I leaned back, rested my head against the wall and muttered, "These fuckers need taking down."

For my pains, I received a bucket load of grunts as I stared straight ahead. Forrest was on edge thanks to my location, but I ignored him after the initial glance, preferring to just stare at a damp spot on the ceiling.

"Are you working on that?" Nyx asked softly, twisting his head to look at me. He was leaning forward, his elbows stacked on his knees, looking like a mixture of The Thinker and a tormented soul in hell.

Considering the MC's name, I thought that was more fitting by half.

"We are," I confirmed. "You?"

"We have Lodestar on it. I think she keeps in touch with someone on your end."

I hummed under my breath. "My biggest concern is them being

everywhere and us not having a pin on any names. Craig Lacey's practically a beat cop he's so fresh with a detective shield. What the fuck kind of information are they going to spew the way of a shitty detective who's only three years into the job and keeps making mistakes?"

"What kind of mistakes?" Nyx asked.

"Guess."

He shot me a dark look. "Racist prick."

"You got it."

"He's still an in."

I shook my head. "Not really." We weren't going to waste time on one of the sheep when we had the Mayor ripe and ready to pluck. Not that I was going to tell Nyx that. Instead, I just informed him, "We've had him under surveillance."

Forrest cleared his throat. "He appears to be a low level runner. At best, a courier. He's been crossing the state lines a lot in an SUV that he hires from the same car rental place over in Brooklyn."

One of the guys, the one Indy had been huddled up against, rumbled, "He has a ride of his own?"

Forrest nodded. "So the SUV shouldn't be necessary, but he pulls these runs every few weeks."

"Drugs?" Nyx queried.

"We don't know. Since we learned his name, he hasn't hired a car."

"Because he knows you're aware of him?"

"No," Forrest dismissed. "It's not time. He has a pattern. When he does, we'll make sure to sweep the car."

"Would it be likely he's carrying drugs? Why use a new detective?" Indy's man argued.

"Who the fuck knows what they're doing," Nyx muttered. "We have to start somewhere."

I pursed my lips, unwilling to tell him about my in with NYC's Mayor, especially when I was about to start stretching my fingers where that particular hypocrite was concerned.

"We're on it, but it's imperative we work together."

"Agreed," Nyx rumbled. "Lodestar seems to believe that there's no high-ranking or low-ranking NWS member."

I frowned. "What do you mean?"

"Just telling you what I've been told." Nyx shrugged.

"I think you're wrong," I said softly, not wanting to cause offense. "At least, I hope you are because that makes them even fucking harder to contain."

He pulled a face. "No denying that."

"Shit." I blew out a breath. "How's your brother?"

"For the moment, they've gotten the bleeding under control."

"I'm relieved to hear it."

Nyx just nodded. "By the time he's ready to be discharged, they'll be letting him out a free man." He cracked his knuckles. "I know I'm not the only brother who's worrying about how that'll go."

"The Sparrows?"

"What's to stop them from coming after him again?" Nyx confirmed.

"Will it be easier to keep an eye on him when he's back?" I stared around the waiting room. "I can make sure there's a Five Pointer on guard here—"

"That's not necessary," Nyx rumbled. "Appreciate it, but we protect our own." He grimaced. "When we can." Meaning that his bro had been left wide open to attack because he'd been the only Sinner in his unit in Rikers.

I wasn't insulted because I knew, if the situations were reversed, we'd have the same attitude on this subject.

"We're going to be looking into how this went down, don't you worry. All of our prison guards who are on our payroll were conveniently off shift at the same time."

Nyx's brows lowered. "Christ. The Sparrows really are everywhere." He swiped a hand over his mouth. "My Old Lady's pregnant, O'Donnelly. I really don't want to spend the first eight years of that kid's life in jail... you know what I'm saying?"

"I do. None of us are going to jail." It just felt like the Sparrows were breathing down our fucking necks no matter which way we turned.

"You can't promise that."

"No, I can't," I agreed, "but I know that I'm going to be working on ways to bring the fuckers down."

"We are too."

"Then we need to make sure we're coordinating. Where's Padraig anyway?" He was our usual liaison.

"He's back in... West Orange." The pause was just enough of a hesitation to let me know he was lying. "We had another situation."

"Situations—they never let up, do they?"

Nyx caught my eye. "They fucking don't."

"Not asking for details, but you need our help?"

He shook his head. "Again, appreciate the offer, but no. Everything's handled."

I nodded. "We're all in the same boat together."

Nyx blew out a breath. "Let's just hope that fucker don't sink."

We were both on the same page where that was concerned.

"You won't hear me—"

Before I could finish the sentence, alarms started blaring, and nurses and doctors rushed in from out of nowhere, piling into the kid's room.

Fuck.

He was coding.

Gritting my teeth, I got to my feet as Hawk, Indy, and Giulia ran in, rushing over to their men's sides, and knowing this wasn't my place, that this was a time for family, I got the fuck out of there with Forrest at my back.

"Think he's gonna die?" I asked Forrest.

"He bled out a lot," my bud said gruffly. "He's gonna be unstable for a while."

I tried to find comfort in that, but didn't find all that fucking much.

"Shit."

"Yeah. Shit."

"What does he know that they wanted to keep quiet?" I muttered, to no one, to everyone. To the universe if it was listening and willing to answer.

"God knows. Let's hope he gets better and he can live to tell us himself."

"Agreed." I grunted, and knowing that being maudlin would get me nowhere, I changed the subject. "You're sure Coullson is going to be there tonight?"

Forrest snorted. "You bet your ass he is."

"Good." I flexed my hands in front of me. "It's time we started putting pressure on him."

"Can do."

His cell buzzed, and as he read the message, I asked, "Problem?" We were putting out fires left, right, and center—it was just one of those days.

"Aidan's been seen heading into the St. Barnabus Community Center."

My brow puckered. "Not St. Patrick's?"

"No."

"Why? It's your job to keep tabs on him," I grumbled the reminder, elbowing him in the side to let him know I wasn't giving him any shit, just yanking his chain.

Forrest heaved a sigh at my messing, and muttered, "I'd explain if you gave me the chance. I've got a guy on Aidan, and then Donny, well, he's been reporting to Finn already so I figured he could keep us in the loop too."

"Finn's been asking after big bro as well?" Donny was on Aidan's crew, not Finn's.

"Don't know why you're surprised. Aidan spends a good three nights a week around Finn and Aoife's place."

I arched a brow. "I didn't know that."

"No, well, I only tell you the really interesting shit."

"And why is St. Barnabus's Community Center interesting?"

Forrest smirked at me. "Because of what's going on inside it."

"Drumroll, please," I mocked. "Don't keep me in suspense, dipshit."

"It's one of those NA meetings but for any and all addicts."

"He's going to support group meetings?" I blurted out.

"Well, don't get excited. This is only the third time he's gone, as far as we know because he can be a slippery cunt, but according to Findleigh, he ain't said jack each time he's been."

My nose crinkled. "Ain't that the point of them?"

"Well, yeah, that's the point, but let's face it, he's gotta build up the courage to actually admit to it. Aidan's not exactly been raised thinking he's infallible, has he?"

"I don't know. Da was harder on him than the rest of us, and he wasn't exactly easy on us," I grumbled.

"Yeah, but to the rest of the world, it's always been 'Junior's shit stinks of violets.' 'Junior's piss is laced with gold.'"

My lips twitched. "Really?"

"You didn't know?" Forrest scowled at me. "That's not like you."

"I know I get sick of the favoritism," I rumbled with a shrug, "but I've never really bothered worrying about what everyone else thinks about the family. They're gonna love us or fucking loathe us—so long as we've got their respect then I'm okay with things." I scrubbed my chin as we finally made it to my car. "Saying that, times had better change I guess. We've got so many fucking turncoats, I keep expecting Da to yell, 'The British are coming.'"

Forrest snickered. "I'd pay to see that."

"You know what, bro? I would too." We shared a grin, then I clapped the roof of my Maserati and murmured, "St. Barnabus is, what? Fifty minutes' ride from here?"

"Give or take a few."

"Throw in traffic..." I crinkled my nose. "Not exactly doable."

"Findleigh was messaging to tell me Aidan's on the move—the meeting's over." He frowned at me. "You want to sit in on a meeting? Don't that go against the code? It's supposed to be anonymous, Bren."

"I know it is, but nothing's anonymous in this fucking world." I hitched a shoulder. "I think it's for the best if I monitor things."

What with Ma talking to a shrink and Aidan potentially dumping a clusterfuck on a group of unsuspecting junkies... someone had to keep the family in line.

"Anyway, let me know the next time he heads there."

"Been going every Friday for a few weeks now." He cleared his throat. "I told Findleigh to get the fuck out of the meeting hall if Aidan starts talking. Not to let his curiosity get the better of him."

"Good. He goes there at the same time?"

"Yeah."

I hummed and made a mental note to stick around that area so I could slip in and listen to whatever shit my big brother was spewing to the masses.

"Tink get the limo sorted out tonight?"

Forrest nodded. "Yeah. I've got Duncan driving you."

"Why Duncan? He's a little high up the ranks for that, ain't he?"

"Boy needs taking down a notch. Getting too big for his own good."

"What'd he do?"

"Got into a couple of fights over the sisters of some runners."

My scowl made a swift reappearance. "He ain't messing around with them, is he?"

Forrest shrugged. "Won't be after those fights."

I snorted out a laugh.

"Want me to stick around here? Or get back to The Hole?"

I pursed my lips. "They don't want us here, and I think Nyx will keep us in the know." I let my gaze drift wide, scanning the hospital on the whole before I murmured, "You have any idea what situation they're trying to manage?"

"The one that has Padraig still back in the boondocks and not deep in our territory where he should be?"

"That's the one," I said dryly, hiding a laugh because only Forrest would consider 'New Jersey' the boondocks.

He shook his head. "No clue. Want me to find out?"

"Not actively. Just keep your ears open."

"Will do, Bren." He tapped the roof of my car, then started to turn on his heel. "I'll see ya later."

"Will do."

I watched him go, relieved that Victoria, Camille's sister, had picked one of Eoghan's crew to be her guard. I needed my best men on the NWS situation, and Forrest was at the top of the tree.

She was family, so I'd have made do with the sacrifice, but was glad I didn't have to.

Climbing behind the wheel, I sank into my seat, then I swept the car for bugs. Just a few months ago, I'd done this every couple of days, now, with the NWS, it was every time I got behind the wheel.

It couldn't be helped, but it was damn boring.

Finding zero listening devices, I let my mind wander. Over the past week, my crew hadn't pulled any moves that made me think they weren't firmly on my side—if anything, they'd further entangled themselves with the family.

Tink and Forrest had helped dispose of the thieves behind the jewelry heists, and Bagpipes had helped me transport Callum to a safer location before I'd ended his miserable life.

When Forrest was like that, when Bagpipes and Tink were as on the fucking ball as always, I felt like a piece of shit for even questioning their loyalties. But no one could be trusted right now.

Not even my fucking brother or mother.

Camille?

I wanted to hope she was different, but only time would tell.

YOU DON'T NEED A PRINCE CHARMING TO SAVE YOU. YOU CAN SAVE YOURSELF. YOU'RE DOING IT NOW. YOU'RE DOING THIS NOW TO STOP YOURSELF FROM TAKING THE PLUNGE. YOU GOT THIS. KEEP ON FIGHTING. IT WILL BE WORTH IT TOMORROW.

THIRTY-EIGHT
CAMILLE

WAS I disappointed that I didn't see Brennan for the rest of the very long day?

Yes.

But... I got to spend most of it with Inessa. After I sent her a picture of my new dresses, she'd come over and we'd converged in the living room, and together, we worked on my hair and nails. Of course, that didn't take *all* day, but catching up did.

We had a lot to make up for, and it was interesting that killing Father was what mended the bridge between us.

Well, partially, at least.

The blood on my hands, on my soul, didn't stop me from enjoying my middle sister to the max.

As she poured me a mimosa, heavy on the orange juice considering I needed to be *compos mentis* for the gala later on, I told her, "It's nice to see you happy, Innie."

Her nose crinkled at the nickname. "Innie? Ugh, haven't I grown out of that yet?"

I grinned at her. "Nope."

She blew me a raspberry, proceeded to take a massive gulp of her drink, which was light on the OJ, before flopping back against the squashy cushions of the sofa. I'd decided to make our base camp here because it was closest to the kitchen—girls had needs, after all.

"You're right though. I *am* happy, which is kind of messed up, considering, ya know, everything."

I shrugged. "You won't see me disagreeing."

Her head rocked back against the cushions for a second, before she tipped her chin forward to frown at me. "What did it feel like?"

I could have prevaricated, but I didn't see much point. We were both glad the bastard was dead—for different reasons, of course. I just prayed she never learned that Mama had been set up by our father to be killed in the most gruesome and horrendous way a woman could be murdered.

I'd do everything in my power to make sure she never learned that horrific truth.

"It didn't feel like anything," I told her slowly, pausing in the application of my false eyelashes. I stopped peering at myself and looked instead into the murky cocktail we were both drinking. "I was... it was like I was in a blackout. I couldn't tell you what it felt like, just that I couldn't stop. Once I started, I had to carry on until it was, well, over.

"I was tired of him being a threat, tired of him tainting every breath we take. When he went to hurt me again, I was so frightened," I whispered, shivering with the memory. "I'd already armed myself, but I didn't think I'd use it.

"It started in self-defense... he went to grab me, and it just clicked in my mind that I didn't have to be frightened of him. I could run and he couldn't catch me, but when he grabbed my hand—" I released a breath, before repeating, "It just clicked in my mind."

"Does it give you nightmares?"

I winced. "I suppose it should."

"Meaning it doesn't?"

"No. I sleep quite well."

Her lips twisted. "Regular orgasms do that for a woman, I guess."

We shared a grin. "How's... everything down below?"

Nose crinkling again, she mumbled, "Almost back to normal. It's been strange not being able to touch him like that." Her gaze turned distant. "I think it's made us closer. I'd tell him again just to stop it from getting worse... so that's something."

"He was annoyed you didn't tell him, wasn't he?"

"Furious." Her cheeks flushed with heat. "I've never seen him so mad, and trust me, I've seen him go postal."

A short laugh escaped me. "I can believe it."

She hummed. "These men... the Irish... they're nothing like the Russians, are they?"

"No," I agreed, "but maybe we just know the wrong ones."

"Perhaps," she muttered doubtfully, and I couldn't blame her.

I thought about our poor baby sister, promised to Maxim, my future freedom leveraged against a wedding band on her finger, and guiltily, I whispered, "We're lucky."

"We are." She cast me a look. "Before I told him everything, about the rash... Eoghan told me he loved me. For the first time."

Happiness filled me. "Oh, Innie, I'm so glad for you." And I was. Inessa deserved all the love in the world. "Let me guess, that made him angrier with you?"

Her nose crinkled. "It did."

I sighed. "Men."

"Men," she concurred, before she pouted. "Why didn't you tell me you were dating Brennan?"

"We weren't exactly chitchatting about each other's love life, Innie. Why would I tell you anything when you didn't want to tell me anything?" I hedged, which made her grumble:

"You could still have said something."

My smile hid the truth in the lie. "It was too early to talk about it."

"Not too early for you to marry him," she pointed out with a laugh. "I know the O'Donnellys move fast, but Christ."

I shrugged. "He liked it so he put a ring on it."

She hooted at that, then said, "I gotta listen to that."

Grinning, I watched as she leaped onto her feet, and when our house computer connected with her phone and Beyoncé blasted through the speakers, I danced a little as I finished with my make-up.

When the song came to an end, she asked, "You'll come to Vespers with me tomorrow?"

"I promise. I doubt the invitation to the family homestead has been reinstated," I said with a laugh, finding that I wasn't all that concerned about Brennan's parents' reception.

Even if Aidan Sr. was insane, I didn't think he'd hurt me like my father had.

She bit her lip, seeming nervous which had me waiting for a difficult question. Only, I didn't get one. Inessa just asked, "Do you think it will be a late night?"

Every night was a late night right now, but that didn't stop life from churning on, or from Brennan being on constant call.

In the time I'd known him, he'd woken me up because he got in so late, and he left way before the sun had a chance to rise most mornings. He didn't exactly live a good life, spending most of his time working, and not exactly at the job he loved.

I didn't think being a made man could be included in that, 'work a job you love and you never work a day in your life' BS.

"I mean, I guess so. Why?" was all I told my sister. She didn't need to know that the second Brennan did get home, he was on me faster than Usain Bolt.

"Well, the in-laws and me have a little ritual now."

"You, Lena and Aidan Sr.?" I blurted out, aghast.

She sputtered out a laugh. "No! Are you crazy? Seeing them on Sundays is more than enough." Her grin turned cheeky. "I meant the sisters-in-law."

"Ohhh."

"Yeah, ohhh. Well, we've started a thing where we go to The Plaza Palm Court and we have brunch together on Saturdays. Just a couple of times a month, you know? I'd like you to be there."

God, it had been years since I'd visited the Palm Court. I'd never wanted to visit again, but turning down this invitation would be stupid when I was working hard to cultivate our relationship.

Hesitantly, I asked, "Are you okay with me attending? I don't want to cramp your style or anything."

"What style?" she asked wryly. "Anyway, before, I probably would have told them you were a bitch, but now? I like you. Weird that it took you killing Father for me to realize that."

I laughed a little. "We really need to stop being okay with this."

Inessa shrugged. "He was a prick. What are we supposed to do? Mourn the bastard who married me off to a man I'd never met? Or the one who pushed you to run away because he wanted to tie you to an ancient creep?" Her grin made another reappearance. "Anyway, the way we live, the way our men make their livings, it'd be pious and hypocritical of me to condemn you for it."

"When you put it like that—"

Her nod was stout. "Exactly." She leaned forward. "Guess what."

"What?" I whispered.

She tapped her nose. "Have you heard of The Whistler?"

I blinked, then frowned when I thought about that name. "It rings a bell. Is he a sniper or something?"

"Yep, he's a sniper." Banked heat flared to life in her eyes. "Eoghan's The Whistler."

A surprised gasp escaped me. "No way."

"Way." She bounced on her seat. "Isn't that the hottest thing ever?"

I laughed. "I mean, I guess, if you're into that type of thing which you quite clearly are."

"I guess it'd be funky if you were into that too."

"More than funky," I agreed. "What does Brennan do? In the Points, I mean."

She pursed her lips. "Mostly, I think he's the go to guy to get everyone out of trouble. I think he started off handling some of their shipments, maybe managed their stock of whores, but I think it's morphed over time."

"Into what?" The idea of him working with hookers made my stomach twist. Even though prostitution was as much a part of this life as dying violently.

"Well, a bit of everything. He deals with the gambling dens and the protection rackets too. It's not fair really. He's taken on Aidan Jr.'s jobs, so he has his hands in a lot of pies."

When I thought about his schedule, it fit.

"What's going on with Aidan Jr.? Why has Brennan taken on a lot of his work?"

She leaned closer. "On Aoife and Finn's wedding day, they were shot down in a drive-by shooting. I only learned this afterward, but that was when the Irish made a deal with Father. I was the sacrificial lamb." She pulled a face. "Anyway, in the shooting, Aoife got hit really badly. She almost died. And Aidan, well, he got hit too. Ever since then, he's been hooked on pain meds."

I whistled under my breath. "Shit."

"About sums it up," she agreed. "So, he's a liability, but they all protect him from Aidan Sr."

"Doesn't he know? I mean, he seemed pretty shrewd to me."

"He is, but the guys cover for Aidan. I don't think they want to cause him trouble with their dad."

"That's sweet, I guess."

She shrugged. "Maybe. Depends on if it's making things too easy for him, you know?"

"You think he needs to bottom out?"

"For as long as I've known him, he's been wired. I think he definitely needs a short, sharp shock."

I pondered that. "You know... when I was at their folks' place, I saw something."

"What?"

"Photos—"

She rolled her eyes. "There are, like, thousands of photos, Cammie."

"Yeah, but these ones stuck out to me at the time. One was of Aidan Sr. and a guy who looked like his brother. The other only registered because I recognized Finn from the papers. The pictures caught my eye because of Aidan's reaction to our news, but the next day..." My voice waned.

"The next day?" Inessa prompted, curiosity making her give me her full attention, enough that she switched off her phone.

"When we were in the churchyard, I noticed that they all look alike." I licked my lips. "*All* of them, Innie."

Our eyes clashed.

"You can't say anything to Brennan," was her initial response.

"Why not?" I whispered, unease filtering through me.

"If he finds out, if any of the brothers find out, they'll go crazy."

"I already asked Brennan about the photo, Inessa. He said it was his Uncle Frank."

"Jesus." She winced, admitting, "Aela brought it up the first time we all had brunch together. I'd noticed it thanks to all the photos as well. I'm not sure how the guys haven't put two and two together yet, but they haven't. Maybe they don't see it because they're so close, I don't know, but—"

"Aidan Sr.'s brother is Finn's dad?"

Inessa blinked. "No. *Aidan Sr.* is Finn's dad."

My mouth dropped open. "No way!"

Her head bobbed. "Yes, definitely. Aoife confirmed it."

"Finn knows?" I queried, my voice hushed like people could hear us talking in the privacy of my empty apartment.

"He does," she muttered. "Weird, right?"

"Definitely." Disappointment filled me. "I thought they were so in love."

Inessa seemed to understand what I was saying. "Oh, they are. Aidan's besotted with Lena. According to her, she keeps him happy in the bedroom and it stops him from cheating," she said with a laugh. "This happened in the early days of their marriage, don't forget. Ask Brennan, and he'll tell you all about the 'rolling pin incident.' That was what had Aidan Sr. falling head over heels for her."

"What 'rolling pin incident?'"

"Apparently, she bashed him over the head with one—"

Before she could carry on, an alarm buzzed on my phone, reminding me that I had less than an hour until the limo was on its way. Bagpipes had given me those details, not Brennan. I hadn't heard from him all day.

"God, is it that time already?" I muttered, wishing that the gala wasn't happening because I wanted to know more.

Inessa stretched on the sofa. "I'll let you get on. Eoghan will probably be home by now anyway." She grinned at me. "I think I might let him make it up to me for, ya know, making my whole vajayjay look like it was from another planet."

I winced. "That bad?"

"Cammie, you've got no idea. It was gross. I can laugh now, but..." She shuddered. "Never again. Brazilians all the way."

"Who knew that would be less painful?"

Her giggle made me feel like I was lit up from the inside out. It was so good to hear that, so good to have *this* again.

"That tells you how bad it was." She got to her feet, stretched again, then bobbed down to press a kiss to my cheek. "I don't think I've seen you this content in years, Cammie. I'm so happy for you."

That we were both on the same track had my heart feeling full. I kissed her cheek too, and whispered, "I think we've both found our places."

"I know we have," was her strident reply. "Anyway, I'll see you tomorrow?"

"You will."

"The Plaza, eleven AM. It's okay if you have to cancel, but it'd be cool for you to meet them properly. They're really nice." She pulled a face. "Don't mention what we talked about, though. It might get Aoife upset."

"I'll be there and I won't say anything," I promised her, making a silent vow that I'd stand up to Brennan about this if he decided we were going out somewhere else.

I wasn't going to say that I let him steamroll over me all the time—even if he pretty much did. But I was still finding my footing.

"I can't wait," she said with a little squeal, before she shot me a wave and pretty much danced out of the living room.

When she was gone, the elevator letting out a few beeps as she departed, I peered at myself in the mirror. I'd spent too much time looking into the damn thing, but I wanted to be Brennan's idea of a dream date. Silly, sure, but why wouldn't I want to be that, especially when he was mine?

When Innie had invited herself over for coffee to see my dresses, I'd thought she was a welcome distraction from fretting about Nyx, but that hadn't been the case. I hadn't thought about him or the Sinners once. Compassion for Quin filled me, but that was it. No more, no less, and it was such a weight off my heart to take a step forward without the past shadowing every move I made.

I'd spent months pining for the man, wringing my hands over him and what would never be, and in a week, Brennan had turned my world on its head.

"It's amazing what a couple dozen orgasms will do to a girl's confidence," I muttered under my breath, but my grin was wry as I gave my make-up a final check.

Innie was right—I did look happy.

For the first time in too long, I wasn't digging my nails into my palms, wasn't even tempted to seek out my kit. I didn't doubt that the urges would come and go, but this week, my palms were getting a much needed chance to heal.

Deciding I was done, I wandered down the hall to the bedroom, dropping the bathrobe I'd put on earlier for ease with changing once my hair and make-up was set.

I'd showered before I started getting ready, so I stepped into the garter belt and slipped on my stockings. There'd been no mistaking how much Brennan had loved those, so it made me smile to put on a different set—black silk, with a black and silver filigree detailing on the bands.

That was pretty much it for undergarments.

It was risqué but I didn't care. I wanted the picture he'd painted this morning for me.

I wanted him to be able to slip his hand between my legs and for him to feel my pussy. I wanted to dance with him in a busy crowd, and for him to be able to touch me how he wanted.

Biting my lip at just the thought, making me grateful that I'd yet to apply lipstick, I tried to ignore the way my body lit up but it wasn't that easy. Not when my nips were so erect I could probably hang my dress off them.

Grinning, I eyed said dress as I slipped into it. Like this morning, it cupped my body like it was made for me, and as expensive as it was, it was still off the rack, but you'd never tell.

It swayed and swung with every movement, and the split was just a few scant inches from baring all.

I resettled my breasts, and grabbed some tit tape that would hopefully keep them in place, then looked at myself.

I wore the star pendant that had started this entire madcap journey, the dress, and nothing else, and I looked good.

"You look better than good," I whispered under my breath, accepting it.

Embracing it.

I did.

With my hair curled the way it was, in thick waves that I'd set with a few pins, I looked like Marilyn Monroe—just a skinnier version.

I'd picked up a pair of high heels too, strappy things that were dangerous, and all the more beautiful for it. Just a single strap at the ankle and a point at the toe were all that were keeping me attached to six inches of stiletto.

Everything about today's look was different than before.

BN—Before Nyx.

Then, I'd dressed for the role I was in—whore.

Now, I looked like a star.

I'd been feeling better about myself of late, but at that moment, I was on top of the world. Even had a bounce to my step—which was dangerous in these heels—as I swished out of the bedroom and into the hall.

I'd purchased a pea coat too, obsidian gray silk with a velvet lining to ward off the chill, and as that swirled around my calves as well, I felt like a princess.

It didn't matter that I was about to face New York society, didn't matter that, a quick Google search of tonight's gala, informed me of just how many important people were going to be in attendance—I was Brennan O'Donnelly's bride.

I was untouchable.

The only thing that spoiled my mood was that conversation with Inessa. As I applied my lipstick, I started to wish that I hadn't mentioned Finn now. I knew how it felt to be on the outside looking in. Even if Finn was included, he was a brother by choice, as Brennan had phrased it the other day. When, really, it was of blood.

Withholding the truth of Finn's heritage felt like I was keeping something from Brennan, and with the precarious nature of our relationship, I didn't want that.

I didn't want to rock any boat or make him think I was holding stuff back from him.

Trust—he'd asked for it. Loyalty—he was trying to earn it.

I wasn't going to reward that by lying to him.

The buzzer sounded, rupturing my concerns for the moment, and I used the house computer to turn everything off before making my way to the console table where I'd already prepped my purse with extra lipstick and my cellphone, so I grabbed it then headed onto the elevator.

The mirrors gave me a three-hundred-sixty degree view of myself. I flushed a little, but I knew I'd never looked so good, and it was with confidence that I made my way out into the garage.

The limo was waiting on me, but Bagpipes wasn't.

I frowned at the stranger who introduced himself as Duncan. I felt like a fool, but I took a step back, not wanting to risk it as I secured myself in the elevator by heading for the third floor.

As the doors closed on me, I saw the driver's surprise, but I quickly texted Bagpipes who promptly replied with a picture of the man who was supposed to be chauffeuring us tonight.

Recognizing he was the driver waiting by the limo, I decided to brazen it out by walking over to the vehicle like I hadn't just taken shelter in the elevator, and smiled at him as he opened the door for me once more.

The limo left for the party and I messed around on my phone for a few minutes as the car seemed to take us off Manhattan and toward Bed-Stuy. I was still nervous, especially when I remembered Brennan saying that he wasn't sure who he trusted anymore, and even though Bagpipes had been nothing but kind, my heart skipped a beat when Duncan pulled up outside a building.

One I didn't recognize.

One I didn't know.

It fit my dress, though, seeming to be like something from the thirties. Curious, I peered out onto the facade of what was evidently a club, but relief filled me when Brennan made an appearance.

As he strode toward the limo, it was a wonder I didn't see stars.

"My God," I breathed, feeling flushed and excited all at the same time, but grateful too that he didn't have to see me fangirling over him like he was Benedict Cumberbatch and I was a Cumberbitch.

He wore a tux, a sparkling white shirt with plackets and onyx studs. His bow tie was in perfect alignment, and his shoes gleamed.

Men always had it easy at these events. They just put on a special suit and they looked dressed up, only Brennan was something else. A whole other league. One of his very own.

I didn't know what it was about him, what hit me like a sucker punch to the ovaries, but he did it every time, and I wasn't sure I'd ever get sick of it.

Duncan climbed out of the limo, rounded the back of it, and held open the door for my husband who dipped his chin in greeting at the driver, before slipping inside to join me in the swanky ride.

There was a ring of lights running down the length of the vehicle, but that didn't really illuminate anything, so I wasn't surprised when he didn't see me, and instead grumbled, "Camille?"

I smiled. "I'm over here."

"Why?" was his wry retort. "Aren't you going to say hello?"

"I can say that from over here," I teased, grinning into the shadows. "Plus, this way, I won't have to fix my lipstick before we leave the limo."

"Ah, a woman's work is never done." He chuckled, but it was darker than usual, ripe with the day's tensions, and rich with his mood—whatever today had heralded, it hadn't been fruitful, and for whatever reason our attendance at the gala was necessary, that wasn't cheering him up either. "I still think you should come and say hello."

"And I think you should look at me first before you ruin what I spent all day making beautiful for you."

It was those two words that would seal the deal.

For you.

I knew what he was like. Even in such a short space of time, I could read him like he was one of my favorite books.

I heard some fumbling, then his cellphone screen blinked on which preempted his flashlight. I half-expected him to use that to spotlight me, but he didn't. Instead, he aimed it at the console which had a small inset area for placing drinks, before he flipped a stronger light on in the cabin.

My eyes took a second to adjust, as did his, and when he caught sight of me, deep in the shadows, I watched his expression change.

From fatigued and drawn to alight with lust.

Bright with energy.

Almost incandescent with it in a way that made the lights superfluous to requirements.

I wouldn't lie that I'd picked my pose intentionally, and I didn't want to maintain it for long either. My chest muscles were already starting to burn, but it was worth it for that look.

Leaning back against the banquette seat, my elbows were digging into the cushions which I knew accentuated my cleavage. My legs, impossibly long thanks to the high heels, were crossed, and the skirt of my dress had swung free, exposing all of them to his gaze.

I felt like a siren, one whose call beckoned only him, and I watched as he leaned forward, rumbling, "Spread your legs, Camille."

"You'll muss me up," I complained half-heartedly.

A swarthy grin creased his jaw. "Down below, maybe. I'll make sure you look pristine everywhere else."

A breathy moan escaped me, and it was beyond my control to contain it as I obeyed—what fool wouldn't?

I let my legs part, the knees spreading even as I kept my feet tucked together, and watched as he slid along the cabin, down the seats, before he reached me at the other end.

When he dropped to his knees, I moaned with delight as he immediately buried his face in my pussy. My hands dug into the cushions as he dove for gold and found it within seconds, his tongue lashing my clit like he wanted my orgasm more than he wanted his next breath.

I could hear my juices, could hear how wet I was, and fuck, it felt so good, so right, that I didn't even care that Duncan could probably hear us behind the privacy screen.

All that mattered was how delicious this was.

I knew, all evening, he'd scent of me. My pussy juices around his lips as he spoke with the bigwigs of Manhattan. As we rubbed shoulders with the rich and famous, he'd be coated in my arousal—

Boom.

My thoughts, my needs, his wicked tongue, and the combination of his fingers thrusting into me and a day's worth of waiting for this had me exploding with the fastest climax in the record books.

It made me feel like I was both imploding and exploding as I reared up, belly muscles tensing as I hunched forward, my hands dragging through his hair as I tried to pull him off, but he wouldn't let me. He just carried on and on, taking me higher and higher until I wanted to scream with both wonder and distress.

When he knocked me toward that edge again, I hovered there, endlessly, so close to falling over...

He stopped.

And I stared at him.

Bewildered, befuddled, just dazedly gaping at him, wondering why he'd denied me.

For a second, I couldn't understand what he was doing, then I saw his cock make an appearance between us. It was thick and red, pulsing with need, his pre-cum dripping from the tip. He slid the head through the folds, coating him with my juices, before he pushed into me.

I was so wet that my pussy offered no resistance as he tapped out, filling me full, and I let loose a keening sound as my head flopped back against the cushions, uncaring if it messed up the long, flowing waves of my hair, not giving a damn so long as he carried on fucking me.

One hand went to my lower stomach which he palpated, and the other went to my clit. I let my legs cross around his back, so that my heels could dig into his ass whenever he pulled out too far, as he worked me back to where I'd been without him. Except empty never felt so good as being stuffed with his cock.

He started to fuck me. Hard, fast. Rough. But I didn't mind. Didn't give a damn. I needed this, needed *him*. Everything he had to give was mine. It belonged to me, just like he did.

He was mine as much as I was his.

My pussy clamped down around him at the thought and a choked cry escaped me as my climax blossomed inside me, bursting free like a gust of wind sending the frothy seeds of a dandelion floating through the air.

I clutched at him even as he pulled out, but before I could complain, he grabbed a hold of his cock and before my bewildered eyes, jacked off. With his spare hand, he shoved my skirts aside, then gritted his teeth, clenched his jaw, forcing the sinews in his throat to pop up as he came all over me. My pussy, my pubis, my lower belly.

Everywhere was anointed with him.

A growl escaped him as the last few spurts of his cum covered me, thick white trails that ran starkly across my skin, contrasting with the glistening folds between my legs which were drenched with my own arousal.

Our harsh, panting breaths were all that could be heard in the cabin of the limo, and even then, the sound of my heart pounding in my ears was louder still.

The sensation of being claimed, of being *owned* by him overwhelmed me to the point where I could have burst into tears. Stupid, or not, my emotions raged at a fever pitch around this man. *Around my husband.*

When he reached down and started to rub his seed into my flesh, I caught his eye, willing him to say it, to whisper the word I was coming to associate with him, the only word that would keep those tears at bay…

And like he heard me, like he knew what I was thinking, he smirked at me, so cocky, so in fucking control that I almost wanted to slap him because I was anything but…

"Mine."

Which was, I was coming to realize, the only thing I wanted to be.

A shaky breath escaped me before I whispered in return, "Yours."

Possessiveness flared in his eyes, a rich starkness that made me preen under his gaze as he reached into his pocket with sticky fingers and pulled out a handkerchief. He wiped his fingers as clean as they could be, earning my eternal thanks because, as much as I wanted to clean them for him, fixing my lipstick in this light would be a nightmare.

With that done, he pressed the cloth between my legs then raised it to his nose. Before my eyes, and with my cheeks growing hotter still, he sniffed it and rumbled, "Delicious."

Heart fluttering, I watched as he tucked it back into his pocket, then pulled out a small ring box—something I gathered from the size alone.

He was still between my thighs, my cunt was still on show and my lips were parted as he placed the box low on my pubis. With that done, he pulled a longer one out of his side pocket, this one more for a bracelet.

I watched as he reached for my left hand, twisting it slightly so he could press a kiss to my ring finger, before he murmured, "I have a feeling we'll always do things ass backward, Camille."

I blinked at him. "I rather like the way we do things."

"Only 'rather,' hmm?" he teased gruffly, making my lips twitch as he opened the ring box.

No fumbling with this man. He was as confident as ever as he revealed an eternity band that was like no other.

This wasn't thin and dotted with diamonds. This was thick. Six diamonds, over a carat each, stacked side by side, nestled between more diamonds that made up the rest of the rim. It should have been gaudy, but it wasn't. And my engagement ring slotted perfectly into it, letting me know that it was a matching set.

"It's beautiful," I whispered, sitting up slightly.

I didn't even care that my pussy was on display, just wanted that ring on my finger.

His ring on my finger.

As he slipped it on, I swore to God, it felt like he slipped on a seal of ownership. Neither of us wore wedding bands, and yes, that felt strange to me, but that he'd one-upped that with an eternity band... well, it shouldn't have lit me up from the inside out, but it did. It truly did.

Such extravagance wasn't necessary but it made me feel like I belonged. Not like a woman who'd trapped him, but like he really meant it when he said I was his. *Forever.*

I clenched my fingers around it, not surprised that it fit perfectly as I stared at it, overjoyed with what I was seeing.

For all my sins, I knew jewelry. I knew that I was wearing something that cost over a quarter of a million dollars...

His hands moved, snagging my attention, and I saw him slip on a ring too. A simple titanium one, but it was there nonetheless.

He was claimed.

That ring told the world he was mine.

Speechless, my eyes wet with emotions I couldn't express, I watched as he opened the other box, the distinctive pop of the hinge ricocheting around the cabin, and found myself looking at a matching tennis bracelet and choker.

"Let them all know who you belong to," he rasped, his voice a snarl, the words hungry and eager and everything I needed to feel whole.

Dressed in his diamonds, and coated in his cum, there would be no other belle of the ball tonight.

Only me.

THIRTY-NINE
BRENNAN

TO SAY Camille looked like a million dollars was underestimating the worth of a million dollars.

She looked like a pin up, a model, and a porn star combined. Throw in some Marilyn Monroe glamor, I was the luckiest fucker at the gala with her on my arm.

Shame the whole event was a farce.

I knew for a fact the Davison's Hudson River Clean-Up charity was a way for the chairman of the foundation to launder cash to filter through his Ponzi scheme.

But we'd only be here long enough for her picture to be taken, for the world to know who she was and who she was married to, to know that I wasn't on the market anymore. *That was it.*

This was my way of killing a couple of birds with the same stone because, on top of that, Coullson would be here, and I was getting sick and fucking tired of being in the dark where the Sparrows were concerned.

An organization that far-reaching would have its sticky fingers everywhere—the Mayor's pants included.

Though tonight's event served a purpose, it was the last place I wanted to be. After the trip to the hospital, I'd wasted too many hours at *Elemental*, setting up cameras with Conor in the private wing of the club. I figured we'd caught Coullson that way, another Sparrow might tumble into our web if we were lucky.

It had been dirty work, tedious too, and the gala looked set to be like every other fucking party in New York City, understaffed, with shitty canapés that filled the beak-like mouths of the perennially underfed socialites, with music that was too loud and lighting that was too low.

Once we made it off the red carpet, the flash of the thousands of cameras blinding us both, I steered us into the crowd.

"You eaten today?"

Her lips curved. "Yes."

The smile had me shaking my head. I wasn't sure why, but she seemed to like me at my most growly—and yeah, that was a fucking word. She smiled when I thought she'd glower, and whenever I figured she'd tell me to back off, she just melted into my arms.

Literally.

And then I melted all over her.

Which was why my cum smeared her cunt and her juices still coated my mouth.

Call me a filthy fecker, I'd take it. But I'd take it alongside the acceptance that society's trappings, all this bullshit here, meant fuck all to me.

I knew what mattered most, and this crap here was just glitter and no substance.

Rather than lead her toward the area where the wait staff were slipping among the crowds, trying to feed people their meager offerings, I moved her toward the dance floor.

Hauling her into me, I slipped my arms around her waist as she tucked herself close against my front, her hands coming up to clasp my neck.

What was it about this woman that made me want to bury my face in her throat like I was at prom again? Dancing to Seal's *Kiss from a Rose* with my latest squeeze.

Except, Camille wasn't a squeeze.

She was so much fucking more—too much more. More than I'd anticipated, than I should have wanted.

My dick argued, but then, the little head never did have much sense in these things, and where Camille was concerned, it was particularly fucking thick.

In more ways than one.

With her snuggled up against me, I murmured in her ear, "You know what Coullson looks like?"

She tensed up. "The Mayor?"

"Yeah."

"He's the reason we're here?"

I hummed under my breath in confirmation. "You see him?"

She tipped her head to the side, not enough to stand out, which confirmed my belief that she could be sneaky when she wanted to be.

"No."

"Keep an eye out and let me know if you do, okay?"

"Will do," she murmured, and I felt the resolve in her, like now she had a purpose, she'd give it her all.

I shook my head at the thought, then, as we danced, decided to talk to her, rather than just have her keep an eye out like I was for the schmuck who was our principal reason for being here.

It was good to have her in my arms, and I could have just held her and danced, but I liked her—it came as a surprise to me too. She had an amusing sense of humor, wasn't weighed down with apathy, laughed freely at me even when I was being serious, and had a take on the world that was quite refreshing. Of course, that was her youth coming into play.

It was only at times like these when I felt every single fucking one of the sixteen years between us.

"You should get a hobby or something," I told her softly. "Keep your mind occupied. You're too smart to just be okay with shopping for clothes and waiting for me to get home." I winced. "You can't be happy doing that volunteering shit, either."

I wasn't sure why I'd anticipated an argument, but I didn't get one. Instead, I had my mind blown as she revealed, "I *am* happy doing that. I've been homeless, Brennan. I know what that feels like. I have time on my hands so why wouldn't I help out other people in that situation?"

"You've been homeless?" The knowledge was like a bullet to my brain.

"Less than a week all in all, but that was enough." She shivered as she tucked herself tighter into my hold. "It was horrible."

My arms tightened around her as if that would be enough to keep her safe but it wasn't. It never would be. She'd had to go through that. All on her fucking own.

Vasov deserved worse than a pyramid to the skull.

"When?"

"My first few nights in New Jersey, I didn't really know what to do. I ran away after a bad argument with Father." She sighed. "I was so dumb. I didn't plan anything, didn't save up my allowance, just took a chance to escape.

"It worked, but I was screwed when I got away. I managed to find work in a restaurant shortly after though, so I had some money in my pocket for accommodation. I had to share a studio with four others at the time, but it was better than the streets.

"Then, it was just me and another girl. Do you remember I told you about the one who cut out with the rent? The landlord tossed me out, and I wasn't... well, I thought I could fix things up for myself. I couldn't. That was when I went to the Sinners."

Rage whirled inside me but I only let it out into our hug, holding her close, protecting her from her memories.

"Anyway, that's in the past."

"Where did you even find out about the damn soup kitchen? Bagpipes said it's nowhere near your old place or ours."

She shrugged. "That day at the clerk's office. They had a community bulletin board, and there was a flyer asking for volunteers."

God, I remembered now. Forrest bitching at me in one ear while Camille folded up a pink flyer, tucking it into her pocket after.

"Anyway, with the horses and then the soup kitchen, that'll keep me busy, but that's why I wanted to get my room ready—"

"Ready for what?"

"My projects."

I pulled back to look at her. "What kind of projects?"

She shot me a sheepish look. "I like crafting."

"Crafting," I repeated with a frown. But when she ducked her head, hiding from me, I tutted, and lifted a hand to cup her chin and encourage her to look into my eyes once more. "I ain't being an asshole, babe. I don't know what crafting consists of. Unless, are you gonna start brewing beer down there?"

She snorted. "Craft beer." Her chuckles made me grin at her, pleased I'd made her laugh. "No. I'm not going to be making you your own IPA."

"Shame," I said wryly. "I'd like that."

Her lips twisted. "Maybe I'll add it to my list. I go through phases." She sighed. "It will be nice to be able to do what I want without hiding it. It's not like Mary wants me to watch her clean the bathroom, so my time is my own when you don't need me."

That she knew the lay of the land without me having to say a word was one of the advantages of her having being raised in the life.

Even if I wished, for her sake, that she'd had a better start than what she had. More so now that I knew she'd had to sleep on the goddamn streets. A week or not, that was totally out of order.

"Agreed," I told her gruffly, "so, what's this crafting?"

"Can be anything and everything. I like crocheting," she admitted on a whisper, like she was confessing to a sin. "But I also love gem art, and making greeting cards, and other kinds of paper crafting." She shrugged. "Before, I couldn't afford it, and I really missed it. It's always kept me busy, but more than that, it makes me happy."

"Well, that's all that matters." I wasn't sure if I'd ever been happy, but somehow, that was bearable when I thought about her feeling that.

The notion hit me then that I wanted the best for her.

I might not be that, but it was within my power to give her everything she needed. Everything she deserved.

God, she'd been homeless. This queen, *my* queen... Fuck.

My arms tightened around her, using the dance as an excuse to cling to her, as if that alone would keep her safe.

"So," I teased, "this gem art sounds expensive."

Another chuckle escaped her. "You don't use real gems."

"That's a relief," I teased, hiding my shaky grin in her hair as she slapped my shoulder. But mere seconds after she slapped me, her hand crumpled the back of my jacket. "Coullson?" I guessed.

"Over by the ice sculpture."

I moved us around, making it look like a part of the dance and peered around the floor.

At the outer perimeter of the room, there were tables that were awaiting the auction that would be happening before the night was out. People moseyed around that area, eying up the lots on display, while, in front of the stage where the auctioneer would stand, that was where people were dancing.

For the moment, the lights were dim, but I saw the ice sculpture for the first time once I squinted away from the smoky dancefloor, and saw that Coullson was standing there with a woman who looked like she had a stick up her ass.

No wonder he needed Frederica to get his rocks off.

Speaking of... I spun Camille around in a few circles, trying to see if my plant was in place.

When I found her, on the arm of some no-hope Z-lister, I carried on looking, hoping she'd see me and would catch my eye.

It took a while, but she did, and we nodded at one another before I started guiding Camille over to where Coullson and his wife were.

In her ear, I murmured, "This can't be helped, Camille."

"I'll try not to listen," she said wryly, picking up on what I was telling her.

"I'm not about to treat you like you're a moron. We both know you're not that."

She stiffened a little. "Do we?"

"Oh, yes, we definitely do. I've seen you with that New York Times' crossword."

Though she'd tried to hide the hobby from me, like it was a dirty secret, I'd discovered her appreciation of the cryptic crossword and had taken out a subscription so she could have a copy delivered every morning without having to leave the apartment. It kept her safe and stopped Baggy bitching at me about being a paperboy.

"That doesn't make me a genius," she disregarded.

I shrugged. "I don't know how you answer all those clues."

"I just like puzzles."

I shook my head, our hair brushing against each other's as I murmured, "Well, closing your ears ain't doable, babe, but I wouldn't do this if I didn't have to."

"I get it, Brennan."

I tilted my head down, pressing a kiss to her cheek, before I whispered, "Game on."

She nodded, then when I spun her away from me, she did so with flair, like it was planned, before she curled into my side just inches away from the table where Coullson and his wife were standing.

The second he saw me, his nostrils flared in agitation and he cut his wife a glance, before tugging at his collar.

"Marjory, I need to talk business."

She heaved a sigh, but was evidently a career politician's wife and just shot me a resentful look before disappearing.

"You've got her on a tight leash, I see," I told him with a smirk. "If you ask her to bark, does she?"

"Don't you dare disrespect my wife," Coullson snarled, and a vein started throbbing at his temple.

"Disrespect her? I'm doing nothing of the kind. I mean, you were the one who disrespected her by sucking Frederica's—"

"Shut up!" he hissed, peering into the crowd like everyone was listening to our conversation.

I ignored the self-important prick, and instead, twisted around, found Frederica in the crowd and pointed. "Our mutual friend has missed you, Coullson. She wanted a chance to meet up with you—"

"Oh, my God, he's here," Coullson rasped, the hot pink flush on his cheeks disappearing as he stared at Frederica, turning him a pasty shade that made bread dough look as colorful as a rainbow.

I sneered at him, "Yeah, *she* is, watch your fucking pronouns, you hypocrite."

He tensed. "You have no—"

Because his opinions meant nothing to me, I steam-rolled over his objection, snapping, "I've got it on good authority that she knows most of your schedule. That's the trouble when you've got a mistress. They tend to know all the little ins and outs of your life—" Camille tensed up at my side, but I ignored her. "—you should remember that the next time you decide you don't want to play nice."

The Mayor tugged at his necktie again, that vein at his temple throbbing like the bassline at a dubstep party. "Play nice? What you want from me, ratting 'them' out, will end up with me dying."

"I doubt that. You're still the Mayor, my man. Still in a position of power, well, that is until that little photo makes its way around the papers... I'm not sure what your core demographic voters will think about their Mayor not only frequenting seedy sex clubs but—"

"I think I'm going to be sick," Coullson whispered under his breath as he placed his hands on the cocktail table, the fingers bleeding white as he tucked them around the edges, leaning over and bowing his head like he could puke up his dinner there and then.

"No need to vomit," I murmured softly, silkily. "You know what I want. A name... a contact. Some pertinent information about our mutual friends."

Coullson clenched his jaw. "They'll kill me."

"For a man like yourself, who's all image, all hypocrite, I'd think it's better to die with your reputation intact than to live with your life in shreds, don't you?" I moved closer to him, so close that he could feel my breath on his cheek. "And let's not forget about how miserable I can make your life. You'll wish you were dead if you don't help us."

For a second, I wasn't sure if it was going to work. If we weren't going to have to abduct him and torture the information out of him.

It was turning out to be one of those months. Torture here, torture there, torture every-fucking-where.

But Coullson caved in, muttering, "Ainsley McKenna."

I frowned. "That it?"

"That's all I've got. You asked for a name, there you go. He's my point of contact." His jaw turned white as he ground his teeth together. "Now, I have social obligations to see through."

"Rude prick," I muttered as he stormed off, taking the opposite direction to where Frederica was standing.

"Rude?" Camille arched a brow at me. "You're lucky he didn't punch you."

My top lip quirked up in a smile. "Thought your ears weren't working."

Her nose crinkled at the bridge. "I tried."

"And failed?" I shook my head as I grinned at her, unable to be angry at her when she looked so fucking cute. I surprised myself by reaching up and rubbing the tip of my pointer finger between her brows in an attempt to erase the frown.

Her eyes were as wide as the moon as she looked at me, and because I saw way too much in them, I dipped my chin and shifted focus.

Reaching for my phone, I pulled it out and sent Conor a text:

Me: *Got a name.*

Conor: *Coullson sang?*

Me: *Like the sparrow he is. Ainsley McKenna.*

When he didn't reply immediately, but I saw the two ticks indicating he'd seen the message, I tucked my phone away and asked, "Mrs. O'Donnelly, would you like to dance?"

She blinked at me. "We're not going straight home now your business is done?"

I knew my eyes were twinkling as I stared her up and down. "And waste that dress?"

Her grin made me feel like I was being blasted by the sun after a lifetime of being in the dark, and because that was way too fucking poetical for a Friday night, I decided to stop thinking and to start doing.

When she held out her hand for me, I snatched it up and together, we headed onto the dancefloor and we danced until dawn.

TODAY WAS A GOOD DAY. TOMORROW WILL BE TOO. RINSE AND REPEAT, CAMILLE. YOU GOT THIS.

FORTY
CAMILLE

I WAS nervous when Inessa ushered me deeper into The Plaza, directing me to The Palm Court, a pre-foyer lobby with tables where people were drinking coffee and eating brunch.

It wasn't my first time here—Mama had brought me for my thirteenth birthday for afternoon tea. Because of it, I'd never had any desire to come again. I could still remember her pouring us coffee from antique coffee pots, decorated with the tiniest of flowers, telling me that I was growing up now and that such an adult treat was something I would appreciate.

I hadn't, not really. I'd have preferred to go for ramen, but I hadn't had the heart to tell her. She'd been so excited, so full of life. That was her though. She was always like that. Always so bubbly and vivacious. I hated that I didn't really remember her that way, just that mental image I had of finding her dead.

"Cammie!"

Jerked from my memories when Inessa grabbed my arm, I grimaced in apology when I saw Aoife and Aela smiling up at me. "Sorry, lost to my thoughts."

Distress freezing her in place, her fingers tightening to the point of pain around my arm, Inessa gasped. "Oh my God, how could I forget?"

I shot her an embarrassed look. "It's okay, Innie."

"What is it? What's wrong?" Aoife queried, her concern clear.

"Our Mama brought Cammie here the birthday before she died." She winced. "I'm so sorry, Cammie."

"Don't be," I told her calmly, slipping into one of the spare seats and wishing I hadn't let the past tug away at me. "It's okay."

"Hardly," Aela denied. "We can move to another part of the hotel—"

I shook my head. "Please, no. It's a nice memory. It made me think good things to remember her this way."

Innie bit her lip and I knew what she was thinking too.

Aoife did as well, apparently. "I remember the news... You found her, didn't you?"

I cleared my throat. "Yes." Then, because I desperately needed to change the subject, brightly, I declared, "Thank you so much for letting me tag along with Inessa. I really appreciate it."

Aoife laughed. "You're not tagging along. This is the O'Donnelly sisterhood! We have to have some place where we can bitch about our men." Her nose crinkled when Jake started wailing. It was only then I saw he was sitting in a car seat, rocking away like he was trying to burst out of jail. "Speaking of... this one is driving me crazy at the minute."

Shyly, I asked, "Would you mind if I held him?"

"Be my guest. He might not like it though," she said wryly. "He's like his dad. Possessive.

"Don't be offended if he tries to come to me. He's like a monkey when he wants to be."

"I won't." I watched as she unfastened him from the car seat then squatted down to pick him up before hefting him over to my lap. He immediately started wailing for Aoife, but when she went to grab him, I hushed him and sang, "*Kalinka, kalinka, kalinka moya! V sadhu yagoda malinka, malinka moya. Sosenushka ty zelyonaya—*"

He calmed.

Almost instantly.

I laughed a little, carrying on singing until he turned to look at me, big eyes peering at me before he grabbed a lock of my hair and started tugging. I patted his fingers and bobbed him on my knee, as Inessa murmured, "Cammie always was good with kids."

Aela's brows rose. "What's she singing?"

"It's a really famous song in Russia." She grinned as my pace increased. "Every time you finish the chorus, you repeat it and get faster each time."

When Jacob started cackling as I bobbed him in time to the beat, I let the song come to an end.

"Kid, you can't be serious. You want me to learn Russian to keep you quiet now?" Aoife complained but she was chuckling as she watched us.

I grinned at her. "I can send you the lyrics if you want."

She snorted. "I'll never be able to say all those words."

"I can teach you." I shrugged. "We grow up knowing that song. It's a dance and everything."

"Maybe he'd like me to learn that as well. Pre-nap entertainment," she said wryly, watching as Jacob settled against me, his fingers twining in the star pendant I wore, seemingly content to just play with it for now.

"Better than Netflix," Inessa agreed with a laugh. "He's got taste. We might do things oddly to you in the West, but I think we're pretty cool."

Innie and I shared a grin, but I just said, "We have to be when it drops to below freezing in the Fall."

She rolled her eyes. "Har-Har-Har."

I smirked at her. "I really need a coffee after that. I didn't expect to start singing today."

"You never know what's going to happen when you've got kids. Be prepared for every eventuality," Aoife joked.

Aela nodded. "You're not wrong. I remember when Shay was that age. Jesus, he kept me up through the night and slept all day. Little monster." She smiled a little, then patted her stomach. "Speaking of babies, I have news, ladies."

"No way!" Inessa blurted out. "You're pregnant? Already?"

Aela shrugged. "The timing is terrible, but is there ever a right time in our world?"

I shook my head because truer words had never been spoken. "Congratulations, Aela."

She grinned at me, her smile lighting up her eyes. "Thanks."

Aoife reached over. "Congrats, honey. I bet Declan's thrilled."

"He is." She pulled a face. "It's not ideal but I'm actually happy about it. I just need to tell Shay. That's something I'm not looking forward to."

"There's almost a ten-year gap between me and Victoria," I told her softly. "It won't be easy. I remember being pretty jealous."

"Well, Shay's at that stage now where he's too cool for everything and anything. Especially now he's at this new school and Brennan and Conor are taking so much interest in him. I'm not fascinating enough anymore," she grumbled, but she was laughing too. "I'm hoping he won't be that upset."

"If he is, he is. At least he can beat the crap out of Brennan if he has to," I teased.

Aoife waggled her brows. "I still can't get over the fact our Brennan's *married*. Sheesh. We never saw that coming, did we?" She pointed a finger at Inessa. "And you, not saying a damn thing about it? Girl, what's that about?"

"I didn't know!" Inessa defended herself, raising her hand to wave over the waiter.

"We kept things on the downlow," I demurred as the server came and handed us menus. After we put our orders in, I carried on, "It was all very spontaneous, you know?"

"More romantic than I'd have thought Brennan was capable of," Aela teased.

"They're all romantic in their own way," Aoife argued. "You just have to learn how to see it."

"You won't hear me complaining," Aela retorted. "Just saying it how it is."

"Look at those rings, though." Aoife whistled under her breath as she stared at the hand I'd wrapped around Jacob's belly.

I flushed as Innie teased, "Brennan's version of a big stamp of ownership."

"Well, that's one way of doing it," Aela said wryly, before she leaned forward. "Forgive me, Camille, but I knew one of Brennan's girlfriends when I was still in school. She said..." She leaned over the table some more. "...he was really big."

"Aela!" Aoife chided, but her interested gaze turned my way.

Inessa snorted when I shot her a pleading look. "Well, Cammie, is he?" she teased. "Is he rocking a Hulk dick?"

"It's not bright green," I grumbled. "What do you want me to do? Pull out a ruler and measure him?"

Aela snickered. "You could for me. I've always been curious."

"Why?" Aoife questioned, her tone bewildered.

She shrugged. "For art."

I blinked at her. "What?"

"Aela's an artist," Inessa explained. "She's really talented."

"You mean, you wanted to paint my husband's penis?"

Aela grinned. "Well, I wouldn't say no."

"Oh my God," Inessa guffawed. "Cammie, if you could see your face."

"I know you want to paint the guys for Lena, Aela, but I don't think *that's* the kind of portrait she'd like," Aoife teased, making the others laugh.

"I thought you guys would be kind of mean to me because I was the new girl and everything. I never thought we'd be discussing my husband's dick," I retorted waspishly, unashamed to be hiding my face by looking down at Jacob.

"Why would we be mean to you?" Aela chuckled. "We've got to stick together, Cammie."

Aoife grinned. "Girl power."

My nose crinkled. "If you say so."

"So, is it massive?" Aela peppered.

When the others started laughing, I just joined in.

But I didn't tell them… if it was down to me, nobody would ever know the size of my husband's anaconda other than me.

And if that sounded possessive, well, so be it.

FORTY-ONE
CONOR

AINSLEY MCKENNA.

A name I thought I'd never hear again.

A name I prayed I'd never hear again.

White noise.

I was used to living with it, used to its constant whine inside my skull but two words had amped up the volume.

Two words had destroyed a lifetime's worth of calm.

Lodestar: **aCooooig? You there?**

Most people thought hacking involved sitting at a computer and typing really fast, mostly because that's how Hollywood portrayed it. Jonesing off on big screens, all stacked up on top of each other, impossibly hot nerds whooping and cheering as they got the girl while never taking into account how fucking long it took to break into databases and websites and the like.

Any self-respecting hacktivist knew that wasn't the way of it, but nobody I'd ever communicated with—and I communicated with *a lot*—had ever understood like Lodestar.

That was why I'd sent her candy corn.

She'd mentioned once that she liked it, so, why wouldn't I send a couple of pounds of the stuff to her?

I figured the feeling was mutual when, a few days later, a package of

Lemonheads showed up at my place. If I'd have been wearing a hat, I'd have tipped it to her. A mutual kudos—she knew where I lived, and I knew where she lived—but also, she'd remembered my candy preferences too.

Despite my appreciation for her skills, for her snark, I had no real desire to talk to her—

Lodestar: **I know you're online.**

aCooooig: **If you know I'm online, then take a hint.**

Lodestar: **When a woman sends you her body weight in lemon candy, she deserves a morning after call.**

aCooooig: **It's not a good time.**

Lodestar: **Why not?**

aCooooig: **Because.**

Lodestar: **You're very communicative today. *Insert sarcasm here***

aCooooig: **That's why I didn't answer. I don't want to piss you off.**

Lodestar: **...**

I frowned, wondering what the hell that was supposed to mean.

Lodestar: **You care if I'm pissed off?**

aCooooig: **Isn't that what friends do? Care about each other?**

Lodestar: **Hmm. I suppose so. All right then, if that's what we are... then what's wrong?**

aCooooig: **I told you already. I don't want to talk about it.**

Lodestar: **Means you should.**

aCooooig: **Since when?**

Lodestar: **Since forever.**

I growled under my breath, and as tempted as I was to kick her out of my computer, which she'd managed to break into, *again*, I didn't.

I just closed my eyes a second, trying to reconcile that the white noise that had been plaguing me was a little quieter thanks to her interference.

Lodestar: **Come on. Tell me. I might be able to help. Is it to do with the Sparrows?**

aCooooig: **I guess.**

Lodestar: **Narrow it down.**

aCooooig: **I've got a name for a potential Sparrow agent.**

Lodestar: **Great! Tell me. I'll hunt them down with you.**

aCooooig: **It's not possible.**

Lodestar: **To hunt him down? Dude, we're the fucking BEST around. Seriously, if we wanted, the Pentagon would be our bitch.**

aCooooig: **You know how I know I'm an adult?**

Lodestar: **Irrelevant, but I'll bite.**

aCooooig: **Because the prospect of busting through the Pentagon's firewalls no longer gives me a boner.**

Lodestar: **A proud moment in your life, I'm sure.**

My lips twitched. aCooooig: **Absolutely.**

Lodestar: **Spill the beans. Give me the name.**

aCooooig: **There's no point.** *Thank Christ.*

Lodestar: **Why not? Shit, it's like pulling teeth with you today. When you said it wasn't a good time, you really meant it.**

aCooooig: **Surprised you haven't figured out that I usually mean every word I say.**

Lodestar: **Hmm, fair point. Tell me the name!!**

aCooooig: **Like I said, there's no point. The guy's dead."

Lodestar: **That's annoying. We don't have enough ins.**

aCooooig: **No, we don't.**

Guilt hit me when I thought about a massive 'in' that we had, but it would involve sharing information that we were keeping tied up.

But Lodestar wasn't just *anyone,* was she?

Lodestar: **So, that's what pissed you off?**

aCooooig: **No. Not that the fucker's dead. Just... I used to know him.**

Lodestar: **The Sparrow agent? Well, that doesn't come as a surprise. They're everywhere.**

aCooooig: **Yeah. He wasn't a good person.**

Lodestar: **Let's hope he's rotting in hell.**

aCooooig: **I hope the Devil's biting his cock off then making it grow again then biting it off once more.**

Lodestar: **Ouch. I thought men were sensitive about their dicks. I've never understood that. You talk about the time you kneed someone in the balls, and every guy in the vicinity cups his junk and groans.**

aCooooig: **That's because you hang out with bikers. Mobsters have more decorum.**

Lodestar: **Oh? What do you guys do?**

aCooooig: **Pretend our balls aren't aching too.**

Lodestar: ***snorts***

aCooooig: **True story.**

Lodestar: **That was pretty graphic though.**

aCooooig: **You want graphic? I hope the Devil's teeth are sharp and pointy. And when he gnaws down on the fucker's dick, that it doesn't snap off. He has to really dig those teeth in and drag it off.**

Lodestar: **Yikes. You've given this a lot of thought.**

aCooooig: **I have.**

Lodestar: **Did this person hurt you?**

aCooooig: **He caused a lot of problems in my family.**

Lodestar: **He did? How?**

aCooooig: **It doesn't matter.**

Lodestar: **It does. Tell me. I won't tell anyone.**

aCooooig: **Not even Maverick?**

Lodestar: **Is that jealousy I hear?**

aCooooig: **Maybe. But you can't hear anything, can you? Unless you've hacked into my speaker system.**

Lodestar: **There's no need to be jealous.**

I noticed she didn't say anything about my speakers, so I made a mental note to do a sweep later.

aCooooig: **Isn't there?**

Lodestar: **No. He's like a brother to me now.**

aCooooig: **You want to fuck your brother? Where are you from again? West Virginia?**

Lodestar: **OMG, take that back. West Virginia is an awesome place.**

aCooooig: **I'm just being mean.**

Lodestar: **I can tell. And I'm from Delaware.**

aCooooig: **With leanings to West Virginia apparently.**

Lodestar: **My dad took me to live there for a while.**

aCooooig: **Why?**

Lodestar: **Why not?**

aCooooig: **Fair point. LOL.**

Lodestar: **Fair is what I do. Okay... how about this: I'll tell you a secret if you tell me what this guy did to cause trouble with your family.**

aCooooig: **What kind of secret?**

Lodestar: **My real name.**

aCooooig: **No way.**

Unease filled me.

aCooooig: **You could lie.**

Lodestar: **I'll send you a copy of my driver's license.**

aCooooig: **You take me for a fool? That will be a fake too.**

Lodestar: **Hmm, true. Okay, how do I convince you of my real ID.**

aCooooig: **You were in the Army.**

Lodestar: **You want personnel records?**

aCooooig: **Yes.**

Lodestar: **This had better be worth it.**

aCooooig: **Sadly, it is.**

Lodestar: **Which email?**

When she listed five of my email addresses, I had to shake my head at the power move.

aCooooig: **Yeah, yeah. I get it. You know my emails.**

Lodestar: **:P Just a reminder not to dick me around.**

aCooooig: **The first one.**

Lodestar: **Okay. Sent.**

I quickly switched screens to my internet browser, logged onto that particular email, and found one waiting in my inbox.

Nerves hit me, which was a ridiculous reaction, but I'd been talking with her for a while now. Anonymity, even if it was relative with someone like her, was something that we all shielded.

Even the Lemonheads had come for 'aCooooig.' That was thanks to my penthouse being held in a trust so no one knew who owned it. Otherwise, she'd have had my real name too.

For all that, she was the only one who'd ever breached my code. *Ever.* I had to respect her for that if nothing else.

When I opened the email, my brows rose. She'd blacked out the picture, but her records were there. At least, some of them. She'd censored other parts as well, leaving me with the information she wanted me to know.

Star Sullivan.

What interested me the most?

Who her daddy was.

Brows high as I recognized the name, a dash of excitement overtook the muted white noise in my ears for a second as I replied: aCooooig: **Your father was Gerard Sullivan?**

Lodestar: **He was.**

aCooooig: **Guess that explains why you moved around a lot.**

Lodestar: **Yup.**

aCooooig: **Christ. Well, I'm impressed.**

Lodestar: **Don't be. He wasn't the best man, but he was a brilliant dad.**

It took a hell of a lot to put stars in *my* eyes, but dayum. Gerard Sullivan? Excuse me while I fangirled.

aCooooig: **Lol. Candid as always.**

Lodestar: **Yep. Worst day of my life was when he died, and after what I've been through on my tours of duty, that's really saying something.**

aCooooig: **I'll bet. Mom 'unknown?'**

Lodestar: **I'm a miracle birth."

aCooooig: **LMAO. You're certainly something.**

Lodestar: **Just because you don't know her name doesn't mean she's unknown.**

aCooooig: **I know. I was only teasing.**

Lodestar: **Come on then, tell me the truth.**

She made it sound so easy.

aCooooig: **I've never told anyone this before.**

Lodestar: **If you haven't, then how did it cause your family any trouble?**

aCooooig: **Because my brother caught us.**

Lodestar: **Your brother caught you doing what?**

aCooooig: **I wasn't doing anything.**

Lodestar: **Hmm. You're still being cryptic. So, it was being done to you?**

aCooooig: **Yes.**

Lodestar: **Bad things?**

aCooooig: **The worst.**

Lodestar: **How old were you?**

aCooooig: **Seven.**

Lodestar: **Christ, aCooooig.**

Conor: **Call me Conor, Star.**

Star: **Conor, you're forcing me to read between the lines here, but I can figure it out... I'm so sorry.**

Conor: **It's okay.**

Star: **No, it's not. It's really not. Nothing about that is okay.**

Conor: **It is what it is.**

Star: **Who was he?**

Conor: **A temporary priest at our church.**

Star: **Fuck. FUCK. Oh, shit, I'm so fucking mad right now.**

Conor: **Star, there's no need to be. It was a long time ago.**

Star: **A long time ago? You were seven and that fucker molested you. No wonder you want the Devil to gnaw his cock off. Okay, I'm gonna add to that. He also gets hot pokers and jams them up his asshole.**

Conor: **And he has to use the hot pokers as a stool.**

Star: **So he's impaled on them?**

Conor: **Totally.**

Star: **Did it happen often?**

Conor: **He was there for a month while our regular priest went on a pilgrimage to Lourdes. It was toward the end of that placement.**

Star: **That didn't answer me.**

Conor: **I was naive.**

Star: **God.**

Conor: **It's okay.**

Star: **STOP. SAYING. THAT. Unless you want me to ride into the city, hijack your system again, and come and visit you so I can shake you—seriously, stop saying that.**

Conor: **I don't know what else to say.**

Star: **Say you're fucking angry.**

Conor: **I am.**

Star: **That doesn't seem angry enough.**

Conor: **I AM.**

Star: **That's a little better. I still want to drive over to hug the shit out of you though.**

A part of me wondered if that would be such a bad thing, but I didn't let myself dwell on it because I didn't have time.

Conor: **Can the shit be hugged out of someone, though?**

Star: **If it's done right, sure.**

That probably shouldn't give me a boner.

What else could she 'do' right?

Star: **How did he die? Did you kill him? I wouldn't blame you.**

Conor: **Now, I wish that I had. But no. One of my brothers found us, and he acted on my behalf.**

Star: **I'm glad. Very glad. I hope the bastard suffered.**

Conor: **I hope he did too.**

Star: **Who told you this guy was a Sparrow? Was he messing with you?**

Conor: **I have to think that he was.**

Star: **You know what this means, right?**

Conor: **Yeah. Someone knows that name would bother me.**

Star: **It's likely. Bastard.**

Conor: **Do you feel like this situation with the Sparrows is a rabbit hole? Only, at the other end, it isn't Wonderland but Rikers?**

Star: **For a long while, bringing these bastards down is the only thing that's kept me going. If I end up at Rikers, I'll be happy so long as those fuckers end up there with me too.**

Conor: **You think it's possible?**

Star: **I'm going to give it my best.**

Conor: **The Mayor's a Sparrow.**

Star: **Coullson? Christ! How did you get that info?**

Conor: **A Fed agent told us under duress.**

Star: **Holy shit! This is big.**

Star: **Wait. Crap, he's the one who told you about the priest, isn't he?**

Conor: **He is.**

Star: **Fuck.**

Some lead he was. Conor: **Yeah, fuck.**

FORTY-TWO
BRENNAN

"YOU'RE KIDDING ME."

Forrest shook his head. "I don't know where he is, Bren."

"Fuck." I hissed the curse under my breath, then in a wave of rage, wiped my hands over my desk, sending everything pouring onto the floor. Laptop, desktop, pens, paper, everything went flying.

Amid the chaos, I let my fingers curve over the sides, with my knuckles aching, I rasped, "I'm going to have to speak with Da."

"I'm sorry, Bren. We had Duncan and Franklin on him. You know they're good at that shit."

I gritted my teeth before I raised a hand and said, "Just leave, Forrest. It's no one's fault. Just..." I blew out a breath. "Just get outta here."

Tink muttered, "Bren? You still want me to take O'Reilly's corpse to the pig farm?"

I didn't look up, just kept my head bowed as I rumbled, "Yeah. Get rid of that before it gets us in the shit."

"You telling your da about him?"

"No."

"Okay. I'll make sure no one sees."

"Good."

I heard the door open and close and knew only Bagpipes would be remaining. "Still no word from Conor?" I rasped.

"No."

"Fuck, I'd ask if this morning could get worse, but let's face it, I have to talk to my fucker of a father so yeah, I know for a fact it will." I snarled under my breath before I straightened up. "If Conor's gone AWOL on us, then we need info on this Ainsley McKenna."

"Census records?"

I pulled a face. "That's a needle in a haystack, ain't it?"

"Ainsley's not a common name. McKenna is, sure, but not Ainsley."

"True. Give it a try. No worries if you don't come up with anything."

"You're being surprisingly forgiving today," he tried to tease, but I wasn't in the mood for it.

"Don't, Baggy. Just don't."

"Sorry, Bren," he said gruffly. "I'll get on it."

"Thanks, man."

"You sure it's wise not to tell him about Callum?"

I shook my head. "I can't handle the fallout. It won't be worth it either. He'll just go apeshit and it'll affect his judgment more than it already is."

"He's a high-ranking son, Bren. His going missing will make waves."

"And I'll deal with them as it comes. We're already drowning," I rumbled. "What's one more tsunami?"

He grunted, but didn't argue because he knew I was right.

"Shall we start spreading rumors?"

I peered over at him. "What kind of rumors?"

He shrugged. "Just a word here, a whisper there. Casting aspersions on the people he comes into contact with?"

The idea had merit. "That might be wise. Then, it'll seem like one of his non-Five Pointer contacts killed him. Or, maybe, that he ran to avoid something."

Bagpipes nodded, then tapped his nose. "Leave it with me."

Gratitude filled me, followed quickly by shame. I'd doubted him, Forrest, and Tink, but these were the only bastards I could trust.

"Thanks, man."

He shrugged. "No big deal."

Temper still kindling, even though he'd doused water on it with his idea, I reached for my landline the second he shut the door behind him, connected a call to Da, and placed it on speaker.

When it rang a few times, I almost hoped the bastard wouldn't answer, but I should have realized that was wishful thinking.

"Bren?"

"Yeah." An awkward pause hit because I knew he wasn't feeling bad about what he put Camille through, and I was very *much* feeling bad about it.

"You got news for me?" he rumbled when the silence extended with neither of us saying a word.

"I got a whole lot of jack shit. This fucking rat's nest is driving me insane. Whichever way I go, there's something going down. It's like living in a conspiracy theory."

"That's exactly what it is," Da agreed. "Want to start at the beginning? You know I cut you a lot of sway, so I stay out of the loop until you key me in but you ain't done that for a while."

Thanking God for small mercies that he had no idea how in the dark he was, I muttered, "That kid, Quin, you got out, you remember the detective who framed him?"

"Lacey? Some chick's name, right?"

"Yeah, Craig Lacey. We've had a tail on him for a while, trying to figure out his role in the group. He's only a small fry in the 42nd, still considered a rookie from what Forrest hears, but the Sparrows use him as a courier to cross over into Jersey.

"Anyway, before we brought him in, we wanted to wait until he pulled another haul across the state line, maybe use that to blackmail him if whatever he's carrying is illegal, but we think we've figured it out.

"Those thieves behind the robberies squealed. Said that some Five Pointer told the brains of the operation that Hummel's wasn't protected by the Points anymore."

"What?" Da snapped.

"According to them, Hummel's is involved in something shady, Da. Are you in on it?"

"If I was, then you'd know about it, boy. What's he cutting us out of?"

"I don't know. I don't even know the fucking Pointer who told them that shit," I lied.

"You didn't get it out of them? Leave them to me."

"Only the brains knew and he died with his trap firmly closed."

"Fuck," my father howled. "How could you be so clumsy?!"

"Getting that shit out of him about the shady dealings was hard enough," I snapped, unapologetically lying once more about Callum O'Reilly, mixing up what both he and the thieves had told us, "but he dropped another name."

"Craig Lacey."

"Yeah."

My da's heavy breathing sounded down the line.

"We're starting to think that his haul is related to the robberies. Those gems had to be fenced somewhere, and even though the robbers gave us a number, it was a dead end." Here came the kicker. "He dropped his tail this morning." I closed my eyes, waiting on the explosion, and when it came, I just gritted my teeth at the verbal bombs he hurled my way. When his rant was over, I snapped, "If you're done, I have some good news."

"Oh, you do, do you? What the fuck would that be, Bren? Have you figured out who's behind this fuckfest but decided to let them go free because they said sorry?"

My top lip curled into a sneer. "Fuck off, old man. I'm as knee deep in the trenches as you are. I'm pulling my weight and doing what I can to unravel this mess. I can't do any more than I already am."

A gust of air was my answer, before he rattled out, "What's the good news?"

"We got a name from Coullson."

"You sent it to Conor?"

"Yeah, but he's not picking up his phone."

"Probably on a bender. You know what he's like when he's on that damn computer," Da dismissed, and his leniency with Con, though I was glad for his sake, pissed me off.

Fucking favoritism.

"Yeah, probably."

"What's the name?"

"Ainsley McKenna."

Silence fell at that, then he muttered, "Why does that sound familiar?"

I cocked a brow he couldn't see and asked, "Really? If you figure out where you know it, clue me in. As it stands, I've got Bagpipes going to the Census, and I'm going to ask the Sinners to use their contacts to find this guy."

"No, don't share the name with them."

"Why not? We need to find this bastard. At the moment, he and Coullson are all we've got. Caro Dunbar ain't reliable. I don't know how long she's got left but she came to The Hole complaining about picking up a tail."

"She has. One of us."

"You could have told me," I snapped.

"Like you tell me everything?"

My nostrils flared with anger, but I just bit off, "Well, she's safe then."

"As safe as a double-timing rat can be." He grunted. "Okay, keep me in the loop about this guy Coullson dropped. This McKenna."

"I will."

I didn't say bye, neither did he as I slammed the phone down on him and he probably did the same to me.

For a second, I stared at the mess I'd made in my office, then I twisted around, plunked my ass on the side and stared out the window at the shit heap outside this building.

The sensation of drowning was hard to overcome.

I hadn't shared everything with him, because he was enough of a lunatic without me adding to that by telling him the Sparrows were behind the drive-by at Finn's wedding, and that Ma had picked up a tail along the way as well.

We were getting nowhere fast with the Sparrows, and all I knew was that their reach, their *touch* had been directly affecting my family for years without us even knowing it.

Finding their nest had never been more important, but it had never felt more impossible either.

FILTHY SEX   445

THE SKY IS REALLY BLUE TODAY. IMAGINE NOT BEING ABLE TO SEE THAT AGAIN. TRY NOT TO MAKE TODAY THE LAST CHANCE YOU GET TO ENJOY IT.

FORTY-THREE
CAMILLE

AS I WRAPPED a scarf around my hair, I watched as Bagpipes rounded the block and pulled onto the street that housed the Russian Orthodox Church Inessa used.

It was new to me.

Instead of the place where Mama had always gone, one that was deep in Russian territory, we were on the border of Irish and Russian territory instead.

It didn't take a genius to wonder why that was.

If Eoghan was the control freak Brennan painted him as, her being this close to Russian territory was a massive concession in and of itself.

"Text me when the service is over. I'll be in the vicinity."

It was one of the few times I'd let Bagpipes drive, but then, that was because we had a convoy of guards with us.

"Okay. Will do."

"Good. Don't go out into the open until I text you to tell you I'm waiting."

"I don't see what the problem is," Inessa grumbled, her blonde hair tucked into a headscarf as well. "I've been coming here for ages and it's in our territory. I switched when Eoghan asked me to."

Bagpipes and I shared a glance in the mirror. "Did she really just ask such a dumb question?"

I winced. "I think she might have forgotten about the Pakhan's death."

Victoria shoved Inessa in the side. "How could you forget about Papa?"

Inessa pulled a face. "Well, he's just not that memorable. Anyway, who's going to do anything in a church?"

"You weren't around for Finn and Aoife's wedding or its aftermath," Bagpipes said wryly, "but I'm sure you've heard a lot about it. The sanctity of church doesn't exactly mean much nowadays. Anyway, you'll have guards going in with you, but Forrest and I will be watching the perimeter. We're more concerned about external forces."

I nodded, just inwardly sighed because I didn't want to come here, period. It seemed unnecessary, but who was I to question Inessa's need to reconnect with her faith? That she wanted to include me was a gift I didn't intend on besmirching. Even if I thought she was nuts.

Hell, we all did crazy things from time to time, and going to church wasn't usually classified as a way of letting one's hair down.

I thought I'd have preferred for her to request we visit a sex shop together, or to go to a strip club, but nope, my sister had to be boring.

As he pulled up outside the church that was foreign to me, I climbed out and smiled down at Victoria when she tucked her arm into mine.

"I'm surprised you're here," she said on a whisper, peering out of a Hermès scarf that was not in her usual shade of dull, but a hot pink that made her look more her age than the Jackie O get-up she was wearing.

"Why? Because I'm a heathen?" I whispered back.

She giggled. "No, because you think this is all mumbo-jumbo like me."

I pulled a face. "Don't let Innie hear you say that."

Her sniff had me laughing. "I can have my own opinions."

"You can, but you shouldn't diss her faith. We all have our crutches. This is hers."

Victoria hummed as she stared up at the looming building. The red brick facade made the green copper domes stand out even more. Whenever I went to an Orthodox church in the States, I always felt like I could be in Moscow.

Not that I missed the city. I'd never really liked it there, even if I'd always appreciated Father's house which was tucked away in the Rublyovka suburb.

"I guess we do. Mine's studying."

"Is that why I haven't seen you all week?" I placed my hand on top of hers and squeezed. "You've been studying?"

I'd been dying to visit her, but Inessa hadn't invited me over to her place, and I didn't want to impose. When Victoria had ignored the texts I'd sent, I'd just let her get on with it. I couldn't force a relationship on her. Rebuilding what I had with Inessa was gift enough, and letting Vicky have her space was something I prayed she'd appreciate in time.

If she was going to be candid with me now, though, I had to hope that I hadn't been wrong. You caught more flies with honey than vinegar, after all.

"Yes, plus I—"

When she fell silent, I prompted gently, "Are you settling in at Inessa and Eoghan's?"

She bit her lip. "I feel bad, Cammie."

"Why? Don't you like it there?"

She peered up at me, her expression miserable. Just as my heart clutched, she whispered, "It's so nice there."

That had me blinking. Relief whacked me in the face. "That's great, isn't it?"

"Well, it is, but that's why I wanted to come here today."

"Because you like where you live now?"

She shook her head. "Because... I mean, I didn't want it to happen, Cammie. I really didn't. I promise."

"I believe you," I said softly.

"What do you believe?" Inessa asked as she finally climbed out of the car too. We all rushed up the stairs toward the front entrance with its high stone arches once Bagpipes merged back into traffic as Victoria admitted:

"I think I'm glad Papa's dead."

Inessa and I shared a look.

"That's terrible, isn't it? What kind of monster is glad their father died?" she mumbled sadly.

"You're not a monster," I told her, squeezing her hand again. "He was the monster."

Once we were under the cover of the front entrance, we headed into the vestibule. There, amid the crowd of worshipers just waiting to flock into the church itself, I stopped her, turned her to me and wrapped her in my arms. Holding her tightly, gladness swelled inside me. Not just because she let me, not just because she hugged me back, but because I'd done this. I'd given her this freedom. I'd ridden her of the pest who'd forever plague her, who would have destroyed her life when she had so much to live for.

At some point, I knew Maxim would come calling, wanting his debt repaid, but I vowed to myself, to God in *his* temple, that I'd make sure Maxim got to know Victoria. That he'd make her fall for him, would court her and cherish her. If he didn't, I'd make sure *he* was the one who paid for it.

Inessa released a soft cry before she huddled around us, hurling herself into the hug, and for a couple of seconds, I thought I knew what heaven actually felt like.

I was accepted.

I was back in the circle.

I was with my sisters—my family, the only family who were tied to Mama, and it felt good. Better than good. It felt like I was finally warm again.

Tears pricked my eyes, and I wasn't ashamed of them. Wasn't ashamed of any of the things I'd done in the past two weeks.

I had blood on my hands, but for the first time in forever, I felt like I could breathe. I felt whole. I felt like I had a future, because that bogeyman of my past was no more.

Pressing a kiss to Vicky's head, I reached behind me to squeeze Inessa's hand, and as I did, I heard a mocking voice that sent loathing hurtling through me.

"What a touching display."

Innie and Vicky tensed up, but I didn't.

It served me right to think I could have some peace when Abramovicz was still roaming this world.

If I had a gun in my hand, I'd have pointed it at him and pulled the trigger.

Church be damned.

Bagpipes had a point—it really wasn't the sanctuary it used to be.

Shoulders straightening, I twisted around to face him. The sight of his wobbling jowls, those beady eyes, and the mutton-chop sideburns were enough to inspire ridicule, but this man was dangerous. Laughing at him would come at one's own peril.

What was even more dangerous?

The dozen men who were waiting on us, and the lack of a crowd which told me they'd headed in for the service, leaving the Bratva footsoldiers behind.

We were surrounded by them. Encircled.

Bagpipes had been wrong, after all. The threat wasn't external, but *internal*.

Throat tight, I rasped, "I didn't think you were a believer, Denis."

"Oh, it's funny what death and grieving will do to a man. The Pakhan's loss has affected us all in many ways. For me, I've made it my solemn duty to ensure the people responsible for his death pay for their sins." His lips twisted into a snarl. "Contain them."

Two words.

That was it.

The Bratva were an army, after all. They didn't care that we were the ex-Pakhan's daughters as they rushed us, especially as, from the Sovietnik's words, he believed we'd helped the Irish kill Father and he'd brainwashed these *boyeviks* into believing that too.

With four men to each of us, I knew the odds of escape were impossible, but we had to try. *I* had to try. In some things, I might be passive, but where my sisters' physical security was concerned, I sure as hell wasn't.

The *boyeviks* were some of the largest I'd seen and I didn't recognize a single one of them. Father had been pulling men in from Moscow to make up for the losses in the war against the *Famiglia*, so a lack of recognition came as no surprise, but even if we *had* known them, they wouldn't have helped us.

They had their orders.

I kicked out at the four footsoldiers who surged into my perimeter like a quartet of sharks, a shriek escaping me as one hauled me around the abdomen, trying to lift me in the air like I was a bag of potatoes. I raised my legs high, swinging them up before I let them drop, my feet colliding with his knees which buckled.

As he went down, I did too, but someone else was there, waiting to grab me. I elbowed him in the stomach, screaming bloody murder in the hopes that the guards Bagpipes said were in here for our protection would come running, but no one did.

Victoria shrieked and squealed as the men started hauling her away, toward the temple itself and not the foyer, and her screams for help had me twisting and bucking in the *boyevik's* hold.

My hands snapped out, aiming for anything and everything I could. Punching. Pinching. Slapping. Smacking. The men growled, their faces turning bright pink as they loomed over me, exertion making them more aggressive.

When one slapped me, I felt it to my bones. Felt my teeth shake in my mouth, rattling as if they were M&Ms in the wrapper.

Dazed, they dragged me back, but I heard Abramovicz roaring at the men to hurry up, just as I saw Inessa knee one guard in the balls. He went down as she reached out and grabbed another's dick, squeezing hard enough to turn him into a soprano. Her fire gave me energy, and I renewed my efforts even though my ears were ringing.

With two of her attackers down, I knew she had a chance at escaping, so I didn't kick out at the men who were hauling me away. Arms banded around my stomach again, lifted high off the ground against one of their chests, I kicked at the *boyevik* nearest to me who was on Inessa.

It was luck, maybe I'd been blessed with some of that now I was Irish by marriage, but my heel glanced off one guard's neck. Scraping a long line down his nape which had him twisting around, his hand clapping to cover the scratch.

"RUN!" I screamed, watching as Inessa, like the wildcat she was, managed to dart out of the way of her final guard. As she fled for the entrance, the top steps that led to the sidewalk, two from my group rushed after her.

With a final glance at me, apology and fear etched into her expression, she sped up.

An elbow to the temple stopped me from knowing if she made it. If she escaped. I didn't even have a chance to pray to the God I didn't believe in anymore that she made it out safe.

YOU HAVEN'T FOUND YOUR PURPOSE
YET. WHAT A WASTE OF A LIFE IT
WOULD BE IF ALL YOU'D DONE WITH
IT WAS WASTE IT.

FORTY-FOUR
CAMILLE

I HAD no idea how long I was out. Twenty minutes, an hour. I knew it couldn't have been much longer than that because, wherever I was, behind my eyes, I could still see a faint light, which made me think twilight was waning.

Groaning as I pried them open, I felt the bitter beat of drums in my head, the slice of pain that felt like my optic nerve was being cut in two, and I let them focus on their own time, peering around my vicinity as I tried to judge where I was.

My brain wasn't so fried that I didn't remember what had happened, so I had to assume that Abramovicz had brought me back to the compound.

"Victoria!" I whispered under my breath, fear throttling me as I remembered she'd been dragged away first.

"I'm here, Cammie," came her soft, fearful reply, the words more of a whimper than the ballsy snap I was used to hearing from her when she wasn't drowning in grief and guilt.

I twisted around, damning my head for the ache battering me, and in the meager light, found her, huddling in a corner. Legs pressed tight to her chest, sandwiched into the narrow space, she practically oozed terror.

Scraping my knees as I crawled toward her, I whispered, "Are you okay?" My body protested the move, but it had to get with the program, so better to start now than never.

She blinked at me. "I should be asking you that. You've been out of it for ages."

"Did they get Inessa?"

"I don't think so. They never brought her with you." Her bottom lip quivered. "I only knew you were alive because your boobs wobbled."

Despite the situation, I let out a rusty laugh. "You been checking out my tits, baby sis?"

She giggled, her cheeks turning pink, but she hid her face in her lap, and whispered, "Cammie, I really thought you were dead."

I closed my eyes a second, but shoved back my pain as I moved to her side, and lifted an arm to hold her as best as I could with her position.

"Brennan will come for us," I reassured her. "We won't be here for long."

"You don't know that," she whispered miserably.

"I do."

"They k-k-killed the Irish guards," my baby sister whimpered, turning her face into my throat. "When they hauled me out of there, I saw them."

Grief filled me at the losses the Irish had incurred because of us, because of Inessa's whim, but I whispered, "That won't stop Brennan." Resolve filled me, strengthening my voice, because Brennan wasn't simply a Five Pointer. He was my husband.

He'd said I was *his*.

I had to have faith in that.

I knew he'd also said that he'd keep me safe... that hadn't worked out, but it was impossible to keep someone safe in our world. The only way to ensure that was to never leave the apartment. *Ever*. And even then, if the vantage point was right, there was always the possibility of a sniper shooting.

Unaware that my brain was churning, she just sniffed, and because I couldn't sit here, twiddling my damn thumbs as Bagpipes would say, waiting for whatever Abramovicz was going to toss our way, I asked, "Where is *here*, Victoria?"

I peered around the darkening room and found that we were in a complete and utter blank canvas. No toilet, no sink, no furniture. Just the floor, the gray walls, a window that confirmed night was approaching, a bare lightbulb overhead with no wall switch I could see, and a door.

Talk about hospitable.

"I think we're at the compound in Bushwick." She tipped her head to the side. "If you listen, you can hear the steelworks. This one runs twenty-four hours a day."

I did as she said, and could definitely hear something. I'd never have said it was the steelworks though, but it was the only info we had so I took it as gospel.

"Shit. I don't know that place at all. If we were at home, I'd know of two ways to breach the perimeter."

She shot me a look. "You do?"

I arched a brow at her. "Of course." Then I shook my head when I saw she didn't believe me. "Honey, you weren't old enough to want to sneak out yet. You'd have found them in time."

"I wouldn't have dared anyway," she whispered, and when I looked at her, I saw that.

She was an odd combination of spitfire and prim. Even though Father was dead, she still wore her pearls and a smart blouse and skirt, kitten heels too, but I knew, that when it came to it, she'd have the guts to stand up for herself.

Which made me think of the church.

"Why didn't you fight them, Vicky? I saw you face off with Brennan. Why did you just let them take you?"

She gulped. "I froze up."

"I'm sorry, sweetheart. I didn't mean to accuse you—"

"Why not? I would. I've been sitting here ever since they dumped us in this place, wondering why I didn't fight. Inessa got away. Maybe if I'd managed to slip out, we could have..." Her voice waned off. "I'm such a wimp. As useless as Papa used to say."

"No, you're not. You were naturally scared," I defended her. "You're only a kid, Vicky. I shouldn't have said anything. I just know what you're like. Beneath the Jackie-O clothes, you're as much of a wildcat as Inessa is."

She bowed her head. "I'm not, Cammie. Inessa has guts. I don't."

"Yes, you do," I argued, then heaving a sigh, accepting that she'd been sinking deeper and deeper into a pity party the longer she'd been left with her thoughts, I muttered, "Is there a way out of here?"

Her scowl made a reappearance at long last. But give me her exasperation over her fear any day of the week. "Cammie, we're in a ten-by-ten room. There are walls, a window, and a door. Unless you're a magician, then no, there isn't a way out. Far as I know, you didn't turn into Houdini while you were away."

"Houdini was an escapologist," I muttered absently as I got to my feet. "Not a magician. More of an illusionist to be fair."

She grunted under her breath at my reply, but left me to it.

The window was about two feet above my head so some light filtered in but I couldn't see out. There were bars and, from the slightest of glints, I thought there was broken glass on the outer ledge too.

I didn't bother with the door. I knew there'd be a guard, and if not a guard, then a lot of locks to which I had no key.

Taking a couple steps further back, I tried to see if there was anything in the skyline that would confirm we were in the Bushwick compound, but I didn't notice jack. Nothing except for some trees which sheltered us enough that it would get darker sooner in this place.

My head ached, my face did too from that nasty slap I'd gotten, and my stomach muscles were twinging from the moves I'd pulled back there—me and body weight exercises were not the best of friends—but I was alive, I knew Inessa was safe, had faith that Brennan would come for us, and I had to protect Victoria in the interim.

With my heart whirring like it was a merry-go-round on triple speed, I paced, moving from one corner to the next, only avoiding Vicky who was huddling up again like a little tortoise. I hated that she was in this position, hated, even more, that it was easy to revert to those moments when Mama had been killed.

We'd made it to the safe room.

She hadn't.

The panic, the fear, the heart-pounding tension was all the same, but somehow, I knew I was more scared now than I had been back then because Vicky was in danger and I couldn't protect her.

This felt like a safe room, but we were the opposite of that. Cloistered in here, no one could get to us—apart from the person who had the key.

Abramovicz.

Was there a reason he'd brought us to this compound?

This wasn't the main one. Those were in Brighton Beach. And where was Maxim in all this? Though only a *boyevik* by rank, Maxim had been a trusted guard of my father's. He'd been in the right position to listen in, to gain influence. To muscle in on a rank that should be out of his reach.

In times like these, fortune favored the brave where the Bratva was concerned. Might being right, if he seized power and held it, he could go from holding a low rank to climbing to the top of the tree. Getting higher ranks to bend the knee was another matter entirely, but that was the problem with being king—there were enemies everywhere.

Was that why we were here? Because Maxim had overtaken Brighton Beach and our old home?

The Pakhan's Two Spies were his money man and his security man. Abramovicz was the former and Basil Lukov was the latter. Neither had been very popular with the men... It would make more sense for the two of them to be infighting over who'd be the next Pakhan, but Maxim didn't want to marry Victoria because he was in love with her. He wanted what her name represented. He wanted to marry up.

He had goals.

He wanted the Pakhan's seat.

I knew I was right. All my instincts told me my father's Two Spies had combined forces to fight Maxim, and Maxim was currently winning, otherwise we wouldn't be here. We'd be in Brighton Beach, the Bratva's main seat of dominance in the city.

My hands furled into fists, but the lack of pain didn't resonate with me. I didn't need the pain from my battered palms to clear my mind. I had enough going on inside my body, but that didn't detract from my resolve.

I was of no use to them.

It was Victoria.

They wanted her for the same reason Maxim did—to legitimize their claim in the eyes of the men.

To the New York Bratva, the Vasovs were nobles.

And the one way to take the throne?

To marry the princess.

I didn't know much about Father's business, but I knew that he, Abramovicz and Lukov were it. The leaders. Father hadn't, but I knew his Two Spies had treated the rest of the foot soldiers as if they were *boyeviks,* whether or not the man had a higher position. It was why they weren't popular. I'd seen that through body language alone.

Lukov was already married, though, so he wasn't a threat. If his wife wasn't who she was—Abramovicz's daughter from his second marriage—I knew he'd probably kill her too if it meant getting to Victoria. But while they were allied, his hands were tied, which meant Abramovicz was the one to worry about.

Vicky was only fifteen, but Abramovicz wouldn't care about that. He'd keep her in his mansion, abusing her, tormenting her, holding her captive until she was of legal age to make her his bride.

The thought made me want to howl with outrage.

I would not, *could not,* allow that to happen.

Maybe it was stupid, maybe it was crazy, but I had to act. If I died, then so be it. I'd spent a lifetime trying to convince myself to live, but to protect her, to save her from that fate, I'd gladly sacrifice myself.

And maybe, if the luck of the Irish really was on my side, Brennan would show up in time to save me.

I turned to her, whispering, "Vicky?"

She peered at me, her brow furrowed. "Yeah?"

"No matter what, remember two things." Her frown deepened. "Never forget that I love you—"

"Camille," she rasped, her shoulders straightening in surprise.

"—and *don't,* whatever you do, look."

Back in West Orange, Nyx had given me the nickname of 'the Hoover' because he said I was great at giving BJs... I had to pray that I could earn that rep now. That it would hold me in good stead.

Without waiting for her to reply, knowing this was it for me, I stormed forward, fists raised and I banged on the door, not stopping until I heard someone snarl something in mumbled Russian, before there were heavy footsteps and the distinct clicking of the lock.

I pulled back, knowing the door would open outwards, and I faced down Abramovicz who was sneering at me like he was already the king of the castle.

"Irish slut," he snapped as a greeting. "You're awake."

The door closed behind him to keep us contained, just like I'd hoped, and a light switched on overhead. He was a fat fuck, as unfit as could be, so rushing him in an attempt to escape wasn't impossible. It was his ego and the fact that he thought we were frightened of him that made him step inside at all.

More than that, it was me.

I knew how he looked at me, knew what he was thinking whenever his beady eyes dropped to my cleavage. I could be wearing a nun's habit and he'd slobber all over me.

"I demand to know why you're holding us here," I bit out, straightening my shoulders, relieved when the predictability of this man followed through like night did day. His gaze dropped to my tits. Even though I wore a respectable neckline, my dress had a mid-calf hem and my breasts were covered fully, he still just *had* to look.

"So eager to know your fate," he practically purred. "You think we'd just believe the bullshit Lyanov spewed? Svetlana would have been a fool to have fucked around on Antoni—"

"I saw her with that *boyevik*," Victoria whispered. "I told Papa."

Abramovicz's shoulders straightened as he shot her a look. "What?"

That was news to both of us, but before he could get side-lined, I reached forward and tugged on his hand. When my fingers tangled with his, he stared down at them as I stepped into him. Moving closer so that I could press my fingers to his chest.

"Denis, why are you trying to frighten us?"

He licked his lips, his gaze dropping to my mouth as he rumbled, "You think you can try to ensnare me when you've spent half a decade avoiding becoming my wife?" His mouth curved into a sneer. "You're exactly like your mother. A slut. Your father dealt with her, and it'll be my last honorable act as his Sovietnik to deal with his treacherous whore of a daughter."

Inside, I froze, but outwardly, I carried on in my role. Ignoring Victoria's garbled cry, I moved closer to him, hating myself, but knowing this had to be done. Knowing I had to protect my baby sister.

Somehow, I had my answer.

Father *had* been behind Mama's death.

Even as I wished that I'd been armed with a machete and not a glass souvenir when I'd killed Father, I rubbed my tits against Abramovicz's chest, and whispered, "I was frightened. I didn't want to marry into the Bratva."

"Camille—" Victoria choked out softly, but I ignored her.

"You were born Bratva," he rumbled, ignoring her as well. "You know that means you'll die Bratva."

I peered at him from under my lashes, watching him watch me, his pupils dilating, and his hideous dick hardening against my belly as I let my hands rub over his chest.

"I know," I told him.

"You chose the Irish." His top lip curled into a snarl. "You chose to be a party to their treachery—"

I was losing him.

I dropped my hand to his dick and rubbed him through his pants. He jerked back in surprise, but he didn't push me away like I'd been sensing he was going to do. If anything, I'd thought he was going to backhand me, but I could see the calculation in his eyes. Knew that he'd let me whore myself out before he pulled out the gun he probably had tucked into the back of his pants and blew out my brains.

I was okay with that, so long as it happened on my schedule.

Slowly, I sank to my knees, my eyes on him as his throat bobbed when I moved to grab his zipper.

Slowly, I lowered it, reaching in to grab his cock, to pull it free from his fly.

Slowly, I pressed a kiss to it.

He stank.

Piss and a weird dirt-smell.

I tried not to gag, not just at the stench of him but at the prospect of putting him inside me. My mouth was dry, so dry, but I forced myself to swallow, to try to bring up some saliva, and though there wasn't much, it was better than before.

And then, I slipped my lips around him.

He was small, the only saving grace.

A shocked groan escaped him as I accepted every inch of him into my mouth. His hands went to my hair and he snagged his fingers in it, holding me so tightly that it was painful, but I ignored it, let him relax, let him soften his guard, let him near climax…

And that was when I bit him.

Like a starving dog tearing into a sirloin steak, I bit down hard. My teeth were my weapon, my means of saving Victoria from being raped by this man. I couldn't save her from fingers or dildos, but I could save her from this cock.

If he killed me next, he'd be dickless, and that was all I needed.

A high-pitched shriek escaped him, a wail so loud that it made an air-raid siren look quiet. I could hear the guards at the door scrambling but even as his hands tightened around my hair, pulling at it so hard that I knew he was tearing it out from the roots, I didn't stop.

And I chewed.

They could sew it back on otherwise.

Blood gushed into my mouth, finally making it moist, as I pulled on his cock like it was taffy.

He finally dragged me off, but it was too late.

For both of us.

FORTY-FIVE
BRENNAN

BY THE TIME we were storming the Bratva compound, my shitty day had turned full circle as the bad news just kept on coming.

Six guards had been mowed down by the Bratva.

And while they were family, and I'd mourn them, the devastation that wrought was nothing to the news that my wife had been abducted.

I'd broken promises today.

Camille *wasn't* safe.

Camille, as far as I fucking knew, might even be dead.

I didn't like to think that I was an emotional man. I'd learned a long time ago that emotions made you weak. Sure, I had them every now and then. It was impossible to cut off feelings, impossible to freeze them. The only ones I let through on a regular basis were the love and loyalty I felt for my family, for my Ma, my crew. But emotions were a hindrance. They made you act out. Made you do stupid shit.

Case in point, O'Reilly.

I shouldn't have killed him.

Should have turned him over to Da. Let him deal with that mess.

Instead, the ice man had melted, and he kept on fucking doing it. Had done ever since this Sparrow shit had come out.

And the worst thing of all?

I had feelings for Camille.

My nice, bloodless, loveless marriage of convenience, where I fucked her to get kids—something I'd blown out of the water that first day of being married—and we raised nice, future mobsters together was no more.

She wasn't *nice*.

She wasn't *bloodless*.

And she deserved all the love in the fucking world.

Those were the thoughts that rammed through me as I raised a gun and point blank shot one of the *boyeviks* surging toward me in the forehead. Blood spurted, coating me in it, but I ignored it, instead running through the gates that Maxim had blasted with a bomb whose provenance I didn't want to know, and trying to kill as many of the Russian cunts as I could.

She and Victoria had been gone ninety minutes.

One and a half hours.

Who knew that was all it took to make a man realize the impossible?

Who knew that was all it took to know that my wife of a week was the only woman I ever wanted in my bed again?

Who knew that that wife had somehow burrowed her way into my frozen heart?

A week.

Seven fucking days.

Impossible.

But true, especially in the face of losing her.

I'd been quite happy to let the Bratva destroy themselves as they fought over their next leader, been quite content to stay out of it. Now my promise to Mariska was being fulfilled, the Bratva meant fuck all to me, and knowing that two sides would be trying to snatch the Pakhan's throne, I'd thought in a month or so, there'd be a territory grab. The Irish could swoop in, adjust their territories, and everyone would be happy.

Only, that wasn't what was happening.

Fuck territory.

Fuck a land grab.

A lot could change in ninety minutes. A lot could happen, too. Most of it shit. Especially as Camille was married now, which meant she had no use to Abramovicz. It was Victoria he was after, just like Maxim.

As furious as I was that he had eyes on her, it was only through those eyes that we knew where Camille and Victoria had been taken at all. She was why he was here, and that was why we'd end this. *Today.* Together.

Declan was at my back, and Eoghan was somewhere in the wings, Forrest, Bagpipes, Tink were all here, Duncan, Franklin too. We'd brought over sixty men with us today, and Maxim had hauled in fifty. By his calculations, the cunts in this compound would be outmanned nearly two to one.

Those were my kinds of odds.

All around me, chaos ensued. We weren't soldiers, we were fucking made men, but for our women, *for family*, for brothers that had been killed by these Russian bastards, sacrifices would be made.

I let the madness unfold as I took a glance around the compound.

It was an open drive that led to a warehouse, around it, there were about two dozen smaller outposts. Some looked like they were garages, others looked like storage places.

It was a front, a steel yard, but we were at the back, which was where Vasov's Two Spies, according to the quick sum-up Maxim had given us on the ride over here, had decided to set up their base.

When a Bratva *boyevik* rounded a corner, guns blazing, I shot him in the shoulder. My aim true, I watched as the gun buckled in his hand as he dropped it and I ran over to him, grabbing him by his bad arm and dragging him upright.

"Where the fuck are Camille and Victoria Vasov?"

He spat something at me in Russian, so I raised my gun and shoved the muzzle into the bullet wound.

"You want to keep your arm, you tell me where the fuckers are."

His eyes rounded, which let me know he spoke English, before he rumbled, "One of the buildings in the East quadrant."

"Which way's that?" I snapped, digging the gun deeper into his wound. As he screamed out his agony, he pointed to a building nearby with his good arm. I could see two guards, their guns drawn as they got ready to defend themselves, all while standing close to their post.

I retracted my gun, my attention already on the guards as I blew that fucker's brains out.

With a stealth I wasn't really known for anymore, I moved toward the small building that was being guarded. The men were focused on the bulk of the fray which was taking place in the middle of the compound, but as I moved toward them, their attention shifted.

The second they raised their guns, I raised mine, but I didn't have a chance to get a bullet out. Two pops and they were gone. I twisted around on my heel, knowing Eoghan was watching from his nest, and raised a hand to him in thanks.

We didn't have long—the cops would be on their way shortly, especially as the steel factory was an active place of work—so I hurried over to the building, and yanked at the door. I was stunned to find that it opened.

My jaw clenched down so hard that I wouldn't have been surprised if I fractured my teeth as I took in the scene.

Da had told me once how he'd found Ma. When he was drunk and should have kept his mouth shut, he'd shared things I should never have known, and that was all I'd been able to see in my nightmares for a long while.

Her bleeding and covered in Aryan cum.

But this was different.

I had to remember that.

Neither was Camille Mariska—bleeding and covered in *Famiglia* cum.

Instead, Abramovicz was the one who was bleeding everywhere, his hands on his junk, an endless scream coming from his lips. Victoria was huddled in the corner, her hands and arms over her head as she tried to hide from what was happening, and Camille, my wife, the—no, *no time for emotions.*

No fucking time.

She was on the floor in a sprawl. Unconscious. Her arms and legs were akimbo, but she was fully clothed. Her mouth was covered in blood, and I read the scene real fast as a small, puckered bloody *thing* lay between her and Abramovicz on the floor.

I refused to think she was dead.

I FUCKING REFUSED.

My gun was already high, and I tilted it Abramovicz's way. My bullets missed though because he plunked to his knees before they could find their home, blood loss evidently weakening him to the point of collapse.

I could have just shot him, but I didn't. I picked up that pink *thing* on the ground, well aware of what it was, and strode over to the fucker who'd made my wife's life a misery for too long.

Pinching his nose, which had Abramovicz's dazed eyes darting open and staring up at me, I waited for him to retaliate but he didn't fight me, his mouth just popped open as he curled in on himself, trying to stop the pain and the blood loss—he didn't need to worry about either. He wouldn't be feeling anything soon.

I shoved his dick back into his mouth, punched his chin so his jaw slammed closed around his cock, then pressed the muzzle of my gun to his forehead.

"For Camille," I rasped as the cunt let out a moan, and I squeezed the trigger.

When his brains scattered everywhere, his skull caving in, I took a second to calm myself before I faced the fucking truth.

My heart was in my throat, my lungs were straining like I was underwater, but I made myself twist around, made myself step forward.

She was so still. Her face pasty except for the blood that was already starting to cake on her skin. Clumps of hair were on the floor, where he'd ripped it free from her head, and I begrudged every lost golden lock. Amid that treasure, there was an abandoned gun that Abramovicz must have dropped after—

No.

Mouth trembling, I sank to my knees and pressed a hand to her head. There were bruises there already, blossoming around her temple like obscene flowers, but I whispered her name, needing her to wake up. Needing those beautiful green eyes to stare back at me.

She'd been in my life too short a time to be able to say I loved her, hadn't she?

Men didn't fall in love in a week.

Christ, we didn't fall in love in a month or *six* months.

But as I looked down at her, as I stared at her still form, as I studied her beautiful red-stained face, as I recognized that she was a fighter, just like me, those feelings were impossible to deny.

What else was impossible to deny?

The rage inside me, the fury that she could be taken from me when I'd only just found her.

We should have a lifetime to get sick of each other. Instead, I'd broken my promises to her.

In my head, for the first time since Ma had been abducted, and I'd learned what it was to be a man, I prayed and *meant* it, *"Father, who art in heaven, hallowed be thy name—"*

As the Lord's Prayer whirred in my mind like a song, her eyelashes fluttered, and my shaking hand moved to stroke through her hair. "Camille?"

My voice was hoarse, her name was husky on my lips, but it was a benediction nonetheless.

Her brow puckered as her eyes opened a slither, then she groaned and turned her face into my thigh, moaning, "Brennan?"

"You're safe now, *Mo Anam Cara*," I rasped.

"I knew you'd come for us," she whispered.

Her hand moved slowly, in increments like that was painful, and she covered her eyes a second.

I wanted to ask what had happened, but I didn't want to rush her—

"The bastard pistol-whipped me." Then she stunned me further. Her bright red lips curved. Fucking *curved. Into a blood-stained smile.* "I deserved it."

"What?" I muttered, confused. *Deserved* it? The hell was she talking about?

"Help me up?" I obeyed, propping her up as she asked: "Is Victoria okay?"

"C-Cammie?" Victoria almost skidded as she crawled toward us, throwing herself at Camille who opened her arms with a grimace, which had me wondering if she'd broken a rib or something, before she held her tight, clinging to her as hard as Victoria clung back.

"It's okay, *malyshka*, he can't hurt you now."

Victoria started sobbing, and all I could do was watch as Camille comforted her. Dazed, I stayed in place, propping Camille up, holding her as close as our position would allow, and wondering if God was going to hold me to the promise I'd made him at the end of the Lord's Prayer.

YOU MAY NOT THINK YOU'RE BEAUTIFUL. BUT YOUR SOUL IS. HAVE FAITH THAT SOMEONE WILL RECOGNIZE THAT BEAUTY AND WANT IT FOR THEIR OWN.

FORTY-SIX
CAMILLE

I WAS ACHING, I was sore, but I was alive.
Alive and kicking.
My body was weak from being manhandled, but inside, I felt energized.
I felt like a warrior.
I'd attacked Abramovicz the only way I could, and he'd paid for it.
Dearly.
For what felt like the first time in my life, I hadn't sat around, waiting for someone else to save me.
I'd saved myself.
And Victoria too.
If that meant I had an adrenaline high the likes of which I'd never experienced before, then so be it. I'd deal with it.
Later.
After ducking and diving, Brennan managed to free us from the compound without any more of our blood being shed.
Knowing Eoghan was The Whistler, I assumed he was the one who kept blowing off people's heads if they approached us.
I spotted Maxim on the way out, and knew the way he'd looked, drenched in blood, riding an adrenaline high of his own, would stay with me for a long time. Even worse than any of that was how he'd stared at

Victoria, his gaze glued to her as he watched us leave, covering our exit with his weapon, waiting for anyone to attack us. Well, *her*.

When we made it to an SUV with no plates, its doors wide open, we leaped in and he got us out of the neighborhood before Brennan pulled into a back alley after a short ride. There, he gave me a bottle of water which I used to rinse out my mouth, while he pulled out a change of shirt for himself and for me from the back seat.

Relieved he'd come prepared, I shrugged the tee over my sweater to cover the stains, watching as he bared his chest by dragging his overhead. Blood covered his skin, but it was drying in patches, so when he replaced it, it didn't seep through.

Aware and thankful for his lack of injuries, I grabbed his shirt, doused water onto the back which was clean, and scrubbed my face, aware I must look like the bride of Dracula, and he did the same once I was done, before asking, "Do I look respectable?"

Brennan was born to be the exact opposite of that, but I hid my smile, and told him, "You'll do." He wouldn't raise eyebrows as he drove through the city, at any rate. "What about me?"

He reached over, and I noticed his fingers were shaking as he cupped my chin, tilting my head this way and that as he looked at me as if he hadn't expected to ever be able to do so again.

After what we'd just gone through, it might very well have ended up that way.

That didn't stop my heart from leaping into my throat from the unexpectedly tender caress, but he didn't say anything other than, "You'll do too."

Now our appearances had reverted to some semblance of normalcy, he set off again. The ride took thirty minutes, and as we drove, bubbles of emotion escaped me. Each time, it made them jump, but I couldn't help myself.

"Cammie? What did he mean? How did Papa deal with Mama?"

Those damn emotions bubbled up in my throat again, but this time, it was a mixture of laughter and rage. "He was just spewing vitriol, *malyshka*. Take no notice."

"But—"

Before she could pepper me with more questions, Brennan cleared his throat and said, "We're nearly there."

Grateful that he'd spared me that conversation, I turned my head to the road to watch the traffic pass.

The car didn't stop until we were at, I assumed, Eoghan and Inessa's building.

The three of us, me and Victoria looking a little more battered than when we'd left for church this afternoon, huddled into the elevator and soared upward to his penthouse where Inessa was waiting by the entranceway.

She hurled herself into the small space between Victoria and I, evidently refusing to choose—which, crazy though it seemed, and as much as Vicky needed the love, I appreciated more than she could know.

She huddled into us, cuddling us both, sobbing and crying and shrieking in French and Russian, a mixture of words that were both terrified and furious and relieved.

By the end, I was giggling, unable to stop myself or this giddy high I was currently riding. She pulled back to stare at me, but Vicky merely said, "She keeps doing that."

And I did.

I wasn't sure why, but I'd giggled a few times.

Brennan cleared his throat. "It's just reaction. Shock setting in." He and I shared a glance, his brow puckering as he looked me over.

I could tell I was surprising him, could tell, also, that there was something going on in his head. Something shadowy, something that had nothing to do with today. Or, that's to say, it was burrowed away in his past but the events at the compound had triggered the memories.

When Inessa said, "You always were a weirdo, Cammie," I just grinned at her, finding amusement in her words because they were said with love, not revulsion, which made all the damn difference.

She hooked her arm around Vicky's shoulders and tugged her into her side. "How you doing, short stuff?"

Our baby sister just shrugged, muttering, "I'm okay."

"She isn't," I ratted on her. "I think you should get her in the shower, then tuck her into bed. She needs to get some sleep."

"I'm not a baby," Vicky retorted, but it was half-hearted, like she wanted to argue just for the sake of it but knew we were speaking wisely.

"I know you're not, *malyshka*, but I'm going to do exactly that when

I get home, and I'm not a baby either." I leaned forward, squeezing Vicky's arm, telling her, "You did good today."

She scowled at me from under a floppy piece of gold fringe. "How can you say that? I just huddled in the corner. You're the one who—" She gasped. "She—" Her eyes watered. "You put yourself in danger for me."

"Of course I did," I told her simply, smiling at her. "That's my duty as the eldest."

"But..." Her head tossed from side to side, seemingly of its own volition, not hers. "I don't understand how you could have..." She swallowed. "...done that. Bite him like that—"

"I had to stop him from hurting you. Not just today, but every other day too. What I did was something he might have survived were it not for Brennan, but he'd never be able to use it the same way again." I jerked my chin up. "I made sure of that."

She gulped. "I think I might be sick."

When she darted out of Inessa's arms, running down the hall, Inessa frowned at me. "Cammie?" Her voice wobbled just as her eyes widened. "You didn't."

My mouth tightened. "I did."

"Jesus."

"He had nothing to do with it," I said flatly, but I reached over and squeezed her shoulder. "I'll call you later after I get some rest. My head got knocked around a few times today. I could do with a good night's sleep."

She frowned but nodded, moving into me to hug me again. "How did you do that?" she whispered. "Didn't you gag?"

"I annihilated a threat." I tipped my head to the side. "That's what O'Donnellys do."

Brennan's nostrils flared as our eyes clashed and held over Innie's shoulder as we embraced.

"I'm so glad you got away," I told her gruffly.

"Only because of you," she whispered. "If you hadn't helped me—"

I pulled back and reached for her hands. Squeezing them, I repeated, "It's my job to protect you. I failed you—"

Brennan protested gruffly, "Hardly."

I just shrugged. "I'm glad you got away, I just wish Victoria had too. I wish she hadn't gone through that."

"You went through worse," Brennan rasped, and I shot him a smile, amused and touched that he was defending me. "Come on, Camille, it's time we got you home."

Damn, that sounded good.

Some of my energy had flagged by the time I hugged Innie goodbye, and when we made it back into the SUV, I sagged into the bucket seat, uncaring that I might get car sick, just needing to catch my breath.

"I want to tell you that you should have waited, Camille, that you didn't have to do what you did," he rasped, breaking into the silence and prompting me to let my eyes drift open, "but I'm oddly proud of you for attacking first."

With his gaze straight ahead, his face expressionless, I wasn't sure if he meant that or not. Was unsure if he was disgusted by me and was just trying to make me feel better, but I decided that I didn't care.

I was proud of me too.

It might have been unnecessary as there couldn't have been two minutes between Brennan storming the compound and me attacking Abramovicz but I hadn't known that, had I?

I'd acted. I'd saved Victoria. I'd saved myself.

"Thank you, Brennan," I told him softly. "You didn't have to say that."

His attention darted off the road for a split second, but his scowl was very much in appearance. "I don't have to say that? I let you down today, Camille. I broke—" He swallowed thickly. "I broke my promise to your mother, to you. Fuck." When he rolled to a halt at a stop sign, he leaned over, resting his forehead on his hands which were at the twelve o'clock position on the wheel.

Surprised, I just looked at him a second, unsure of what to do, but I decided to let my instincts reign. They'd helped me out today, after all.

I leaned over, and even though my hands were dirty and speckled with blood, I smoothed my fingers over his hair, cupping the back of his neck as I murmured, "You came for me, Brennan. You could have left us. I'm a wife you didn't really want—"

"'Didn't' being the operative word," he grated out, his head pivoting so he could look at me. "I—I thought I lost you today, Camille. When I burst into that room, you were sprawled out flat. You were covered in blood. I didn't see you breathing. It felt like you weren't. Maybe I was projecting; I don't know. But I just..." He blew out a breath. "I didn't want you. You *were* a promise I had to fulfil, however I can't let you carry on thinking that."

"We've only known each other..." Damn, why was I arguing? This was everything I wanted, and nothing I'd ever expected. Blinking back the tears that had started to prickle my eyes, I whispered, "Brennan?"

"Yeah?"

"We have to move. The horns."

It was an orchestra of pissed-off New Yorkers that serenaded me as, wordlessly, Brennan let me know he had deeper feelings for me. As I let him know the same.

"Fuck them."

My throat felt thick, my eyes still stung, but I whispered, "We don't have to put a name to it. We don't have to even describe it. Just know that I feel the same."

He clenched his teeth, but his words were simple as he said, "I'm glad," and like that, he started up the car and drove us to the apartment.

Once inside, we went straight to his, *no*, our room, and after stripping off, he pulled out his phone and did the most astonishing thing—he turned it off and left it on the bathroom vanity.

We climbed into the shower together, and he tended to me as if I was something precious. Something to cherish. It was unexpected and delicious, and I appreciated him cleaning me as much as I appreciated the show when it was his turn to wash up.

I was exhausted, too drained to do anything but watch, but damn, he was better than *Magic Mike*.

After, he dried me, taking care to smooth the towel over my skin, making sure no part of me was damp, then he even put toothpaste on the toothbrush for me, watching as I spat out a few gross remnants of blood, and then handed me the bottle of Listerine.

When I was cleaned to his satisfaction, he moved us over to his bed. He held my hand as he lowered me between the sheets, then said, "Wait there."

Like I was going to go anywhere.

I closed my eyes a second, and then the next, opened them to find him there, sitting beside me with a bottle of pills in one hand and a glass of water in the other.

Sadly, he'd put on a pair of boxer briefs, I noticed, as I reached for both.

"Take two. It's only Ibuprofen," he directed.

I complied, asking, "Are you coming to bed?"

"I'll lie with you until you sleep."

That was a massive concession.

Huge.

I knew it, so did he.

He wasn't going to call in, get the details on what had happened once he'd left. He wasn't diving straight into business. He was giving me his time, and that was the most precious commodity he had. Which, in turn, made *me* feel precious.

When I'd taken the pills, I laid back once more, wincing as the parts of my head where that bastard had pulled out my hair stung, but watching as he rounded the bed to reach his side. After he'd climbed in, he maneuvered me so I was tucked into him and then he whispered, "This is unexpected."

I smiled because I knew, inwardly, he was thinking that it was unwanted too. But I could forgive that. I thought I could forgive him anything *when* he held me like this, his mouth drifting over my temple like he couldn't believe I was here and needed to reassure himself, *when* he'd come to save me, *when* he'd done as I knew he would—ridden in like the protector he was, to slay my enemies. Now he knew though, I could slay them too.

Rather than say that, I mumbled drowsily, "The best things are, aren't they?"

"I suppose."

Silence fell between us, but my brain was still whirring.

"Abramovicz said my father *handled* Mama." My eyelids fluttered closed to stop the prickling tears from falling.

"He confirmed it? Shit."

"Poor Mama," I whispered sadly.

He bowed his head and pressed a kiss to my temple. "Mariska, you can rest easy now. I've got your girls and I'll keep them safe. No one will ever touch them again. I promise."

I knew neither of us were religious, so his words warmed me, enough that I tucked my face against his chest and pressed a kiss just above his heart.

"Thank you, Bren. I'm sure she heard that." And with that promise of his, a vow that meant so much to him, I rested.

Knowing I was safe.

Knowing he'd hold me.

Knowing that he'd been right that first day we'd met—I was no longer in flight mode, but fight.

Knowing that I'd never been prouder of myself and that I deserved it.

Two enemies I'd taken down now. *Two.* It wasn't a fluke, if anything, a pattern was forming. Luckily for the Bratva, no one else had earned my hatred.

Maxim had better watch himself, though, or he'd become my third...

And then there was Father's Obschak, Lukov...

But for the moment, I felt safe, which was enough to make me sigh with relief and sag into him.

FORTY-SEVEN
BRENNAN

"PLEASE COME," Ma pleaded.

"She's still resting, Ma. She needs to sleep."

"She needs to be around family."

I sighed. "Da wasn't very welcoming before, was he? Why the fuck would I take her into another situation like that when she needs calm and peace?"

I wasn't sure if she did need that, to be honest—Camille kept on surprising me—but I wasn't about to throw her to the rabid dog that was my father just because she hadn't cried once.

During the night, when I'd held her, my eyes wide open, my brain ticking, thoughts blurring as I tried to reconcile how right she felt in my arms with how insane it all was, she hadn't stirred once either. Not a single damn time.

No nightmares, no tears, no recriminations.

Who was this woman?

Her strength bewildered me, even as, inside, it made me want to protect her more. Made me want to do stupid shit like coddle her. I'd never coddled a woman in my life except Ma and that was only because of what she'd been through. That I wanted to do the same with Camille...

I gritted my teeth at the thought.

I'd always been the kind of guy my brothers' women had turned to. They knew they were safe with me, knew I was honorable—I had no idea why they thought that, but apparently they had some kind of fucking radar—but it wasn't in my nature to be soft, just protective.

Ever since Da had told me to treat the women in my life like queens, I'd listened. The difference here was, with Camille, I wanted to be both. I wanted to be softer around her, to protect her, but did she want that?

And was it weird that, at the same time, I wanted her dark and dirty, filthy with my cum? I wanted to fuck her hard, make her scream and cream at the same time. Wanted to drag her to the outer edges of her control.

Could that be done with a queen?

Mistresses, sure. But Camille was my wife. My woman. The future mother of my kids.

My palms grew sweaty as I thought about her in the limo the other day. I had two pictures in my head, that one and then of her on the ground on the compound. The two didn't correlate, but one blew my brains and one made me want to blow my load.

She'd been regal in the limo, and somehow, drenched in blood and unconscious, she'd been powerful too.

Queens didn't bite cocks off.

They waited to be rescued.

Camille hadn't waited for anyone.

My voice was hoarse as I told my mother, "She bit his dick off, Ma."

"I know what she did, son."

I closed my eyes, then reached up to rub them. "When I went into that building, all I could think of was you. That she'd gone through what you had."

She swallowed. "I know."

"But it wasn't her blood."

"Camille was incredibly brave."

"She was. She hasn't cried, Ma. Hasn't gotten upset. If anything, she just slept the whole night through." This, from the woman who self-harmed. Whose palms were a ragged mess of scars... each one a cry for help. "She only woke up about a half-hour ago, and she's singing in the fucking kitchen." I could hear her all the way down in my office.

On my desk, I had the catalogue of coins from the Yakuza, but even they weren't giving me any comfort.

"You should be with her. I only wanted to call because I knew you wouldn't come to the house otherwise, but I'd like you to."

"I'll ask her—"

"No, son. Please. I've spoken with your father. He knows that I'll put arsenic in his meat pie tomorrow if he treats her badly, but I don't think he will. I think she impressed him."

I rolled my eyes. "Jesus Christ."

"Well, it's not every day that a woman will do *that* to save herself, is it?"

"Surprised he doesn't think she's dirty now."

"Take that back, Brennan," Ma snapped. "Did you think he tossed me out of his bed because I was a slut in his mind after those bastards—" She sucked in a breath. "—did what they did to me?"

Bowing my head, I rumbled, "Sorry, Ma."

"So you damn well should be. If anyone understands what you're going through, Brennan, it's your father. And if anyone understands what she went through, it's me. God help me, I never thought what we endured would be visited upon our sons." A noise drifted from her lips, something that sounded suspiciously like a sob. "It really is like they say —the sins of the fathers…"

"Don't get into that Bible shit, Ma. It had nothing to do with you or Da. If anything, it had to do with her father, her family." I reached up and rubbed the back of my neck. "She's not like you. What you went through, she didn't. She's fine."

"I want her to know, today of all days, that she's with family. I never put my foot down with you, Brennan—"

"Don't you?" I interrupted glumly.

"But I have to insist that you bring her here."

I scowled at the coins, wanting to argue, but knowing as well that this was important to her. That she wanted to see Camille for herself, make sure she was okay.

From one victim to another. But Camille didn't feel like a victim. At least, she wasn't acting that way, which was only confusing me more.

I blew out a breath and said, "I'll talk to Camille. I make no promises."

"Thank you, son," was her immediate reply.

She cut the call before I could say another word, and I just rocked in my chair after I placed my cell down on the desk and picked up a Krugerrand.

Running it between my fingers, I raised it to my eye to squint at the marks etched on it.

Krugerrands started being produced in South Africa in 1967, and this one was minted from that year. They weren't precious, but they were worth a hefty amount of change, which was why the oyabun from the Yakuza had gifted them to me.

A bribe...

I hadn't exactly lied to my brothers, but Yamamoto had asked me to keep quiet about a certain someone in my phone list. A certain someone who was his son.

Frederica.

The old bastard was ashamed of his kid, refused to accept what *she* was, and had bribed me to keep quiet about it. I liked Freddie. I'd run across her over the years, and had paid her to get close to Coullson. Yamamoto's issue was that I'd known Frederica back when she'd been Akio. We'd gone to school together.

Pursing my lips, I placed the coin down on the desk and got to my feet.

My office was a simple space, just a desk, a chair, a computer and a painting that, unoriginally, hid a safe.

There was still a blood stain over on the carpet by the window where I'd had Callum tied up for the night, and that was on Tink's to-do list to deal with. I'd already instructed him to get rid of Camille's dress from the night she'd murdered her father. I'd had that stored in my safe too, just in case, but when he came over to sort out the stains, he was under orders to get rid of that as well.

She'd never know that, but it was a true testament to how fucked in the head I was over her that I was willing to destroy evidence—and my leverage—on her behalf.

The painting was of Central Park. I'd picked it up from one of the painters who sold tourists the same images over and over, but I'd liked how this one kid had picked up the light as the sun peeked through the trees at dawn.

Even though I'd bought it years ago, it reminded me of Camille now.

Which was way too fucking sentimental for this early in the morning.

Opening the safe, I pulled out a velvet pouch and retrieved one of my favorites and one of the rarest in my collection. A $4 Stella. There'd only been ten minted at the time in 1880, and this one was from the first strike—it was frosted, a museum-quality piece. In truth, the Smithsonian owned one of the ten, and so did I.

I'd snagged it at auction back in 2013, and I'd been hoarding it ever since.

As I lifted it and treated it to the same gimlet look as the Krugerrand, I pursed my lips before I tucked it into a single velvet pouch that I kept in a desk drawer.

Holding that in my hand, I locked the safe back up, then headed out of my office.

Camille was still singing about paradise being a thousand miles away, and I shook my head as I wended my way to the kitchen where her voice came intermittently with the sound of the blender.

She didn't just sound normal, she looked it.

I'd promised God that I'd actually listen to Doyle's services rather than sleeping through them if he brought Camille back to me, but the last laugh was on me, because I knew she hadn't needed that prayer.

She'd been fine. *Was* fine now.

Even if I couldn't reconcile it.

Last night, when I'd known she was sleeping hard, when my brain was tired of thinking, I'd gone to her bedroom to find the little box she'd hidden in her jewelry case. I'd found it during my first sweep of her room—I wasn't about to invite a stranger into my home without checking everything out.

While the contents of the kit weren't new to me, loaded down as it was with thin razor blades, each one scrupulously clean, tucked beside alcohol wipes, it was the small journal that interested me.

The first time I'd seen it, I'd known what it was. She'd doodled a title onto it: 'Reasons to live.' Not opening that was the only slice of privacy I'd given her, but last night, I'd cracked the seal on that journal. I knew it made me a bastard, but it was hard to reconcile a woman who could harm herself, who had to give herself justifications to live, who'd whored herself out because she didn't recognize she had worth, with the creature who'd been alight with fire yesterday even when she should have been cowering and crying like her sisters had been.

Had it given me any insight into her?

Not really.

I'd betrayed her trust for nothing. I'd learned that she was filled with hope. That, no matter what she claimed, she *was* a romantic. I guessed I'd also discerned an inherent insecurity that went bone deep, one that made me want to shore her up...

Hence the coin.

Once she poured herself a drink, her attention tipped down to the counter, where I saw she had the paper lying flat out in front of her. That was how she saw me watching her, at long last. Muttering, "Classic saying originated by John Donne," under her breath, she'd lifted the pen to her mouth to gnaw on as she thought about her answer.

I knew I needed to work on her survival instincts if she didn't sense a predator like me walking around. And instead of scowling at me with hatred for letting her down, like she *should* have, she dropped the pen and beamed a grin at me.

"Do you want a smoothie?"

Grimacing at the green gunk, I shook my head, letting my eyes drift over her tits and her tiny waist which were revealed in her cami, before I murmured, "You know I'm training Shay to fight?"

"Yeah." She took a sip from the bright, lurid green shake. "I know."

"I want you to come with."

"You want to train me to fight too?"

"Victoria as well, if she'll let me." Hell, I'd hold a self-defense class for all the O'Donnelly women if they'd join in.

She frowned a second, then she beamed a grin at me, bouncing a little in a way that had her tits bouncing along for the ride. "I'd love to! When you talked about it with Shay, I thought it sounded fun."

Fun. Yeah.

"You should have said."

Camille shrugged. "I'm not good at asking for things."

"No, I know that. I guess it's time you learned, hmm?"

Her grin turned sheepish. "It's hard to change the habit of a lifetime."

"Not true. Yesterday's proof of that." As expected, pride lit up her eyes. It both bewildered and amused me, but mostly, I was just relieved. I remembered Ma after the Aryans had done with her. She'd been a broken wreckage. Of course, her situation, her experience was different than Camille's, but either way, they were both survivors.

I remembered how useless I'd felt back then, too.

I'd watched the little sanity my father possessed drain away like water in a bathtub when Ma came home.

The rampage was known the city over. Even the cops hadn't tried to stop that particular war, and I was fucking honored to have taken part in it.

There was a reason there were no remaining Aryan groups in the vicinity—my da had annihilated them all from the East Coast to the Midwest. He hadn't just gone city-deep, he'd gone coast-wide.

"Brennan?" She was there. In front of me. Close enough to touch. To reach out to hold. "I lost you for a second."

Her smile was teasing, but the words resonated.

Because I needed to, I cupped her chin and murmured, "I have something for you."

She shook her head. "I don't need anything."

"I want you to have this." With my free hand, I slipped the pouch onto her palm. Her ravaged palm that was only just starting to heal up. Bright pink striations of fresh skin that had once been torn open by her razor blades.

"What is it?" she asked, not bothering to open it.

Arching a brow at her, I dropped my gaze to the pouch and waited for her to huff, pass over the bright green concoction to me, then let the coin drop out onto her scarred palm. Amused that she'd handed the glass to me when there was a sideboard beside us, I dumped it on there, then returned my attention to her.

She frowned at it, then at me, and said, "Huh."

My lips twitched. "Huh?"

"Never took you for a numismatist."

"I shouldn't be surprised you know that considering you're a crossword buff, should I?" I questioned ruefully, scratching my stubble.

"Nope." Her eyes twinkled. "*Consumable product of melting numismatist's prize.* That was the first time I came across it."

My brows rose. "You remember the clue?"

She hitched a shoulder. "Sure." Unaware she'd blown my mind, she lifted the coin to her eye, before gulping, "1880?"

"I collect all kinds of coins." I frowned at her. "What was the answer to the clue?"

"Rarebit. It's a type of grilled cheese." She blinked. "Why are you giving this to me?"

"I want to do a deal with you."

Warily, she lowered the coin, her gaze drifted to me and back again to the rare Stella with the coiled hair. "What kind of deal?"

"That's my most favorite coin. It's unique. It cost over one and a half million dollars."

"And you're giving it to me?" she rasped, swallowing when she raised the coin to eye height again. I watched as she almost dropped it as she fumbled, before she snatched it back up in her hand—at least her reflexes were semi-decent. That boded well for our training.

"I am. On one condition."

She bit her lip. "What condition?"

"You can cash that in anywhere in the world, Camille. I'd suggest you don't," I said wryly, "I'd *suggest* that you take it to Sotheby's or somewhere like that, because you'll earn more money that way—"

"Is it stolen?" she interrupted.

"No." I couldn't fault her for thinking that. "I have provenance for it. I'll make sure you can access that." I'd have to install a safe that only she had codes for, but it would be worth it. "But at any given moment, you have access to a fortune. If you're careful with it, you could live very well for the rest of your life on that amount of money..."

She blinked up at me, that damn bottom lip of hers back between her teeth. "T-Thank you, Brennan."

"You haven't heard the deal yet," I teased.

Camille gulped and said, "Of course not. Sorry." Then she broke my heart. She reached up and swiped at her eyes.

This woman, this crazy, fucking woman who hadn't cried once yesterday, had wet eyes now.

How I didn't haul her into me, I'd never know. My hands itched with the need to hold her close, to have her in my arms, but this had to be done.

"Don't be sorry," I rumbled, and I gave into temptation and let my hand cup her shoulder. My fingers spread out over the bare skin, and I watched as her body gave her away, just like I hoped it always would—a wave of goose flesh whispered down her bicep.

"What's the deal?" she whispered, peeking at me with liquid green eyes.

"Remember I told you that I'd tie you to the bed if I caught you self-harming?"

She licked her lips. "I remember. You said you'd spank me and make me come hard enough to forget why I was cutting too."

"Well, I recognize that wasn't the right command to make," I drawled, noticing the flush of arousal on her cheeks.

"No?"

"No. That might incentivize it," I told her gruffly, smirking when her cheeks flushed even more. "See? I know you're getting hot just thinking about it, and one day, I *will* tie you to the bed, but I don't want it to be because of that. That's not what we're about." I tipped up my chin. "Unless you don't like how I've treated you in the bedroom?"

Her brow puckered with genuine confusion. "You taught me what a climax is. How couldn't I like that?" She bit her lip. "Unless, *you* don't... want, I mean, maybe you don't like—"

Her goddamn insecurities.

I squeezed her shoulder and told her, "I want you. I don't want anyone else, that's how much I want you, Camille. Any which fucking way you'll have me, but just because I need that, doesn't mean you like it." It didn't mean that a queen wanted to be treated the way I treated her...

She pressed her hand to my chest and then she nearly had my eyes crossing as she purred, "I love what we do together."

My throat felt like an orange was stuck in it as I rasped, "Okay, then. So I'm not going to incentivize this. What we do together isn't going to be reduced to that level."

"What we do together is about you being nasty in the sack, huh?"

"Exactly," I said with a grin, "and you loving every step of my being nasty." My grin softened as I carried on, "Now, my deal is, when you want to cut, you come talk to me. You call me if I'm not home. Or you text me if you don't want to talk—"

"That's not practical," she inserted, shaking her head. "You won't always be able to answer—"

"That's my point, Camille," I rumbled. "I will *always* make time for you, okay?" A gasp escaped her, and I nodded. "Now, the day you decide you can't talk to me, or call me, or text me, that's the day I want you to grab this coin and I want you to sell it so you can make a new life somewhere else."

Her brow puckered. "You wouldn't want me if I cut myself?"

"It's not about wanting you, Camille." I groaned, then grabbed her and dragged her into me. "Christ, can't you tell? I never fucking stop wanting you. It's like you're dosing me up with Viagra or something." I grunted when I saw the pleased smile dancing on her lips. "It's about trust. It's about us talking. The day you can't do that is a day you don't trust me and it's the day I don't deserve to be your husband."

"Y-You said there'd be no divorce."

"And we wouldn't. But that doesn't mean you can't have your own freedom." I swallowed, because the concession was hard to give her. It was only after reading her journal, a small, padded book that was set up funny, each page waiting for a date to be written in, and each one able to house five days, that I'd seen how far back this thing went.

Reading her tell herself that she was lovable, that she hadn't found her purpose yet, that she had to live to make up with her sisters... it had broken something inside me. Something that had already been cracked the day the Aryans took Ma, and I was the reason they'd gotten to her.

"It's the only out I'll give you, Camille," I told her gruffly.

She shocked me—when wouldn't she?—by whispering, "I don't want an out."

"Then always talk to me." I let my hand come up to cup her cheek, allowed my thumb to wipe the single tear track that arced over the curve. So beautifully poignant was it that I felt choked up too. "Always let me in. No punishments for cutting, Camille. No punishments. Ever."

She stepped into me, and I hugged her, holding her close as she whispered, "Just trust."

"Exactly," I rasped. "Lyanov..." My voice waned as she tensed. "He wants Victoria, Camille. I don't know the extents he'll go to to have her as his bride. Far as I know he's from an orphanage in Moscow, so he's trying to buy his way to respectability as Pakhan. I didn't think about the consequences when I dealt with him, but I promise you this, now, after we've had this conversation, the day before she turns eighteen, I'll kill him before I let him have her.

"She wasn't a part of the promise I made your ma, because she wasn't born then, but that doesn't mean shit. She's family. Through her, I'm going to redeem myself and I won't let her—"

She tensed, interrupting, "You'll start a war."

"We're always at war, sweetheart. Ain't you figured that out yet? Life is fucking war."

"I made him promise that he'd court her."

"You think he's got time for that?" I snorted. "He's got three years to turn even more fucked in the head as the power corrupts him. I don't want him anywhere near my family."

Her hand clenched in my shirt. "Abramovicz said something that resonated with me yesterday. You're born Bratva, and you'll die Bratva—there's no escape."

"There was for you and Inessa. You're Irish now," I rumbled, even gladder now that she'd bitten the fucker's dick off after he'd told her that. "We can wed her to one of our men."

"I don't want that for her. I want her to make her choice." She stared up at me, repeating, "I told him that if he wanted her, he had to court her. If she chooses him, then he lives."

"Why let it get that far?"

"A feeling."

"What kind of feeling?" I grumbled.

"Did you see him yesterday? When we drew Victoria outside?"

I thought back to those moments when I'd had to get both of them to the SUV without either of them getting shot. Eoghan had popped off some rounds, saving us from the remaining bastards who refused to surrender, but I hadn't exactly been on the lookout for Pakhan-wannabes who had calf eyes.

"I didn't."

"He wants her."

"So?"

"To be wanted like that isn't something Victoria knows."

"It's pretty fucked up that he wants a kid. I should kill the bastard now."

She growled, "No, not like that. It was as if she was a Christmas present he couldn't afford."

"I thought you weren't a romantic," I chided softly, though her diary had told me otherwise.

"I'm not."

I snorted. "Everything you just said makes no sense unless you are."

Camille huffed. "If he's willing to fight for her, then let him. And if he isn't, and he raises his voice to her just the once, I'll let you kill him."

"You'll let me, huh?"

"Yes." She licked her lips. "I'm a woman who knows what it is to be unwanted, Brennan. I don't want that for her."

Closing my eyes, I tucked her closer then propped my chin on the crown of her head and corrected, "You've *known* what it felt like. Not anymore, Camille. I'll spend the rest of my fucking life showing you if that's what you need."

Her voice was small. "I do."

"Then that's how it'll be."

"No war, Brennan, not with the Russians. Not yet. Promise?"

I heaved a sigh. "Promise. Until you let me loose."

Hearing the smile in her voice made everything inside me feel like I was being hung upside down as she whispered, "That's five promises. If you include last night's too."

"I know. Things are getting out of hand." She laughed as I continued, "I just got off the phone with Ma actually. Da's softened up some. She's invited us over for Sunday lunch because she'd like to talk to you."

"About what?" She didn't tense up, so I didn't think she was saying no.

I cleared my throat. "You were young but most people haven't exactly forgotten about the war with the Aryans."

"God, no, it's legendary."

I nodded. "Ma was hurt real bad, Camille—"

"I think I know, but... what was your promise to your mother, Brennan? Was it to do with the Aryans?" she interrupted.

"Yeah. I vowed I'd never let her down again." Her gaze softened, but before she could say another word, I carried on, "Ma knows what it's like to be taken, Camille. She wants you to know you can talk to her. She wants you to be with family today."

Funny how *that* had her tensing up.

How *that* had her sobbing in my arms.

And funny how I felt like crying too as I held a woman who'd started out a stranger, who'd fucked me so filthy that she'd uncrossed my eyes, who'd shown a resilience and a strength so magnetizing that I felt bound to her in a way that I'd never felt with another person.

I knew what it was to be the man with broad shoulders. To be the one everyone relied on. Who protected the rest, who took the first hit so everyone else could duck.

Somehow, *somehow*, I'd found a woman who knew how that felt too, and that strong creature felt safe in my arms.

I'd tried to live with honor ever since I'd failed Ma, but it was the first time I actually *felt* honored.

I DON'T NEED TO THINK UP A
REASON TO LIVE TODAY.

FORTY-EIGHT
CAMILLE

I WAS nervous when Lena invited me into her country-style kitchen.

This time, I hadn't dressed up to visit with Brennan's family, instead wore a simple pair of black slacks, a thin cashmere jacket above a camisole, and my bracelets that helped me cope with motion sickness for the drive upstate. My hair was tucked into a loose ponytail that I hoped hid the bald patches, while also taking off some of the pressure on my scalp. No one else had dressed up either, and from last Sunday, I knew that wasn't normal.

The men had been in suits, Aela, Aoife and my sister had worn expensive dresses. Now, they sported jeans and sweaters, Aoife had a sapphire-tinted woollen dress on that complimented her hair with cute ballet pumps on her feet, but Aela and Innie wore sweaters, yoga pants and UGGs. Victoria, of course, was dressed like a miniature First Lady, but I took no notice of her. I could imagine her going to a rave dressed that way.

Yesterday, three of the brothers had stormed a compound and gone to war to liberate me and my sister.

Today was about comfort.

Today was about family.

I'd already been greeted by everyone, the brothers and the sisters-in-law like I was a soldier returning home from the battlefield, and even though I'd blushed, their acceptance had mattered more than their praise. Seeing Shay and Victoria being introduced had eased things for me too—teenagers could be cute when they were so awkward.

Unfortunately, the greetings were just the start of things. I'd hoped we'd get right into eating, but Lena had invited us into her kitchen, where she took a seat at the head of the kitchen table.

There, she'd declared, "Join me, Camille, Aoife, Aela, Inessa, and Victoria."

The setting might have been homely and cozy, but her order was as regal as anything else.

I did as she asked, my sisters and new in-laws obeying too, and in the doorway, I saw Brennan looming, waiting for her to call him in.

She clucked her tongue at the sight of him, then waved him into the room.

He surprised me by moving to my chair, gesturing at me to get out of it, taking that seat, then dragging me onto his knee. Lena smiled a little mistily at the sight, while Inessa grinned, and Aoife and Aela shot each other surprised glances, Victoria simply rolled her eyes. Me? I felt a bit giddy at the possessive hold in front of the woman who mattered the most to him.

"Everyone around this table has gone through something that they shouldn't have.

"Aoife, Aela, you know my heart bleeds for what you have both endured. So that's why you're here. Because we need to come together, at a moment like this, to know that we're bound in ways that few families are." She cast Victoria, Inessa and me a glance. "I know what it is to be held hostage, girls. I know what it is to be taken." Inessa started to argue, but Lena raised a hand. "You got away, but you know the fear of being snatched. Of your life sinking to its knees around you as your routine is held against you and used as a means of getting close to you." Inessa's shoulders hunched. "Then, there's my boy, Brennan. He's steeped in guilt for something he didn't do, for a duty that should have never been given to him in the first place, and that's my fault. This, here, is a safe space. For us all."

"Ma, that's not fair to you. You never asked for that to happen," he rasped.

"It's dead fair. I should have told your father to give me a guard for the morning. That task should never have fallen to you. It changed you, Bren. You were my sweet-hearted lad, then you turned dark." Her voice waned, but even as something flickered at the back of her eyes, something I'd seen in Brennan's, she shot us a smile as she repeated, "This is a safe space. The safest in the world. Only Aela hasn't lost her mother," she whispered, shame flickering in her eyes, "and by no means have I been the best one. My boys will agree. I've let their da get away with too much, and I've done things I'm ashamed of. Even this week, I let them down." She sucked in a breath. "But I can keep trying. That's all we can do in this life—try. I'm here, and I'm what you've got, so I'll do my best to do your mothers proud. Aela, whenever you need me, you know I'm here. For you *and* Shay."

"I do, Lena. Thank you. I appreciate that."

She shrugged. "If I can help, I will."

I wasn't sure if I could ever call on this woman who was more like an empress than a mere matriarch, but I whispered, "Thank you, Lena." After Aoife, Victoria and Inessa murmured their thanks as well, I asked, "What happened?"

Brennan tensed beneath me. "Ma's got a dress shop. One of my duties was to take her to her store and to wait for her guard to show up. This particular morning, I was in a rush. I didn't go in. They were waiting on her inside. I didn't know. I just dropped her off... They took her."

Another person might have asked why, but I was born to the life.

Even Aoife, who I knew wasn't like the rest of us, had to know.

Business.

Always fucking business.

"I'm sorry," I said simply, and I reached over to place my hand on Lena's. "Truly, I wish you hadn't had to go through that."

Her smile was half-hearted this time, and her expression wobbled, the strength she projected wavering as her mask dropped. It might have been years ago, but to Lena, it was as close to her as our attack was. "I wish so too."

A booming laugh sounded over in the corridor, making me jump, Victoria as well. Lena's mask reappeared within seconds, but when Aidan Sr. came wandering in, his boys around him, a grin on his face, I wasn't sure if it was a mask, or her exasperation was real enough to jerk her out of the past.

"Must you make so much feckin' noise, Aidan," she complained, even as she raised her chin, tilting her head to the side for him to kiss her there. He didn't obey, well, he *did,* only he didn't leave it there. His mouth collided with hers—I saw a flash of tongue, which was definitely TMI—then he placed a hand on her shoulder and beamed a smile at me.

For a second, I felt like a rabbit frozen in headlights.

For a second, I wasn't sure if that smile promised the same threat as Medusa's glance—that I'd turn to stone.

Then, he cackled and, rubbing his hands together, asked, "Now then, girlie, what's this I hear about you biting off that cunt's cock?"

And as Lena chided, "Aidan, there are children present!"

I shared a look with Brennan and knew, somehow, 'that cunt's cock' was why Aidan had accepted me. Us.

If I'd needed proof that he was insane, I had it.

FORTY-NINE
BRENNAN

SUNDAY LUNCH HAD GONE BETTER than expected, so much so that most of us had stayed overnight.

Only Conor had fucked off back to the city, pretty much as soon as he'd finished dessert. I'd only had the chance to grab him by the arm as he was shrugging into his coat with one hand, hauling his massive laptop case in the other.

Kid looked like he was getting ready to leave for the airport he was in that much of a rush, but before he did, I managed to ask him, "Any news about that McKenna guy?"

He'd shot me a dead-eyed stare, which was unlike him. But everything about lunch had been unlike him.

Quiet, moody, taciturn when he did eventually speak. None of the wry humor, the jokes or the sarcasm we were all used to. Leaving early was unlike him too. Especially when there was a game on.

"He's dead."

I blinked at him. "He can't be. Why the fuck would Coullson give me that name if the bastard's dead?"

"I don't know, Bren. You'll have to ask Coullson that, won't you?"

He'd pulled his arm out of my hold before he'd stormed off to kiss Ma farewell, then he'd left, speeding off down the drive in his Ferrari like he had ants in his goddamn pants.

His weird behavior didn't appear to be noticed by anyone but me, so I let it go, and immersed myself in one of the few times we got together for a full day and night.

Holidays we gathered here and spent the night, but otherwise, we always went home. It was a day for drinking, though, and we all got a little hammered, Da included.

With every drop of single malt he supped—the Glenrothes Camille had bought him, I noted—he got louder and more boisterous, and would start cackling every now and then which we knew was related to how Camille had taken down Abramovicz.

I was glad the rest of them could get a laugh out of it. For me, I knew I'd be scarred for fucking life. Whether Camille would be or not was another matter entirely, but she seemed to find it amusing too. Only Victoria and me didn't, whenever Da's cackles grew loud, she'd hunch her shoulders and would disappear to the bathroom.

Da was definitely not to everyone's taste.

Mostly, I was glad he got slushed simply because it meant I could avoid talking about business.

I knew Mark had to have been making waves about his son, because Priestley must have been worried sick by now. I'd fucked up by killing the cunt, but learning he was behind the drive-by that had my eldest brother spiraling into addiction, that had almost killed Aoife, and that had triggered every single downfall that had befallen us recently—was it any wonder I'd broken?

I needed time.

Time to fix things, and Da getting pissed helped, especially when he talked about planning the funerals of the guards we'd lost yesterday, as the single malt stopped him from getting angry, and just made him weep instead.

I talked to Ma a little, watched the game with my brothers, shot the shit in general, but mostly, I kept an eye on Camille who seemed to fit in fine. She hung out with the other women, and they laughed and joked and cooed over Jake. Aoife and Aela didn't drink, Shay, and Victoria either obviously, but the rest of us let our hair down.

It didn't matter that Da had rejected Camille—yesterday had changed things.

The Russians had gone after an O'Donnelly, which meant his loyalties shifted.

I was glad for her sake, even if the end didn't justify the means.

Sometime during the night, I pulled a Victoria and took a break from the rowdy noise that a big family gathering created. After I went to take a leak, I found myself in the hall staring at the photo Camille had mentioned.

My da with his favorite brother, Frank, in Coney Island.

Like it was fate, a laugh echoed down the hall, one I recognized as Finn's thanks to the deep tenor of his voice.

Finn had been with us for so long that he was like blood now, and this kind of get-together would have been hollow without him, Aoife, and Jake, as much as we felt the lack of Conor today.

But Camille was right.

I'd just never noticed it before. *Why would I?*

This picture had followed us around every house we'd moved into. I'd seen it so often I didn't even look at it anymore, but as I peered into the smoky image, the lack of focus typical of a photo from this era, there was no denying that he and Finn were alike.

Remarkably so.

A fact I could check as, right beside the photo of Frank, there was a new one of Aoife, Finn, and Jacob.

Twins... the similarities were remarkable.

Was he our cousin?

But wouldn't Da have told us?

Scraping my hand over my chin, I backed away from the pictures. We had enough intrigue going on in our lives without me adding to it. But it definitely had a question mark popping into existence in my head.

I'd push it aside, for the moment, but one day, I'd ask. One day, I wanted to know the truth.

That following morning, we left early. I never slept well at my parents' place, and I sure as hell wasn't going to fuck Camille there, so we didn't hang around for breakfast, I didn't even wait for Da to wake up. Just kissed Ma the second she was awake and bustling in the kitchen, her favorite place, and shepherded a still yawning Camille out into the cold light of day.

As we drove back to the city, Camille dozed off, which I was glad about. I'd been awake since four, but I was still trying to formulate my plan of attack.

Visiting Coullson was at the top of today's to-do list. But what I wanted from him was another problem. He'd given me that name under duress. He believed it mattered.

Had someone fed that to him?

Who?

I wanted nothing more when we got back to the apartment to climb into bed with Camille, but I hustled her between the sheets, pleased she was still slightly hungover—apparently, she and Inessa had vodka flowing through their veins because Ma, with sixty years of drinking behind her, got drunker a lot faster than they had.

A part of me wondered if I should wake her, seeing as she'd volunteered at the soup kitchen and it was a cause that mattered to her, but I needed to rush. This was a situation that was putting me on edge, had been ever since Conor had stormed out last night.

After I grabbed some clothes, I set an alarm for a half-hour's time with the house computer so she had the choice of waking up or snoozing it, then got showered and changed in the bedroom I'd given her to use that first night.

When I was ready, I sent Forrest a text: **Me:** *Where's Coullson most likely to be at this time?*

Forrest: *City Hall. Why?*

Me: *Conor says McKenna is dead.*

Forrest: *Fuck.*

Me: *Yeah. Re. Coullson, it's damn early. Are you sure he's there?*

Forrest: *I'm fucking sure. Why ask if you don't think I know my shit? We've been trailing him ever since Dunbar fed him to us.*

Me: *I'm just checking. Calm the hell down.*

Forrest: *Need me to come with?*

I had a feeling something was going on today, but for the life of me, I couldn't remember. A quick glance at my calendar reminded me. He and his wife had been trying to get IVF through a certain clinic, and they'd been on the wait list for eight months.

Me: *Ain't that important. Go on, I know you two have been waiting for this appointment for a while.*

Forrest: *Are you sure?*

Me: *Yes, I'm fucking sure. Now who's the nag?*

Forrest: *Lol. Sorry. I'm nervous. You know I hate this shit.*

Me: *Who could blame you? But don't worry. At least today, you'll get some answers. Let me know how you get on.*

Forrest: *Same goes. I wanna know why Coullson fed us the name of a corpse. See ya later.*

Me: *Speak later.*

With that confirmed, I peered at the time, called Bagpipes and told him to meet me at City Hall.

The ride down to Lower Manhattan was surprisingly quiet thanks to the early hour, but as I approached City Hall Park, that was where it started to get busy.

Busier than usual.

I frowned as I drove around the park, heading toward City Hall itself, but as I did so, I realized why it was busy—there was a massive cluster of police cars, their blue lights flashing, doors left wide open as if there was an active threat underway.

I'd only ever seen such a response like this when there was a shooter situation.

Frowning, I pulled over beside one of the cop cars, where a uniform was speaking into his radio.

When he'd done, I hollered, "Hey."

The cop twisted around to glare at me, but when he saw me, he gulped.

Nice to know my face was that recognizable to the boys in blue.

"Sir," he muttered warily, "you need to move on. This is an ongoing crime scene."

"What happened?" I asked, dismissing his words.

"There's been a murder."

"There has? Who's been killed?" I peered over at City Hall, leaning onto my wheel to get a better angle, taking note of all the cop cars and registering it had to be someone powerful to trigger this response from the boys in blue.

It had better not be Coullson...

The cop tugged on his shirt collar, before he replied, "A guy sneaked into the Mayor's office and..." His mouth worked, his cheeks turning pasty as he gulped. It was clear to me he'd seen the crime scene, and it was also clear to me that he wasn't used to seeing dead bodies.

"And what, son?" I asked, feeling oddly paternal. Had I ever been this much of a fucking rookie?

Still he wasn't that new that he didn't recognize me, because he answered where he'd have told anyone else in the general public to fuck off. "Slit the Mayor's throat," the guy bit out.

My brows rose. "The Mayor's dead?" I repeated, even though there wasn't much inaccuracy in taking a knife to the throat.

Fuck.

Coullson was dead?

Jesus, what a waste of a resource. We'd only just turned the fucker and there he was, eliminated.

The thought resonated with me, and I knew that word was bang on —*eliminated*.

They knew he'd talked to us.

They knew.

The fuckers.

How did they know that?

Goddammit.

Had he told them? Or had someone been listening in? He'd said at the gala they'd kill him for talking to us—seemed as if he'd been right.

Shit.

Barely refraining from slamming my fist into the wheel, instead, I gritted out, "The assailant is still in there?"

"He's holed himself up inside the Mayor's office."

"Is it some nut job?" I rasped. "Some lunatic?"

He shook his head, then leaned into the window. "It was a cop."

And just like that, everything turned in a circle in my head.

This was the reason Craig Lacey had gone missing.

"You guys have a name yet?" I rasped, even though I didn't need to have it confirmed. I just fucking knew I was right.

The Sparrows were tying up loose ends.

The question was, what leverage had they pushed onto Lacey's shoulders to break his back?

When the cop grimaced and affirmed my supposition, I told him, "Thanks for the info, officer."

"You're welcome, sir." He bit his lip. "Please, don't tell anyone I spoke of this with you."

"I won't."

Driving off, I maneuvered away from the clusterfuck of traffic, asked Siri to send Bagpipes a message telling him we had a change of plans and to meet me at The Hole, and was about to call Da with this update when my cell buzzed.

Seeing Eoghan's name flash up, I hit 'accept,' and muttered, "You won't believe what's just happened."

"Neither will you." He hissed out a breath. "You at home or on the road?"

"On the road."

"You anywhere near my place? Can you bring Camille over?"

"Why? What is it? What's wrong?"

"We just got in, and someone's sent Victoria a gift. It's gnarly."

"What is it?" I repeated, confused.

"I don't want to say over the phone."

I winced because I hadn't swept my car for bugs after I'd parked up in my garage, so my hands were fucking tied as well. Eoghan's reminder might have spared us some shit down the line.

"I'm in Lower Manhattan. I'll go and get her and bring her to your place."

"Get Tink as well."

"Tink?" As well as our resident computer, he was our go-to clean up guy. "Jesus."

"Trust me, it's not pretty."

"I'll be about an hour if traffic's kind."

"Just… Christ, just get her here as fast as you can."

The second he disconnected, I rang through to Camille. She yawned, which made my lips curve before she mumbled, "Bren?"

It was the first time she'd called me that, and even though nothing about this situation was good, it made me sigh, a slither of happiness unfurling inside me as I thought about her stretching out in our bed, her arms and legs tensing and relaxing as she curled up amid the sheets.

I'd give my left ball to be there, but instead, I didn't have time.

"Babe, I'm in Lower Manhattan. I'm gonna drive back home, but I need you to be ready to meet me in the garage."

"What? Why?"

"I know you had scheduled to go to the soup kitchen, but Eoghan's just called. He says Victoria needs you. She's had a meltdown."

"What?! Okay, I'll be ready in ten."

Though her voice sounded a lot more alert, I just said, "Well, I'm thirty minutes away, Camille, so don't break your neck or anything."

"What's wrong with her?"

"I don't know. Eoghan didn't tell me." I cleared my throat. "Just be ready, okay? I'll buzz you when I'm about to turn into the garage, so you know to come down."

"Okay, Bren. I'll see you in a little while."

With that done, I sent a message to Tink as well, telling him to meet me at Eoghan's.

I raced through traffic which wasn't as kind to me now as it had been earlier, and when I made it to my building, I did as I said, called her then hung up and pulled into the tunnel that would take me to my section of the garage.

When I made it there, she hadn't arrived, so I leaned into the glove compartment and pulled out the sweeper Con had made for us.

The second I swept it over the dashboard, the device flashed red.

Jaw clenching, I swore under my breath and climbed out of the car. This vehicle had been only two places without my eyes on it—my da's compound and here, a secured parking lot.

Locking it up, the sweeper in my hand, I moved over to the cupboard beside the elevator just as she made an appearance. Even though I knew she'd rushed, she looked a million dollars and as fucking furious as I was, as mad as those bruises decorating her temple made me, I stopped to tug her into my arms and greet her good morning.

When I thrust my tongue against hers, she jerked in surprise, then immediately melted in my arms.

Her reaction to me, her response, like always, blew my fucking mind, but it also cleared it. Made everything feel as transparent as glass.

Before, I'd been working for the family. I'd kill for them, but this was different. This was my family of choice. This was the woman I had to protect, or die trying.

My entire world boiled down to her as she accepted me for all that I was, unequivocally, and at that moment, I accepted her for what she was too—the woman I loved.

There, I'd said it.

Even if it was only to myself.

I pulled back, nipping her bottom lip as a parting tease, before I rumbled in her ear, "I have to check the cars. Mine was bugged."

She frowned. "Did you park up somewhere when you were in Lower Manhattan?"

I shook my head and watched the cogs whirl. "Here or at your father's place?" she muttered, the question more rhetorical than anything else.

"That's my thinking too." I gritted my teeth as I left her to grab the keys for the Maserati.

When I opened it up, the second I did, I swept the device over the car, and found it hadn't been touched.

I almost preferred the idea of my parking garage being infiltrated than Da's compound.

Rounding the car, I held open the door for Camille, beckoning her over. As she slipped into the passenger seat, I called Conor.

As it rang, she muttered, "Don't worry, I'll try to close my ears."

Despite the situation, I laughed, that was when Conor picked up. "Bren?"

"You been on a bender?" I demanded, recognizing that tone of his.

He was wired.

"Maybe. What's up?"

He sounded like he was hopping in his fucking chair—the bounce of the springs in his seat gave me literal confirmation of that.

"My car was bugged at Da's place."

"What?" Conor boomed. "That's impossible. I checked the alarms myself when I was there yesterday. No breaches. None, Bren."

"Well, it's either that or your sweeper's stopped working."

"I'll drive out to your garage, test the sweeper and remove the bug if it's there." He hissed out a breath. "You know what this means, don't you? If the bug is actually there?"

"That a rat at Da's compound planted that shit in my car, and maybe everyone else's as well?"

"Fuck."

"That's pretty much how I feel too." I heaved a sigh. "I'll speak to you later, Con."

"Okay, Bren. Bye."

Disconnecting the line, I called Bagpipes. "Baggy, there's a fuckfest going down."

"When you redirected me, I checked. He's dead?"

"Yeah. The uniform recognized me, told me that the guy behind Coullson's death—" Camille gasped. "—was Craig Lacey."

"No fucking way."

"Unfortunately, yeah."

"They're cleaning up shop."

"Seems like it." I grunted. "They must have pulled some BS move on him. Either that, or he's doing it on his own volition to make a stand? Who the fuck knows."

"Where're you heading?"

"Eoghan's place. Got a family situation going on there."

"Okay. You'll be by later though, right?"

"Yeah. We need to figure out our next move. Everything we did with Coullson was a waste of fucking time."

"That name has to mean something."

"I take it nothing came up at the Census Bureau?"

"Not this year. Or for the ten previous years." Bagpipes grunted. "Long shot, Bren, but do you remember a Father McKenna at St. Patrick's when we were kids?"

Scraping my jaw, I cast my mind back to church. The only trouble was, I rarely paid attention to the nonsense that went down there. "Christ, I can't remember. I can ask Da though."

"Nah, don't bother. It was just, the name rang a bell."

"It's a pretty common name," I pointed out.

"True. Anyway, you get going. See you later."

"Yeah, later." I cut the call as I headed north to Eoghan's building. "How much of that did you try not to hear?" I asked wryly.

"Well..." I shot her a look and saw her nose was wrinkled at the bridge.

Fuck, she was hot.

I knew for a fact she didn't know it either.

I reached over and placed my hand on her thigh. Not to get kinky or to tease, just to connect.

In all honesty, my mind wasn't on sex. I just needed the union.

"Camille, things are going to get ugly."

"Brennan, you said it yourself—life is war."

"You have that coin," I reminded her. "I wouldn't blame you for running off with it."

"Hush," she whispered, her hand cupping mine.

And that was how we drove the rest of the way, neither of us saying a word, both of our hands bound—each of us the other's life raft in a fucking storm.

When we made it to Eoghan's place, Tink was there, waiting in the parking lot. He nodded his head at me, waved at Camille, and as a unit, we headed to the elevator and rode up to the penthouse.

When Eoghan let us in, I immediately saw the issue. There was no way of hiding it.

"Where was it?" I demanded. "Was your security breached again?"

Down the hall, I could hear Victoria sobbing, and I knew Camille had as well, but the box held her in thrall too, otherwise I knew she'd have gone to her sister.

"No. They left it with the doorman who brought it up when he saw we were back."

My brow puckered. "He carried it like that and he didn't call the police?"

Eoghan snorted. "It was in a case, like one of those Uber Eats' carriers the bikers wear strapped to their backs."

That would have contained the smell, I figured. At least, for a short while.

In the center of the hallway was a white cardboard box that was soaked through with blood at the base. Eoghan had tipped off the lid to reveal a severed head. Around the neck, there was a bright blue ribbon which peeked out behind the Ziplock bag tucked between the fucker's lips. The only consolation was that the bastard's eyes were closed.

"What's in the bag?"

Eoghan shrugged. "I ain't touching that shit."

I couldn't blame him, but I still grumbled, "Pussy," as I leaned down and pried it out of the guy's mouth—rigor mortis was a real pain in the ass.

Once I was standing, I opened the bag and cast Camille a look. "Correct me if I'm wrong, babe, but that's Basil Lukov, right?"

"Yeah. It is," she whispered, her eyes perfectly round in her beautiful face as she stared down at the decapitated head of a guy that had just become the next move in Maxim Lyanov's plan to take over the Bratva.

Pulling out the contents from the bag, I realized it was a legal document, and my brow puckered as I read it.

"What is it?" Eoghan asked, folding his arms across his chest.

Good news, I guessed. Sorting out Victoria's legal status in Eoghan's household was on this week's to-do list, but it looked like Mariska had thought of everything.

I, Mariska Vasov, knowing that my husband will outlive me and may not provide adequate guardianship in case of his untimely death for our daughters, Camille, Inessa, and Victoria Vasov, do hereby assign their legal guardianship to Brennan O'Donnelly.

The statement was notarized, signed, and date-stamped.

Rubbing my chin as I realized Mariska's faith in me ran deeper than I probably deserved, I murmured, "Your mother thought of everything."

Passing the note to Camille, I watched as, eyes watering, she read the letter, whispering, "It's dated four days before she died."

Her pain hit me like a hammer to the heart, and I tucked my arm around her shoulders, holding her close as I whispered, "She kept you girls safe. That's all she ever wanted to do."

Camille gulped, before she rasped, "Maxim must have gone through everything in the house to find this."

"Did he know your mother?"

"Yeah. She was good to him." She bit her lip. "She was good to everyone."

I murmured, "Then, if he knew that, he probably also knew that your father wouldn't think to protect you because he was a selfish cunt, and knew Mariska might have dealt with the legalities before she died."

"Vasov isn't officially dead, but it doesn't matter now, does it? Whether his death is ever reported or not, Victoria's safe."

"Lucky," was all Eoghan said.

My lips twisted. "That's the luck of the Irish for ya." I squeezed her. "See? Even the universe knows you're Irish now."

A choked laugh escaped her as we shared a glance, warmth arcing between us, before Eoghan grumbled, "The fuck is this head about?'"

Somber shadows darkened her eyes as both of us accepted the unpalatable truth. Lukov was no longer a threat, because Lyanov was tying up loose ends. He was making his grab for the Pakhan's throne, but more than that...

"Lyanov's started to court your sister," I rumbled, and her shaky exhalation was all the confirmation I needed to know she thought so too.

CAMILLE

FIVE YEARS LATER

WHEN MY CELL RANG, I darted over to grab it, thinking it might be Brennan. I wasn't worried about him, not technically, but I knew he'd worry about me if I didn't immediately answer.

It was ridiculous considering I was in a secure location, and he was in Las Vegas with his brothers and crew for his bachelor party, but ever since we'd been abducted, he'd amped up security for all the women in his family.

Years later, I still lived like I was under constant threat, which meant I had Bagpipes with me at all times, even in the nail salon or a craft store, but I also had another guy in the back seat, monitoring the car when we left it.

When he'd flown down to Nevada, he and Eoghan had ratcheted things up even more, to the point where we couldn't even leave the damn house without taking an army along for the ride.

With us all under the same orders, and because it turned our homes into prisons, we'd agreed to stay at the building the Points used expressly to protect their women, and we were taking advantage of our time stuck together as a pre-bachelorette party, getting everything ready for when it was my turn.

What that boiled down to was that every O'Donnellys' wife was tucked away here, safe and sound, so that their menfolk could go partying.

It was a joke, but we'd get our own back when we left for Key West. They wouldn't be locked up here, and we'd have a lot of guards on us, but I intended to have a bachelorette party worthy of a Netflix film.

Disappointed when I saw it was an unknown number, I wasn't going to answer, but it rang on for a while.

Uneasily, I connected the call, and asked warily, "Hello?"

Only God knew who it might be, but this number was harder to get than the President's.

"Cammie?"

That deep, husky baritone hit me right in the stomach.

Nyx.

Before, a flutter of butterflies would have stirred to life inside me.

Now?

Dread filled me. Regret and irritation too—I'd been such a fool back then. So pathetic. His voice was a flashback I didn't need, but it was also a reminder of how different I was now.

I was no longer Cammie.

I was Camille.

"Please, don't put the phone down," he burst out, making me tighten my hands around my cell, because I'd been on the brink of doing just that.

"What do you want, Nyx?"

"I—" He hesitated. "I know this is stupid, but Giulia gave birth today."

Before Brennan, that would have sent shards of agony throughout my entire being. Now, I could admit that I was happy for him.

Huskily, I said, "Congratulations."

"I just got back from the hospital," he muttered. "I have a daughter, Cammie."

"That's great, Nyx," I told him softly. "I'm happy for you."

And I was.

Genuinely.

"I believe you mean that," he rumbled.

"I do. I always wished you the best." I'd just wanted that best to include me. But everything happened for a reason, and my reason was Brennan.

My smile appeared at that, easing the wariness that had overtaken me the second I registered who was calling.

"I didn't deserve it." He cleared his throat. "I know this is crazy, and I know you probably hoped you'd never hear from me again, but today, I held my baby girl in my arms, Cammie. I held her, and I looked at her, and she grabbed my finger, and I just—

"I realized something."

When he fell silent, I knew it was because the emotional day had hit him hard. For a psychopath, Nyx could get in his feelings quickly.

"What did you realize?" I prompted.

"That if any guy treated her the way I treated you, I'd kill them."

My mouth rounded at that. "What?"

"You heard me. I was a bastard to you, Cammie, an absolute cunt. I'm lucky that O'Donnelly hasn't sent The Whistler after me, because I'd deserve that for what I put you through—"

"It wasn't your fault that I loved you and you didn't love me," I rasped.

"No, but I could have been kinder about it. Instead, I just tossed you out like—" He sighed. "Cammie, I wanted to tell you I'm sorry."

Lips trembling, I whispered, "I don't know what to..."

"You don't have to say anything," he told me as my voice waned, "You don't even have to accept it. Just know that I mean it. I regret what I did to you."

"Thank you." There was nothing else I could say.

He cleared his throat. "Anyway, I'd best get going. I have two boys as well, and it's time for bed... Be happy, Cammie."

"It's Camille," I blurted out.

"Can't blame you. You never were made out to be a clubwhore, Camille. I'm glad you found your rightful place. Have a good life."

"You too, Nyx."

With that, he ended the call.

For a second, I stared blankly at the TV opposite my bed. Whatever his purpose might have been, I could never have imagined it'd be an apology.

And even though he didn't mean anything to me anymore, even

though my heart was so wrapped up in Brennan it was like it beat for him alone, his apology mattered. It wasn't until he said sorry though that I registered how much.

The world was crazier than it had ever been, but life was war as Brennan had once told me, and we had to carry on. That was why, in a month's time, we were renewing our vows. In St. Patrick's. Just in time for my baby bump not to show through my wedding dress. A real wedding this time.

With the only thing that mattered in attendance—family.

Reaching up, I tugged on my bottom lip when my screen flashed on again. I cast it a look, and saw Brennan had sent me a text.

Bren: *What are you doing, beautiful?*

Me: *Nothing much. :) How about you? Having fun?*

Bren: *Not really. Wish you were here.*

I grinned. **Me:** *You'll be back tomorrow.*

Bren: *Don't care. It was stupid to go away without you. Most of these fuckers are drooling over lap dancers, and there's only one ass I want in my face.*

Laughing, I didn't even have it in me to be jealous, because I knew he meant it.

I had his focus.

All of it.

And I *loved* it.

I reveled in it.

He could never be too possessive, could never guard me too zealously.

I'd never felt more alive when he glowered at every man who dared cast me a look, had never been happier than when his fingers found their way under my skirt as we danced at a gala.

Amid this chaos, he did that—he made me happy, and I knew I did the same for him.

Me: *That can be arranged.*

Bren: *Can it?*

Me: *Give me a few.*

Bren: *Do I need to be in my hotel room?*

Me: *You'd better. If you whip that dick out in public and another woman sees it, I'll be the one going homicidal.*

Bren: *You'd better be willing to deal with the boner you just gave me.*

Me: *What do you think? Give me five.*

With a giggle, Nyx completely forgotten, cast to the past where he belonged, I rushed over to the table where I had a collection of things to keep me occupied.

There was a tangle of patterns for my crocheting because I was trying to make baby clothes and failing—who knew things that were miniaturized were so hard to create—and I'd been saving up crosswords because I wasn't allowed to have the paper delivered to the compound. Underneath all that, there was my laptop.

I turned it on, then carried it over to the foot of the bed.

With that done, I reached down and shimmied out of my yoga pants.

As I stared down at my belly, I smiled as I cupped the tiny pooch.

Life was stirring inside me. A life that Brennan and I had created after years of trying. A life that I refused, point blank, to be inveigled in war.

We had eighteen years to change things, to make New York better, and I knew Brennan would for our baby. Just so that he or she never had to go through what he had. What *I* had.

Stripping out of my loose sweater, I clambered onto the bed, opened our messaging service and tapped out: **Me:** *You there?*

Bren: *At the hotel and dying for your cunt.*

I closed my eyes as shivers rushed through me.

What he did to me with those dirty words... Five years on, and he still held me in his thrall.

Shuddering and wishing he was here to take charge of me how I needed, to come on my tits, to fuck me filthy, I positioned myself on the bed.

It was awkward, but he didn't have to know that.

On my hands and knees in front of the screen, my pussy there, in the direct line of the webcam, I reached between my thighs and tapped on the 'video call' button.

For a few seconds, it rang, and then his face popped up. His beautiful, gorgeous face that I saw from between my legs.

He was flushed from a couple of drinks, but whatever he'd been about to say disappeared in a heartbeat as he saw my pussy.

My slick, wet pussy that creamed only for him.

"Fuck," he snarled.

I smirked and slid a finger into my cunt.

"I love you, baby," I said breathily.

"Fuck, Camille, I love you too," he rasped and I heard the sound of his zipper as he pulled out his cock.

When he groaned out his love for me, I sighed with delight as he handed me another reason, on top of the ten thousand others he'd gifted me over the last five years, to be alive.

Which brother will be next?
Read FILTHY HOT here: www.books2read.com/FilthyHot

AFTERWORD

DARLINGS,
So, you came across Camille in Nyx (www.books2read.com/Nyx) and I knew she got a lot of hate simply because of her past, but if you go

and do a search for her name in that book, you'll find that she was always kind, always loving, and always wanting his love. People don't like club-whores in the MC world, but Camille is a genuine diamond, and I hope that your eyes are opened if you do search for her name.

With that being said, I hope this finds you shedding a little tear in hope.

Even in the darkness, there is light. <3

Suicide journals, sadly, are a tool used by people having suicidal thoughts to keep themselves from going ahead with taking their own lives. Not unlike her darling mama, Camille journaled, but hers was to stop her from taking that very final step.

Camille is a lost soul. There's no mistaking that. Suffering with Body Dysmorphia, lost in her grief, with a parent who doesn't care, cutting as her only comfort, I hope you believe that, by the end, she became the big sister she always wanted to be. That she became the woman she deserved to be.

She didn't need Brennan to make her stronger, to empower her—she just needed acceptance. She needed the security of knowing that she was safe. And now she has his love. I, for one, know that Brennan will always cherish his Queen.

I pray that, today, you too are safe. That you know you are loved, because you are. You're in a sisterhood now. Much like Aela, Aoife, Inessa, Camille, and even Victoria—though we both know she isn't destined to be in the Five Points. You are a fan of the Filthy Feckers, along with thousands of others like you. You are strong, you are beautiful, you are proud.

The song Camille sang to Jacob is an old Russian folk song: Kalinka: https://youtu.be/b8nvPjKMDho

Oh, and yes, the wedding Inessa and Eoghan attended was Amaryllis, Ink, Saint, and Keys'. :) If you didn't know, they're from All Sinner No Saint. <3

I hope to see you in my Diva reader group: www.facebook.com/groups/SerenaAkeroydsDivas where you can chat with me on the regular about my releases, but if not... until next time.

And if you're interested in finding out more about Quin, then you should read HAWK, the next book in 'A Dark & Dirty Sinners' MC' series. www.books2read.com/HawkSerenaAkeroyd

If you enjoyed this book, please, if you'd consider leaving an honest review, it would mean the world to me.

THANK YOU.
Much love,
Serena
xoxo

PS. Don't forget, this is the crossover universe's reading order. <3

FILTHY
NYX
LINK
FILTHY RICH
SIN
STEEL
FILTHY DARK
CRUZ
MAVERICK
FILTHY SEX
HAWK
FILTHY HOT
STORM
THE DON (Coming Soon)
THE LADY (Coming Soon)
FILTHY SECRET (Coming Soon)

FREE BOOK!

Don't forget to grab your free e-Book!
Secrets & Lies is now free!

Meg's love life was missing a spark until she discovered her need to be dominated. When her fiancé shared the same kink, she thought all her birthdays had come at once, and then she came to learn their relationship was one big fat lie.

Gabe has loved Meg for years, watching her from afar, and always wishing he'd been the one to date her first and not his brother. When he has the chance to have Meg in his bed—even better, tied to it—it's an opportunity he can't refuse.

With disastrous consequences.

Can Gabe make Meg realize she's the one woman he's always wanted? But once secrets and lies have wormed their way into a relationship, is it impossible to establish the firm base of trust needed between lovers, and more importantly, between sub and Sir...?

This story features orgasm control in a BDSM setting.
Secrets & Lies is now free!

CONNECT WITH SERENA

For the latest updates, be sure to check out my website! But if you'd like to hang out with me and get to know me better, then I'd love to see you in my Diva reader's group where you can find out all the gossip on new releases as and when they happen. You can join here: www.facebook.com/groups/SerenaAkeroydsDivas. Or you can always PM or email me. I love to hear from you guys: serenaakeroyd@gmail.com.

ABOUT THE AUTHOR

I'm a romance novelaholic and I won't touch a book unless I know there's a happy ending. This addiction is what made me craft stories that suit my voracious need for raunchy romance. I love twists and unexpected turns, and my novels all contain sexy guys, dark humor, and hot AF love scenes.

I write MF, menage, and reverse harem (also known as why choose romance,) in both contemporary and paranormal. Some of my stories are darker than others, but I can promise you one thing, you will always get the happy ending your heart needs!

Made in the USA
Middletown, DE
08 July 2023